THE TOTALLY BRILLIANT BUMPER PUZZLE BOOK

This edition published in 2012 by Arcturus Publishing Limited
26/27 Bickels Yard, 151–153 Bermondsey Street,
London SE1 3HA

ISBN: 978-1-84858-450-1
CH002496EN

Author: Lisa Regan
Illustrator: Beccy Blake
Editor: Kate Overy
Designer: John Walker

Supplier 07, Date 0712, Print run 2012

Printed in India

MONSTER MAD

This monster is hopping mad!
But which silhouette matches him exactly?

IN THE SWIM

Which jigsaw piece finishes the picture:
a, b, c, d or e?

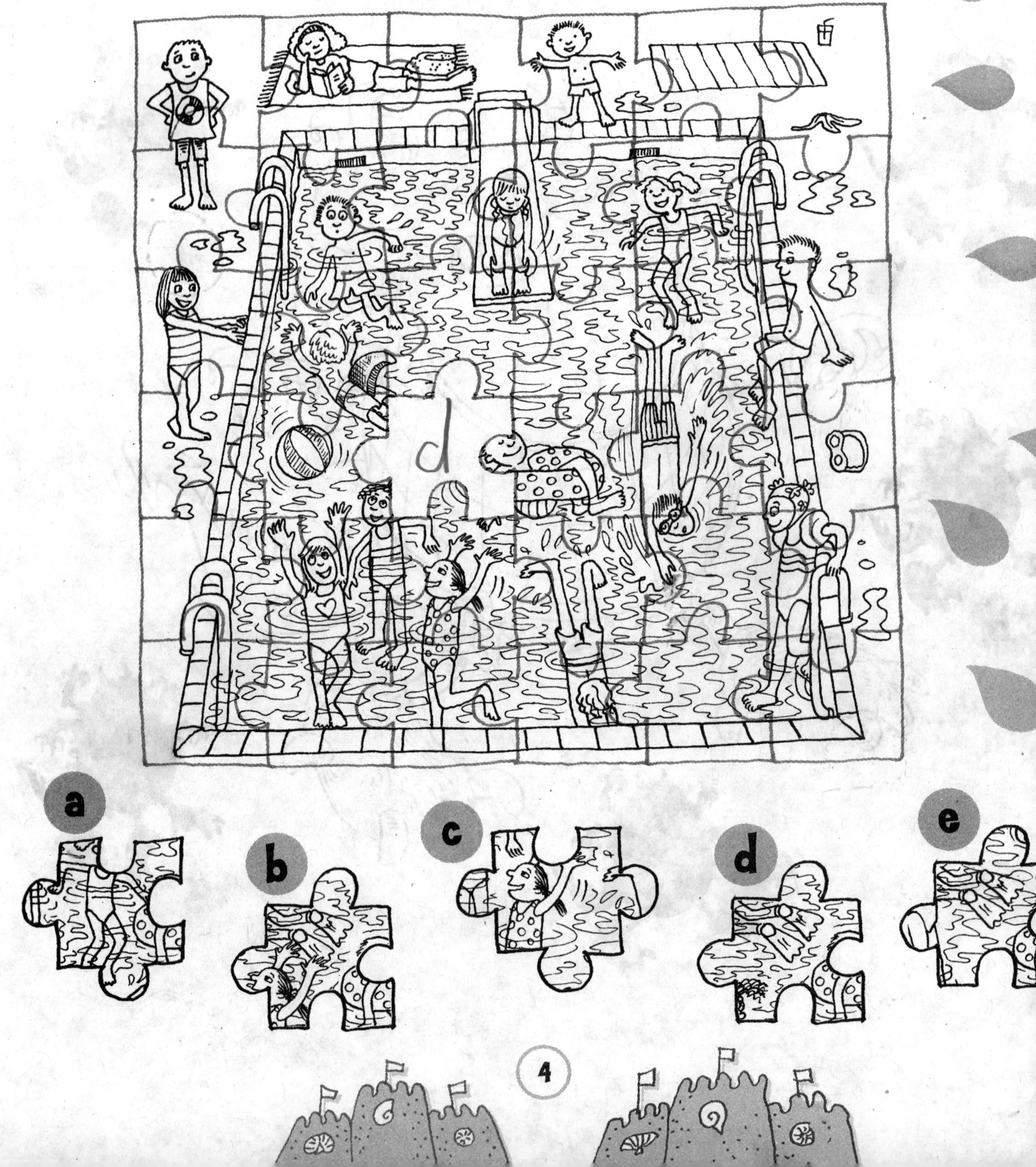

AT THE MATCH

Can you spot which six items are different in the two pictures?

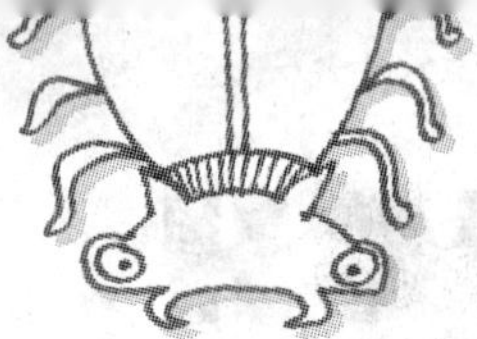

BUGOKU

Solve the puzzle so that every row, column and mini-grid contains each of the four bugs.

MOON WALK

Follow the arrows to guide the spaceman across the planet, without jumping on any craters.

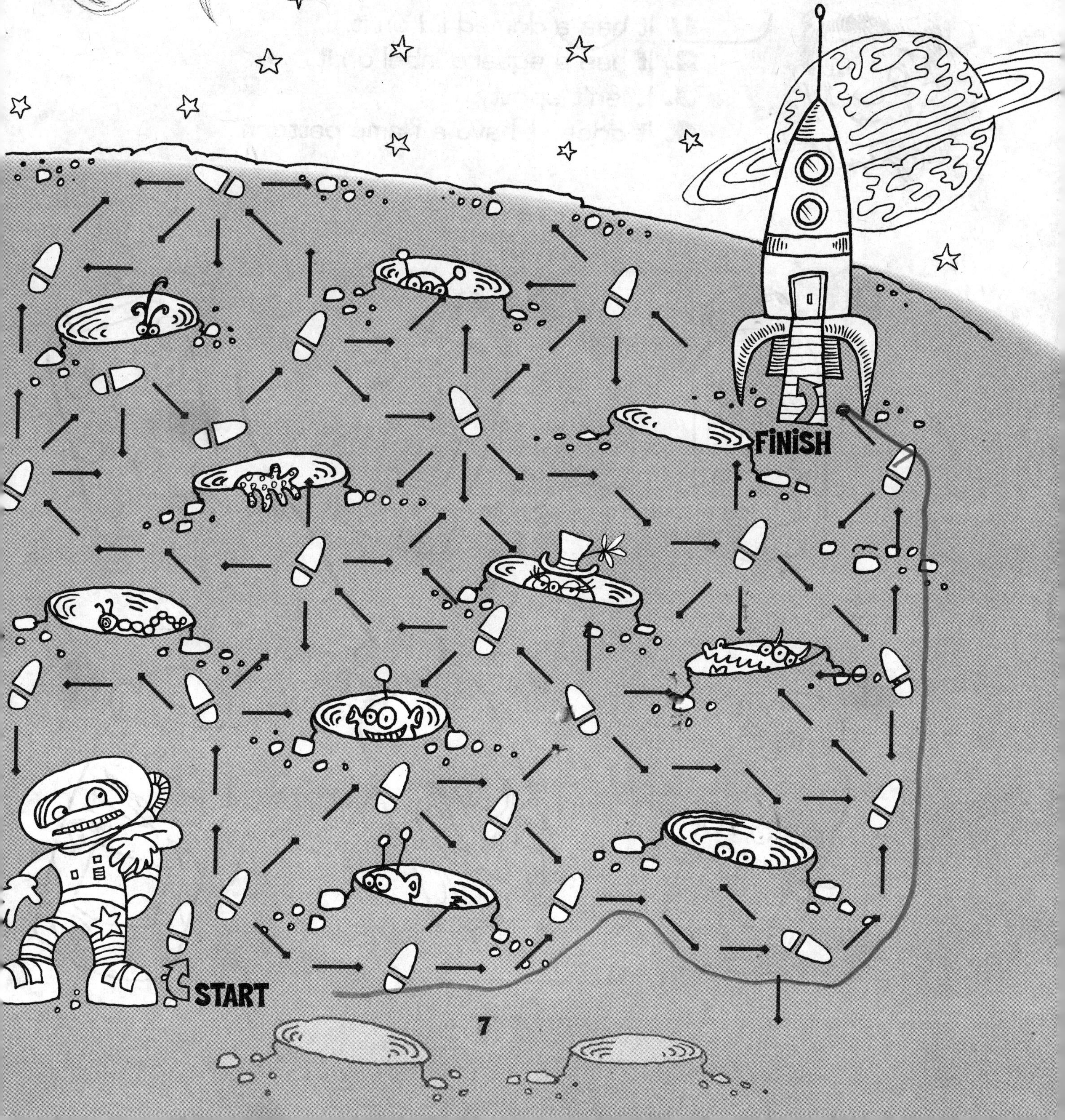

FINISH

START

THIRSTY WORK

Which drinking bottle belongs to Joe? Use the clues to help you work it out.

1. It has a domed lid on it.
2. It has a square label on it.
3. It isn't spotty.
4. It doesn't have a flame pattern.

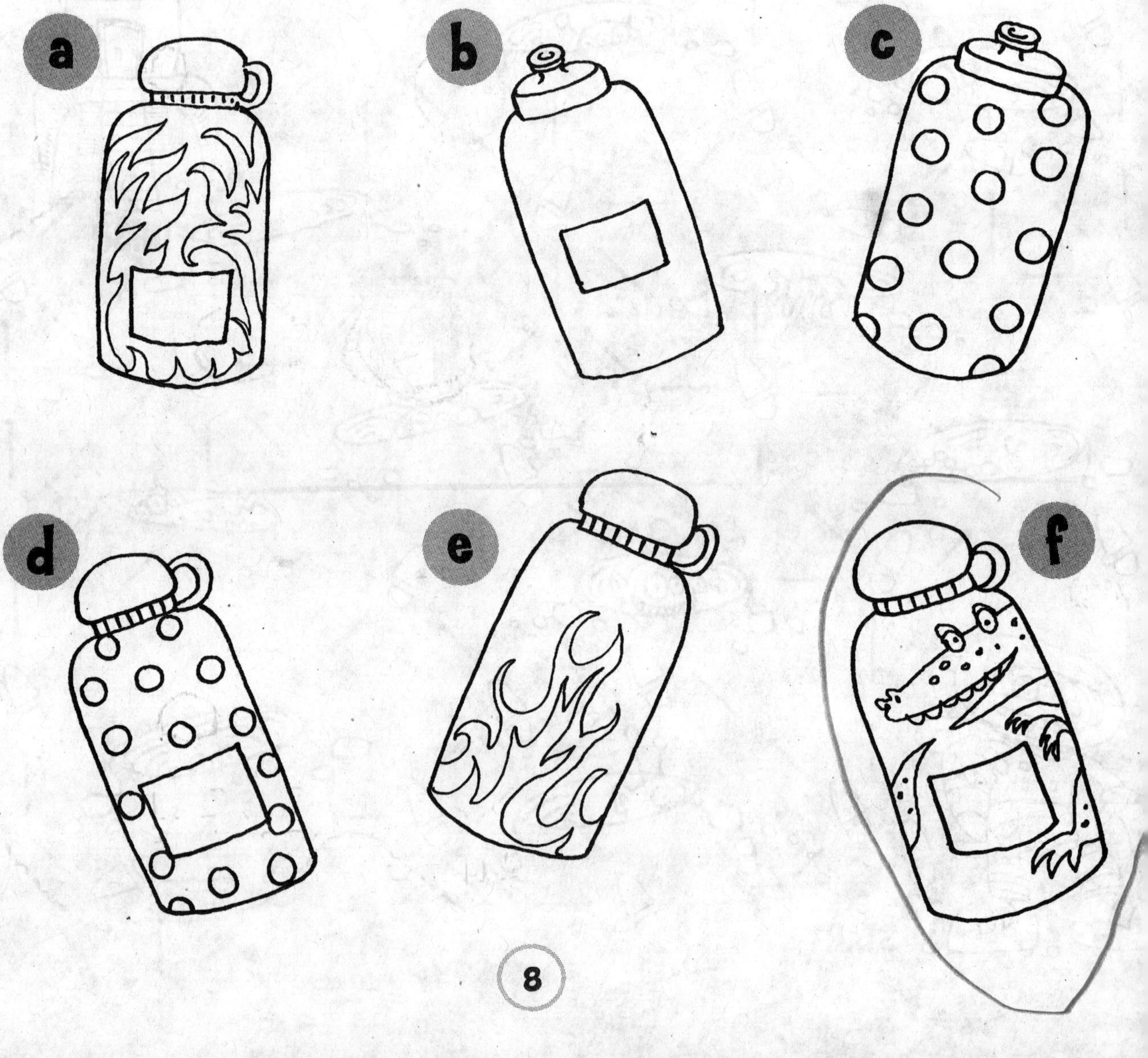

a b c d e f

A DAY AT THE ZOO

These two pictures were taken on a trip to the zoo. Can you see which three people have arrived in the bottom picture?

SPY SCHOOL

Can you work out what this message says?

KNOCK! KNOCK!
WHO'S THERE?
SADIE...
SADIE WHO?
SADIE SECRET
CODE OR YOU
CAN'T COME IN!

These
secset sape

A WALK IN THE PARK

Answer the questions using the grid references from the map.

1. What are people doing in A4 and A5?
2. Which square contains the porcupine?
3. What animals are in squares C1 and C2?
4. Which square is the seesaw in?

CAPITAL LETTERS

Fill in the missing letters to spell five capital cities from around the world. Can you match them to the country they are in?

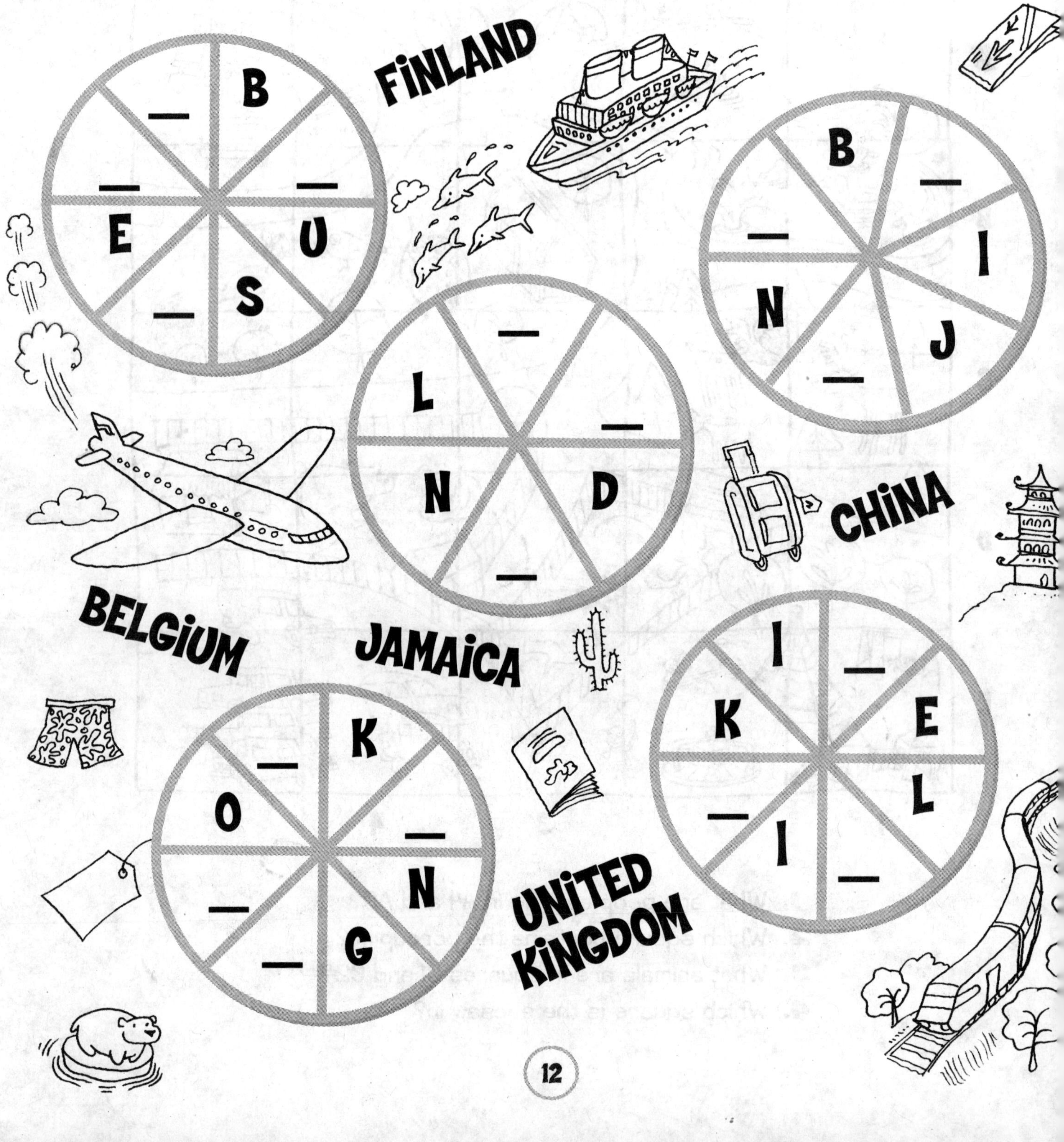

B _ U S _ E _ _

L _ _ D _ N

B _ I J _ N _

K _ N G _ _ O _

I _ E L _ I _ K

FINLAND

CHINA

BELGIUM

JAMAICA

UNITED KINGDOM

UNDER COVER

Help the soldier through the camouflage net by following the numbers that appear in the five times table.

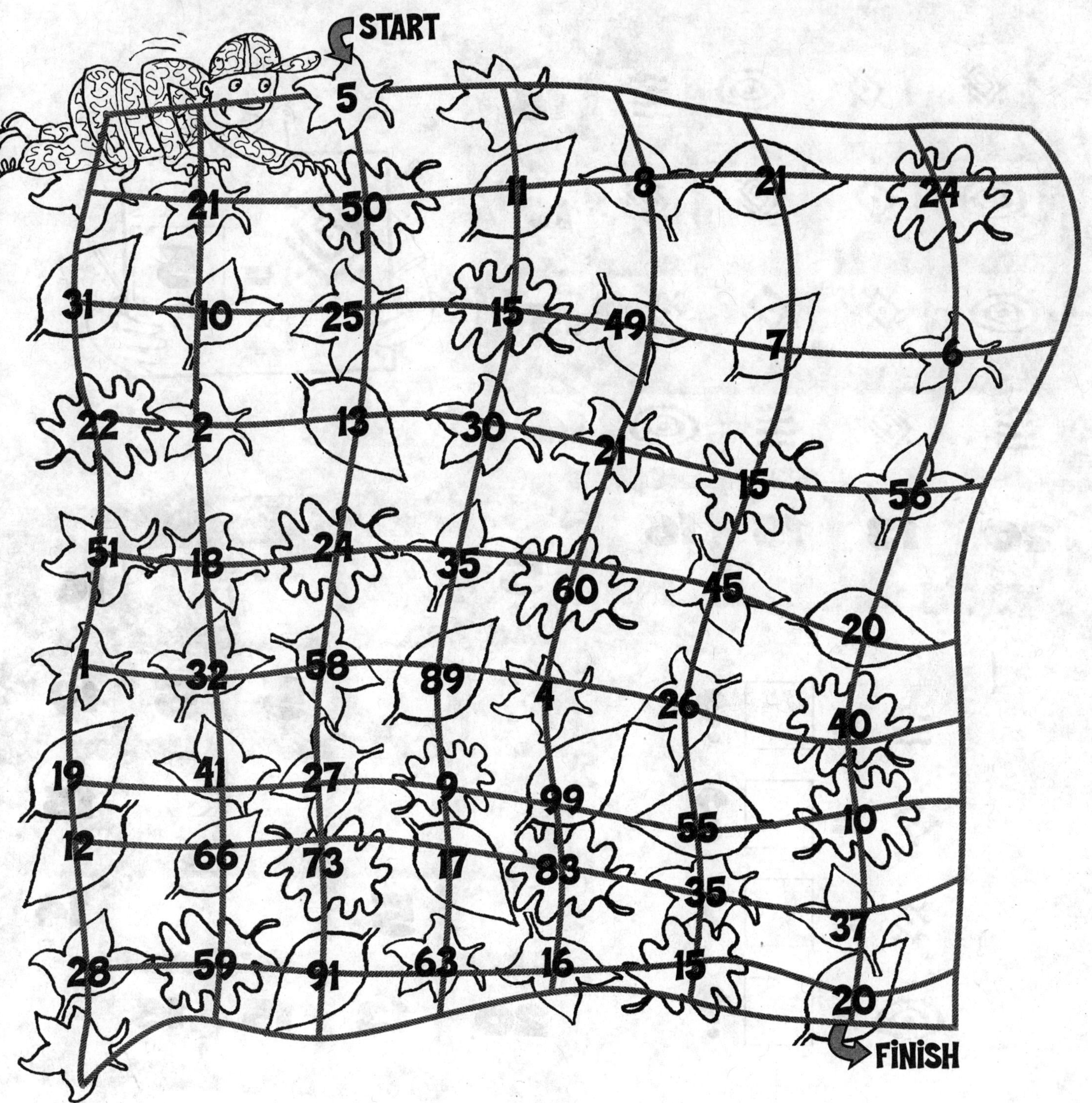

NUMBER CRUNCH

Work out which number is represented by each symbol to make the sums add up on each row and column.

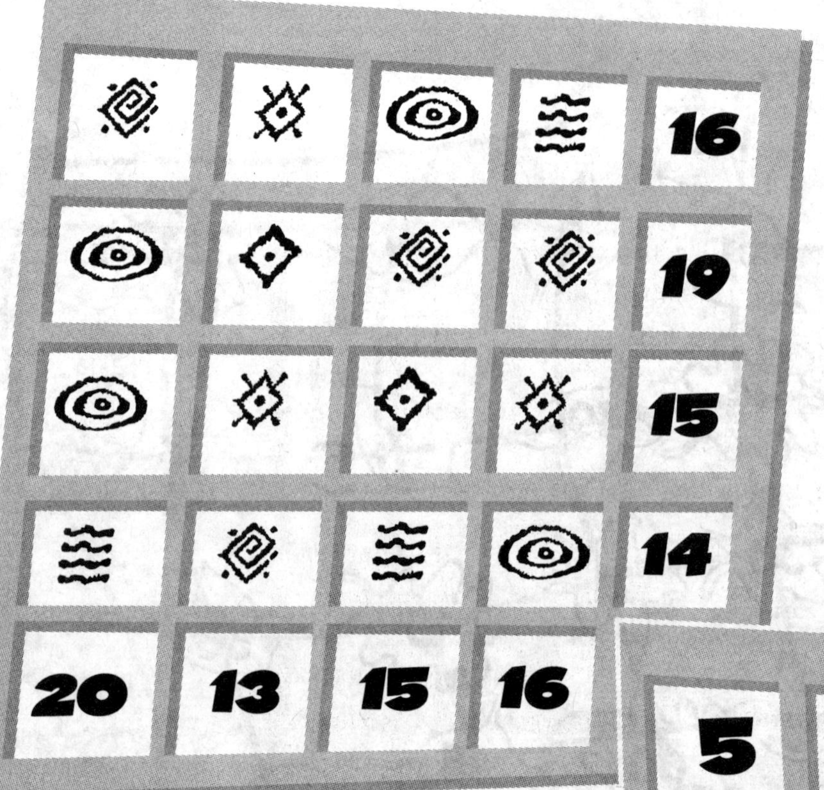

= ?

= ?

= ?

= ?

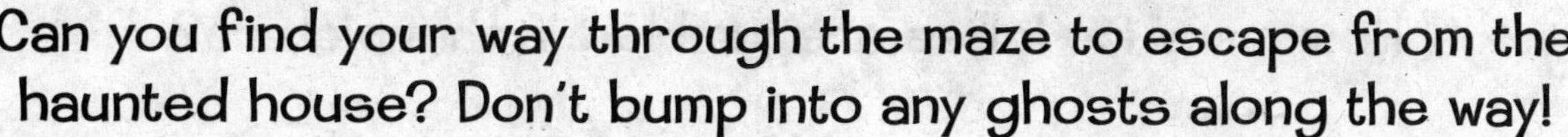

HAUNTED HOUSE

Can you find your way through the maze to escape from the haunted house? Don't bump into any ghosts along the way!

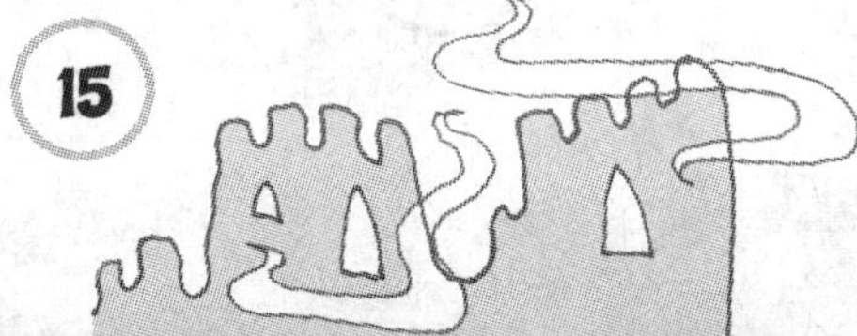

FREEZE POPS

How many ice lollies are jumbled in this picture?

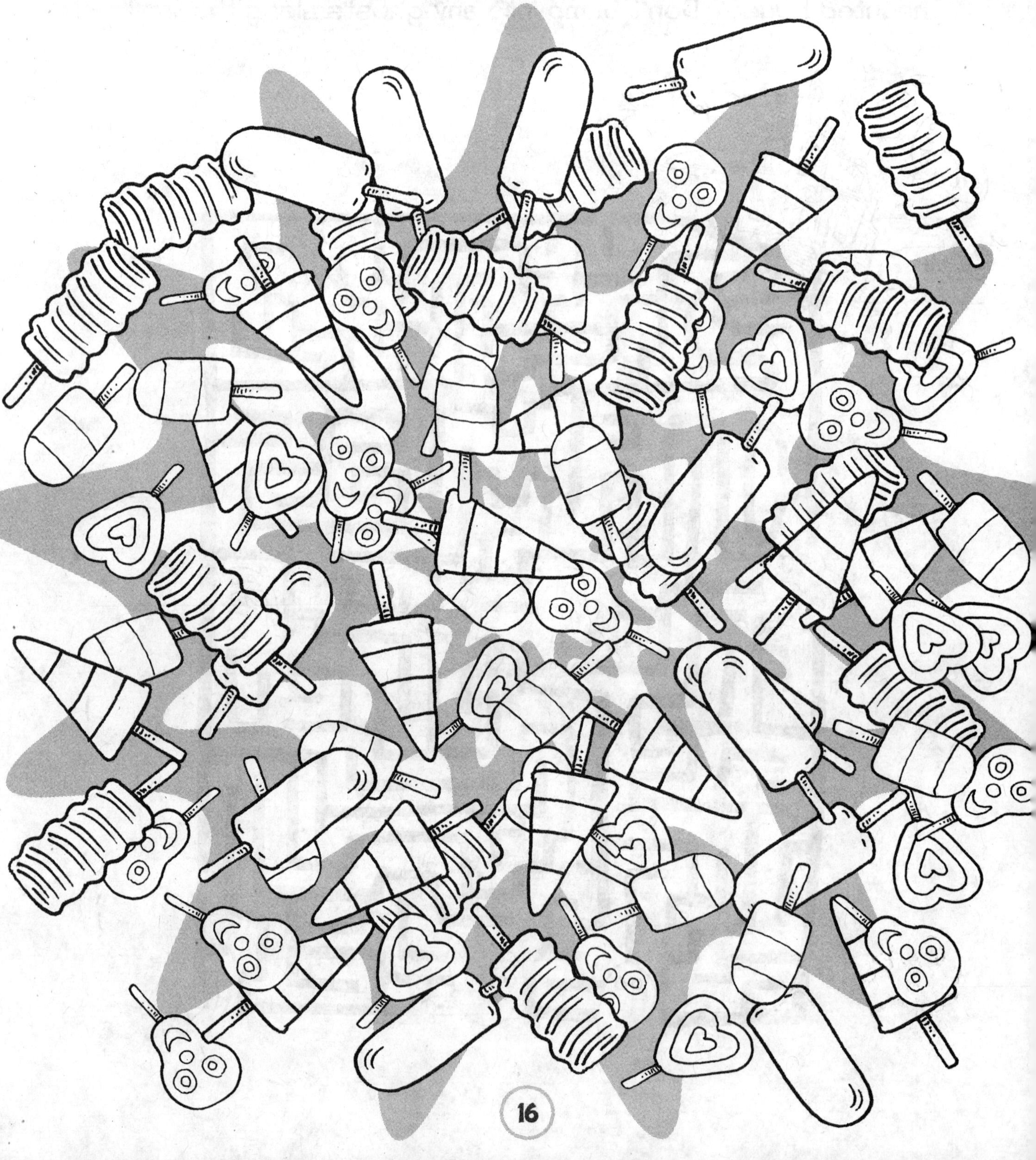

ANIMAL BREAKOUT

Answer the questions to fill in the code and open the hamster's cage so he can come out and play.

1. How many four-legged creatures can you see?
2. How many birds can you count here?
3. How many lizards are there?
4. How many animals here have no legs?

PIRATE PARADE

Only two of these pirate pictures are exactly the same.
Can you spot which two?

a

b

c

d

e

f

ALPHADOKU

Solve the puzzle so that every row, column and mini-grid contains the letters A to F.

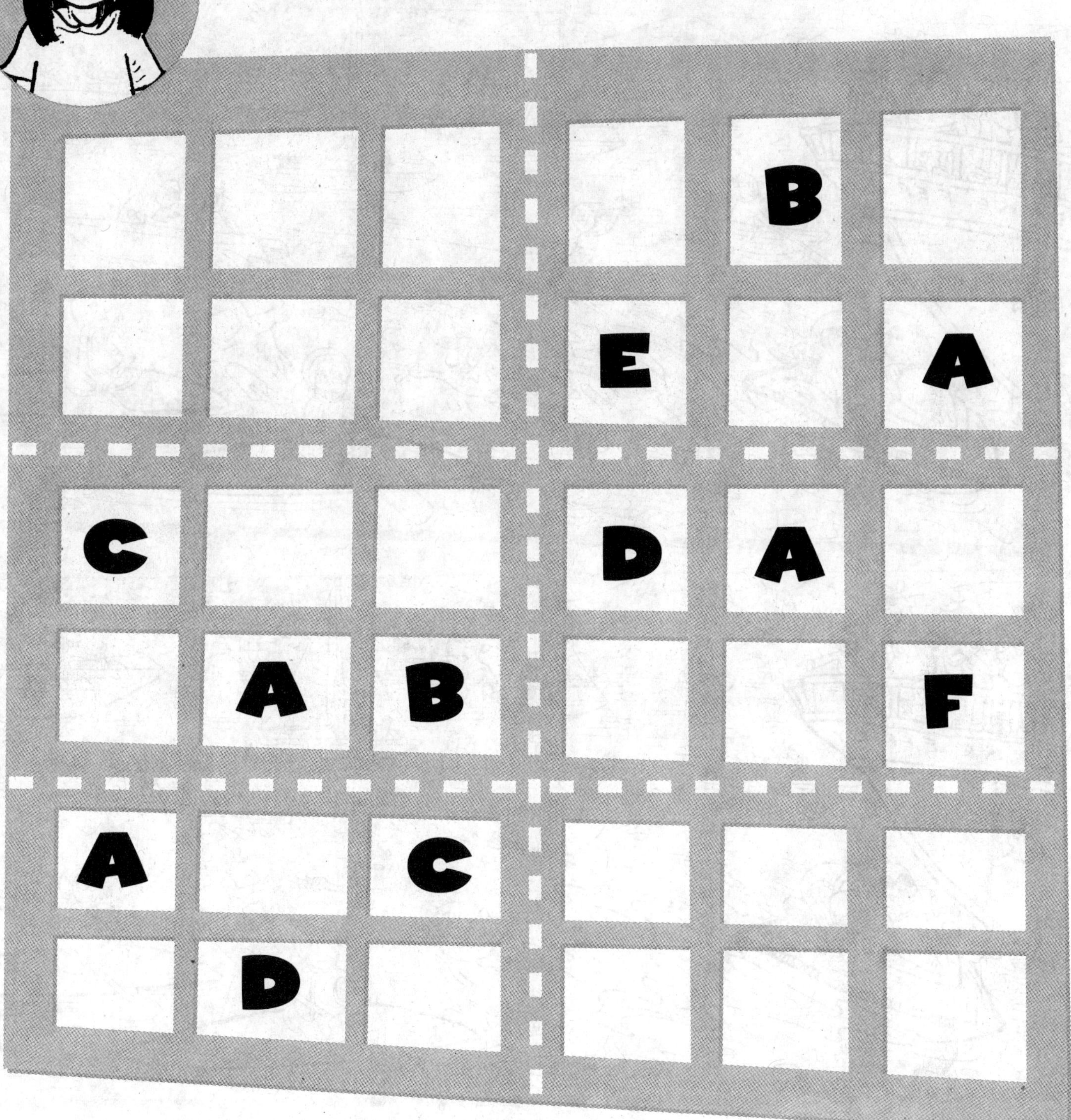

				B	
			E		A
C			D	A	
	A	B			F
A		C			
	D				

SPOT THE DIFFERENCE

There are six differences between these two pictures. Can you circle them all?

MENU MIX UP

Match the boxes in pairs to make the names of ten different kinds of food. One has been done to help you.

~~BAN~~ ATO TOM KEY

POT ORA SAL NUT FLE ROT

PEA BUR NGE ~~ANA~~ ATO

CAR TUR TRI MON GER

B	A	N	A	N	A

WORLD RECORDS

The world is full of amazing places! Can you find some of them in the grid? Look for the names hidden across, down or diagonally.

NILE (longest river)

AMAZON (largest river)

EVEREST (highest mountain)

PACIFIC (largest ocean)

GREENLAND (largest island)

RUSSIA (largest country)

CHINA (country with most people)

SAHARA (largest hot desert)

R	M	A	M	E	T	C	G	R	E	E	C
U	B	N	A	V	S	P	H	N	A	V	H
S	A	I	I	E	E	A	S	I	M	E	B
N	R	A	S	L	R	C	A	Z	A	S	A
E	A	O	S	O	E	I	H	Z	Z	U	I
E	H	P	U	N	V	F	A	I	O	R	K
R	A	G	R	E	E	N	L	A	N	D	A
G	S	R	C	I	F	I	C	A	P	A	L
M	S	G	R	U	S	E	V	I	H	C	E
A	M	A	Z	S	Z	M	A	C	P	T	V

PLANET SIX

Fill in the missing numbers on the spaceship so that you count through the six times table.

ODD ONE OUT

Which of these toucans is the odd one out?

GRIDLOCKED

The mini-grid only appears once in the whole of the larger grid. Can you find it?

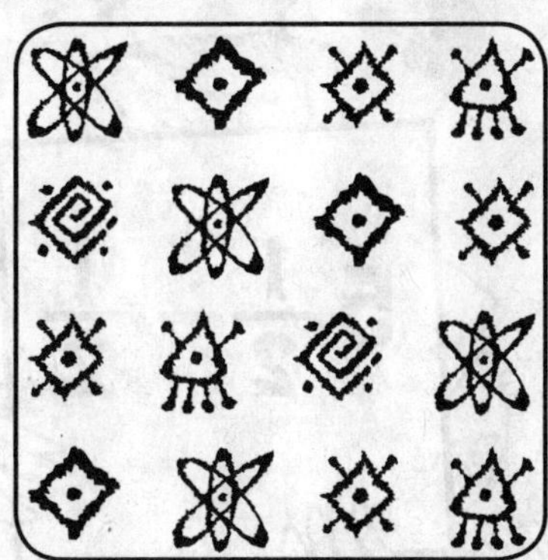

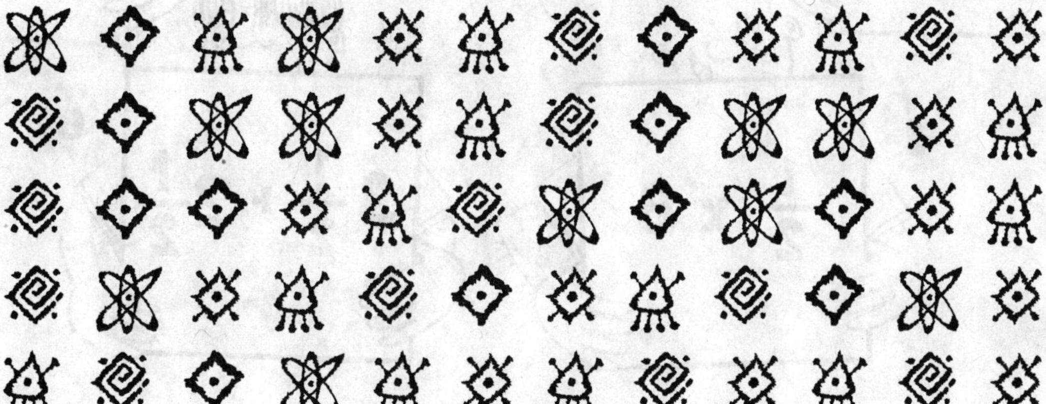

FOOTBALL FRACTIONS

Which football shirt should each player wear?

CLASS ACT

Put your memory to the test by studying the picture for three minutes, and then turning the page to see how many questions you can answer correctly.

CLASS ACT

How much can you remember about the picture on the previous page?

1. What is shown on the board?
2. Is the teacher a man or a woman?
3. How many children are in the picture?
4. What time is it?
5. What is on the windowsill?
6. How many children are wearing sweatshirts?
7. What classroom pet did you see?
8. How many coats are hanging up?
9. What pattern is on the wellington boots?
10. What shape is the pencil case?

FAIRY TALES

How many words of three letters or more can you make up from the letters below? Two are listed to get you started.

ONCE UPON A TIME

1 TEAM

2 POTION

3

4

5

6

7

8

9

10

11

12

SUDOKU

Solve the puzzle so that every row, column and mini-grid contains the numbers 1 to 6.

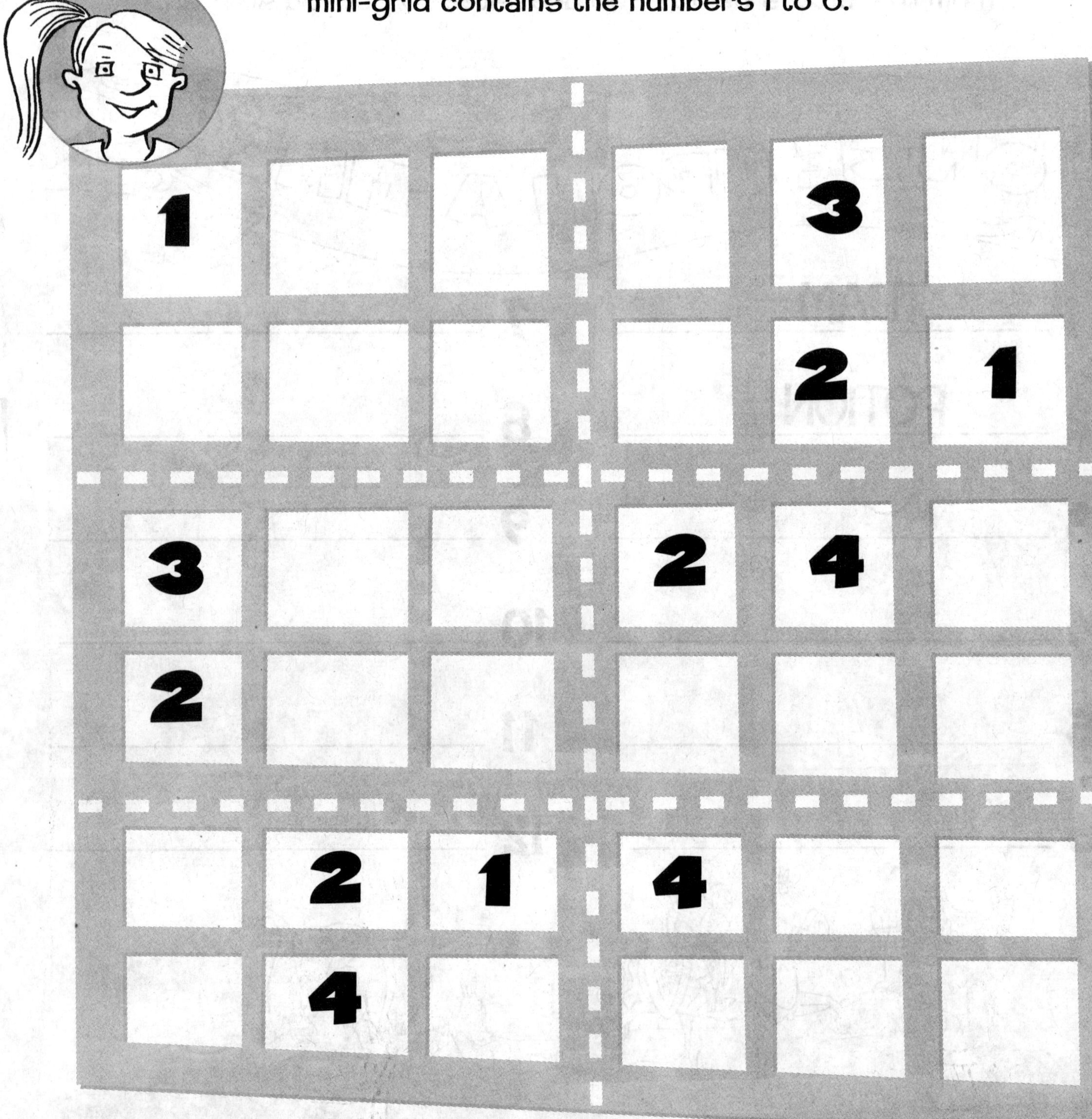

1				3	
				2	1
3			2	4	
2					
	2	1	4		
	4				

OUT OF ORDER

Can you rearrange the six pictures so that they tell the story in the correct order?

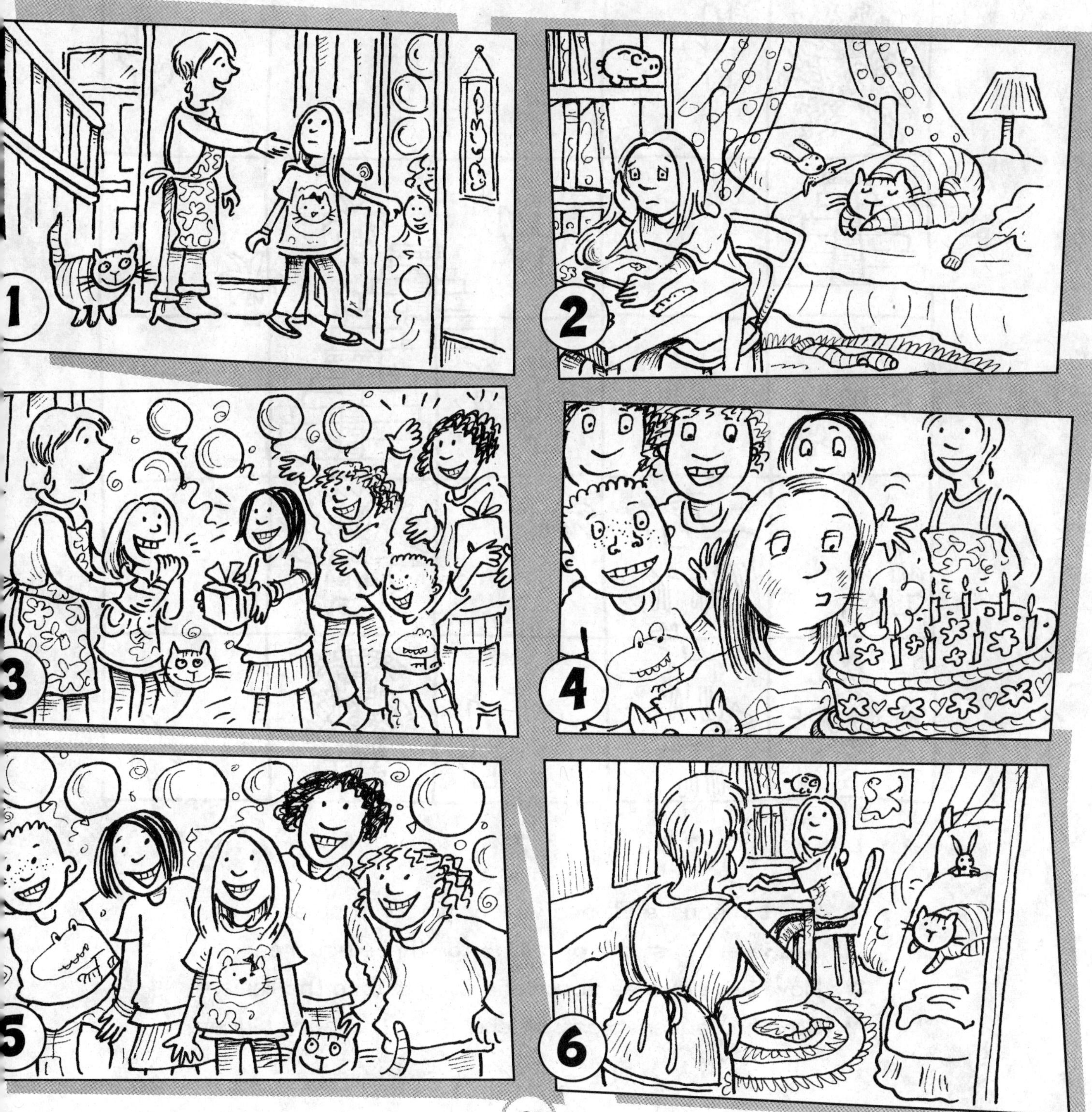

TREASURE HUNT

Follow the directions to find out where the Inca treasure is buried.

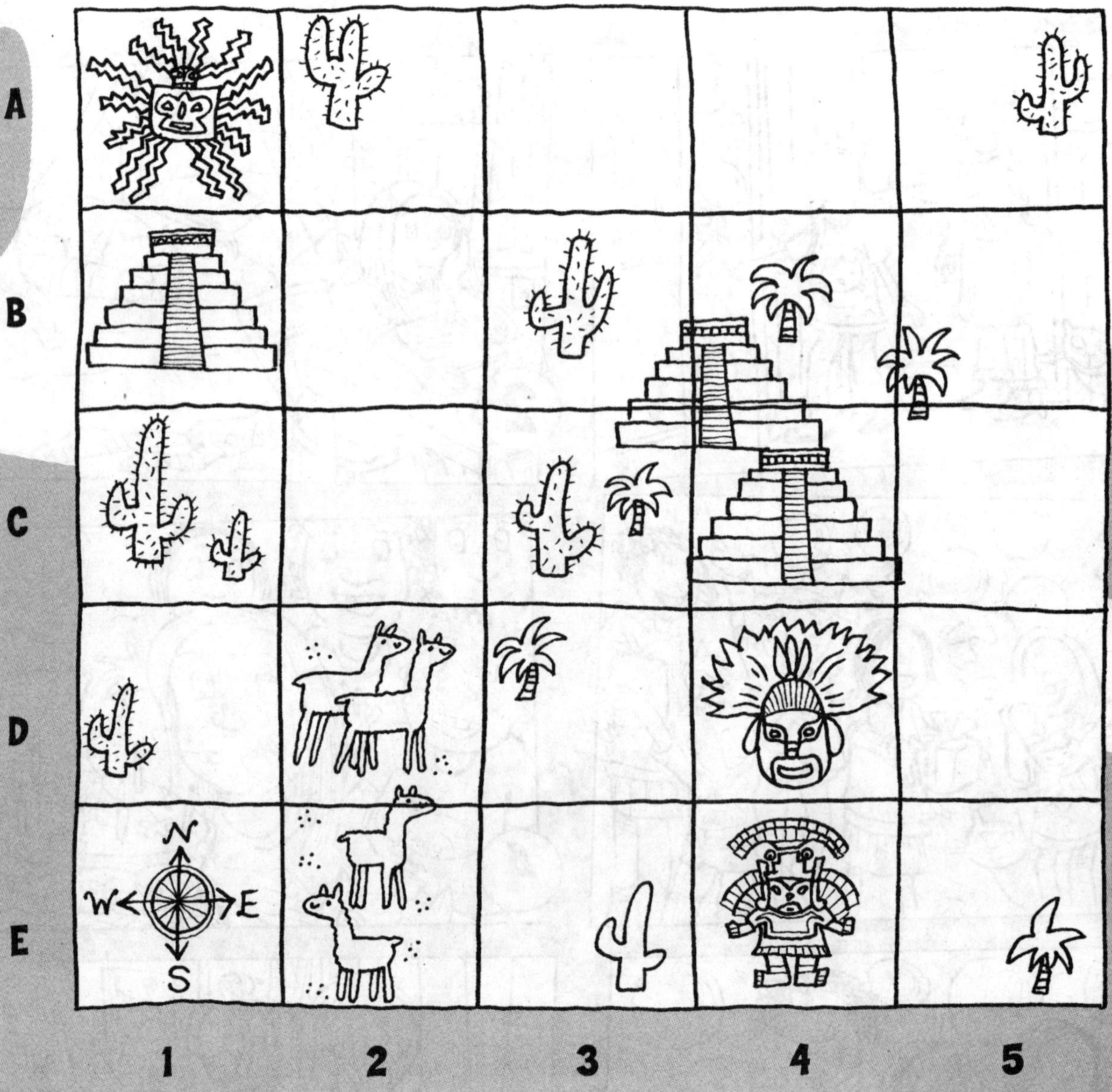

	1	2	3	4	5
A					
B					
C					
D					
E	N W E S				

1. Start in square E5 and walk north for four squares.
2. Head west past the pyramids for three squares.
3. Move two squares south and stop before the llamas.
4. Step one square west. Where is the treasure hidden?

DOUBLE TROUBLE

Starting at the X each time, use every other letter to spell the names of four birds. The remaining letters spell out four more birds.

TIGER TABLES

Help the tiger cub find its mother by counting up in fives, starting at the number 5.

20	15	10			85	90	95
25	30	START 5			80	105	100
40	35	60	65	70	75	110	115
45	50	55	190	185	170	165	120
210	205	200	195	180	175	160	125
215					150	155	130
FINISH 220					145	140	135

DINO-DETECTIVE

The spy has to collect a hidden package from the Dinosaur Museum. Use the code to work out which exhibit it is hidden behind.

A	❀
B	✺
C	✱
D	❄
E	❅
F	❆
G	✳
H	✼
I	❃
J	❉
K	✽
L	●
M	◯
N	■
O	❏
P	❐
Q	❑
R	❒
S	▲
T	▼
U	◆
V	❖
W	◗
X	✶
Y	✹
Z	✺

PLANE SAILING

Look at the main picture and then work out which of the smaller pictures is the view you would have of the same scene from a plane.

a

b

c

d

e

f

ON THE MOVE

Can you unscramble each set of letters to find the transport words?

YCCBLIE

TARRCOT

THACY

RANTI

NEAREPOLA

SPOTEDABE

ROBOTMIKE

POTLICEHER

FEEDING FRENZY

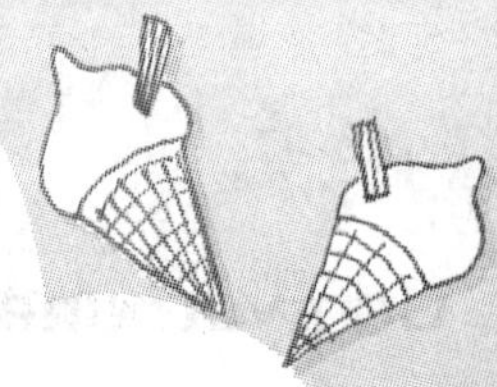

Chris has bought ice creams for everyone!
But which silhouette matches him exactly?

ZOO SHOPPING

Ben wants to get something from London Zoo's souvenir shop. Answer the questions to find out what he can buy.

1. How much will he spend if he buys a baseball cap and a giraffe toy?
2. How many pencils can Ben buy with £3?
3. What costs more, three large elephant toys or two snow globes?
4. If Ben gives the shopkeeper £5, how much change will he get if he buys a baby elephant toy, a pencil, a badge and a card?

ALPHADOKU

Solve the puzzle so that every row, column and mini-grid contains the letters A to F.

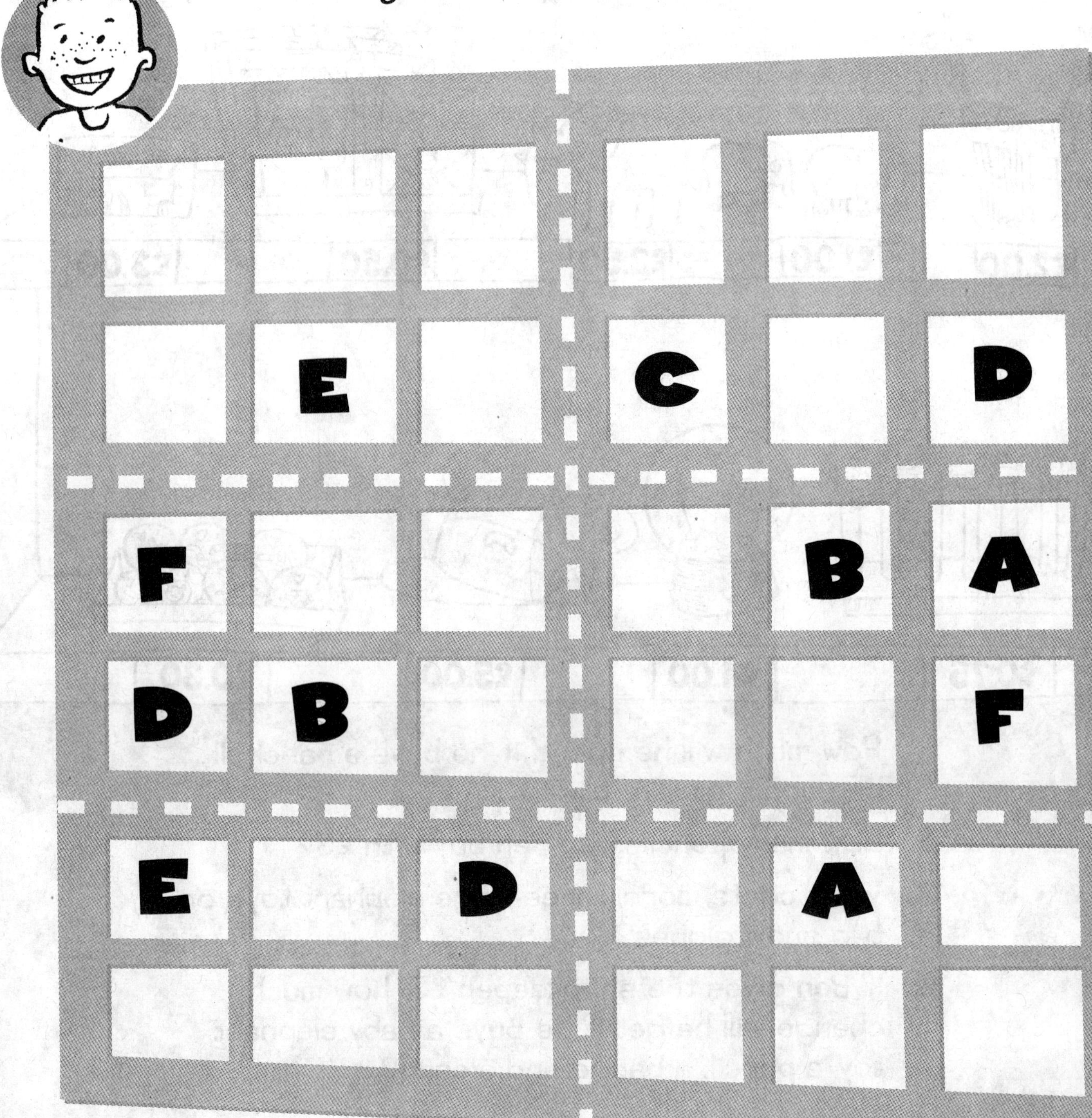

	E		C		D
F				B	A
D	B				F
E		D		A	

WHAT NEXT?

Study the sequence of pictures carefully and work out which cow finishes the pattern: a, b or c?

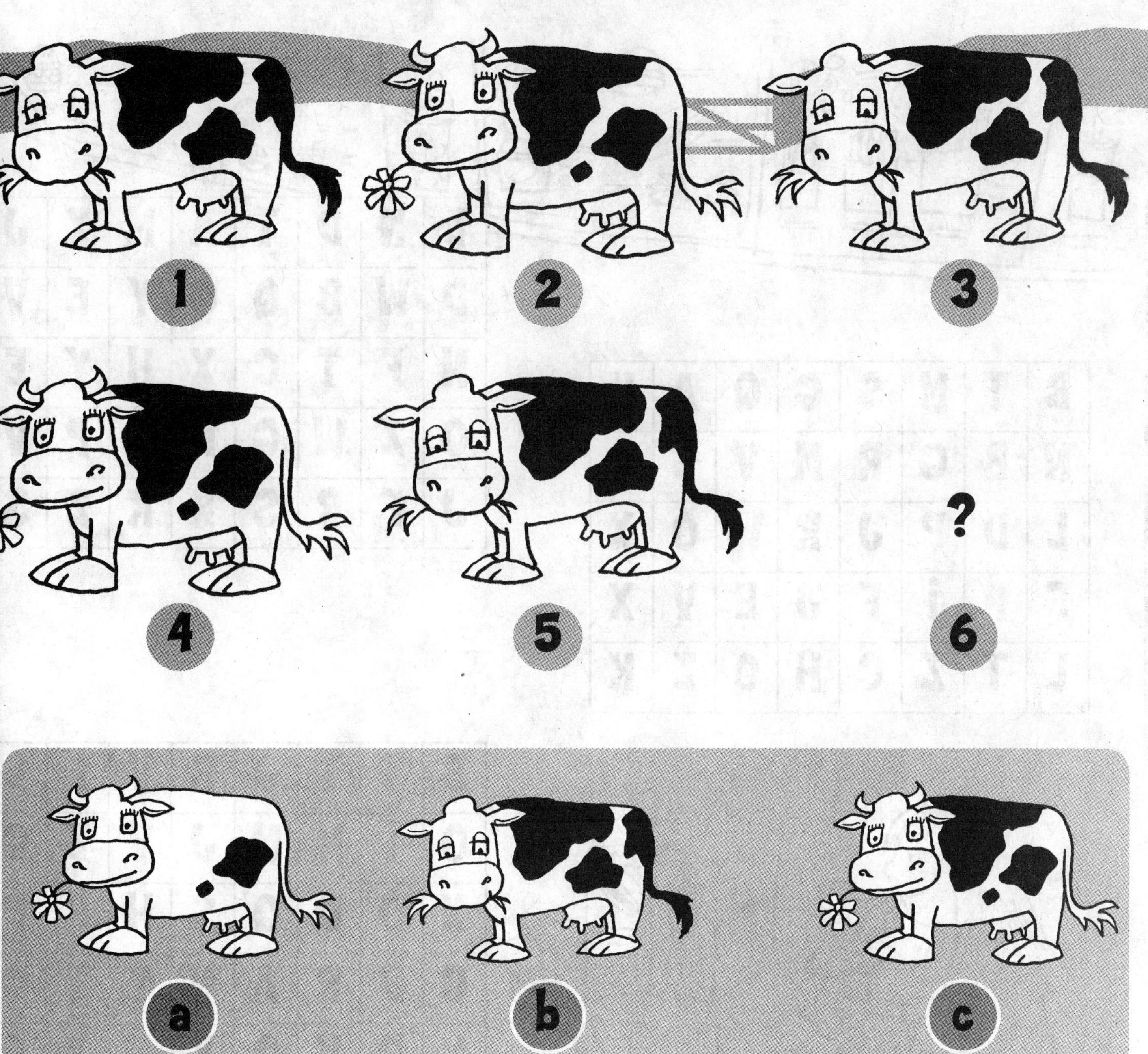

FOOD FOR THOUGHT

In each grid, cross out any letter that appears twice. The remaining letters spell out three items you might find on a menu.

L	N	D	T	A	M	X	J
D	W	B	Q	G	Y	E	V
N	F	T	C	X	H	Y	E
O	Z	W	G	K	Q	P	V
J	F	R	S	R	K	Z	S

B	T	M	S	G	Q	A	K
N	B	G	R	M	V	E	Q
L	D	P	J	R	W	O	X
F	P	I	F	J	E	V	X
L	T	Z	C	H	O	Z	K

B	T	T	J	B	V	F	L
O	I	M	M	J	V	Z	G
X	O	D	Q	S	H	P	P
C	D	R	A	N	Y	Z	G
L	R	K	Q	Y	N	X	E

HOLIDAY HUNT

Use your eagle eyes to spot each of the items on the left-hand side of the page, hidden in the main picture.

Find these!

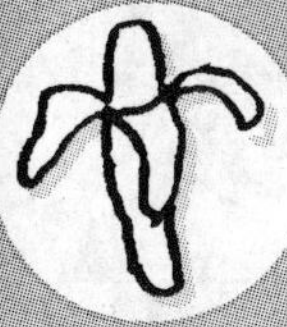

GRIDLOCKED

The mini-grid only appears once in the whole of the larger grid. Can you find it?

SPY SCHOOL

Use the coded alphabet to work out where the spy is going on her next assignment.

FEEDING TIME

Answer the questions to fill in the code and let the zoo keeper into the enclosure to feed the snake.

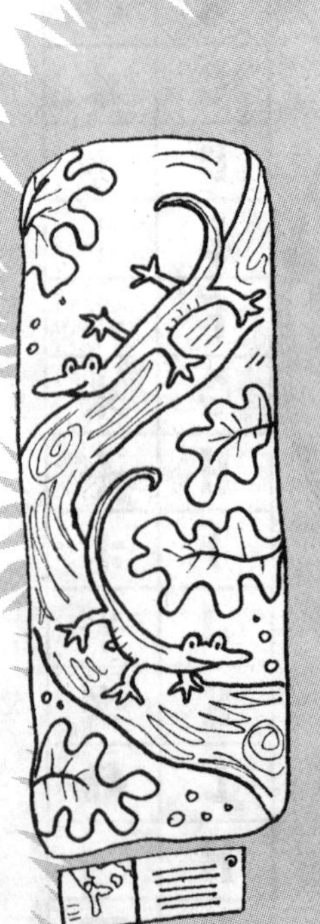

1. How many enclosures contain lizards?
2. How many legs does a stick insect have?
3. How many frogs are there?
4. How many animals here have four legs?

CAMPSITE CHALLENGE

Look carefully at the top picture, and then decide which five things have changed in the bottom picture.

SPACED OUT

Fill in the missing letters to spell six things that you can find in outer space.

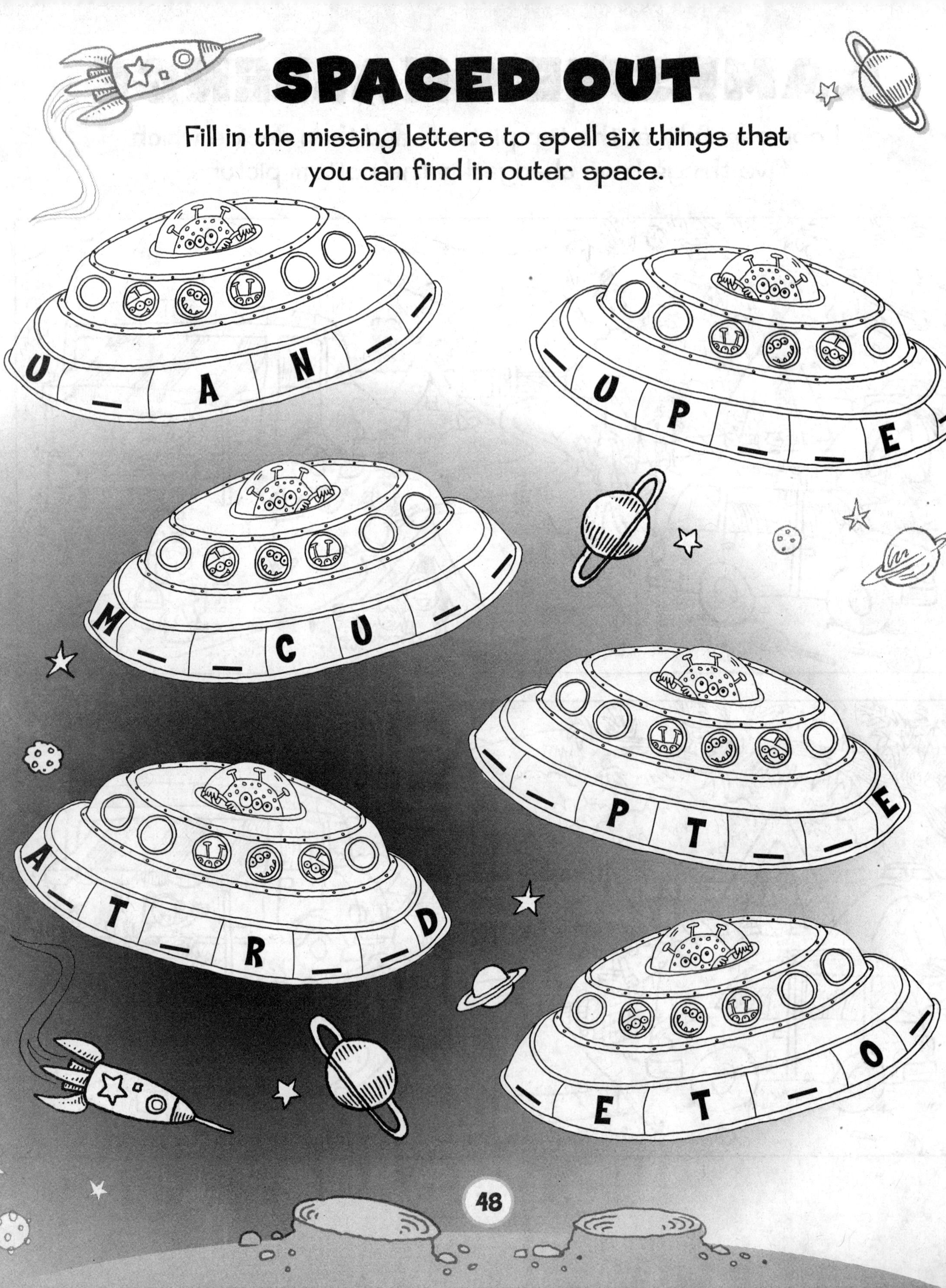

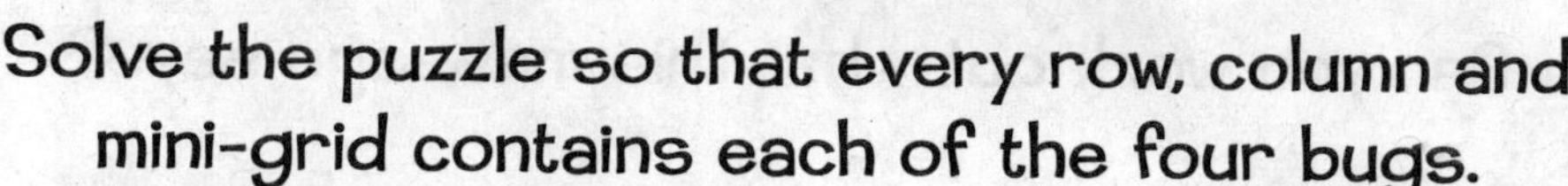

BUGOKU

Solve the puzzle so that every row, column and mini-grid contains each of the four bugs.

SPY SCHOOL

Can you work out what this message says?

PIECES OF EIGHT

Which jigsaw piece finishes the picture: a, b, c, d or e?

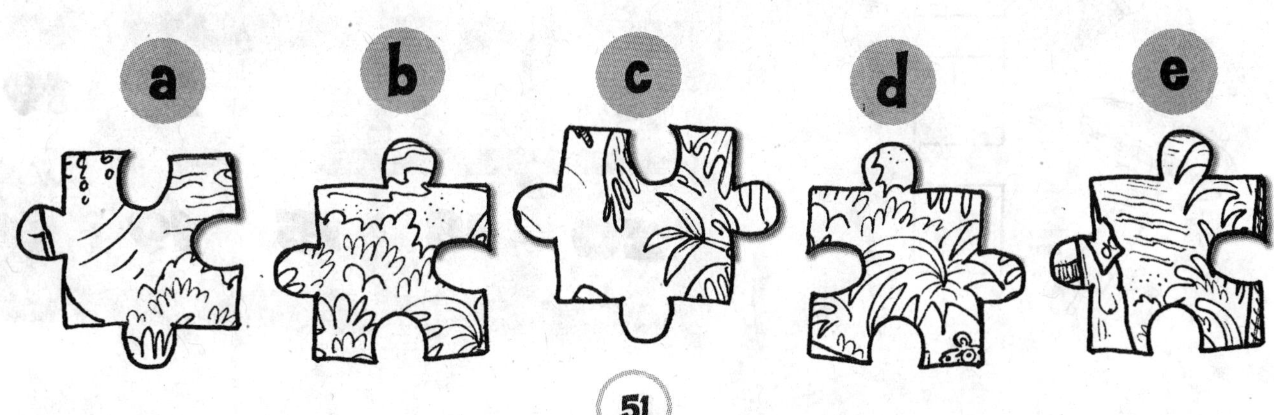

SNACK SUMS

Work out which number is represented by each piece of food to make the sums add up on each row and column.

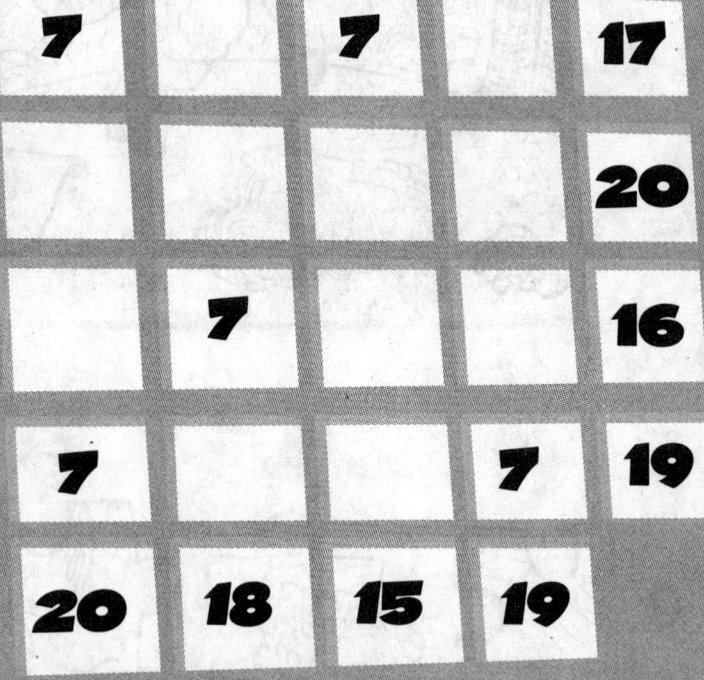

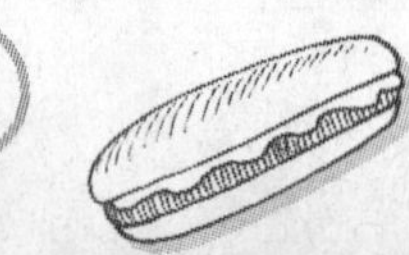

DOUBLE TROUBLE

Starting at X each time, use every other letter to spell the names of four sports. The remaining letters spell out a different activity.

FOURASAURUS

Fill in the missing numbers on the dinosaur so that you complete the four times table.

BLAST OFF!

Which of these space shuttles is the odd one out?

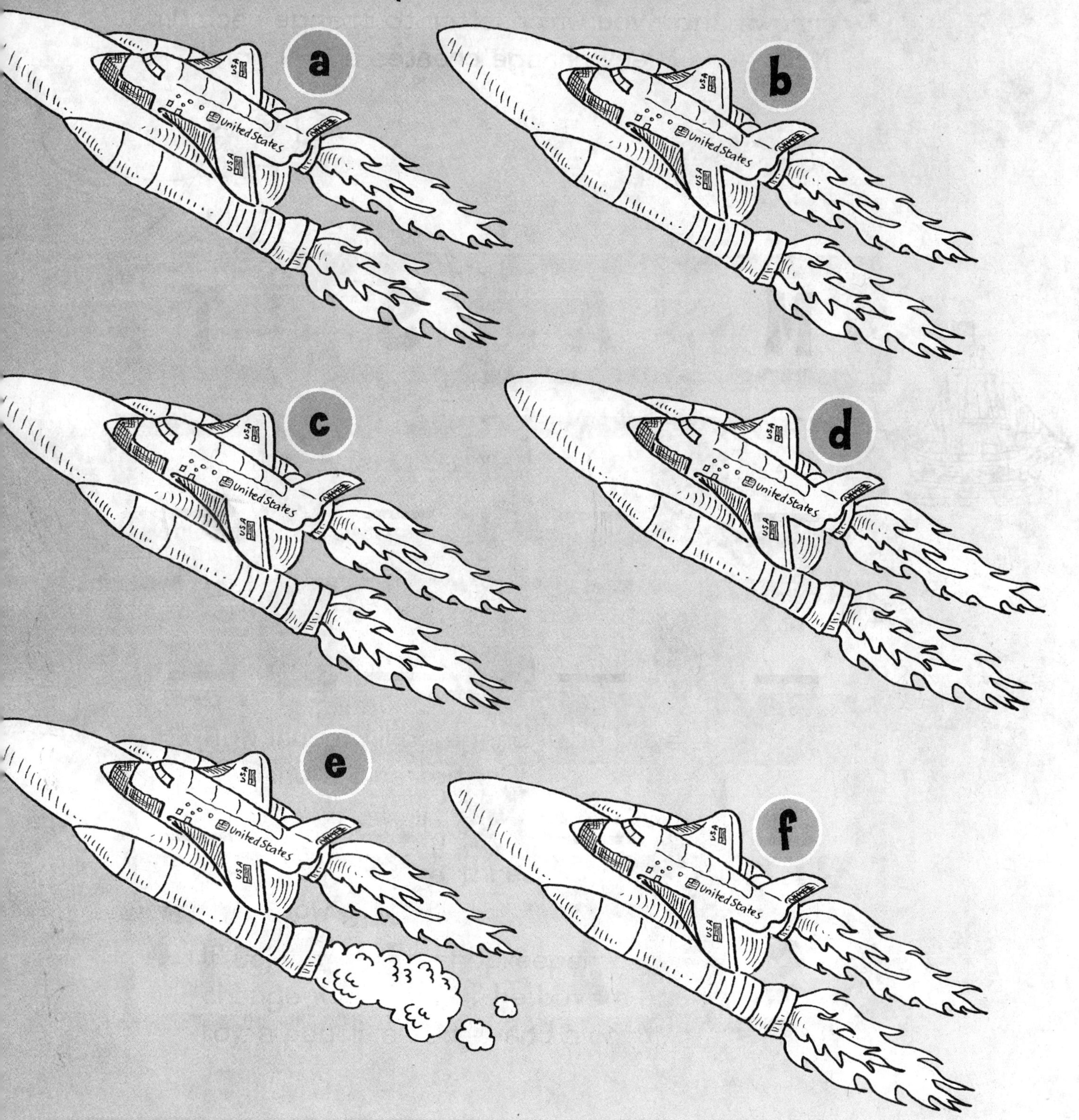

RIGGING RIDDLE

Change the word MAST to the word SAIL one letter at a time. The arrows show you which letter to change each time. Make sure every change creates a real word.

M A S T

_ _ _ _

_ _ _ _

_ _ _ _

S A I L

NUMBER MAZE

Answer the sums correctly to work your way through the grid of numbers.

START

5 ↓	13 – 3	16 ↓	7 x 2	8 ↓	24 ÷ 6	5 ↓	7 – 1
8 + 3	14 ↑	4 + 4	16 ↑	30 ÷ 2	11 ↑	10 x 1	1 ↑
11 →	4 x 2	8 →	12 – 6	19 ↓	18 – 7	3 ↓	4 x 2
15 ÷ 5	6 ↓	9 + 7	6 →	10 ÷ 2	20 ↓	4 x 7	5 ↓
7 ↓	1 x 11	13 ↓	4 x 8	5 ↓	8 – 2	16 ↓	6 x 3
6 x 6	← 2	18 ÷ 9	← 22	11 + 11	← 40	9 ÷ 3	← 1
36 ↓	3 x 4	 19 ↓	20 ÷ 5	 6 ↓	21 – 5	 0 ↓	18 – 11
14 ÷ 7	 5 ↓	30 ÷ 6	 8 ↓	24 – 8	 3 ↓	7 x 5	 15 ↓
2 →	30 – 18	 12 →	3 x 3	 7 ↓	13 + 11	 14 ↓	40 ÷ 4
27 ÷ 9	← 43	16 – 7	← 9	8 x 3	← 50	11 x 3	← 6
		9 ↓					

FINISH

ELEPHANT RIDE

This elephant is fit to carry a king! But which silhouette matches it exactly?

ANIMAL MIX UP

Match the boxes in pairs to make the names of ten different animals. One has been done to help you.

~~MON~~ UAR RUS MOT GER

OTE BiL HON GiB BAD WAL

MAR PYT ~~KEY~~ COY

BON TLE TUR JAG GER

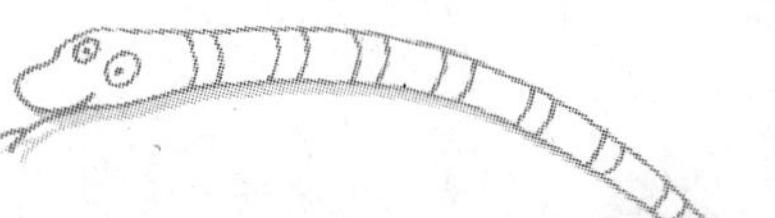

ALPHADOKU

Solve the puzzle so that every row, column and mini-grid contains the letters A to F.

F				B	C
	B	C			
	C		A		B
B				F	
			B	A	
A	E				F

STATION SLEUTH

Test your memory by studying the picture for three minutes, and then turning the page to see how many questions you can answer correctly.

STATION SLEUTH

How much can you remember about the picture on the previous page?

1. How many taxis are waiting outside the station?
2. What time is it?
3. Where is the closest train going to?
4. How many suitcases are on the baggage trailer?
5. What is the man on the bench doing?
6. In which direction do you go for the toilets, left or right?
7. What is printed on the T-shirt of the man by the train?
8. What is on sale in the shop at the back of the station?
9. What musical instrument can you see?
10. What platform numbers can you see?

FAIRY DUST

Only two of these fairies are exactly the same.
Can you spot them?

ENDANGERED SPECIES

Some of the world's most amazing animals are in danger of becoming extinct. Can you find these eight in the grid? Look for the names in capitals hidden across, down or diagonally.

ELEPHANT | **PANDA**
GORILLA | **RHINOCEROS**
LEOPARD | **TIGER**
ORANGUTAN | **WOLF**

E	L	E	P	N	T	L	O	E	P	A	D
L	E	A	A	A	Y	I	D	U	G	X	R
W	O	T	W	T	N	A	G	T	W	E	A
A	X	O	O	U	R	D	U	E	O	C	P
E	L	E	F	G	U	O	A	T	R	Y	O
F	O	L	T	N	A	H	P	E	L	E	E
D	R	E	I	A	O	R	P	H	A	N	L
U	A	S	O	R	E	C	O	N	I	H	R
G	N	R	H	O	O	N	R	H	I	P	O
B	T	I	C	H	E	G	T	A	H	A	Y

A BUG'S LIFE

Help the bug munch its way through the apple maze.

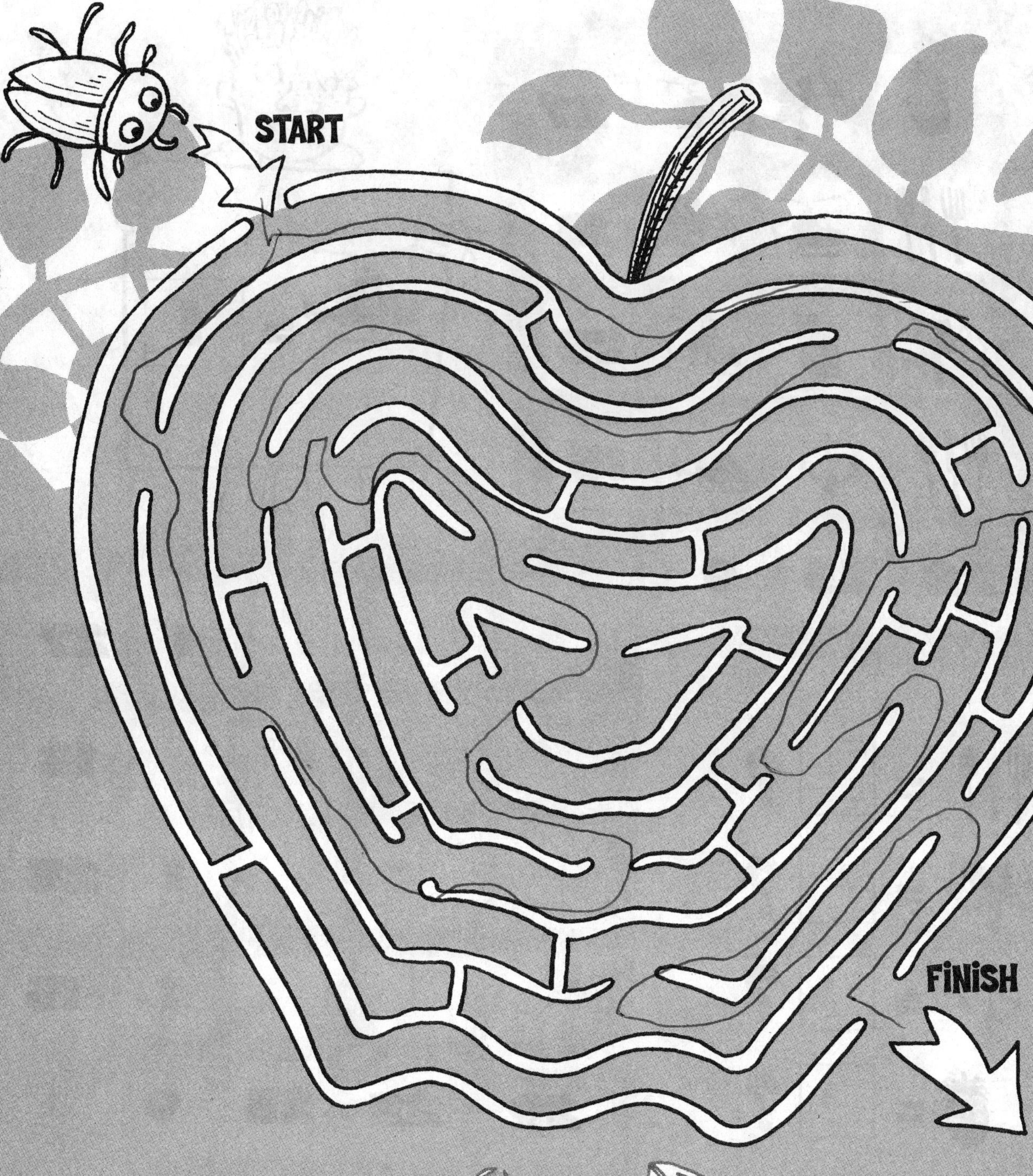

START

FINISH

NUMBER CRUNCH

Work out which number is represented by each symbol to make the sums add up in each row and column.

= ?

= ?

= ?

= ?

OLYMPIC GAMES

Answer the questions using the grid references on the map.

1. What sport can you watch in D1 and D2?
2. Which square is the diving pool in?
3. Where should you go to watch archery?
4. Which sport is directly below the gymnastics arena?

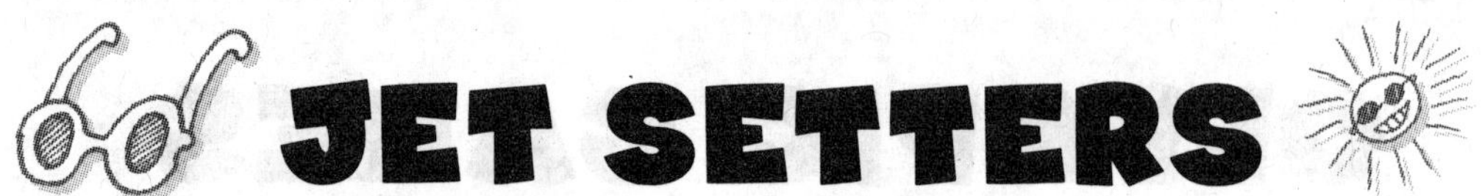

JET SETTERS

How many words of three letters or more can you make up from the letters below? Two are listed to get you started.

AROUND THE WORLD

1 HEART

2 TOWER

3

4

5

6

7

8

9

10

11

12

MAGICAL MARVIN

Help the magician find his rabbit by counting in threes, starting at the number 3.

START

30	27	24	21	18	9	6	3
33	48	51	54	15	12		
36	45	60	57				
39	42	63	72	75			
		66	69	78			
		93	90	81			
102	99	96	87	84			

FINISH

RIDE 'EM COWBOY!

Yee-ha! Which of the silhouettes exactly matches the main picture?

FOODOKU

Solve the puzzle so that every row, column and mini-grid contains each of the four foods.

FLOWER FAIRIES

There are six things in the top picture that are not in the bottom picture. Can you circle them all?

SPY SCHOOL

Use the coded alphabet to find out where the spy needs to visit for his next rendezvous.

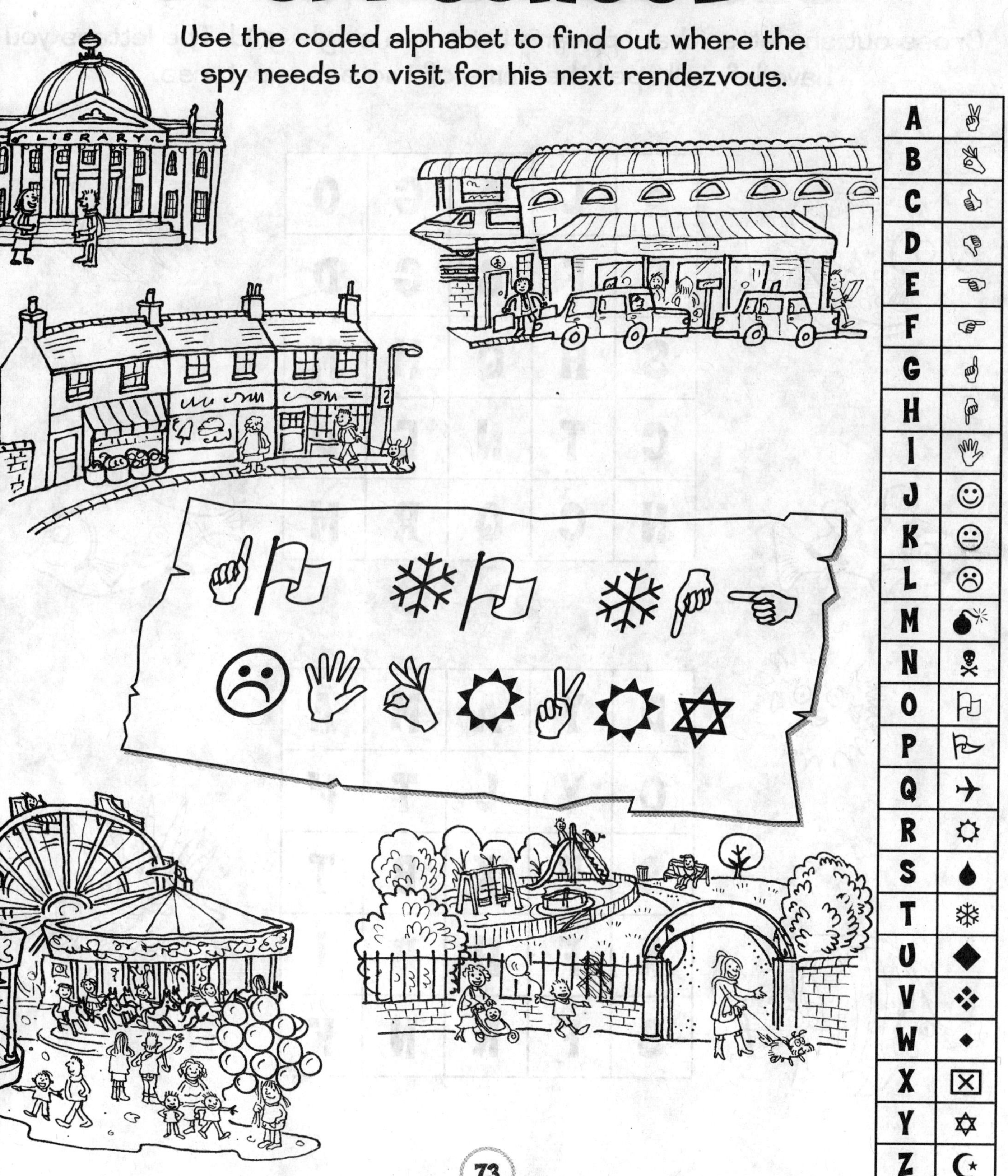

SEA LIFE SQUARES

Cross out any letter that appears twice in a single grid. The letters you have left will spell the name of two sea creatures.

A	L	A	G	O
F	F	B	G	D
S	H	Q	H	M
C	T	N	E	D
N	C	Q	R	M

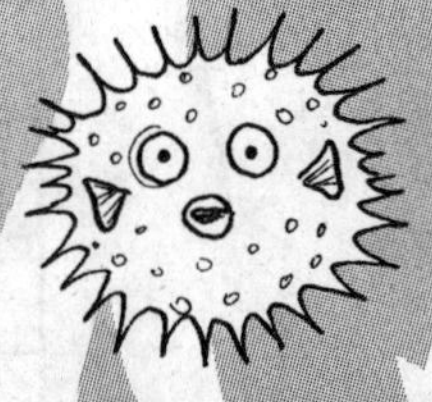

D	Y	A	M	A
O	Y	L	T	M
S	P	X	B	T
X	F	H	B	i
S	F	K	N	K

CRAZY CRABS

Find a route through the crazy crabs, following them in this order all the way through.

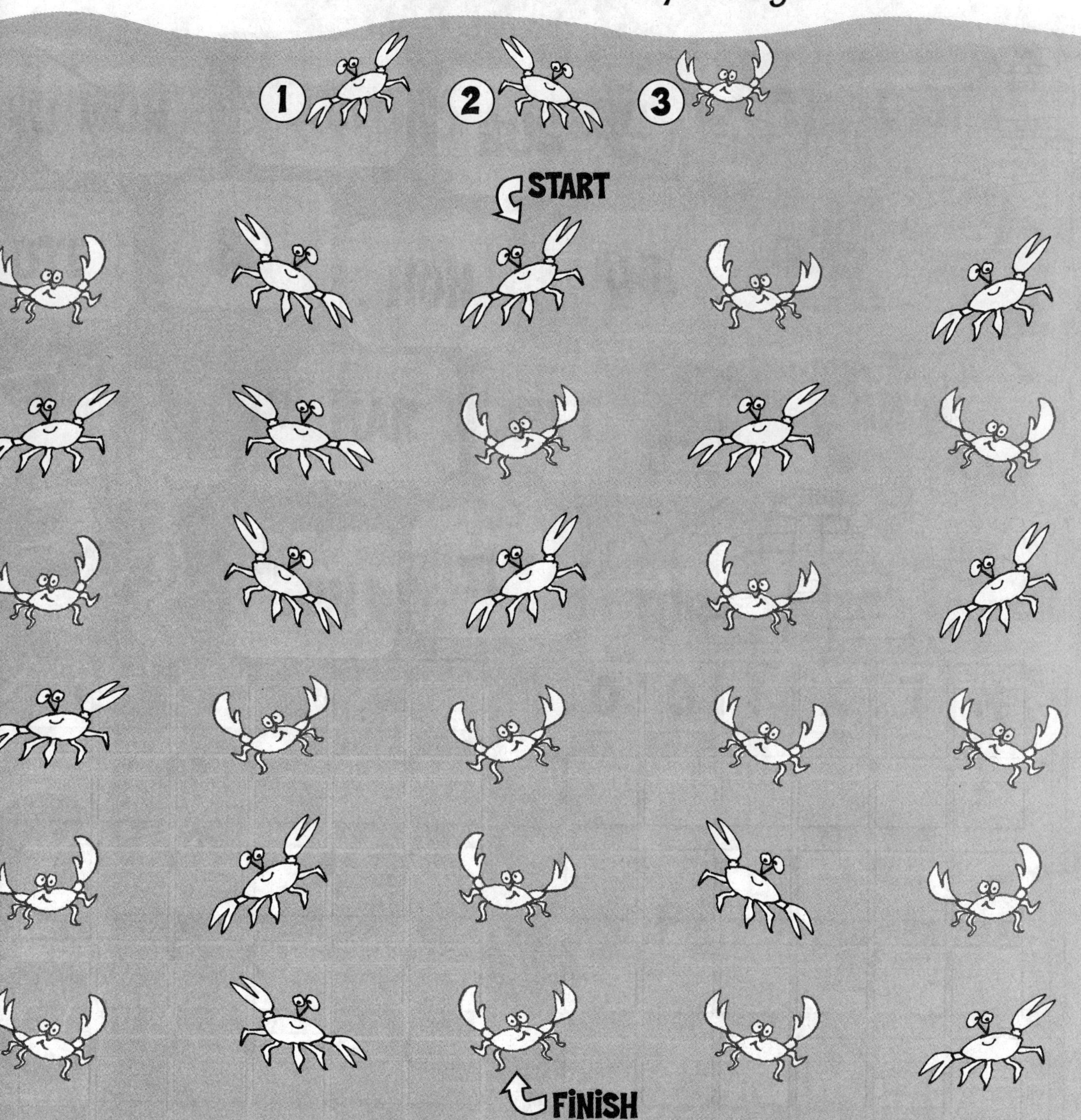

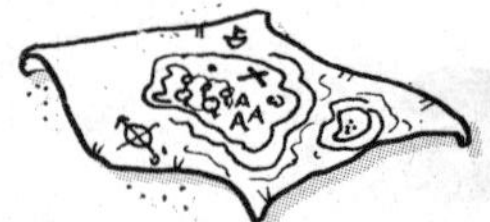

MAP MIX UP

Match the boxes in pairs to make the names of ten different countries. One has been done to help you.

FRA	AiT	DEN	CAN	ECE	TUR
	iCO	SiA	KEY	POL	GRE
AND	NCE	ADA	iSR	SWE	
	MEX	KUW	AEL	RUS	

M	E	X	i	C	O						

MONSTER TRUCK

Which jigsaw piece finishes the picture: a, b, c, d or e?

a

b

c

d

e

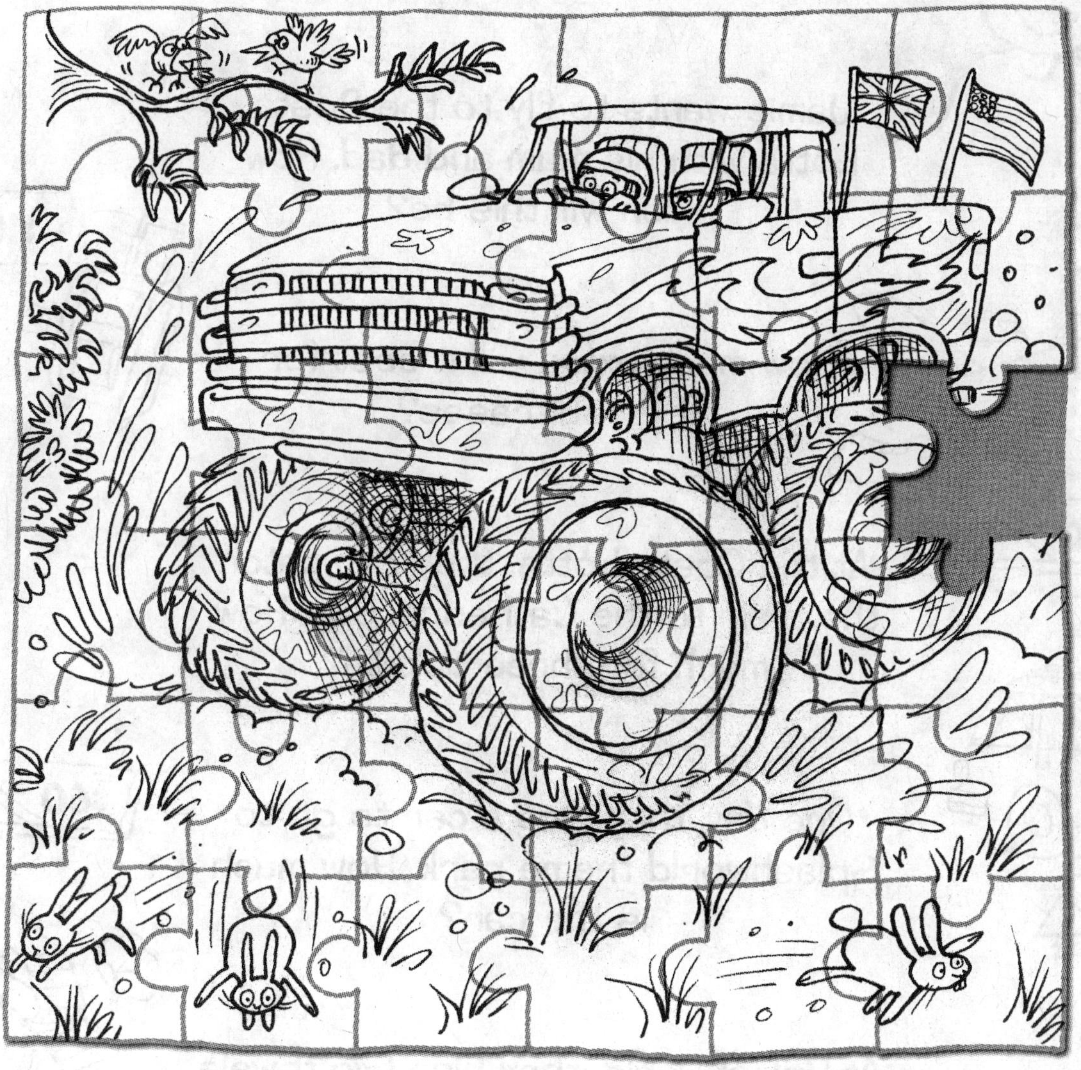

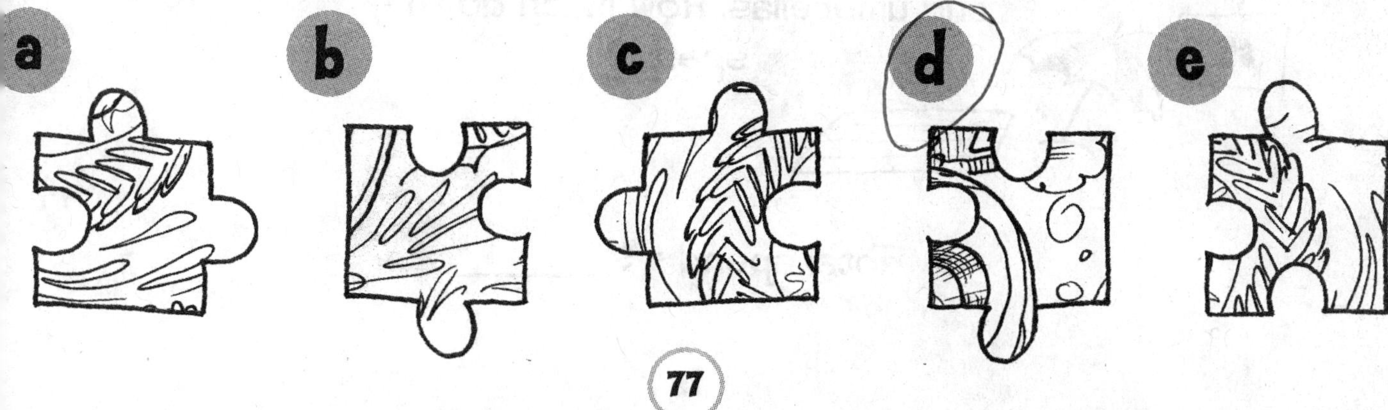

TAKING A TRIP

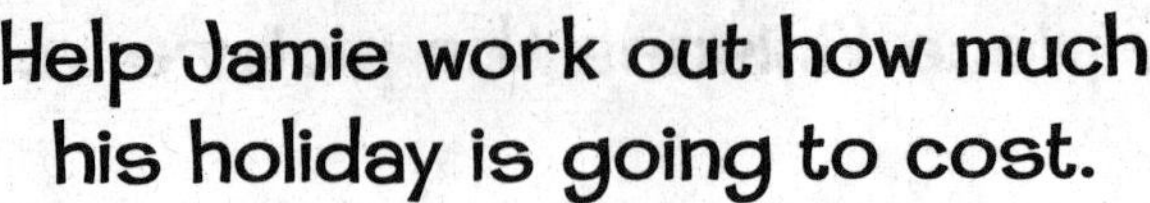

Help Jamie work out how much his holiday is going to cost.

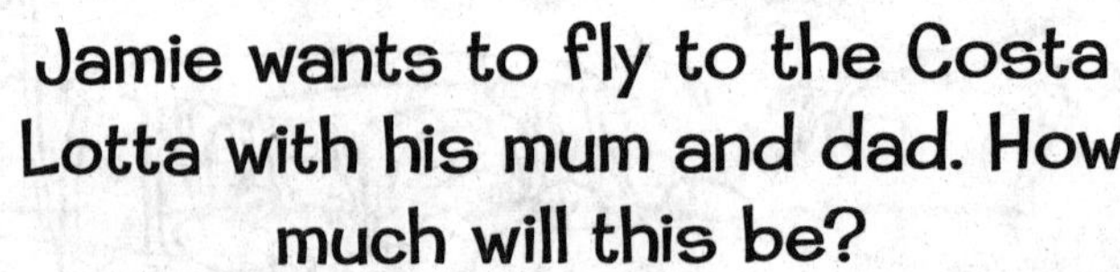

Jamie wants to fly to the Costa Lotta with his mum and dad. How much will this be?

$100

How much extra will it cost for four suitcases?

At the Costa Lotta, they can catch the train to the Cathedral City. How much for three tickets?

One day, they hire a car to go to Splashworld theme park. How much is the car?

At Splashworld, they hire two towels and umbrellas. How much do they spend?

$5

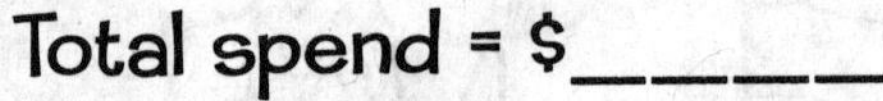

Total spend = $______

WHAT TO WEAR?

Which T-shirt does Emily want to wear today?
Use the clues to help her choose.

1. She doesn't want a plain one.
2. She's not in the mood for stripes.
3. She wants one with a white background.
4. She doesn't want one with a star on it.

a

b

c

d

e

f

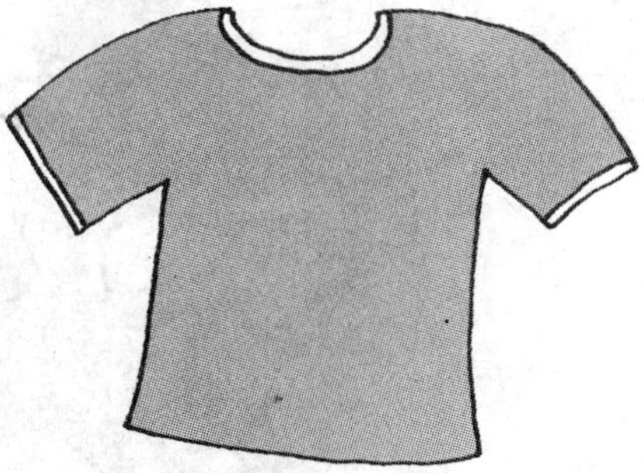

CLIMBING THE WALL

Use the nine times table to help Josh make his way up the climbing wall. Don't take a wrong turn!

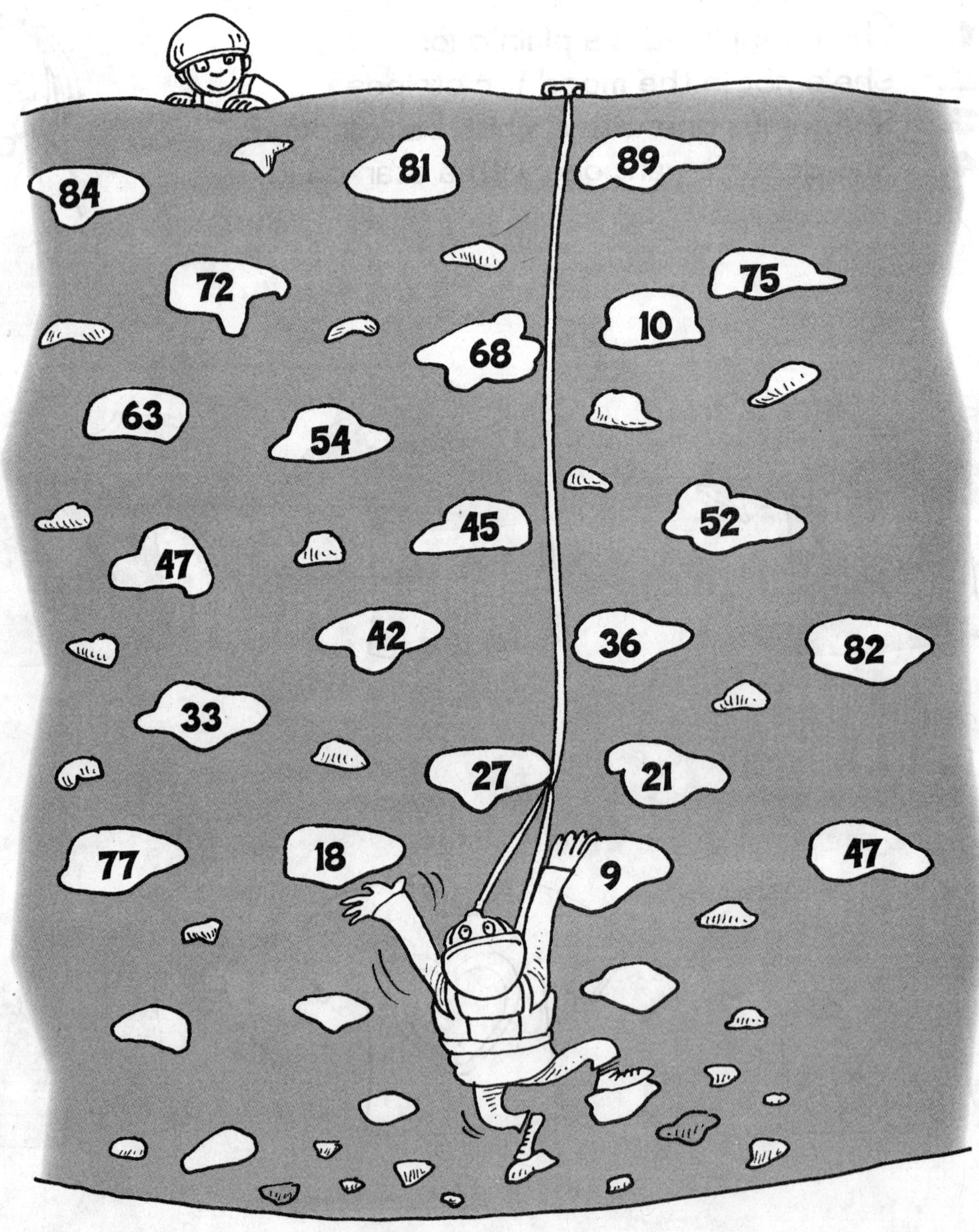

TIDY UP TIME

Mr Sprout the gardener has been raking up leaves. How many can you count in the pile? How many hidden bugs can you count?

SPOT THE DIFFERENCE

There are six differences between these two pictures. Can you circle them all?

SUDOKU

Solve the puzzle so that every row, column and mini-grid contains the numbers 1 to 6.

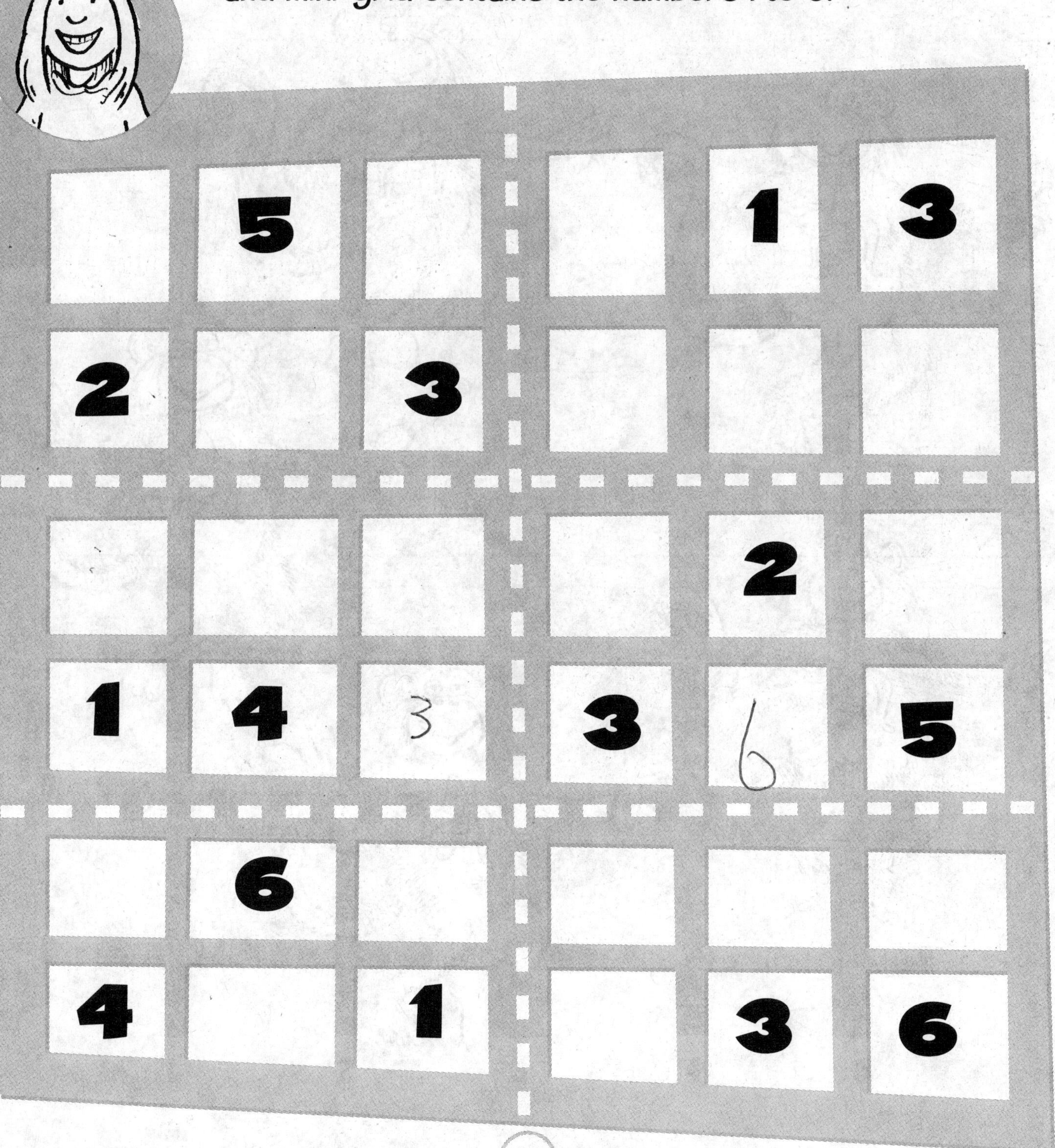

	5			1	3
2		3			
				2	
1	4		3		5
	6				
4		1		3	6

CHEEKY MONKEYS

Which of these monkeys is the odd one out?

a

b

c

d

e

IN THE LAB

Look at the main picture of a science lesson and then work out which of the smaller pictures is how the lesson would look from above.

TROPICAL PARADISE

Use your eagle eyes to spot each of the items at the foot of the page, hidden in the main picture.

SPY SCHOOL

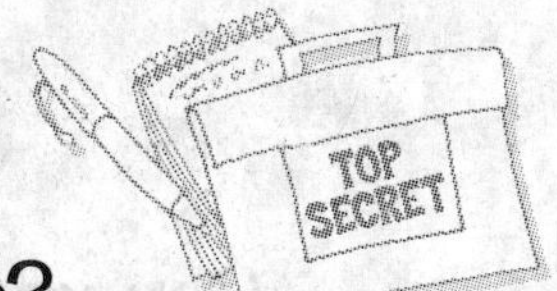

Can you crack the code to find the joke?

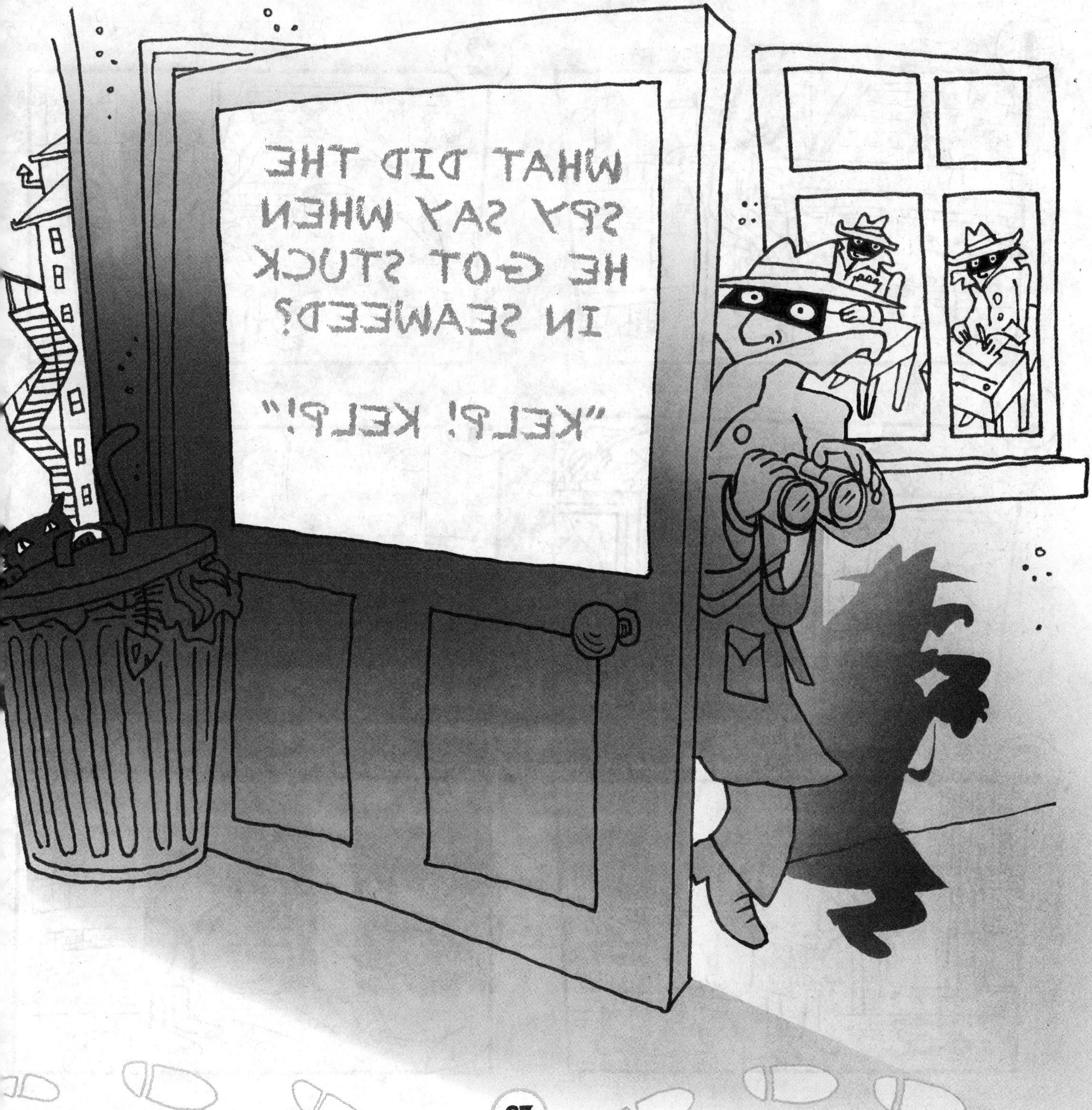

WHAT DID THE SPY SAY WHEN HE GOT STUCK IN SEAWEED?

"KELP! KELP!"

OUT OF ORDER

Can you rearrange the six pictures so that they tell the story in the correct order?

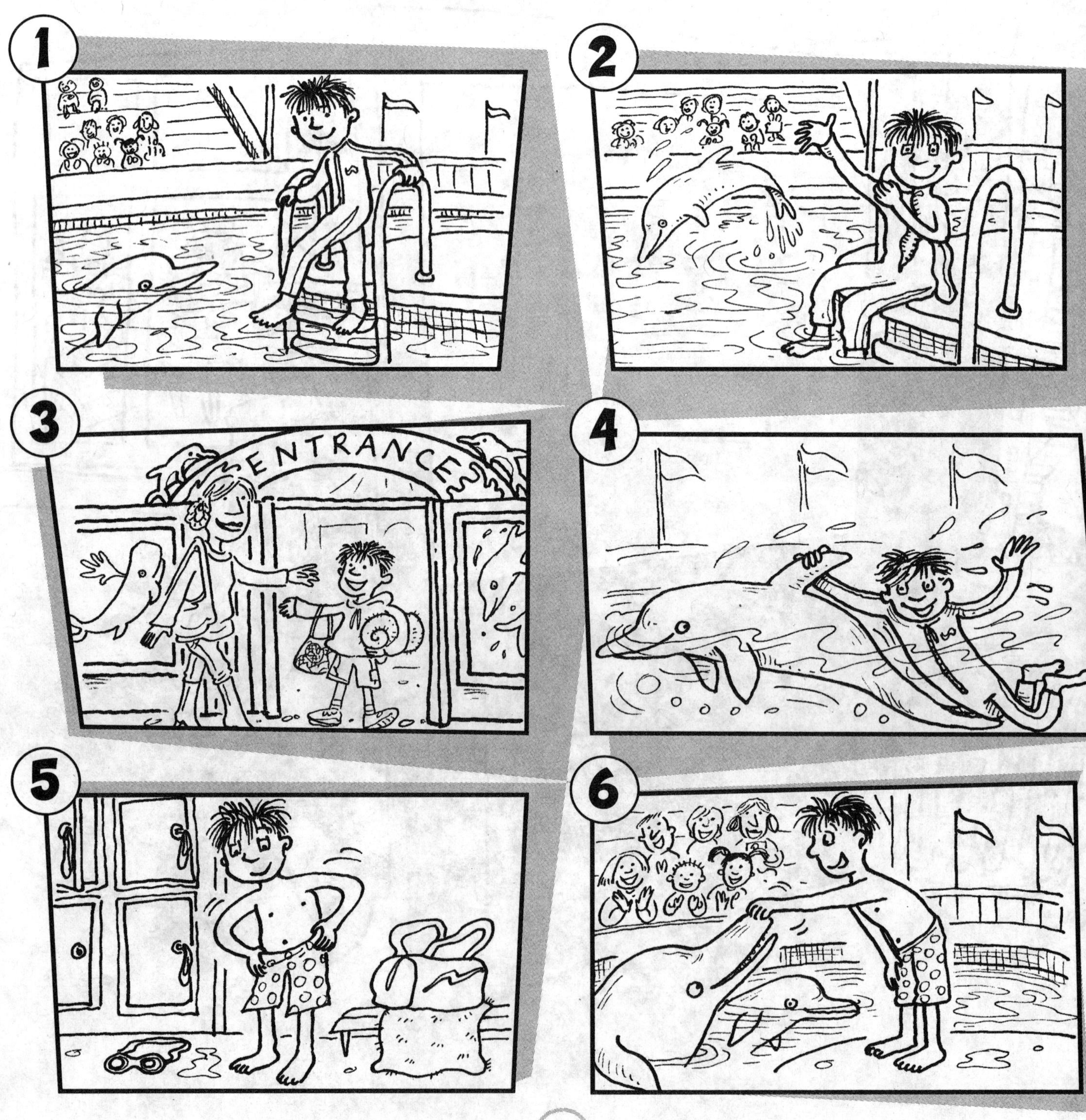

GRIDLOCKED

The mini-grid only appears once in the whole of the larger grid.
Can you find it?

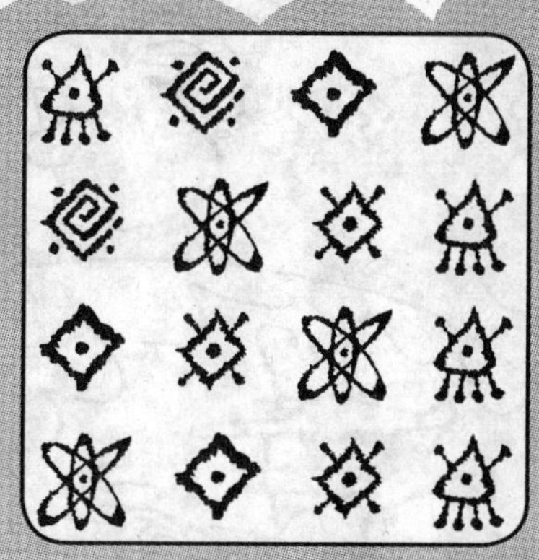

JEWEL THIEF

Answer the questions to fill in the code and allow the spy to find the stolen jewels!

1. How many jewels are on the vase?
2. How many bags of money can you count?
3. How many gold ingots are in the biggest pile?
4. How many necklaces are there altogether?

FLYING FUN

Put your memory to the test by studying the picture for three minutes, and then turning the page to see how many questions you can answer correctly.

FLYING FUN

How much can you remember about the picture on the previous page?

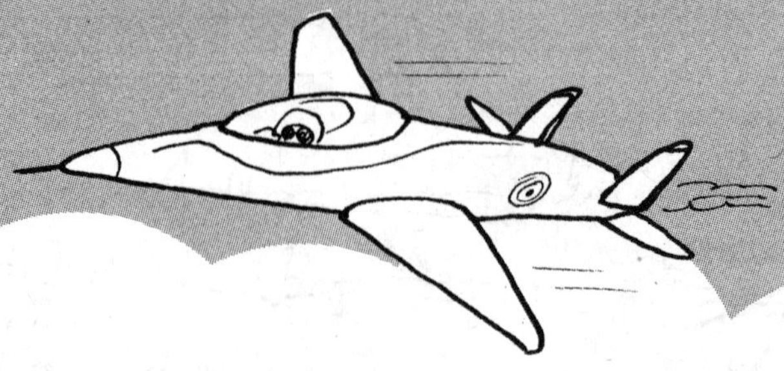

1. How many planes are flying in the diamond formation?
2. Is the helicopter flying or on the ground?
3. How many flags are at the entrance?
4. How many parachutes can you count?
5. What pattern is on the lady's bobble hat?
6. What two types of food are on sale?
7. How many long trails of smoke are there?
8. What day is it?
9. What number is on the helicopter?
10. How many people are using binoculars?

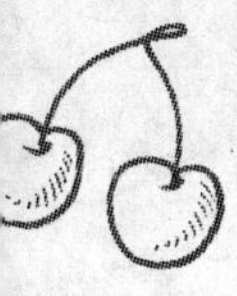

DELICIOUS DESSERTS

Only two of these ice-cream sundaes are exactly the same. Can you spot them?

a

b

c

d

e

f

BUGOKU

Solve the puzzle so that every row, column and mini-grid contains each of the four bugs.

TREASURE HUNT

Follow the directions to find out where the ancient treasure is buried.

1. Start in square E5 by the babbling brook.
2. Walk two squares west past the castle.
3. Head north two squares to the ancient church.
4. Turn west in the direction of the burial mound and walk for one square.
5. Head north one square. Put an X to mark the treasure!

CREEPY CRAWLIES

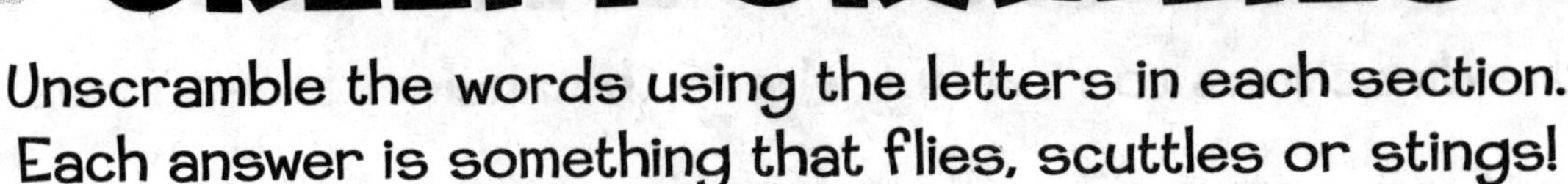

Unscramble the words using the letters in each section.
Each answer is something that flies, scuttles or stings!

L B E M B E E B U	D R Y I B A L D
T E I D E P N C E	T F U L T B E Y R

FIRE DRILL

Help the fire engine join the firemen at the practice building by counting in fours.

START

				4	8	12	16
				72	68	64	20
116	112	100	96	76	80	60	24
120	108	104	92	88	84	56	28
124	128					52	32
136	132					48	36
140						44	40

FINISH

LIBRARY CODES

This spy has been sent to the library to pick up his next message. Use the code to work out which section he must visit.

A	
B	
C	
D	
E	
F	
G	
H	
I	
J	
K	
L	
M	
N	
O	
P	
Q	
R	
S	
T	
U	
V	
W	
X	
Y	
Z	

PLAY TIME

Can you spot which five items are missing in the bottom picture?

ALPHADOKU

Solve the puzzle so that every row, column and mini-grid contains each of the letters A to F.

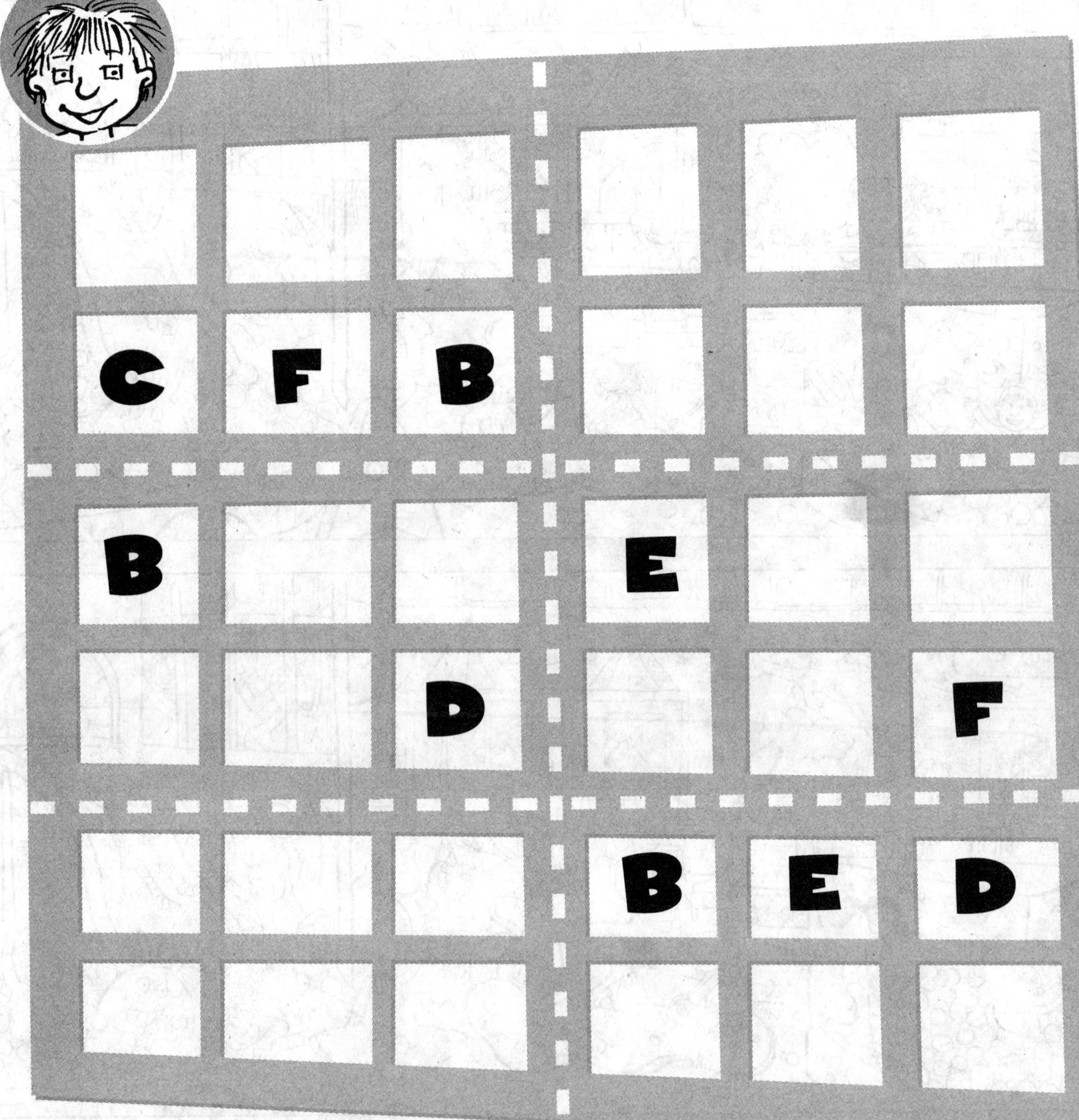

TOTALLY TROPICAL

How many tropical fish can you count on this page?

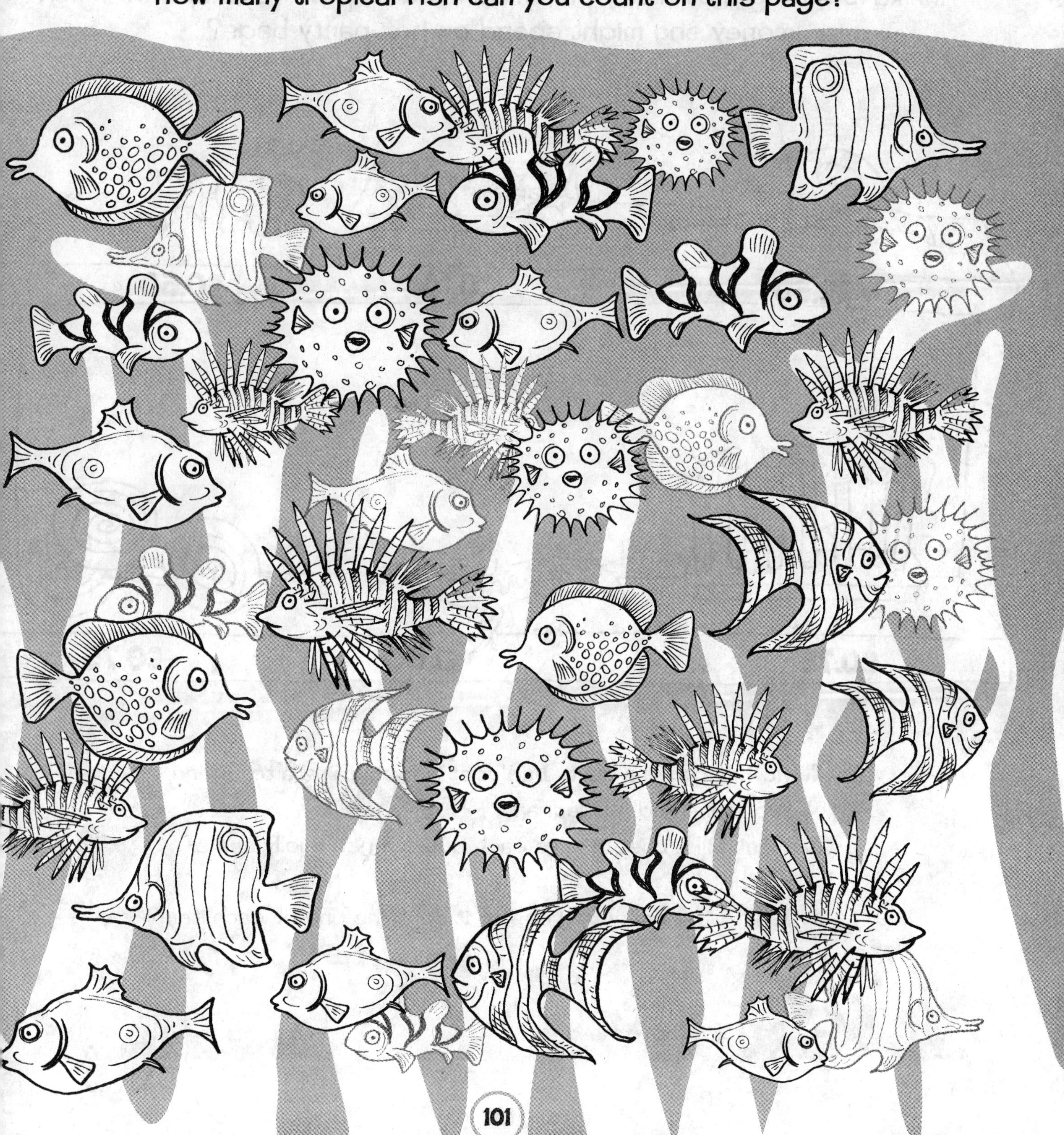

PARTY BAGS

Annika is having a birthday party. Can you help her add up how much money she might spend on her party bags?

1. How much will a party bag cost if it contains a toy lizard, two stars and an elephant?
2. What will it cost to give each guest a hat, a lolly and a pencil?
3. What will a party bag cost if it contains one of each item?

FANTASTIC GYMNASTICS

Look at the people in this gym class. They've moved round a lot between pictures! Can you see two new people and two people who have left?

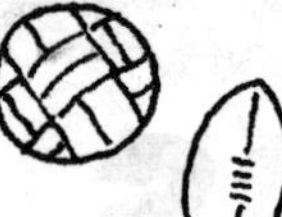

SUMMER OLYMPICS

Can you find these ten Summer Olympic events in the grid? Look for the names hidden across, down or diagonally.

ARCHERY
ATHLETICS
BADMINTON
BOXING
DIVING
FENCING
HANDBALL
ROWING
SWIMMING
TENNIS

F	I	B	O	F	E	N	C	I	N	G	C
E	A	H	A	N	D	B	A	L	L	F	R
N	T	X	R	D	G	G	O	I	W	S	O
M	H	S	C	I	M	N	R	X	I	A	W
I	L	W	H	V	B	I	U	N	I	R	I
N	E	I	E	I	O	H	N	A	B	N	N
G	T	M	R	N	X	E	B	T	H	O	G
B	I	T	Y	G	T	A	O	H	O	A	X
O	C	E	A	S	W	I	M	M	I	N	G
X	S	I	N	G	H	A	N	D	F	Y	Y

WHAT NEXT?

Study the sequence of pictures carefully and work out which statue finishes the pattern: a, b or c?

CASTLE CAPERS

Answer the questions with the grid references from the map.

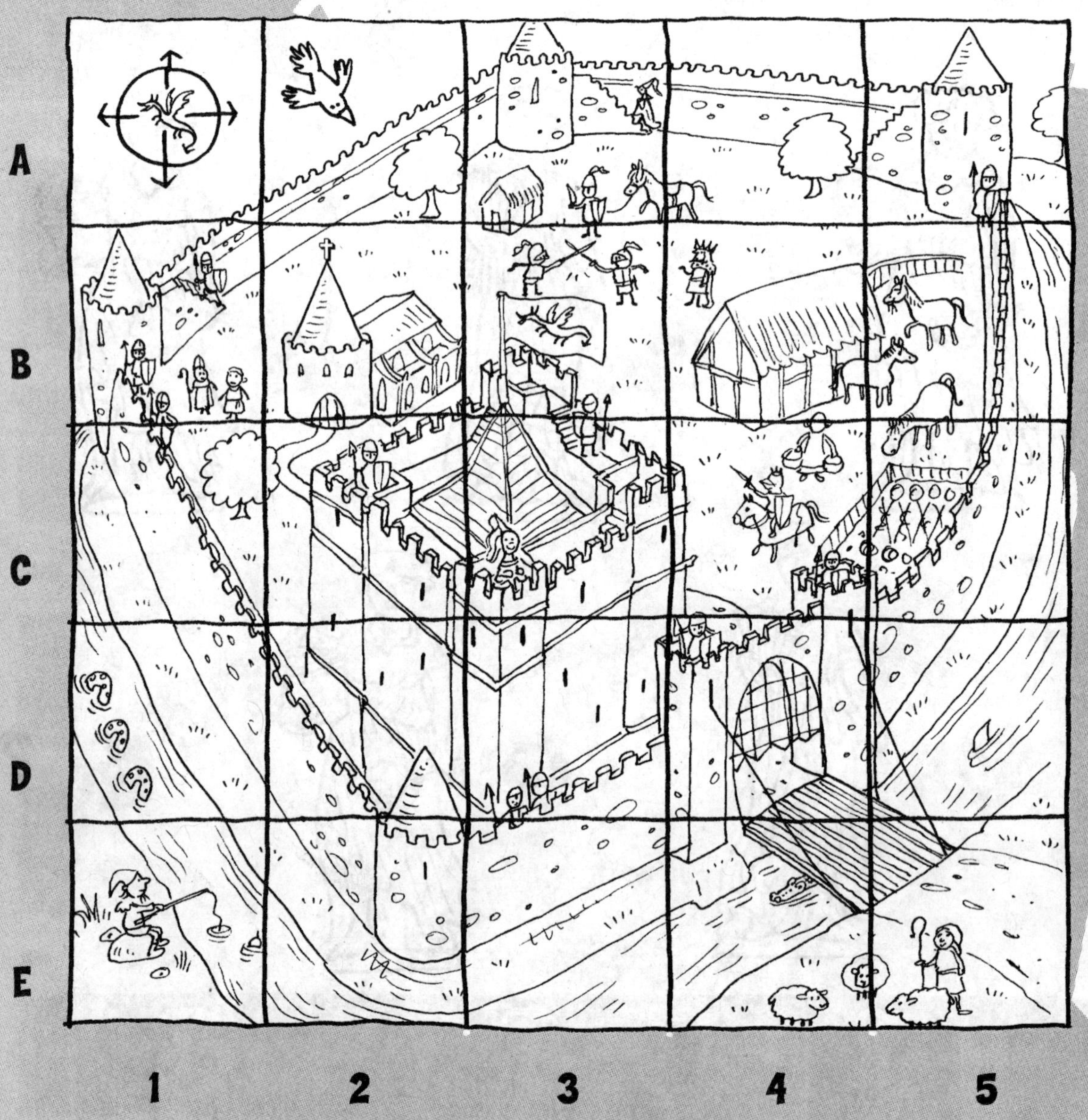

1. What building is in square B2?
2. In which square is the portcullis?
3. Which square does not have a guard tower: B1, E3, A5 or A3?
4. What animals are kept in the building in B4?

COOL CALCULATIONS

Work out how much it costs to buy all the tasty treats in the circle.

CHILL-OUT TIME

Can you guide the girl through the maze to have a well-deserved lie down on the beach?

BIRD BRAINS

Match the boxes in pairs to make the names of ten different birds.
One has been done to help you.

~~TOU~~ PUF PAR KEY EON

KOO TUR THR PIG FAL

MAG FIN CON ROT CON

DOR USH PIE CUC ~~CAN~~

T	O	U	C	A	N

SPOT THE DIFFERENCE

There are six things in the top picture that are not the same as the bottom picture. Can you circle them all?

 # FOODOKU 

Solve the sudoku puzzle so that every row, column and mini-grid has each of the four foods in it.

RAINY-DAY PUZZLE

How many words of three letters or more can you make from the letters below? Two are listed to get you started.

1 STRONG

2 GROSS

3 ______

4 ______

5 ______

6 ______

7 ______

8 ______

9 ______

10 ______

11 ______

12 ______

FAIRY TALE

Which jigsaw piece finishes the picture: a, b, c, d or e?

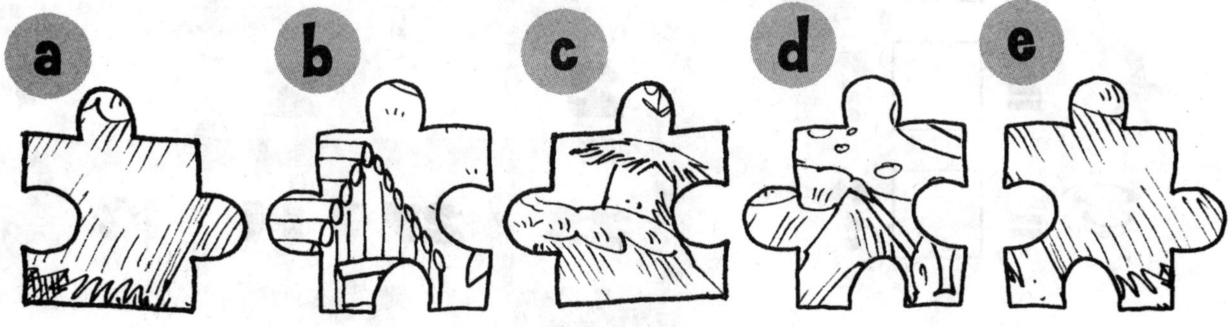

NUMBER CRUNCH

Work out which number is represented by each symbol to make the sums add up on each row and column.

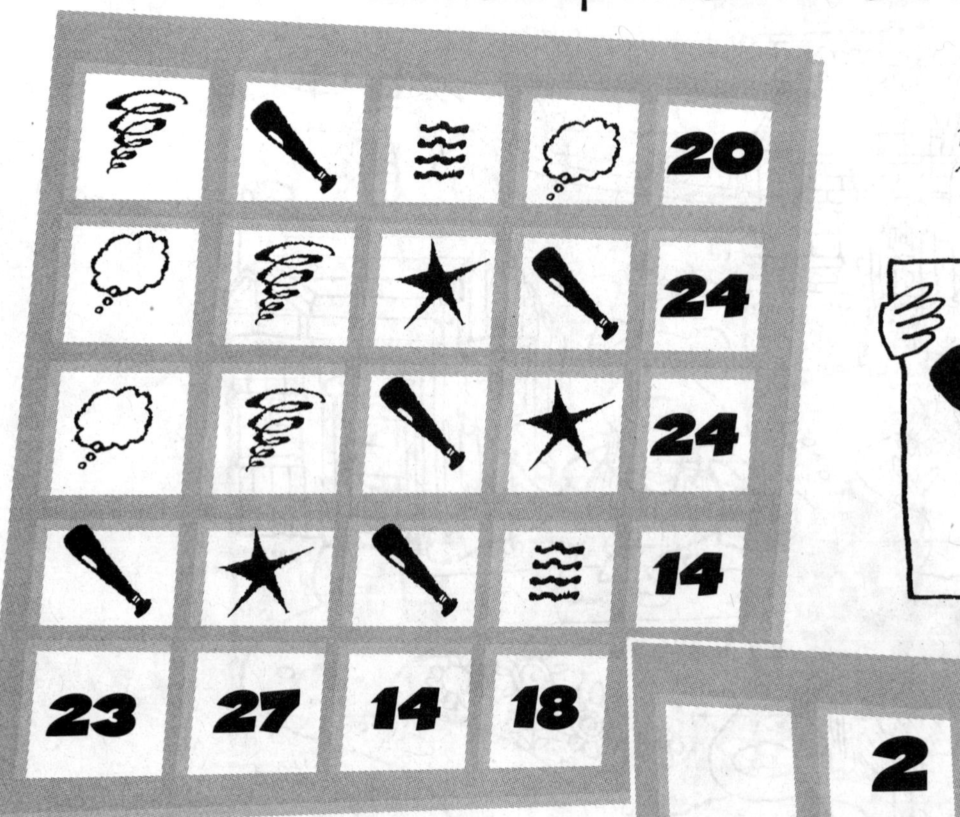

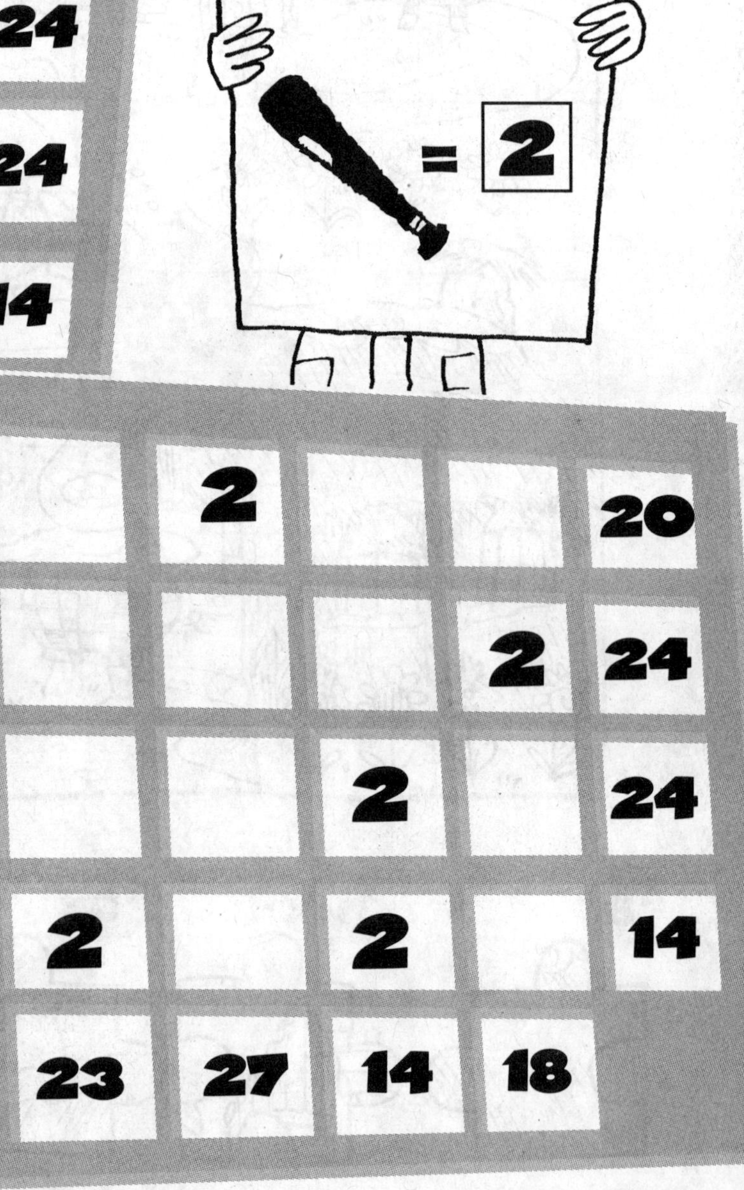

= ?

= ?

= ?

= ?

DINO CLUB

This spiny dinosaur is on the prowl! But which silhouette matches him exactly?

a

b

c

d

e

POPSICLE PUZZLER

Find a route through the popsicles, following them in this order all the way through.

1 2 3

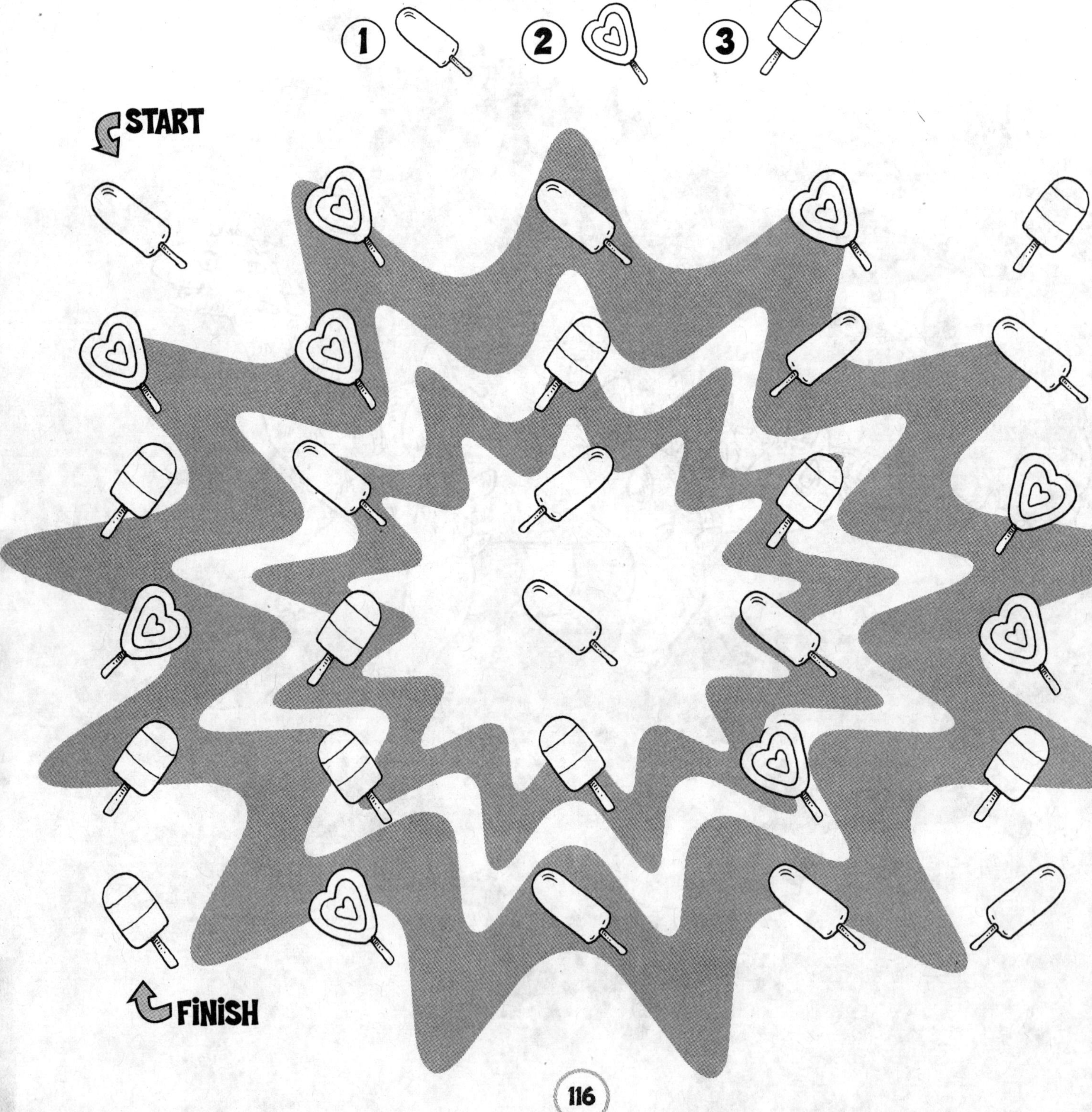

OCTOPLUS

Do each of the sums held by the octopus to fill in the number code and unlock the treasure chest.

TREASURE HUNT

Follow the directions and put an 'X' where the pirate treasure is buried.

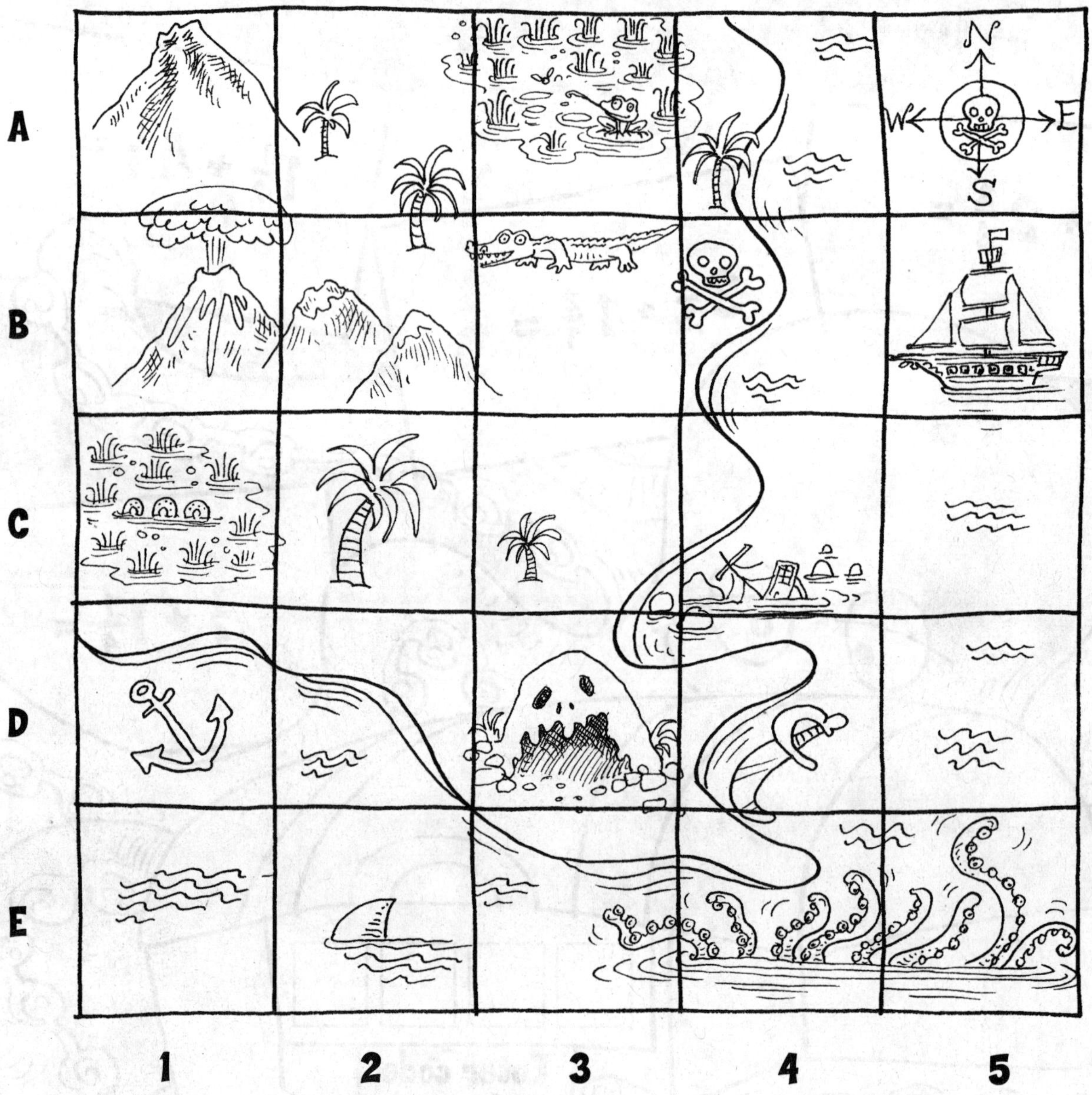

A

B

C

D

E

1 2 3 4 5

1. Set sail to Cutlass Cove in square D4.
2. Proceed on foot to Skull Cave in square D3.
3. Head due north three squares to the swamplands. Be careful not to sink!
4. Walk two squares west and one square south and start to dig!

SPY SCHOOL

Can you work out what this message says?

WHAT DO YOU
CALL A SPY WHO
HIDES AT THE
BEACH?

SANDY!

IN A TWIRL

Fill in the missing numbers on the gymnast's ribbon to complete the eight times table.

BEAUTIFUL BUTTERFLIES

Which of these butterflies is the odd one out?

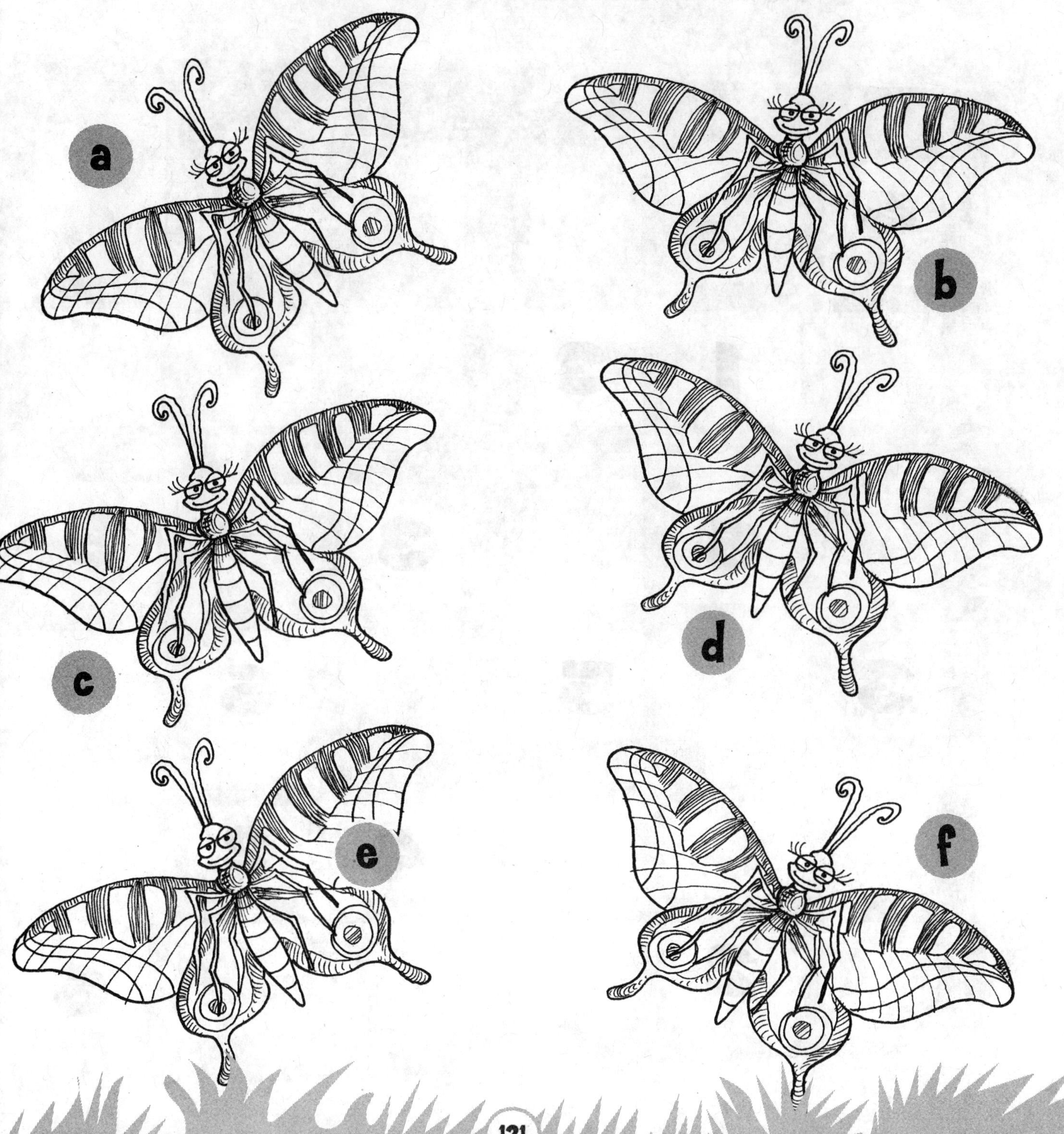

SUDOKU

Solve the puzzle so that each row, column and mini-grid contains the numbers 1 to 6.

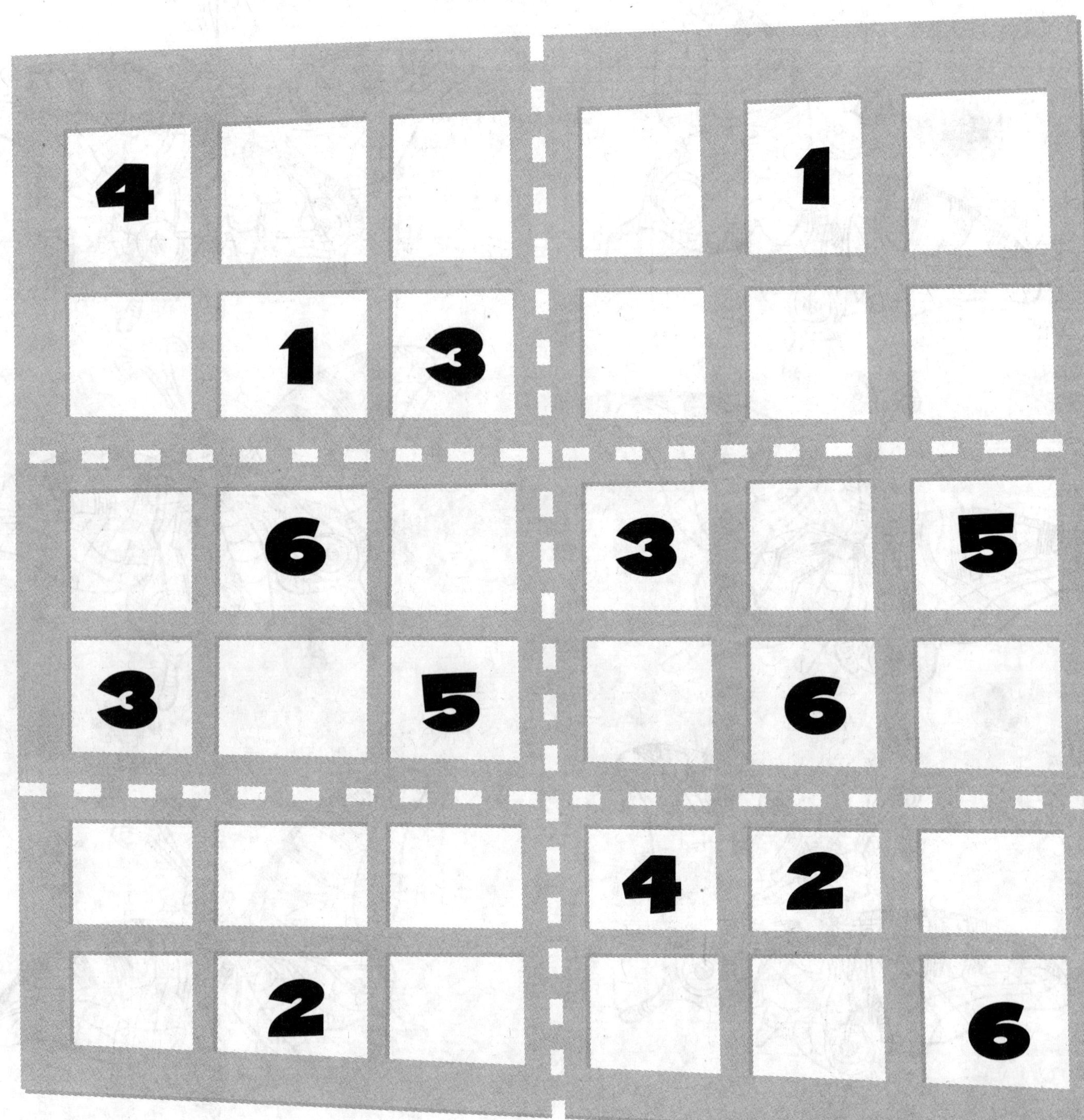

FAST FOOD FRAZZLER

Put your memory to the test by studying the picture for three minutes, and then turning the page to see how many questions you can answer correctly.

FAST FOOD FRAZZLER

How much can you remember about the picture on the previous page?

1. How many baseball caps can you see?
2. Is a man or a woman pushing the baby buggy?
3. Which toilets sign can you see: ladies or gents?
4. What two foods are on the menu on the table?
5. How many people are sitting at the table?
6. Is the server at the counter a man or a woman?
7. How many straws are in the drink on the table?
8. What is directly behind the rubbish bin?
9. What toy is the little boy holding?
10. How many people are wearing glasses?

GRIDLOCKED

The mini-grid only appears once in the whole of the larger grid.
Can you find it?

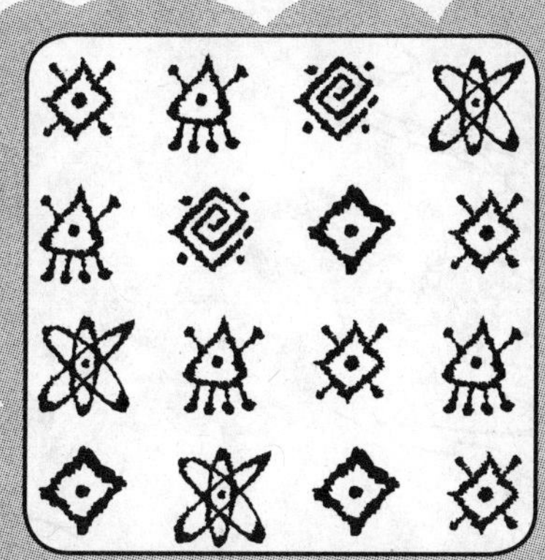

FIRE STARTERS

Only two of these dragons are exactly the same.
Can you spot which two?

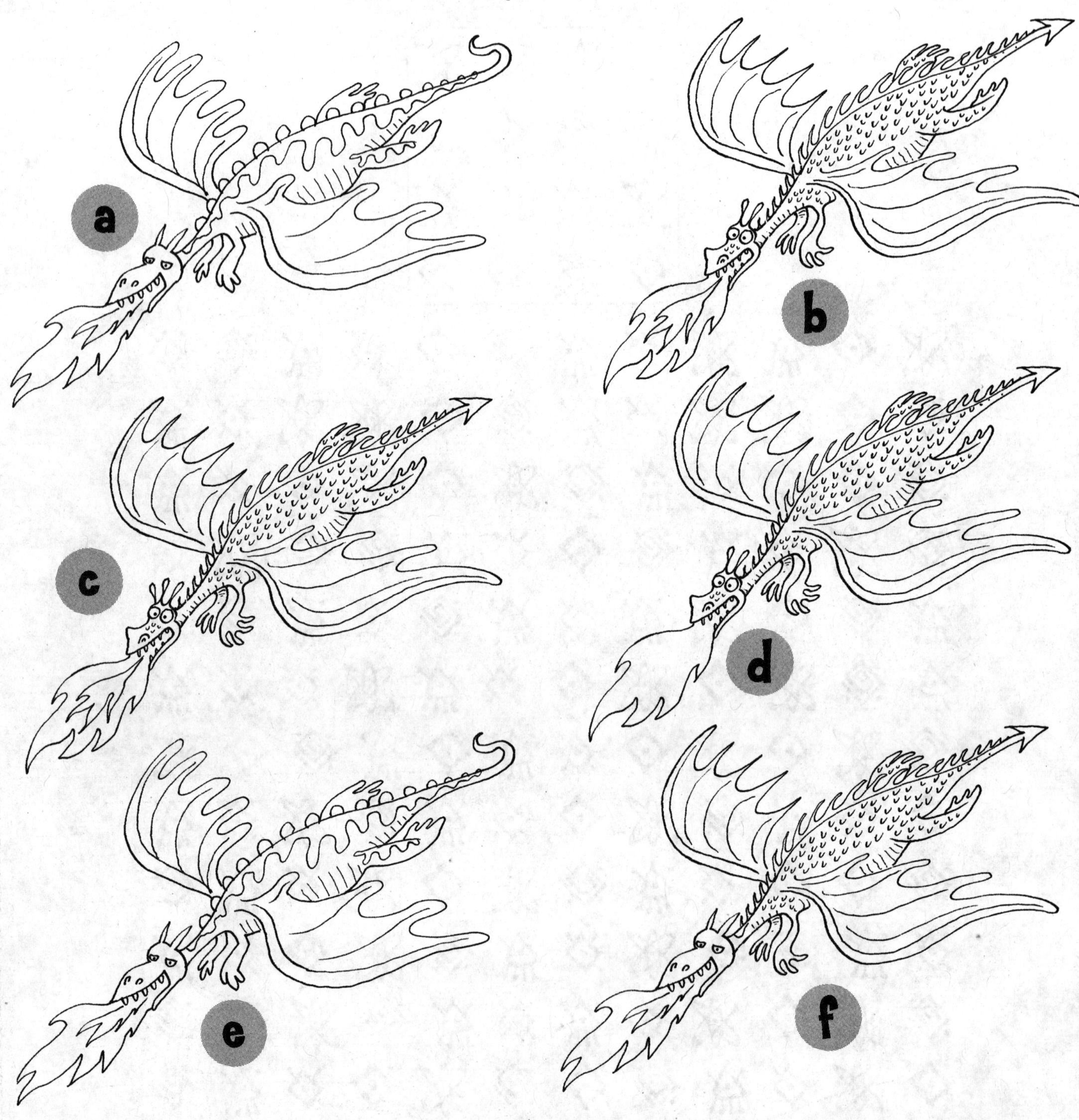

OUT OF ORDER

Can you rearrange the six pictures so that they tell the story in the correct order?

SHOPPING TRIP

Answer the questions with the grid references from the map.

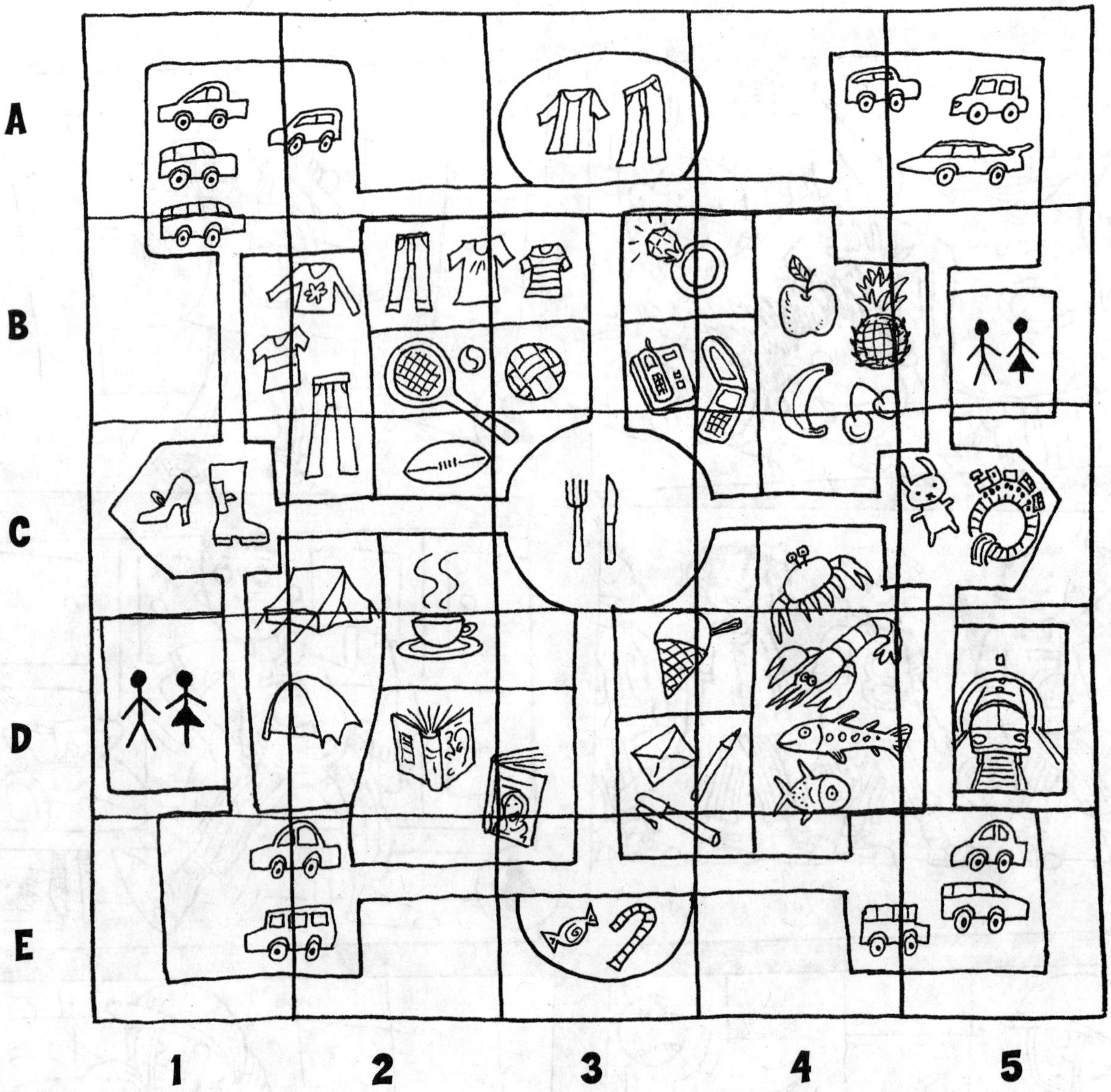

A
B
C
D
E

1 2 3 4 5

1. Which square does not have a car park: A1, E1, D1 or E5?
2. Which square is the shoe shop in?
3. What kind of shop is in A3?
4. Which square is the sweet shop in?

SNAIL TRAIL

Can you fit each of the creepy crawlies from the list into the spaces on the snail shell? The shaded spaces show the last letter of one word and the first letter of the next.

GLOWWORM

HORNET

TERMITE

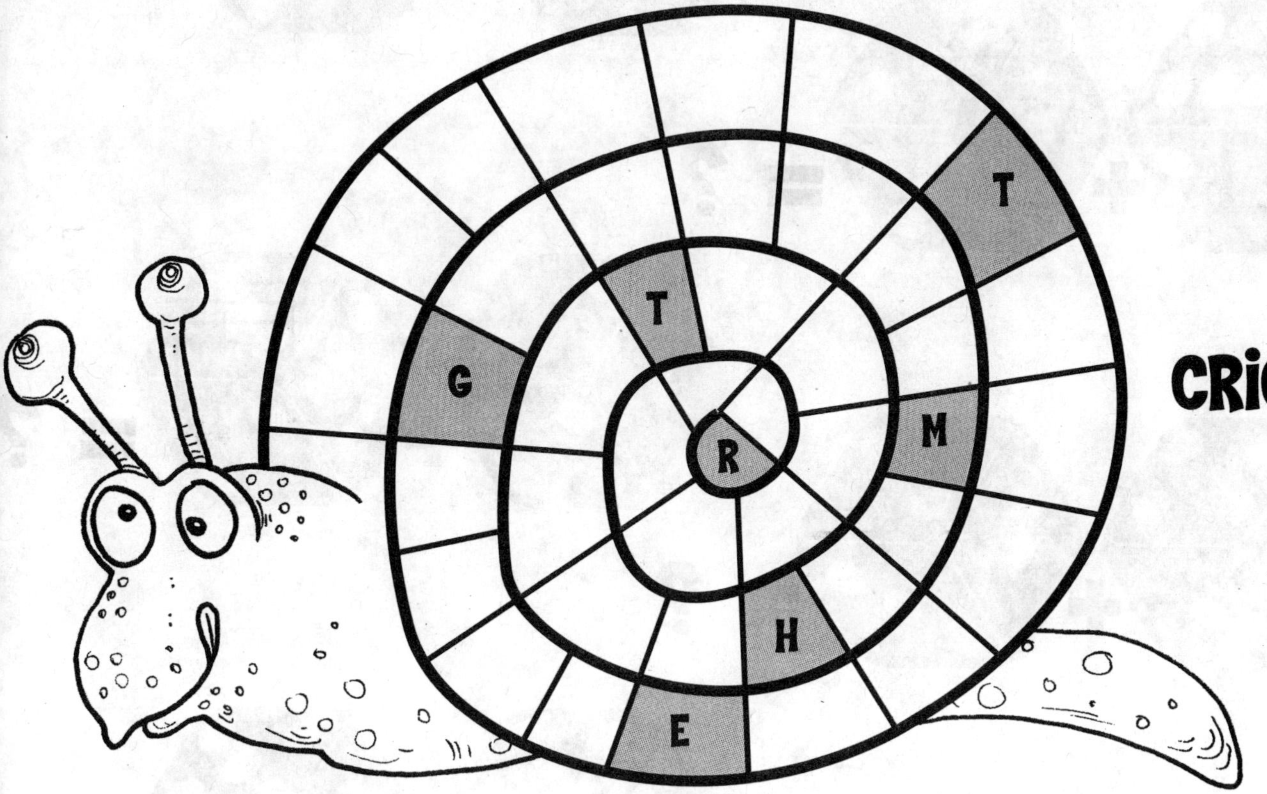

T

T

G

CRICKET

M

R

H

E

MOTH

EARWIG

TREEHOPPER

ROLL THE DICE

Use the numbers from the dice to finish off the sums.

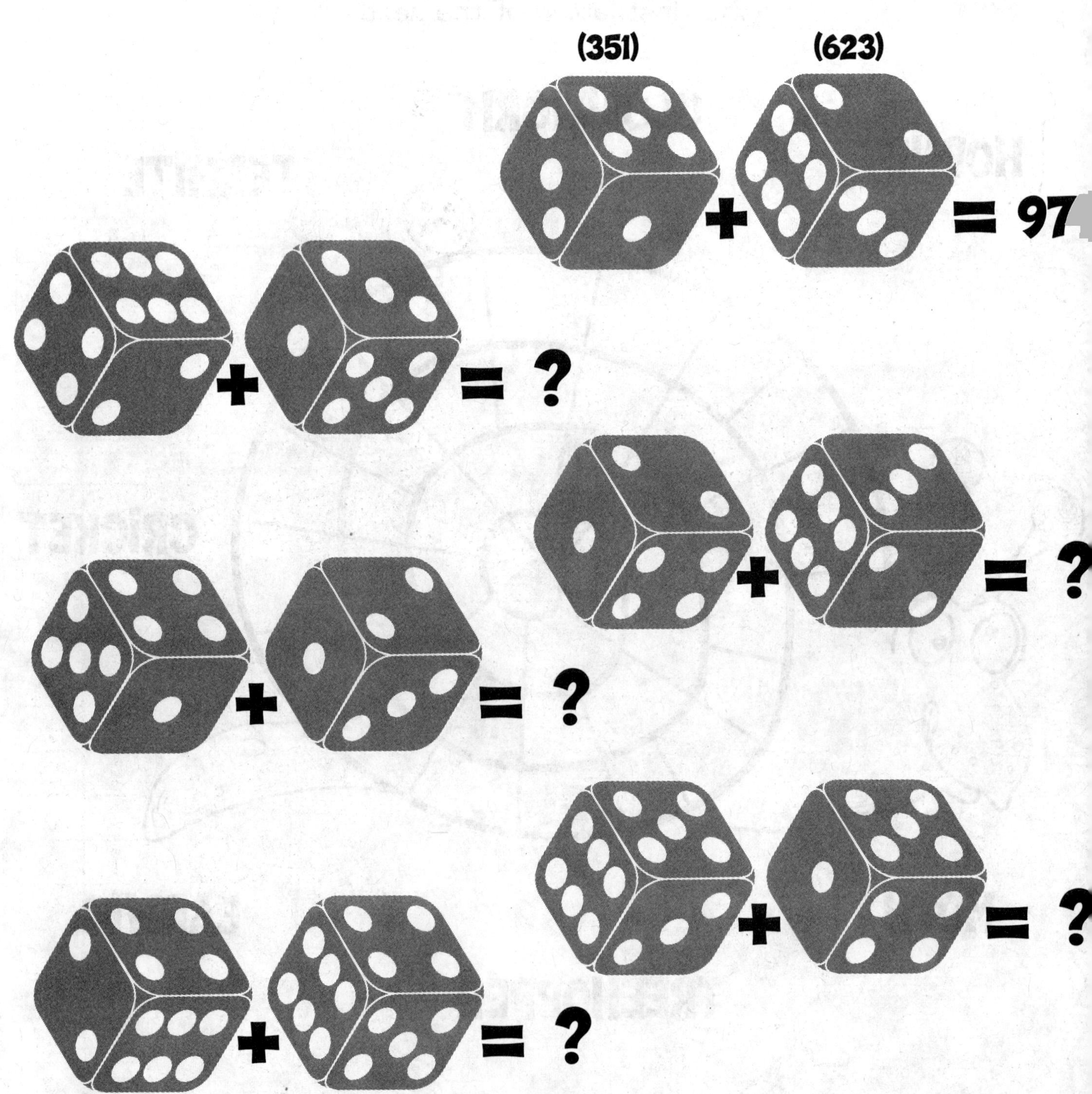

JUNGLE FEVER

Use the coded alphabet to find out which part of the tropical house the spy must visit to meet her contact.

A	✌
B	👌
C	👍
D	👎
E	☜
F	☞
G	☝
H	☟
I	✋
J	☺
K	😐
L	☹
M	💣
N	☠
O	⚐
P	⚑
Q	✈
R	☼
S	💧
T	❄
U	◆
V	❖
W	⬥
X	⌧
Y	✡
Z	☪

CIRCUS SEVENS

Find your way from the trapeze artist to the ringmaster by counting in sevens, starting at the number 7. Are you ready for a challenge?

	1	17	12	28	35	42
		11	16	21	25	49
			START 7	14	33	56
37		41	44	52	50	63
	FINISH 105	98	91	84	77	70
			96	90	79	75
			100	95	83	88

WITCH NEXT?

Study the sequence of pictures carefully and work out which witch finishes the pattern: a, b or c?

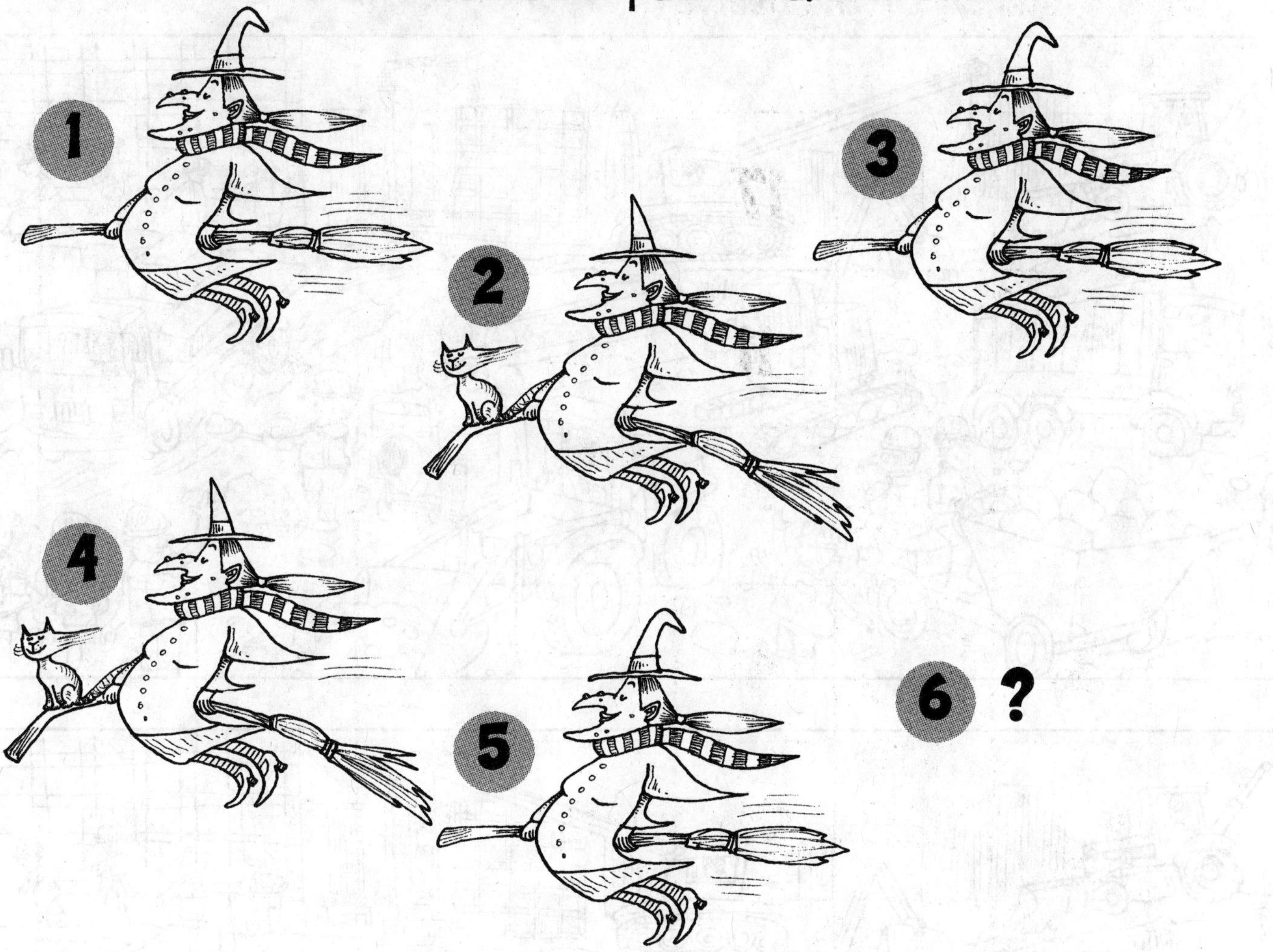

1

2

3

4

5

6 ?

SPOT THE DIFFERENCE

There are six things in the top picture that are not the same in the bottom picture. Can you circle them?

NUMBER CRUNCH

Work out which number is represented by each symbol to make the sums add up in each row and column.

= ?

= ?

= ?

= ?

CAMPING TRIP

Change the word HIKE to the word CAMP one letter at a time. The arrows show you which letter to change each time. Make sure every change creates a real word.

GHASTLY GHOSTS

How many ghosts are haunting this page? How many bats are fluttering among them?

PARTY PUZZLE

Use your eagle eyes to spot each of the things on the left-hand side of the page, hidden in the main picture.

PAINTER'S PALETTE

In each section, cross out any letter that appears twice. The remaining letters spell out three colours.

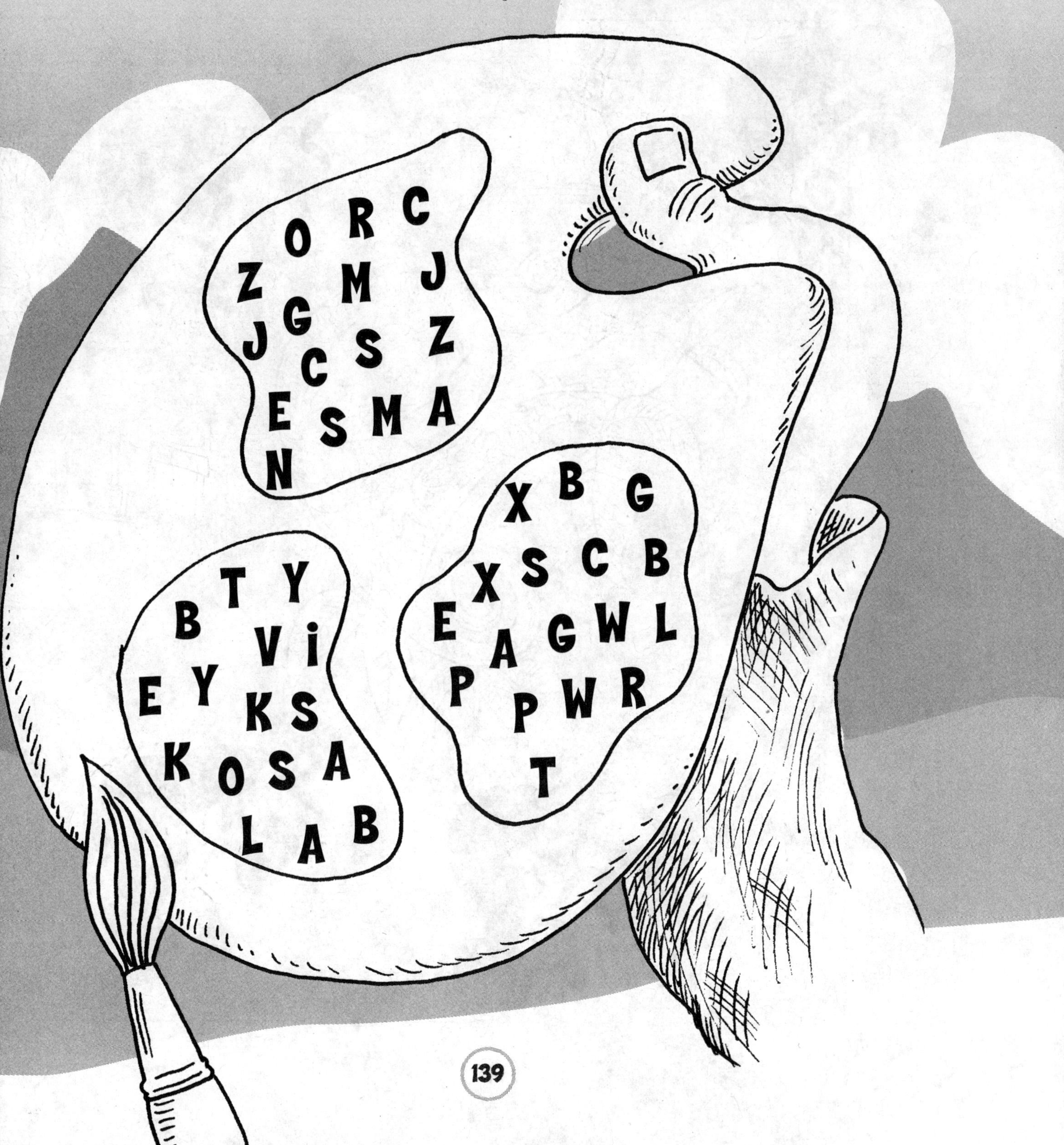

ALL CHANGE

This chameleon is eyeing up his lunch! Which of the silhouettes exactly matches the main picture?

FLYING FARTHEST

Add up the numbers on each jet trail to see which plane has flown the farthest.

FOODOKU

Solve the puzzle so that every row, column and mini-grid contains each of the four foods.

TRACK SIDE

Can you spot which five items are different in the right-hand picture?

HIDDEN GNOMES

How many times can you find the word GNOME in the grid?
It only appears across or down, and forwards not backwards.

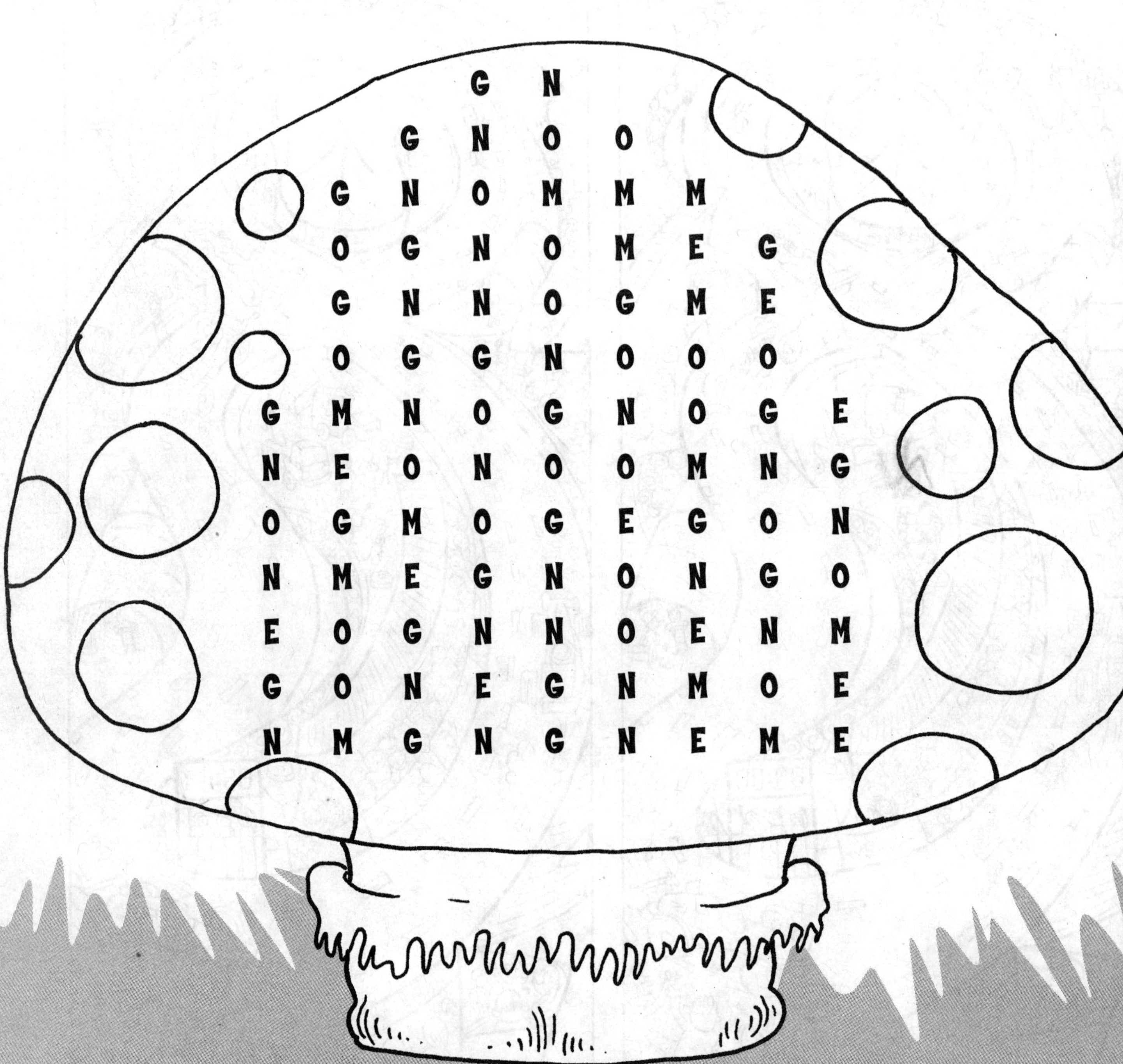

TEEPEE TEASER

Which of these teepees do you need for your camping holiday?

1. It has zigzags on it.
2. It doesn't have spots.
3. There are no bird pictures on it.
4. It has triangles around the bottom.

FARMER BEN'S HEN

Help Farmer Ben drive his tractor through the maze to find his lost hen.

EATEN EIGHTS

How many apples has this worm eaten? He's only guilty of munching those from the eight times table.

JUNGLE TREASURE

Follow the directions and draw an 'X' where the treasure is buried.

1. Start at the watering hole in square A4.
2. Head south past the waterfall for two squares.
3. Stride west from the roots of the giant tangle tree for three squares.
4. Walk two squares south to avoid the tiger, and then two squares east.

BUGOKU

Solve the puzzle so that every row, column and mini-grid contains each of the four bugs.

BEAT THE TEACHER

The teacher can't work out the answer to this maths problem. Which of the clever students has got it right?

GARDEN PARTY

Look at the main picture of Charlie's garden and then work out which of the smaller pictures shows how it would look from above.

a b c d e f

PET CITY

Can you find ten popular pets hiding in the grid?
They might be written across, down, diagonally, backwards or forwards.

MOUSE SNAKE PARROT RABBIT DOG
CAT GERBIL LIZARD HAMSTER GOLDFISH

FANCY THAT!

Look at the people in fancy dress. They have all moved round between pictures! Can you see two new people and two who have left?

TROPHY CABINET

Find your way through the trophies following them in this order all the way through.

JURASSIC PARK

How many words of three letters or more can you make up from the letters below? Two words are listed to get you started.

DIPLODOCUS

1 CLOUD

2 SOIL

3 ______

4 ______

5 ______

6 ______

7 ______

8 ______

9 ______

10 ______

11 ______

12 ______

SPY SCHOOL

Can you work out what this message says?

WHY DID THE
SILLY SPY GO TO
NIGHT SCHOOL?

HE WANTED TO
LEARN TO READ
IN THE DARK.

AT THE BALLET

Only two of these pairs of ballet dancers are exactly the same. Can you spot them?

SKI RUN

Fill in the missing numbers on the flags to complete the 11 times table.

SPOT THE DIFFERENCE

There are six differences between these two pictures.
Can you circle them?

DOWN ON THE FARM

Answer the questions using the grid references from the map.

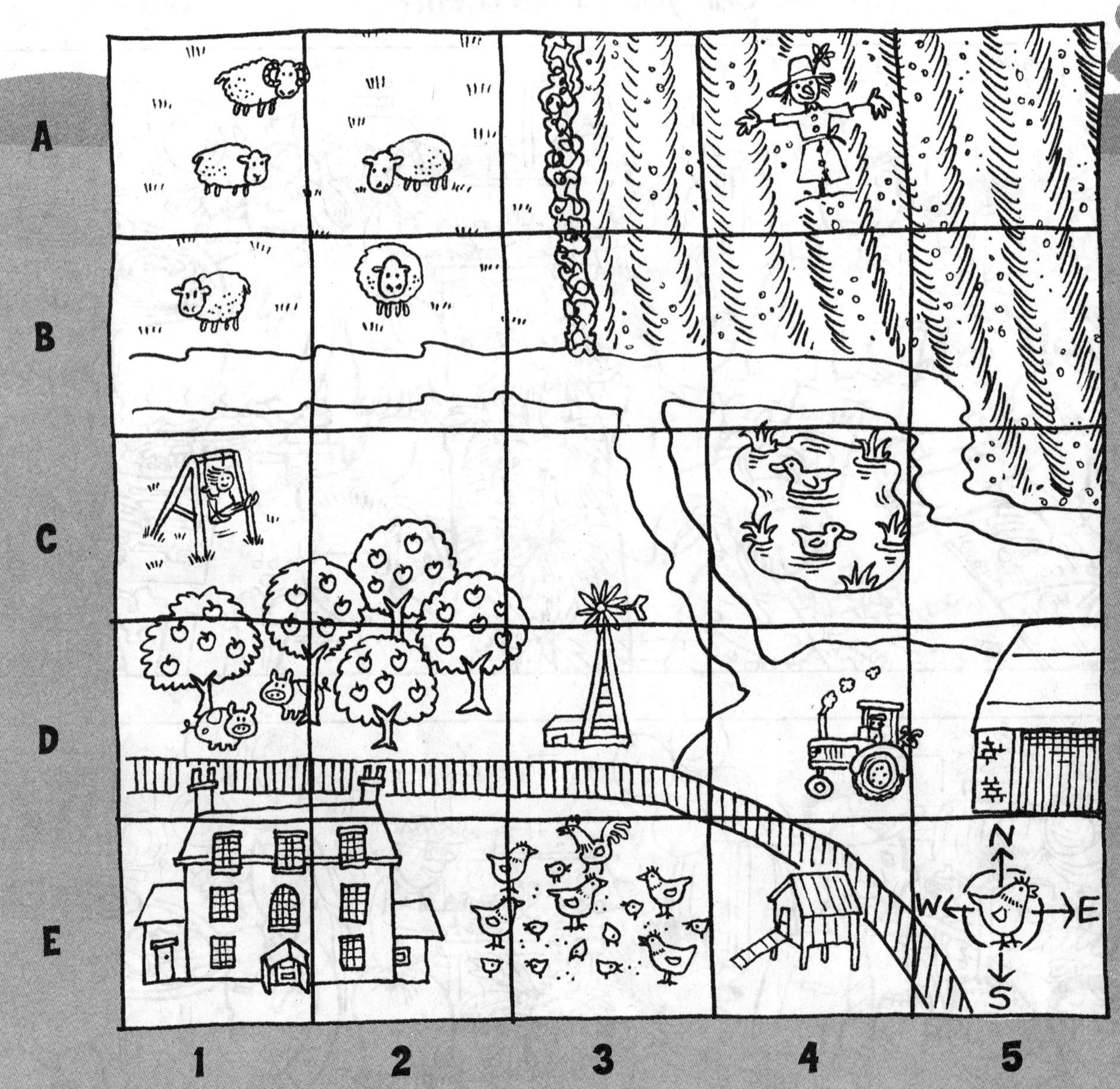

1. What is in square A4?
2. In which square is the tractor parked?
3. How many sheep are in B1?
4. Which three squares have birds in them?

LE PUZZLE

No, it's not French, but all the answers to the clues end in '-le'. Each of the letters in the shaded squares is a double letter, too, to help you.

1. You're doing one now.
2. Keep your drink in it.
3. A kind of laugh.
4. A rhyming puzzle.
5. Not very big.
6. Rain on the ground.
7. Part of a war.
8. Boil water in this.

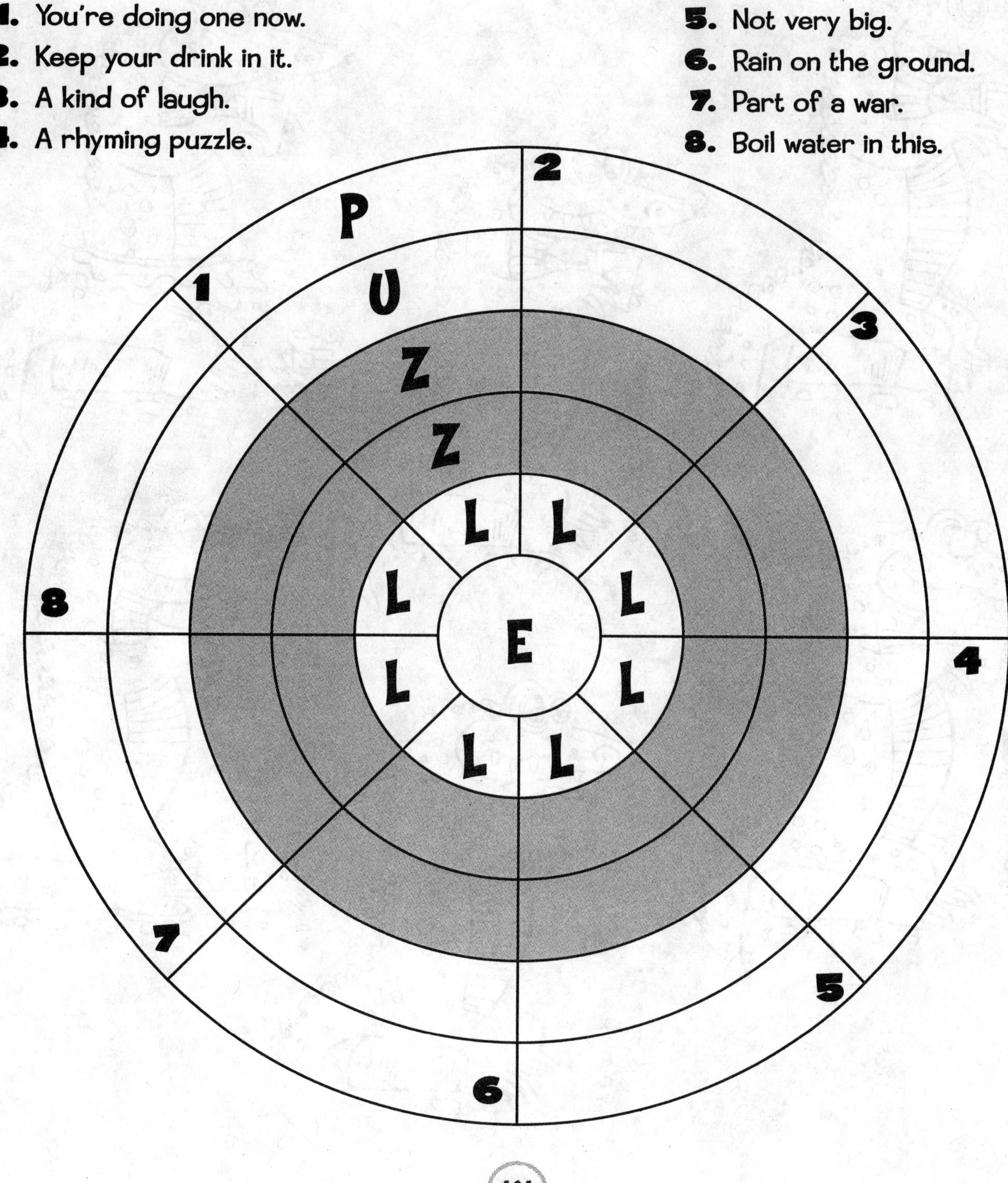

PLAYING SNAP

Which two of these crazy crocodiles are the same?

SWEET TREAT

Put your memory to the test by studying the picture for three minutes, and then turning the page to see how many questions you can answer correctly.

SWEET TREAT

How much can you remember about the picture on the previous page?

1. How many flowers are on the gate?
2. What is the witch holding?
3. Who is on the left of the picture, the girl or the boy?
4. How many windows are there?
5. What is growing in the vegetable patch?
6. Which part of the cottage is made of choc-chip cookies?
7. Is there smoke coming out of the chimney?
8. What animal is next to the cottage?
9. Are the children holding hands?
10. How many spiral lollipops are there?

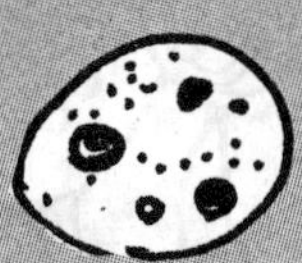

SPY SCHOOL

Use the coded alphabet to find out what message both spies want to see.

A	✌
B	👌
C	👍
D	👎
E	☜
F	☞
G	☝
H	☟
I	✋
J	☺
K	😐
L	☹
M	💣
N	☠
O	⚐
P	⚑
Q	✈
R	☼
S	💧
T	❄
U	◆
V	❖
W	⬥
X	⌧
Y	✡
Z	☪

KAYAK COURSE

Which kayaker scores the most points paddling through the gates?

AT THE AQUARIUM

Libby is at Sydney Aquarium and wants to buy a toy to take home. Answer the questions to help her.

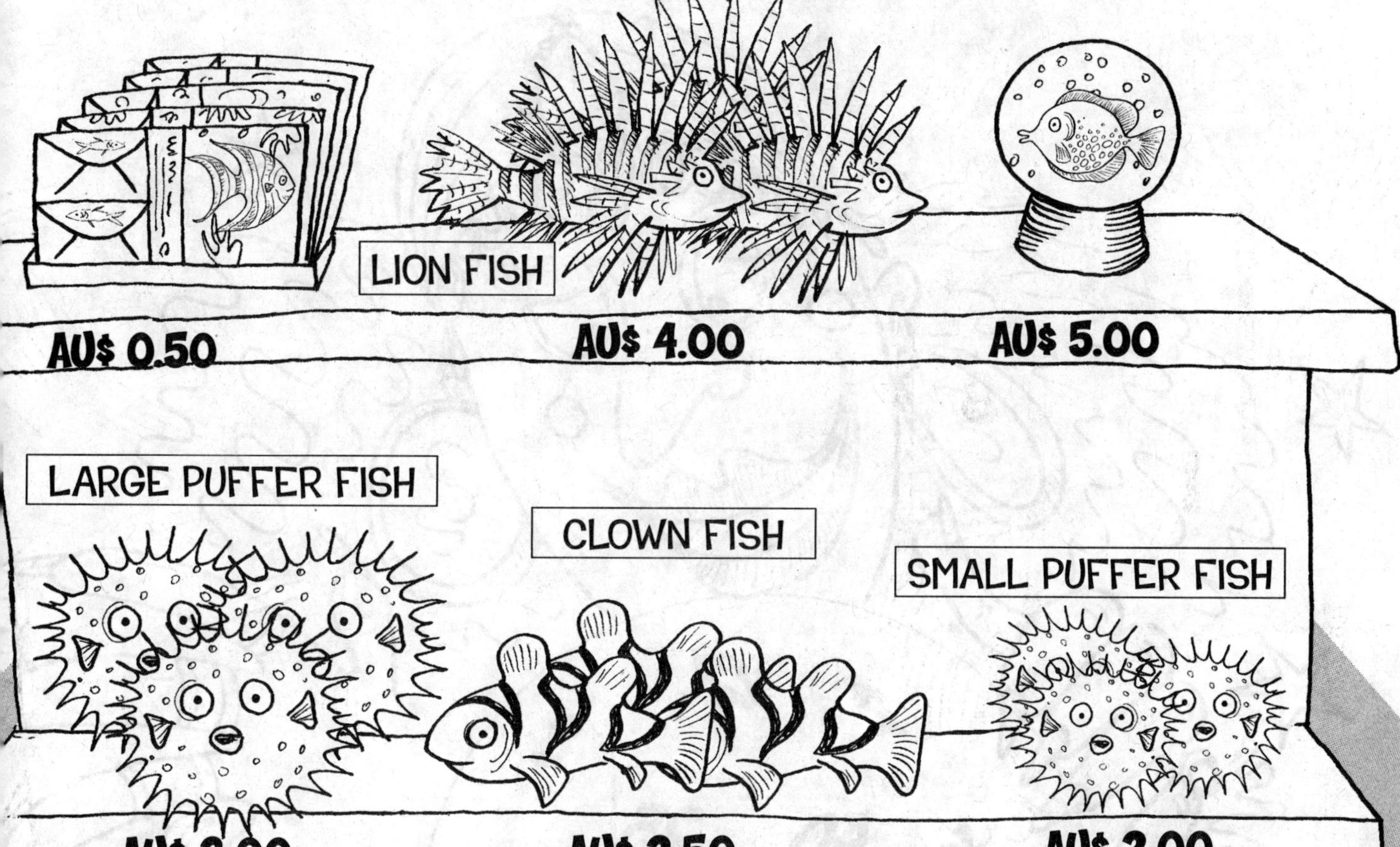

1. How much does it cost for a clown fish and a lion fish?
2. Which costs more, two lion fish or three small puffer fish?
3. How many postcards can Libby buy with AU$5?
4. How much change will Libby get from AU$10 if she buys a globe and a clown fish?

FOUR-TUNE TELLER

Which of the numbers in the crystal ball are part of the four times table?

FAIRY TALE

Which jigsaw piece finishes the picture: a, b, c, d or e?

a b c d e

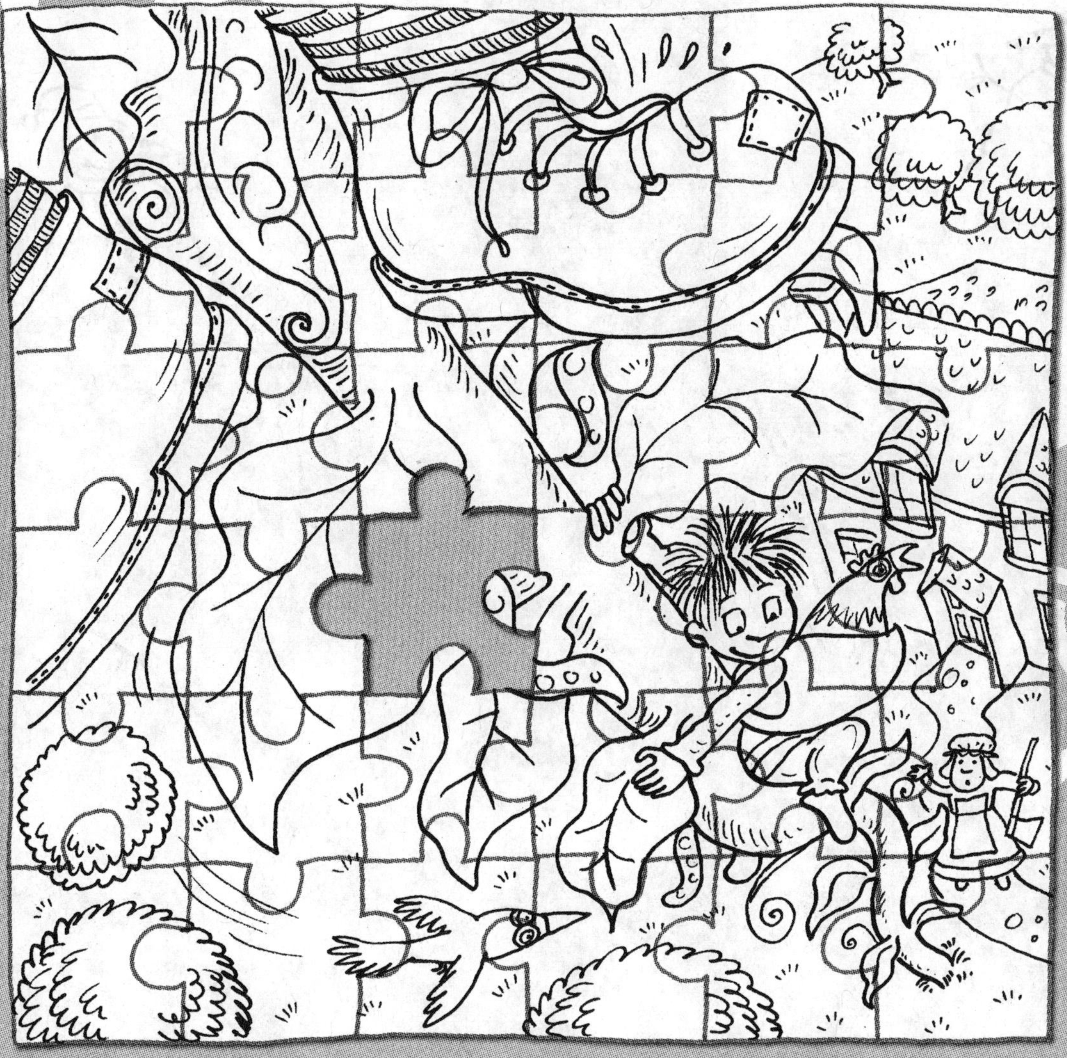

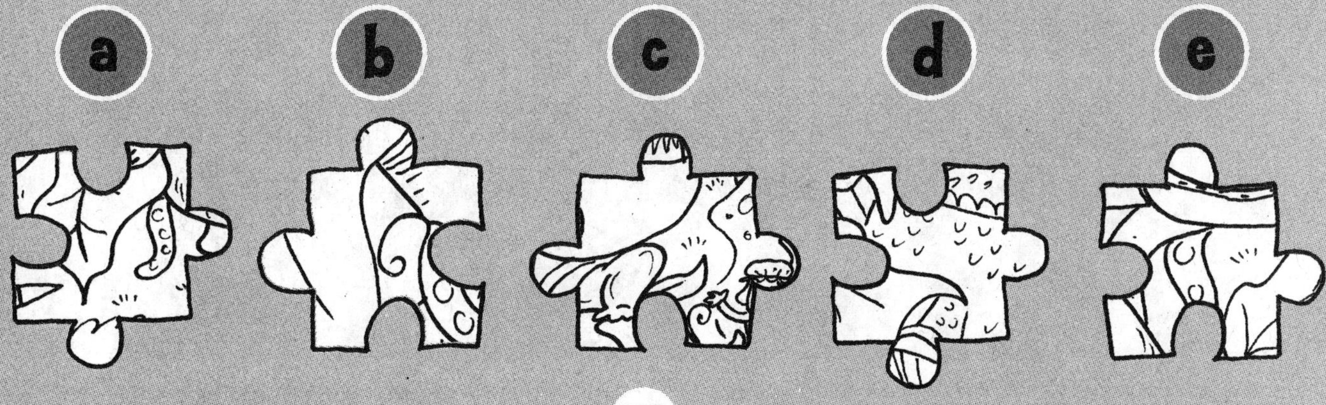

LET IT SNOW!

The mini-grid only appears once in the whole of the larger grid.
Can you find it?

PRETTY POLLY

How many words of three letters or more can you make from the letters below? Two are listed to get you started.

BRAIN TEST

Change the word EASY to the word HARD one letter at a time.
The arrows show you which letter to change each time.
Make sure every change creates a real word.

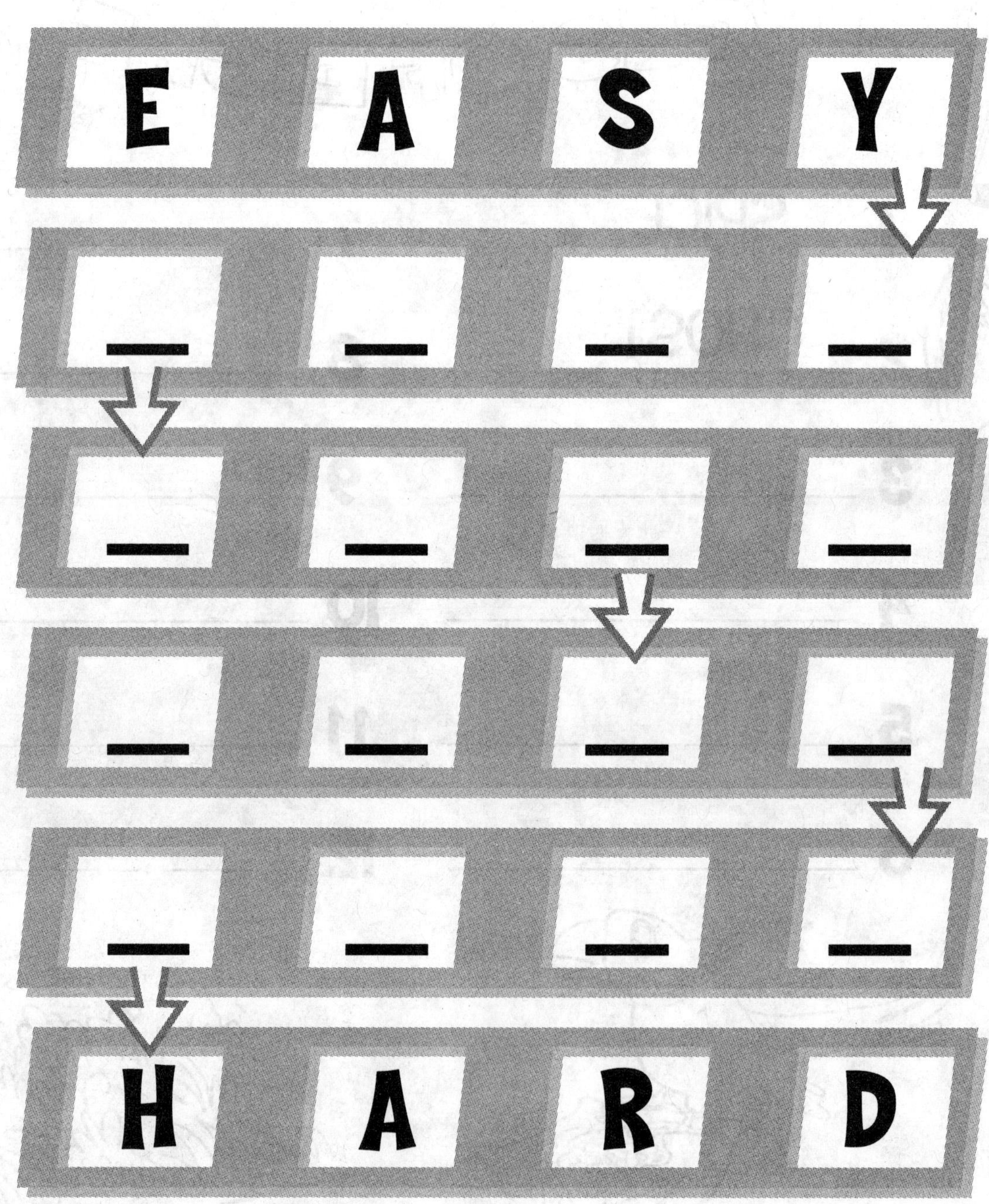

NUMBER CRUNCH

Work out which number is represented by each symbol to make the sums add up on each row and column.

				23
				29
				28
				23
27	20	26	30	

= 10

= ?

= ?

= ?

= ?

			10	23
		10	10	29
10				28
	10			23
27	20	26	30	

FAIRY TREASURE

Follow the directions and draw an 'X' where the treasure is buried.

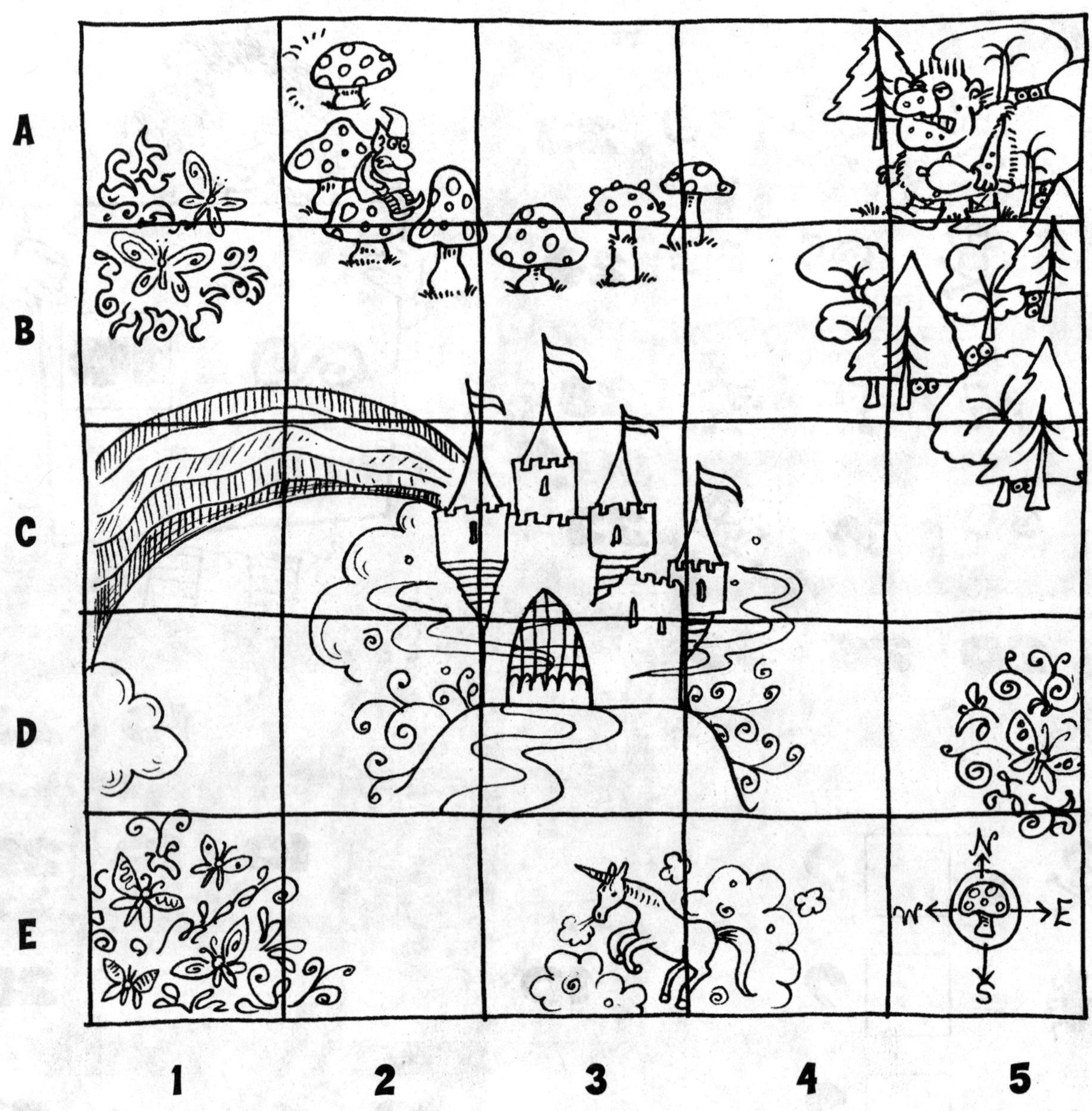

1. Start inside the fairy ring in A3.
2. Skip one square east, then three squares south, avoiding the Black Forest.
3. Fly three squares west and pass under the rainbow.
4. Go two squares north. The treasure is hidden under something insects like.

ALPHADOKU

Solve the puzzle so that every row, column and mini-grid contains the letters A to F.

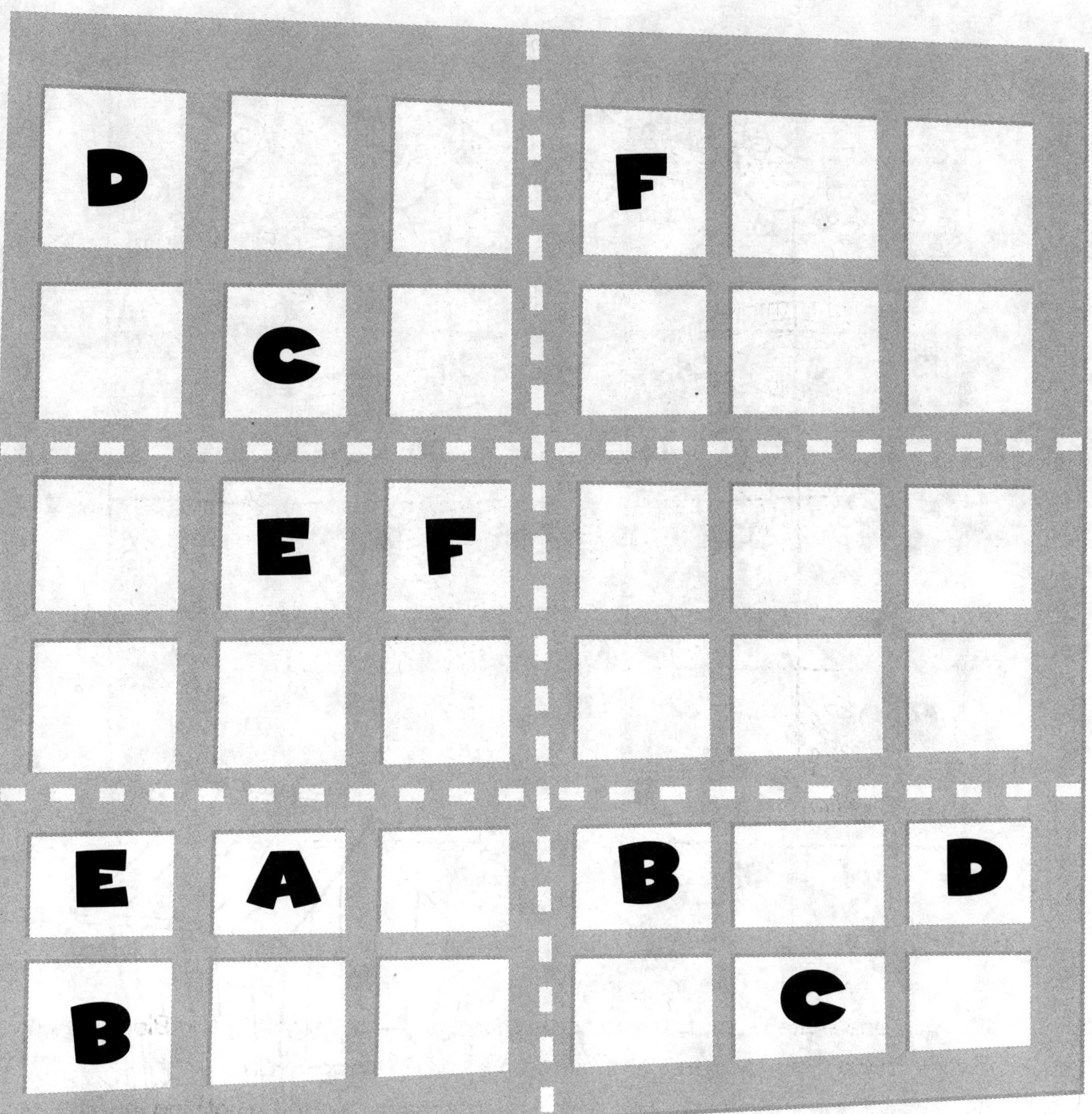

SIX CHICKS IN A FIX

Help the chicks through the farmyard to their home by finding a path using numbers from the six times table.

ANIMALS OF THE WORLD

Fill in the missing letters to spell six animals. Can you match them to the continent they most commonly live in?

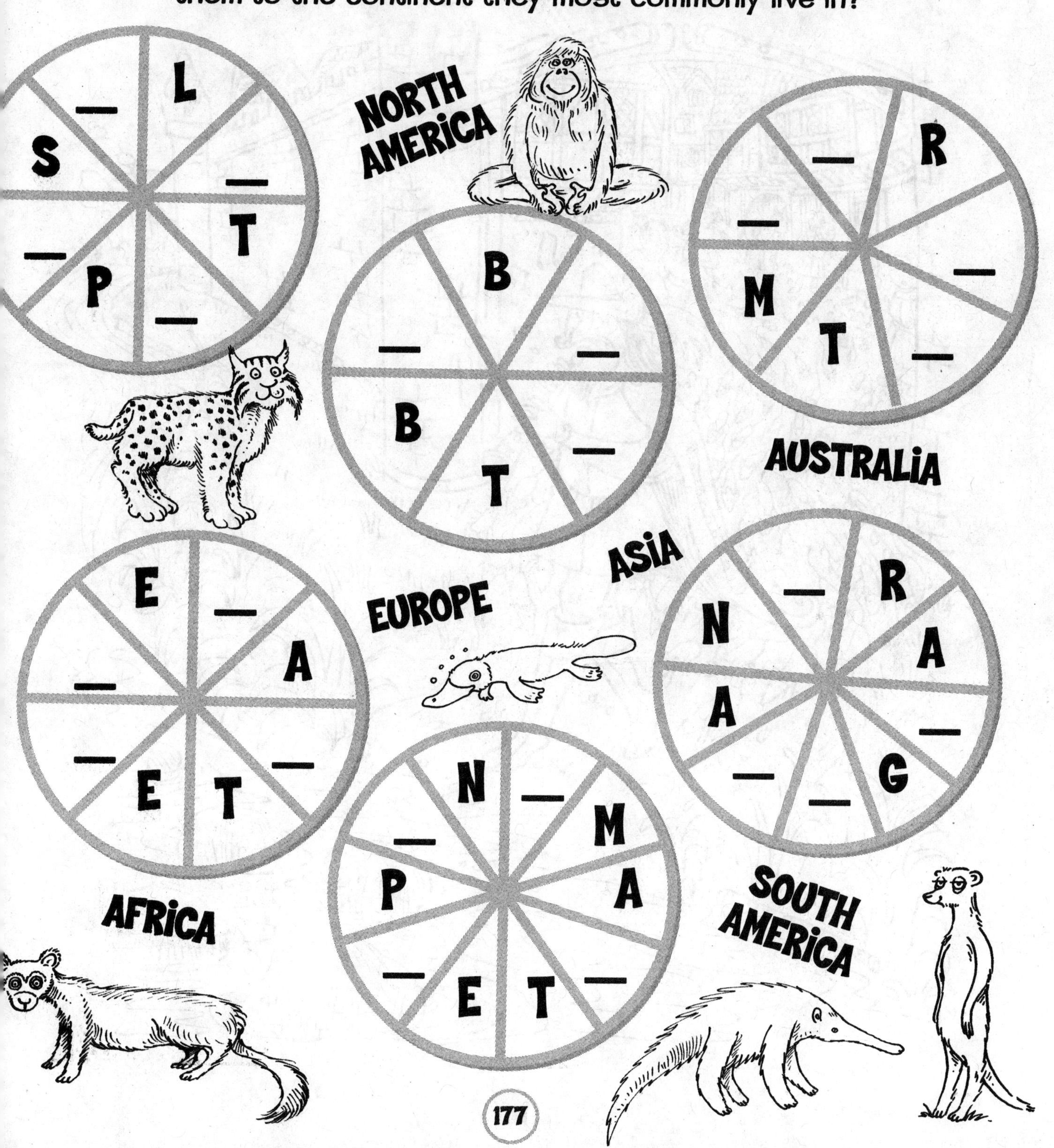

HIDE AND SEEK

How many recorders can you spot in this picture?

GOING APE

Take a careful look at the picture to see if you can spot all of the items from the list.

Find these items!

MISSING MONSTER

One of the monsters from the top picture is missing in the bottom picture. Can you spot which one it is?

PIRATE PAIRS

All of these pirates have an identical twin - except one. Can you find him?

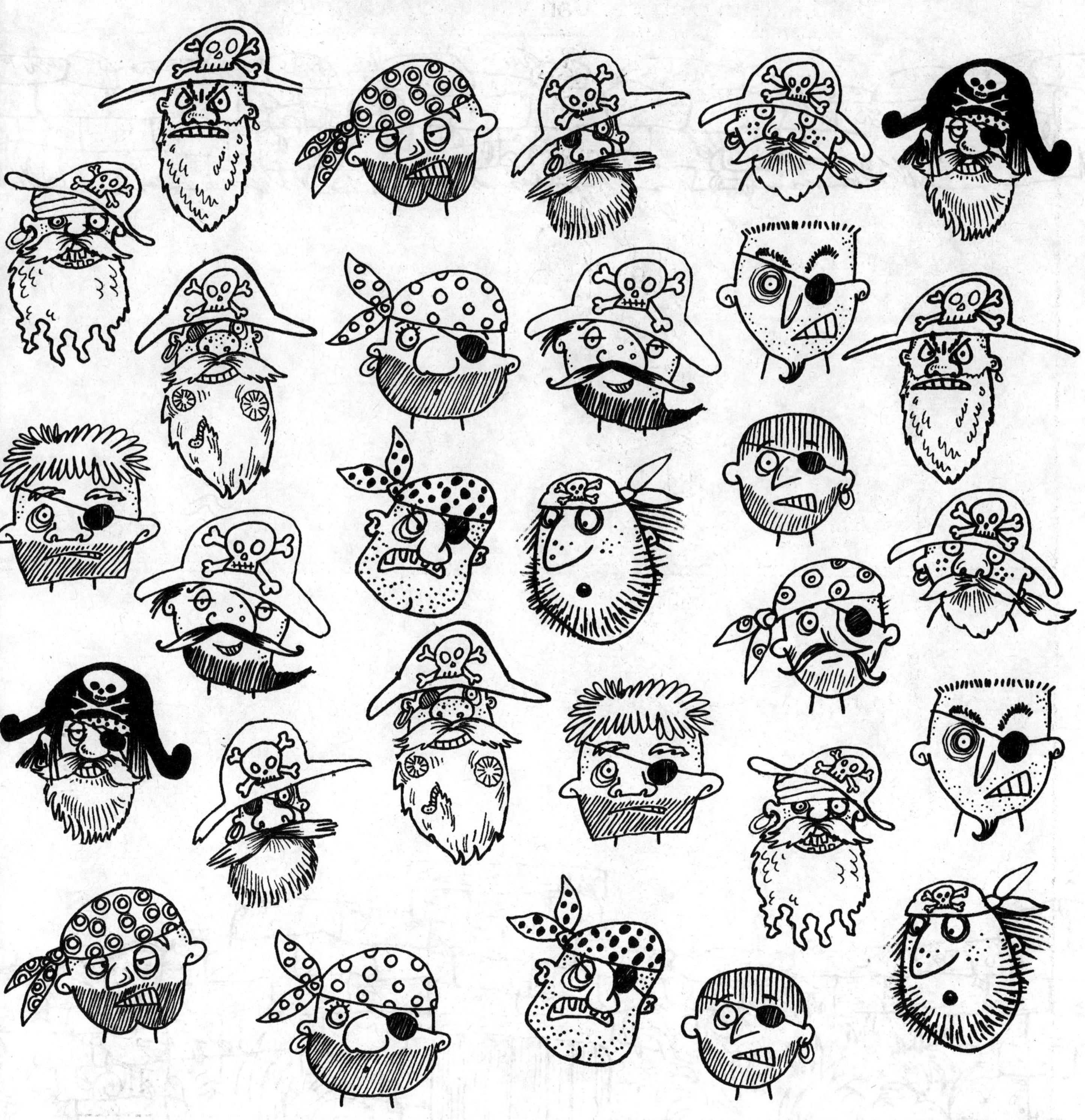

THE SECRET GARDEN

What would you love to see if you found a secret garden?

ALL MIXED UP

Match the boxes in pairs to make the names of ten different plants, trees and flowers. One has been done to help you.

~~TUS~~ TLE GUS BAM LET

WIL BON NET SAI CRO

ORC LOW BOO ~~CAC~~ HID

CUS FUN VER CLO VIO

C	A	C	T	U	S

GOTCHA!

What has this monster spider caught in its giant web?

JURASSIC JOKE

Use this decoder to work out the answer to the dino-joke.

A	B	C	D	E	F	G	H	i	J	K	L	M	N	O	P	Q	R	S	T	U	V	W	X	Y	Z
Z	Y	X	W	V	U	T	S	R	Q	P	O	N	M	L	K	J	i	H	G	F	E	D	C	B	A

What do you call a dinosaur that smashes everything in its path?

GBiZMMLHZFiFH DiVXPH!

_ _ _ _ _ _ _ _ _ _ _ _ _   _ _ _ _ _ _ !

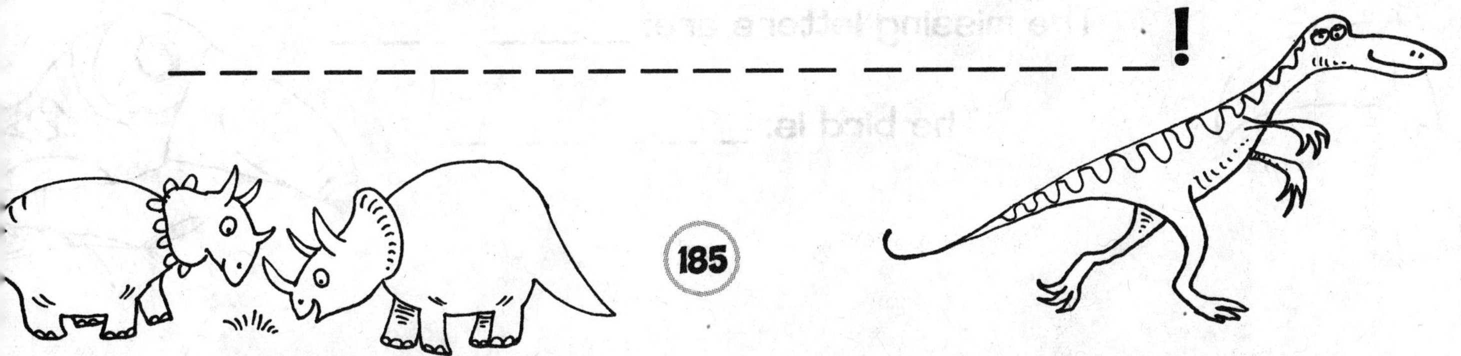

EGGS-ACTLY

Some of the letters of the alphabet are missing from these eggs. Work out which they are and then use them to spell the name of a bird.

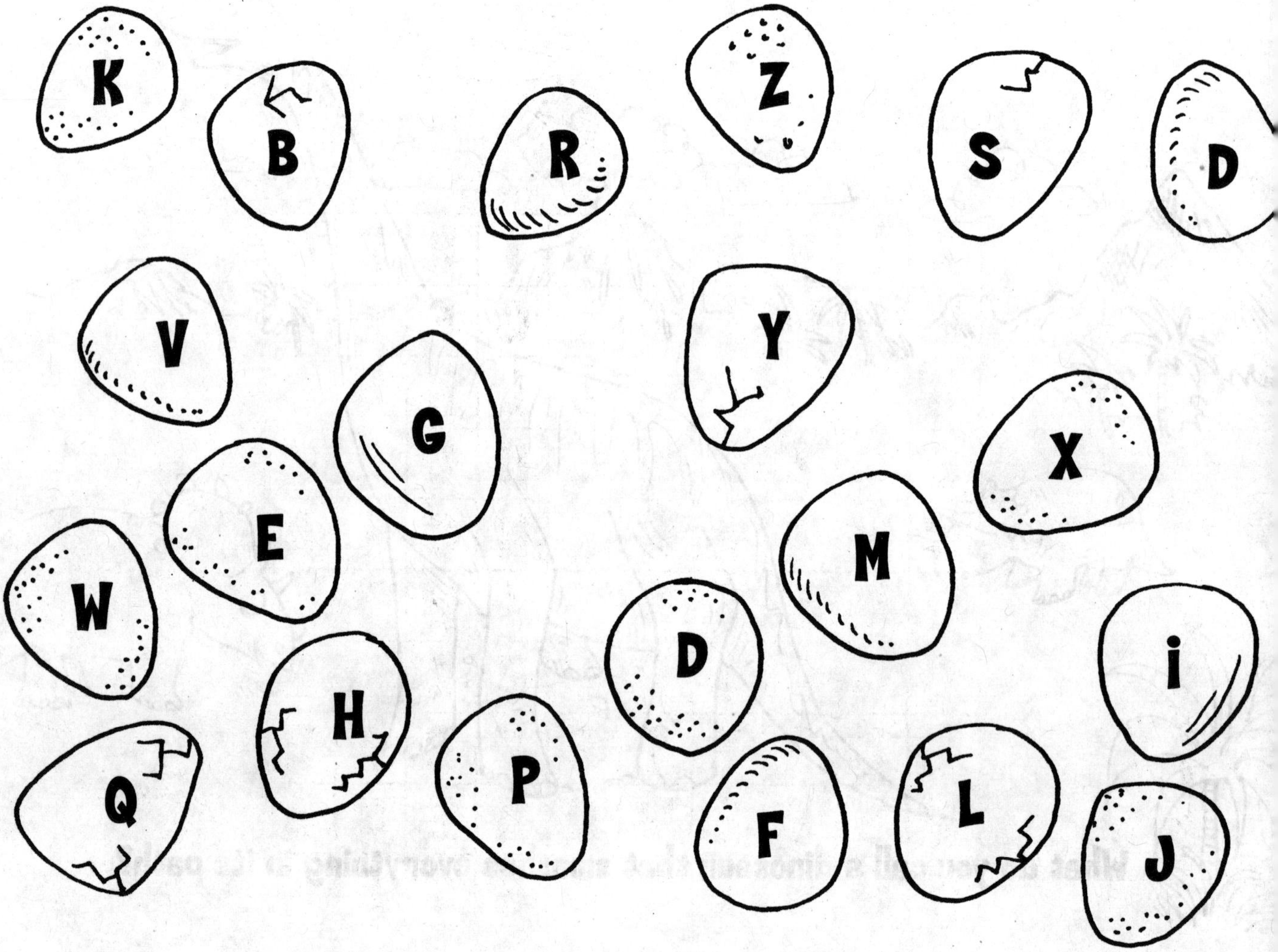

K B R Z S D

V Y G X

E M W D i

H P Q F L J

The missing letters are: _ _ _ _ _ _ _

The bird is: _ _ _ _ _ _ _

WEIRD SEARCH

Find ten weird or creepy creatures hidden in the grid. There are no clues to help you!

Z	L	V	A	M	P	I	R	E	G
W	L	W	I	Z	L	G	F	G	Z
O	I	O	A	G	L	L	H	N	O
E	E	Z	G	H	O	U	L	A	M
W	W	Z	A	W	R	W	G	I	B
O	G	W	E	R	T	I	W	T	I
L	G	R	I	E	D	Z	E	R	E
L	E	R	Y	T	E	V	R	A	R
W	E	E	E	W	C	A	E	M	A
W	G	H	T	S	O	H	G	E	W

POLLEN COUNT

How many smaller flowers make up the four big flowers?

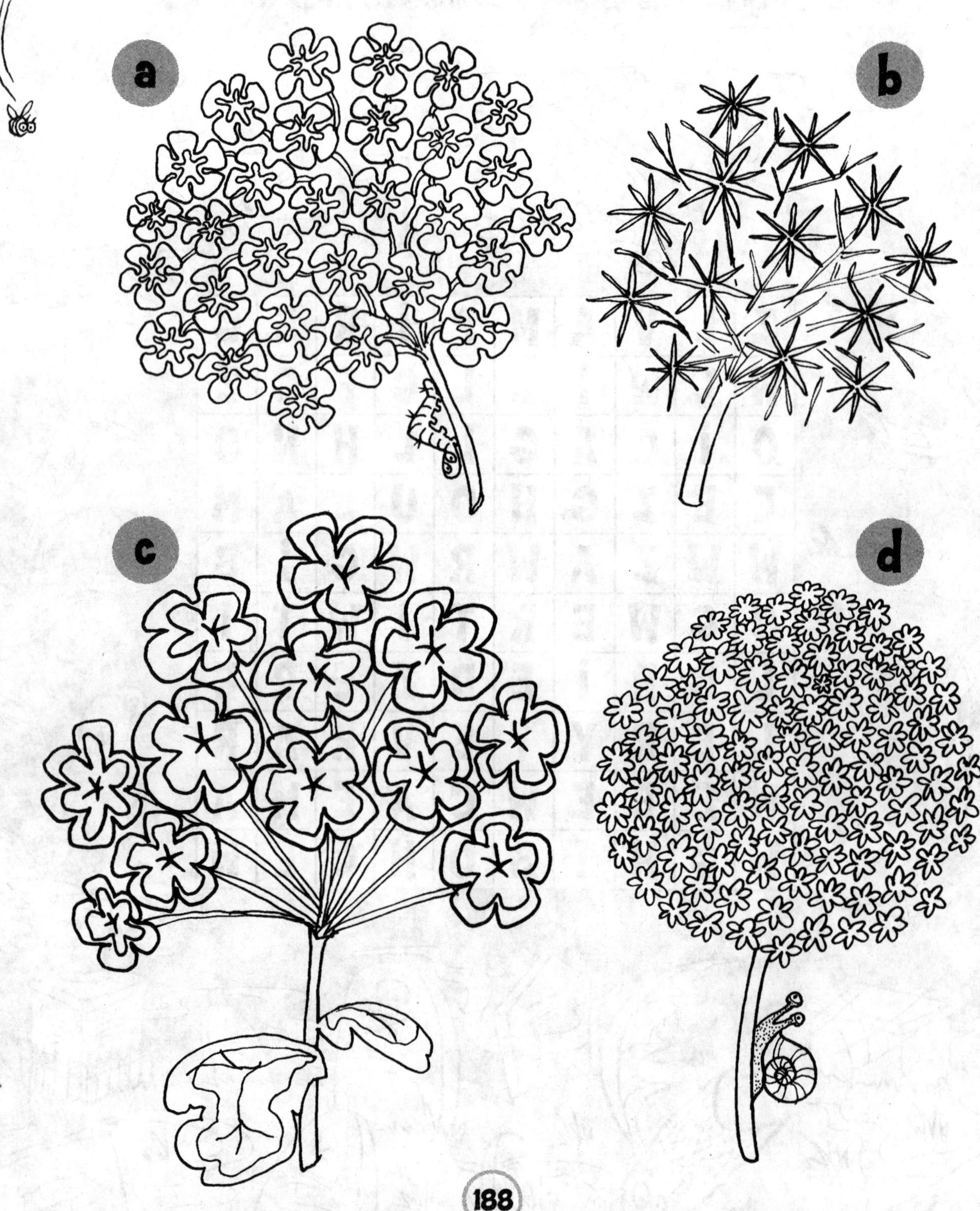

BIRDS GALORE

Fill this scene with as many different birds as you can think of.

OUT OF THIS WORLD!

Only one of these alien actors can make it in the movies. Which of them is going to star in the next blockbuster?

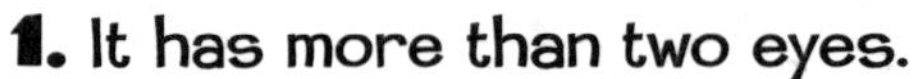

1. It has more than two eyes.
2. It has two legs.
3. It has only one head.
4. It isn't wearing any clothes.

a b c d

e f g h

ARMOUR PLATING

This dinosaur needs some protection - can you add it?

SEEING STRIPES

Which of these zebras is the odd one out?

THE NAME GAME

On each line, find the letter that appears in every name.
Use these letters to spell the name of the old pirate!

GIO	EGBERT	CRAIG	OGDEN	_
BJORN	OWEN	CODY	JOHN	_
NATHAN	DANTE	NOEL	ANDREW	_
FAIZ	ZAINAB	EZRA	OZZY	_
CALEB	DALE	BLAKE	AARON	_
ALI	BAILEY	LAWSON	RIDLEY	_
TONY	NOAH	OLAF	DIEGO	_

BUTTERFLY BONANZA

Which of the butterflies has numbers on its wings that add up to exactly 100?

POND DIPPING

What amazing creatures have you found in the water?

PIRATE PEDRO

Draw the pirate that belongs to this parrot!

TRICERATOPS TRAIL

Work out the sums on each Triceratops and find a path to the jungle by hopping on dinosaurs with 3 as the answer.

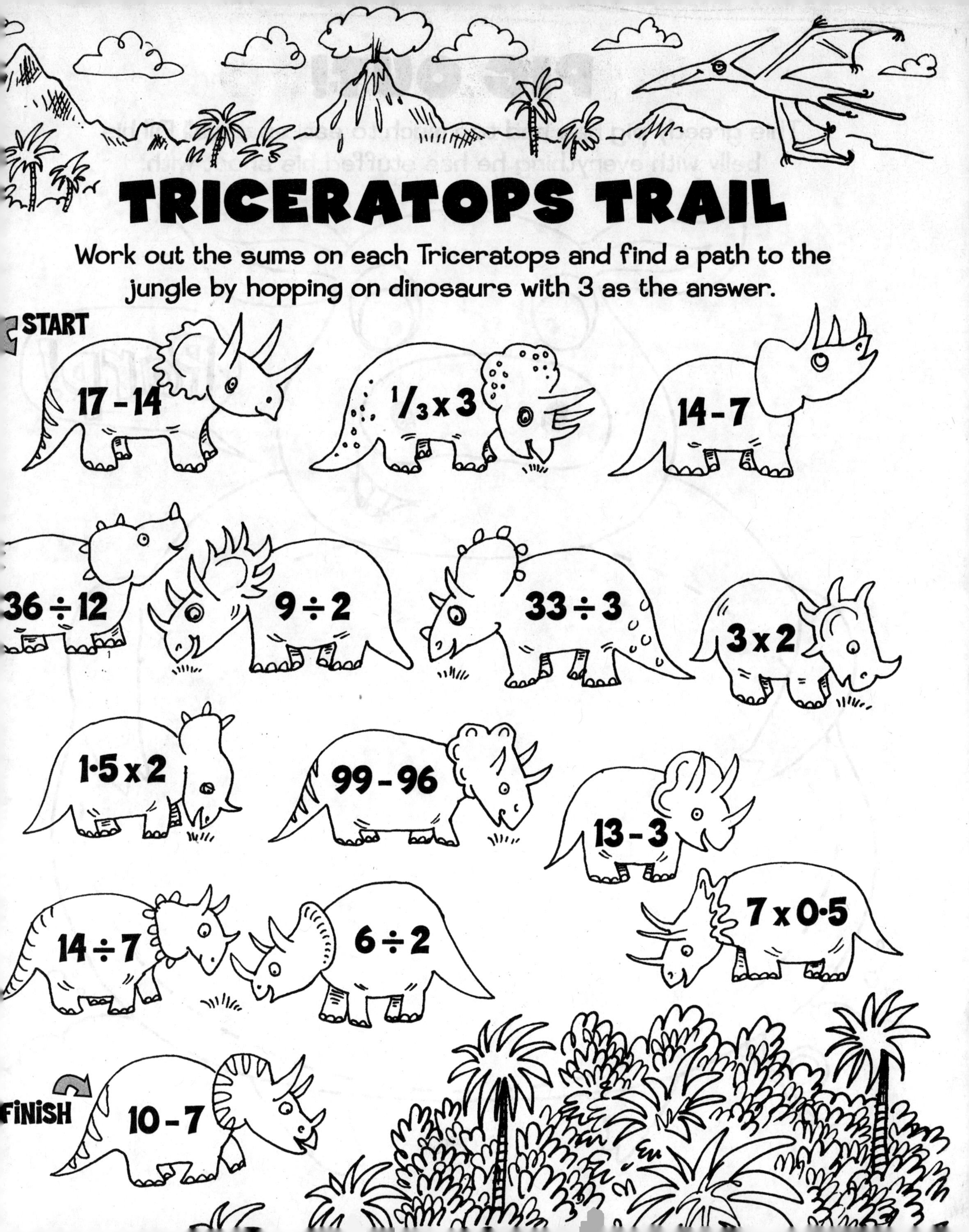

PIG OUT!

This greedy pig has had too much to eat, as usual! Fill his belly with everything he has stuffed his snout with.

IN A MUDDLE

Help Pirates Stoppit and Shuttup untangle the ropes to spell out the name of the island they are sailing to.

PRINCESS PETS

Draw a selection of cute or exotic pets for Princess Padmani.

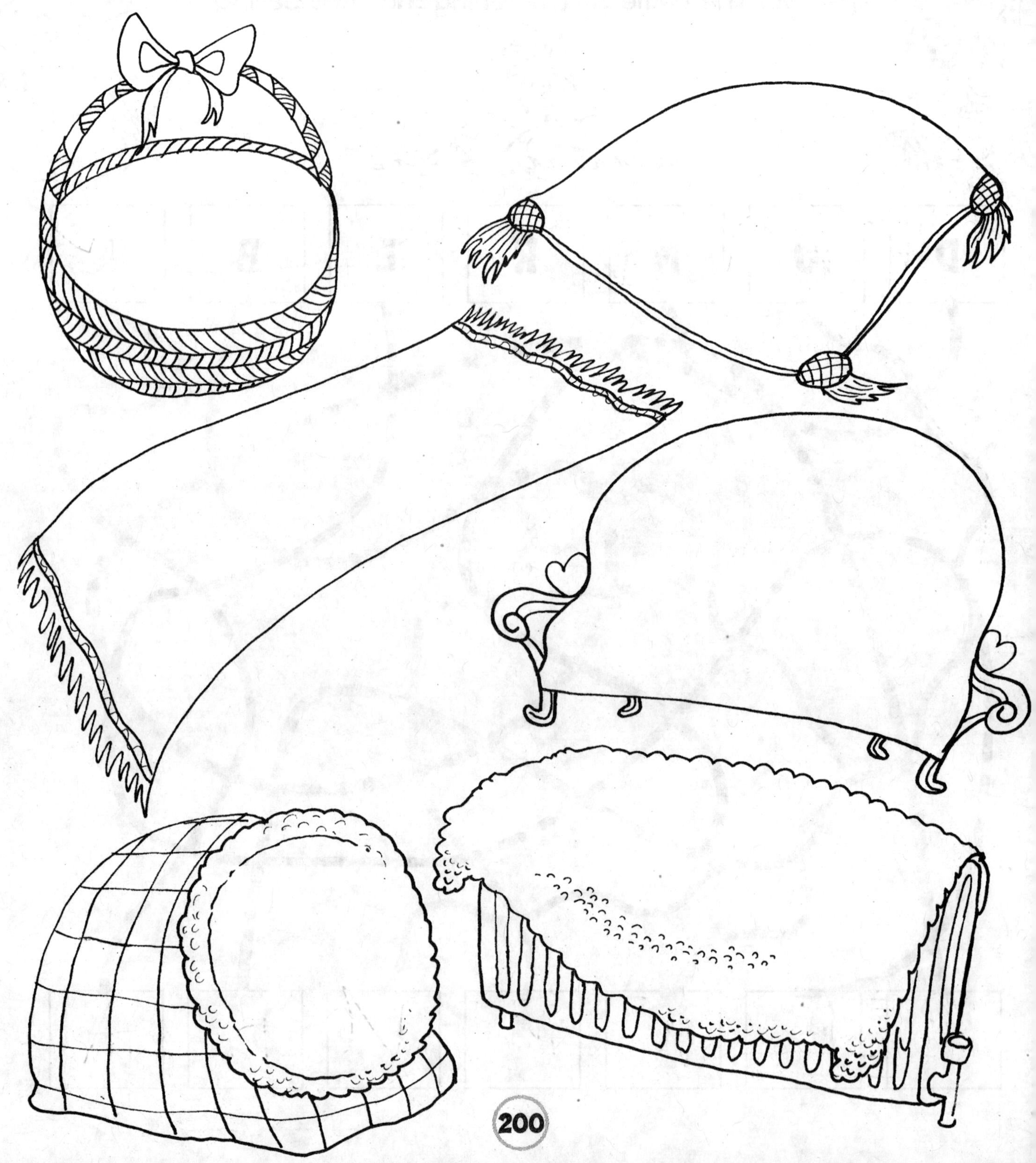

BIG IS BEAUTIFUL

Work out each sum to find which of the giant water lilies has the biggest number.

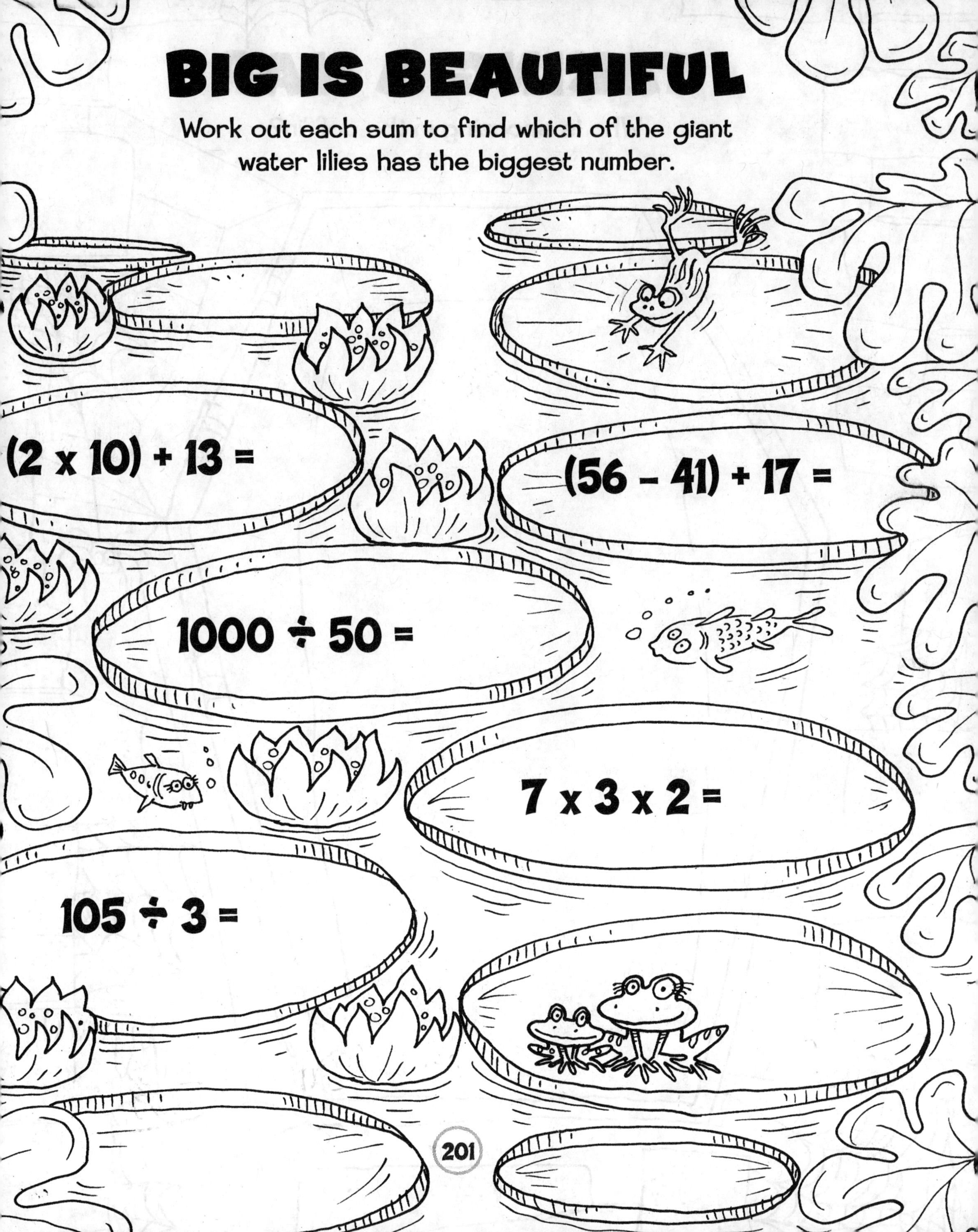

TAKING A NAP

Who is snoozing in the coffin?

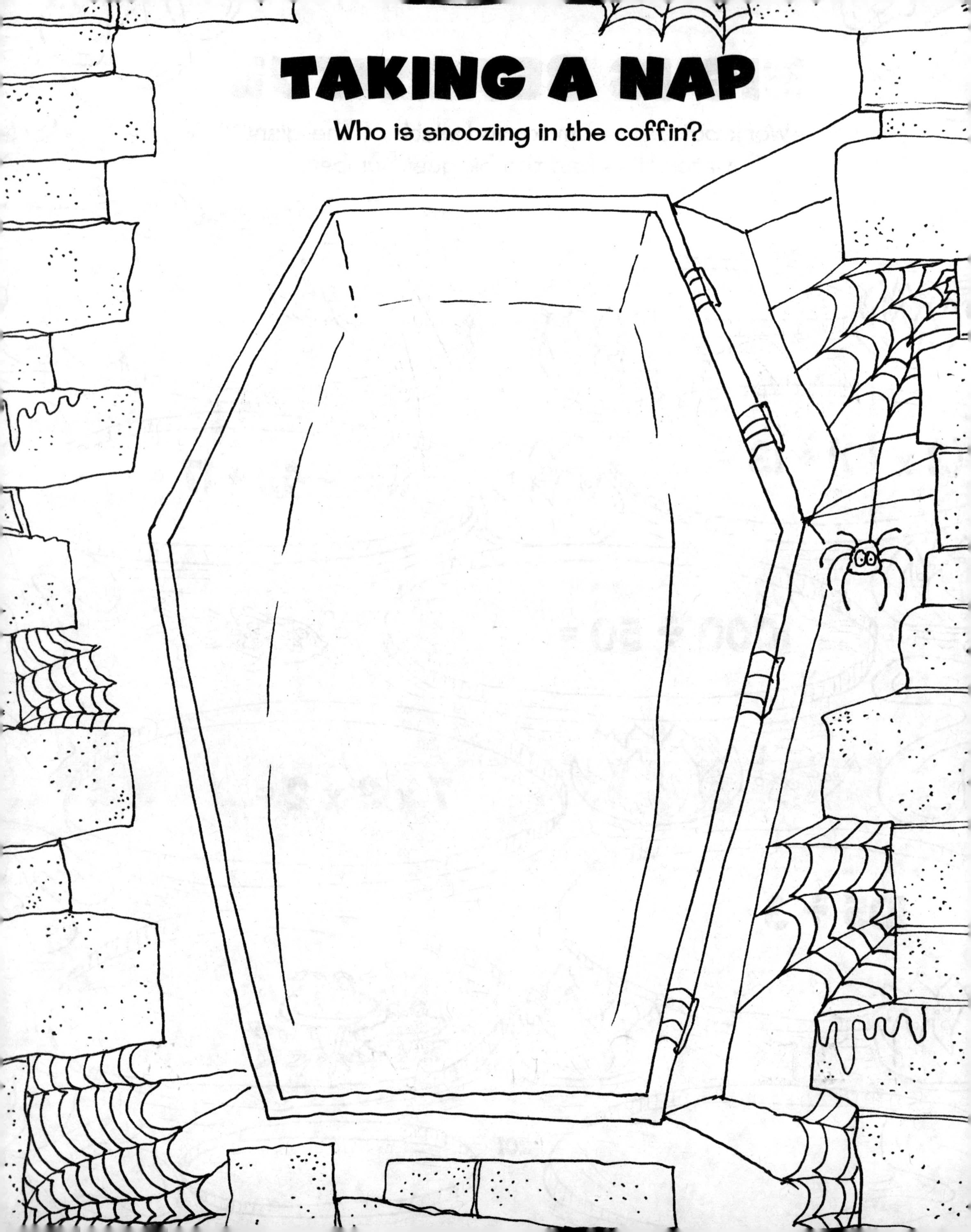

MUNCH TIME

Which of the jigsaw pieces finishes the puzzle?

THE RIGHT FIT

Write the listed creatures in the correct place in the grid, and the circled letters will spell another animal.

AARDVARK	CHIPMUNK	FLAMINGO	MONGOOSE
BULLFROG	ELEPHANT	HORNBILL	PARAKEET

	O						
							T
	A						
			M				
		R					
			P				
							E
	U						

EYE SPY

What you think Pirate Pedro can see through his telescope?

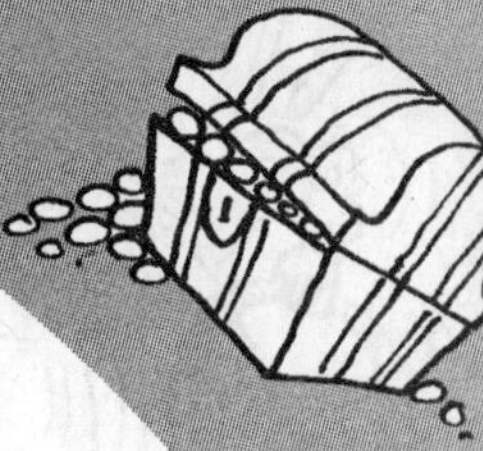

FAIRY FOOD

Which of the toadstools is safe for Fairy Freya to pick?

It doesn't have spots.
It hasn't got a dark stripe
around the edge.
It hasn't got a pointed top.
It has a thin stalk.

HONEY TRAP

How many of the bees are heading back to the hive?

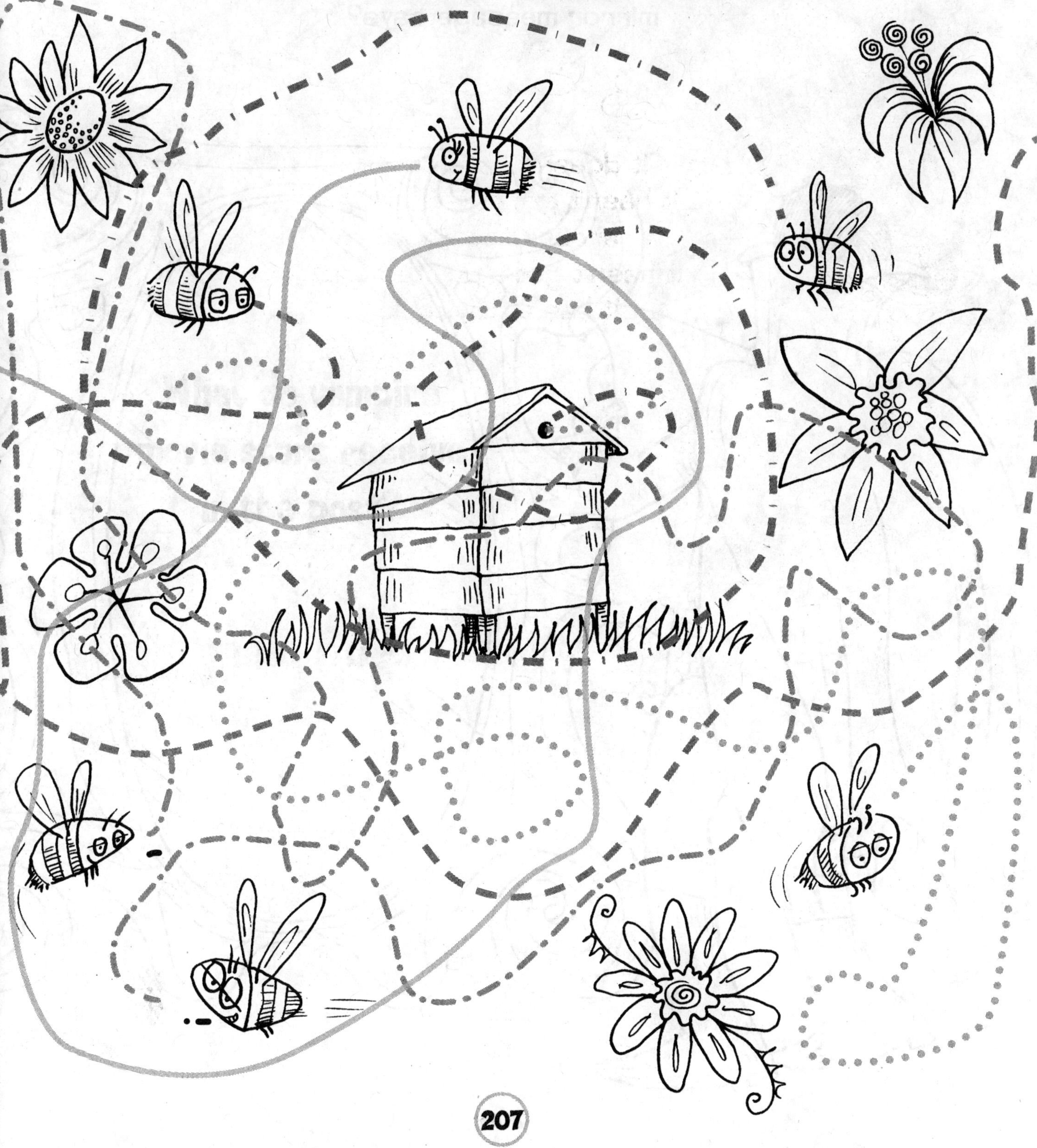

ON REFLECTION

A vampire has no reflection... but can you read what the mirror message says?

DINO DESIGN

Draw your favourite dinosaurs onto these clothes.

FEEDING TIME

Write down the letters shown by the minute hand, then the hour hand, for each listed time. They will spell the names of the animals being fed.

MAGGOTY MATHS

Fill in the answers to the sums on the maggoty biscuits.

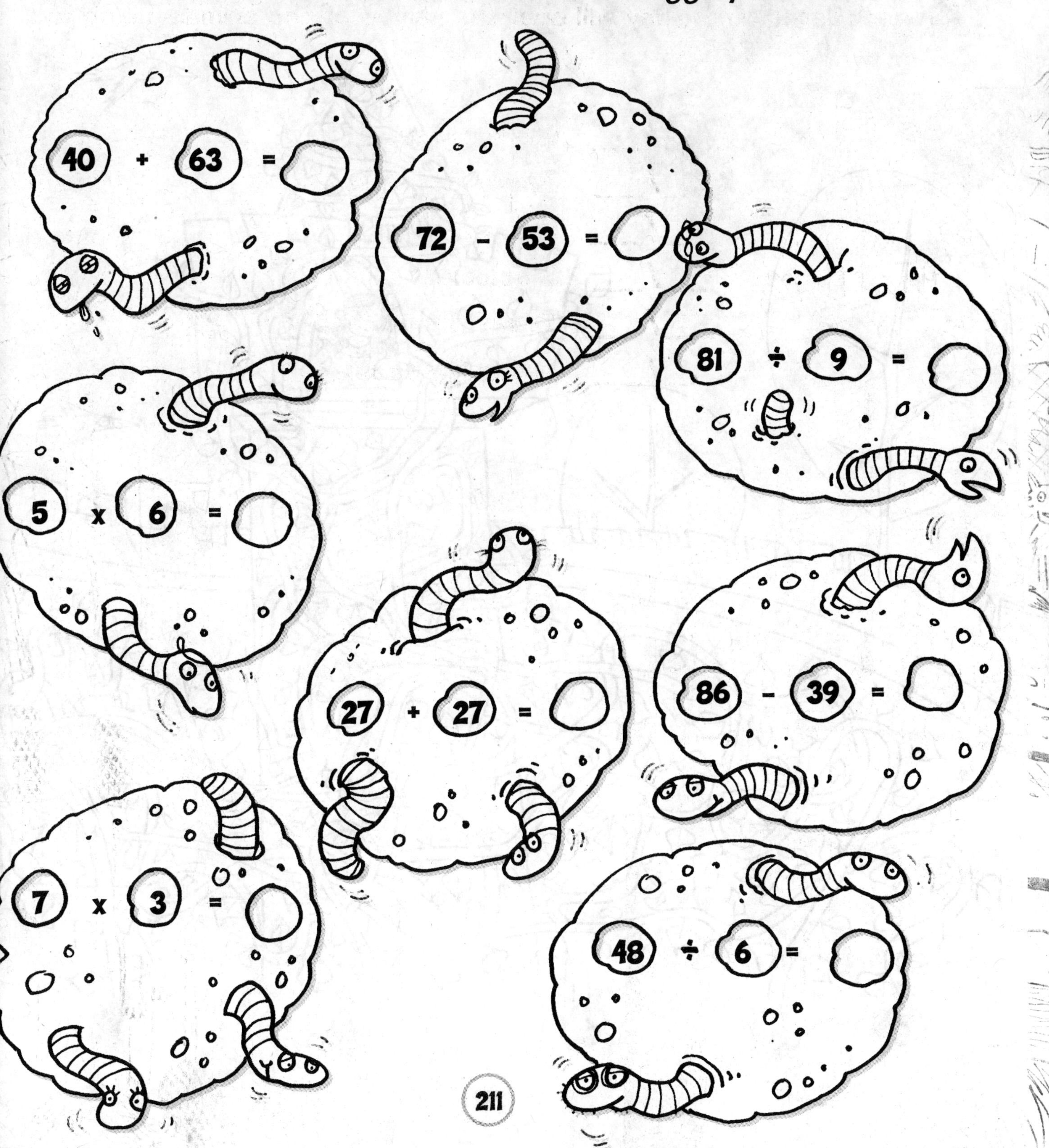

IVORY TOWER

Which of the strands of ivy leads all the way to Princess Isadora?

A BIRD'S EYE VIEW

Look at the main picture of the botanical gardens and then work out which of the smaller pictures is how it would look to a bird flying overhead.

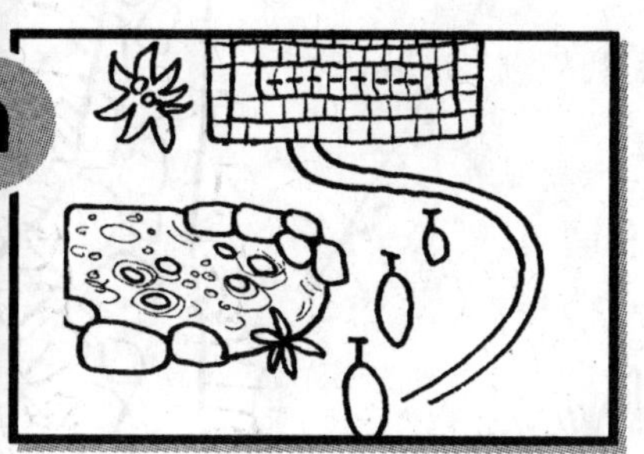

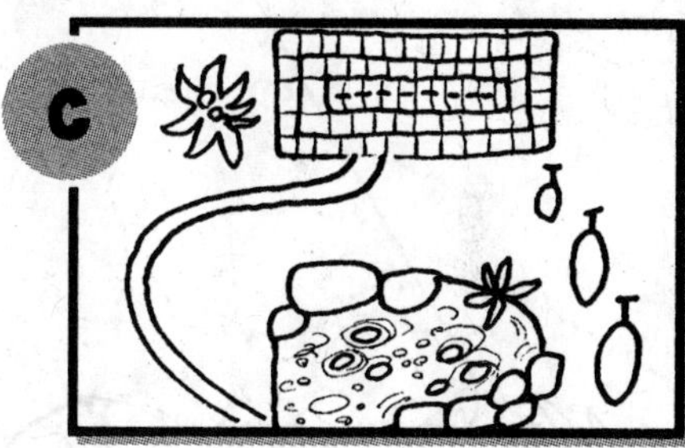

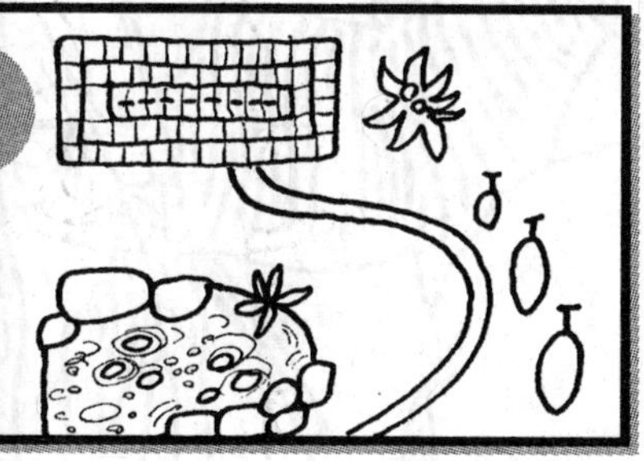

ANIMAL ALERT!

Watch out, there's a wild animal about! Design a road sign to warn drivers that something unusual may be crossing ahead...

MEGALOSAURUS MATHS

Put the meat-eaters into pairs that both have the same answer to their sum.

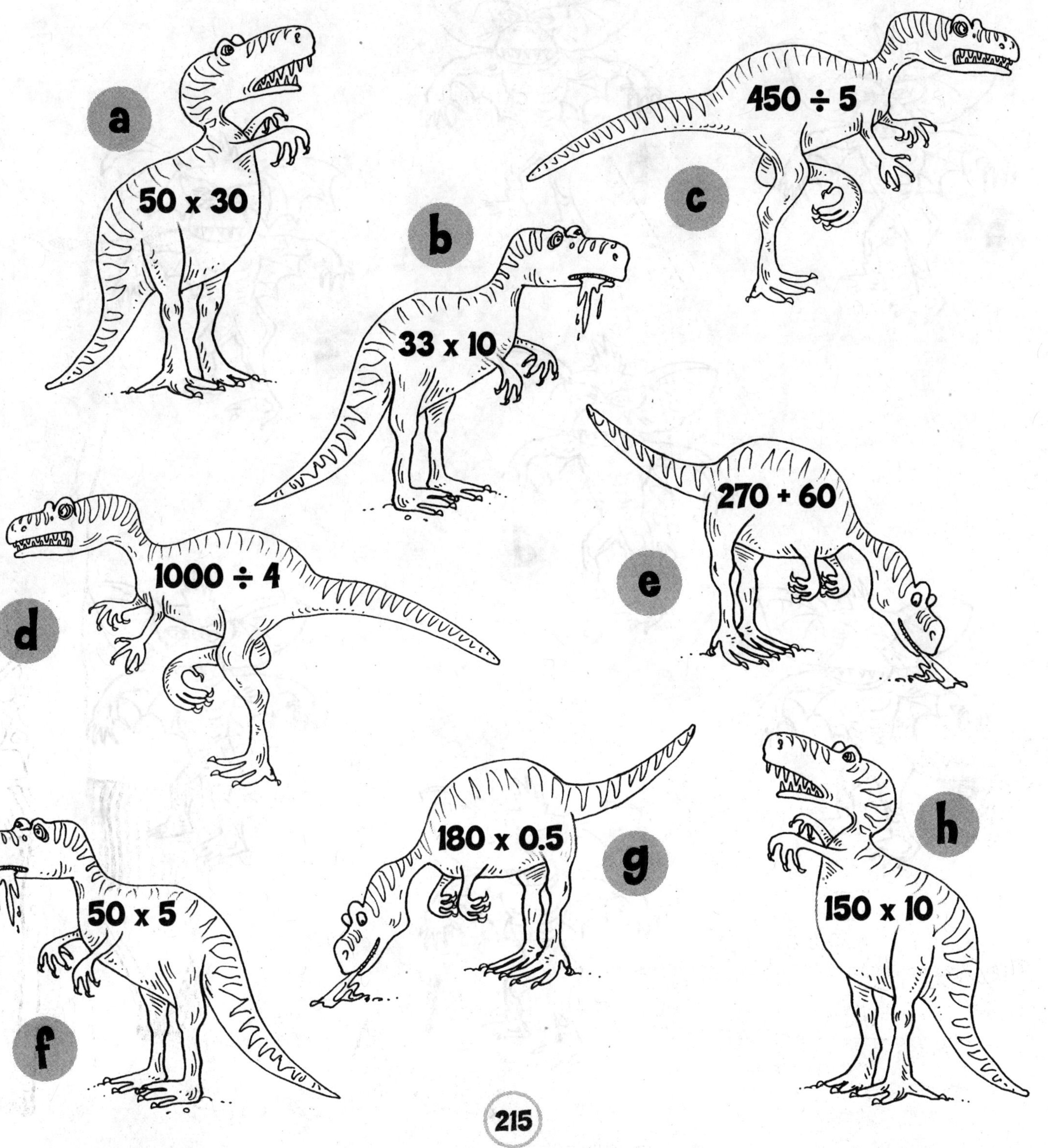

MONSTER MATCH

Only two of these monsters are identical. Can you see which two?

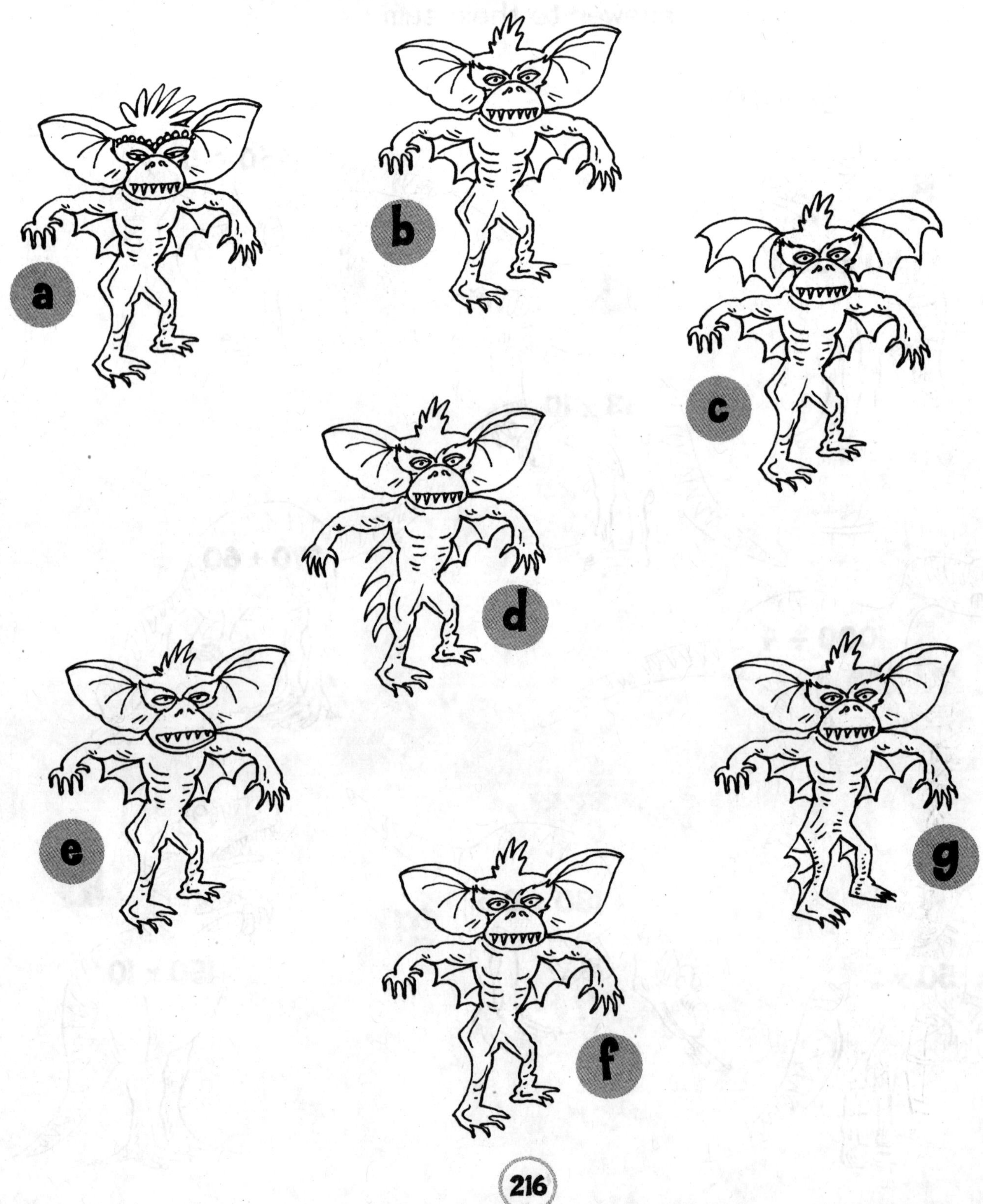

LAND AHOY!

The pirate ship has sighted land. Can you spot ten differences between the two pictures?

DANDELION CLOCK

Use the letters on the seeds with four wings to spell out what time it is.

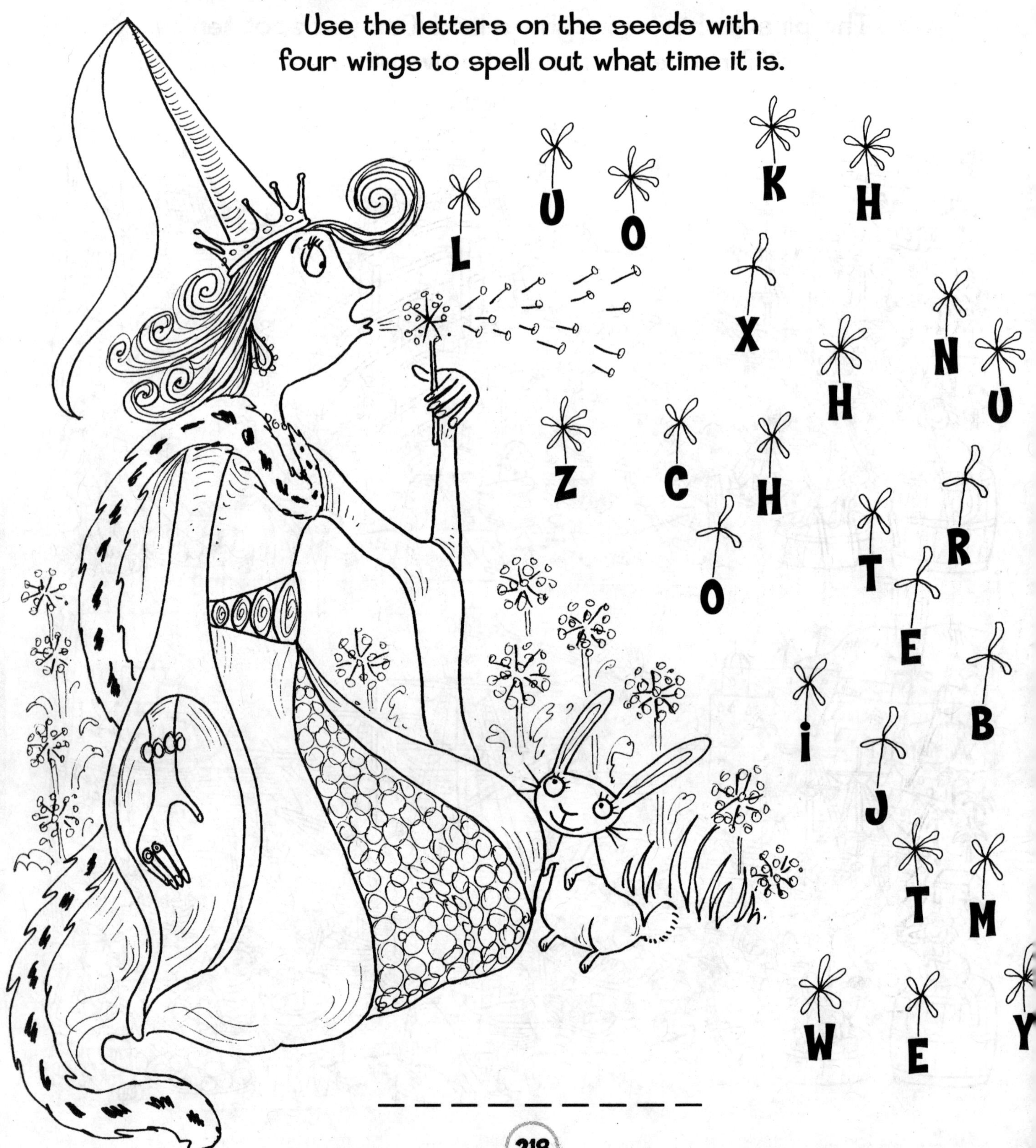

_ _ _ _ _ _ _ _ _ _ _

A-MAZING

Work your way through the rings on the tree trunk to get to the centre.

SCAREDY CAT

What has frightened this cat?

DINOSAURS AND DRAGONS

How many dragonflies can you count in this scene?

PAIR UP THE PETS

Use the clues to put ticks and crosses in the grid and work out which person has each pet, and what colour it is.

1. Freddie's pet doesn't meow.
2. Luke has a black pet.
3. Freddie's pet isn't brown or a dog.
4. The boys have the cat and the hamster.

	dog	cat	hamster	white	brown	black
Annika						
Luke						
Freddie						

JUNGLE ISLAND

Imagine you have landed on a faraway island.
What - or who - is hiding in the jungle?

SHOE SHUFFLE

Princess Pedora is tidying her room. Can you find three shoes that aren't in pairs?

GOING UNDERGROUND

Follow each path and choose the correct trails to spell the names of three burrowing mammals.

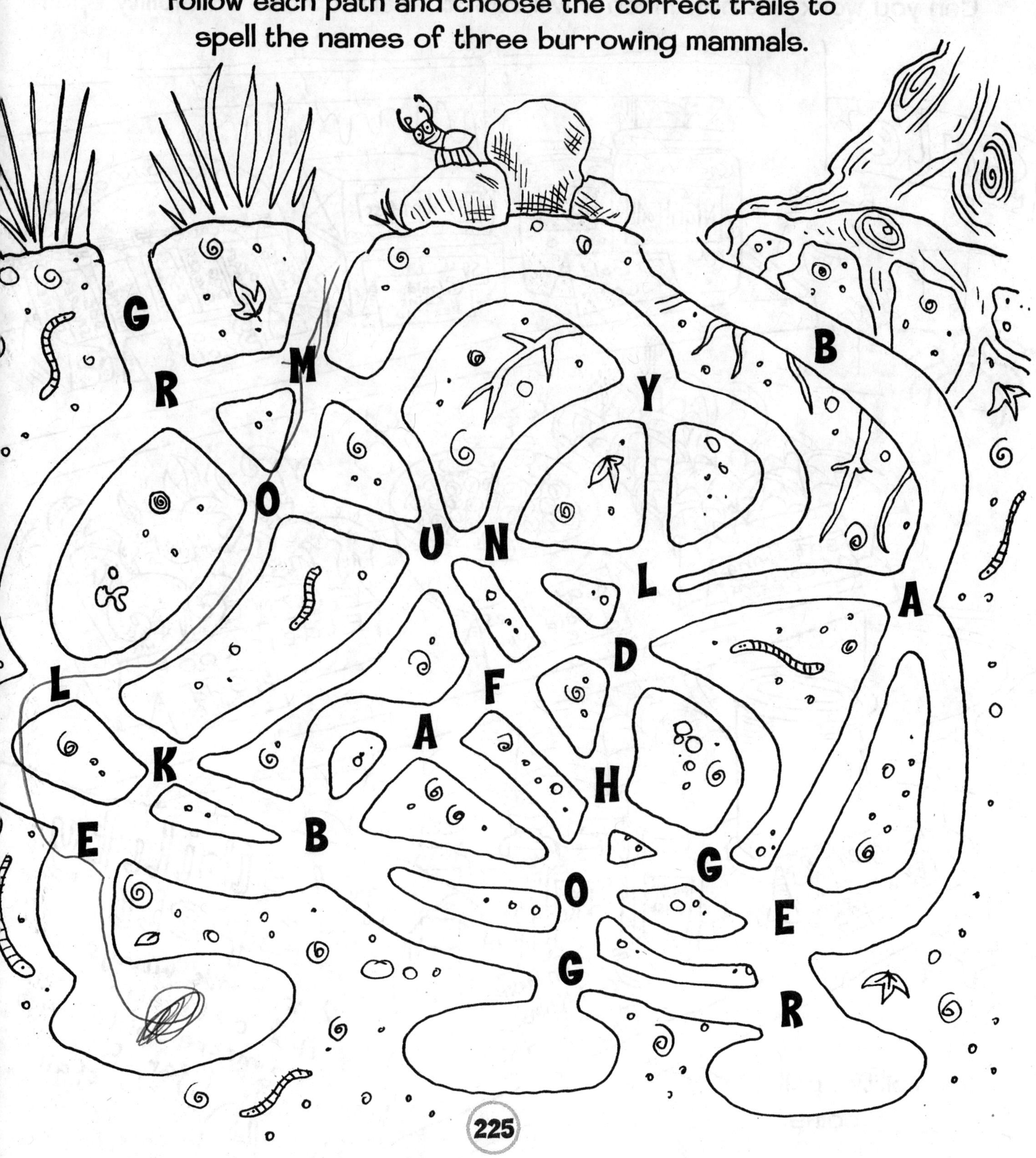

SPELL SHOP

Can you work out how much it will cost to make up this invisibility spell?

Invisibility spell =
_ _ coins

MIGHTY MIX UP

What would a T. rex and a Brachiosaurus look like if they got mixed up?

THINK ABOUT IT...

Use the code to work out the answer to the joke.

What shape is a parrot that has flown away?

The answer is: _ _ _ _ _ _ _ _

MINI BEASTS

Which mini beast finishes the sequence here: a spider, snail or beetle?

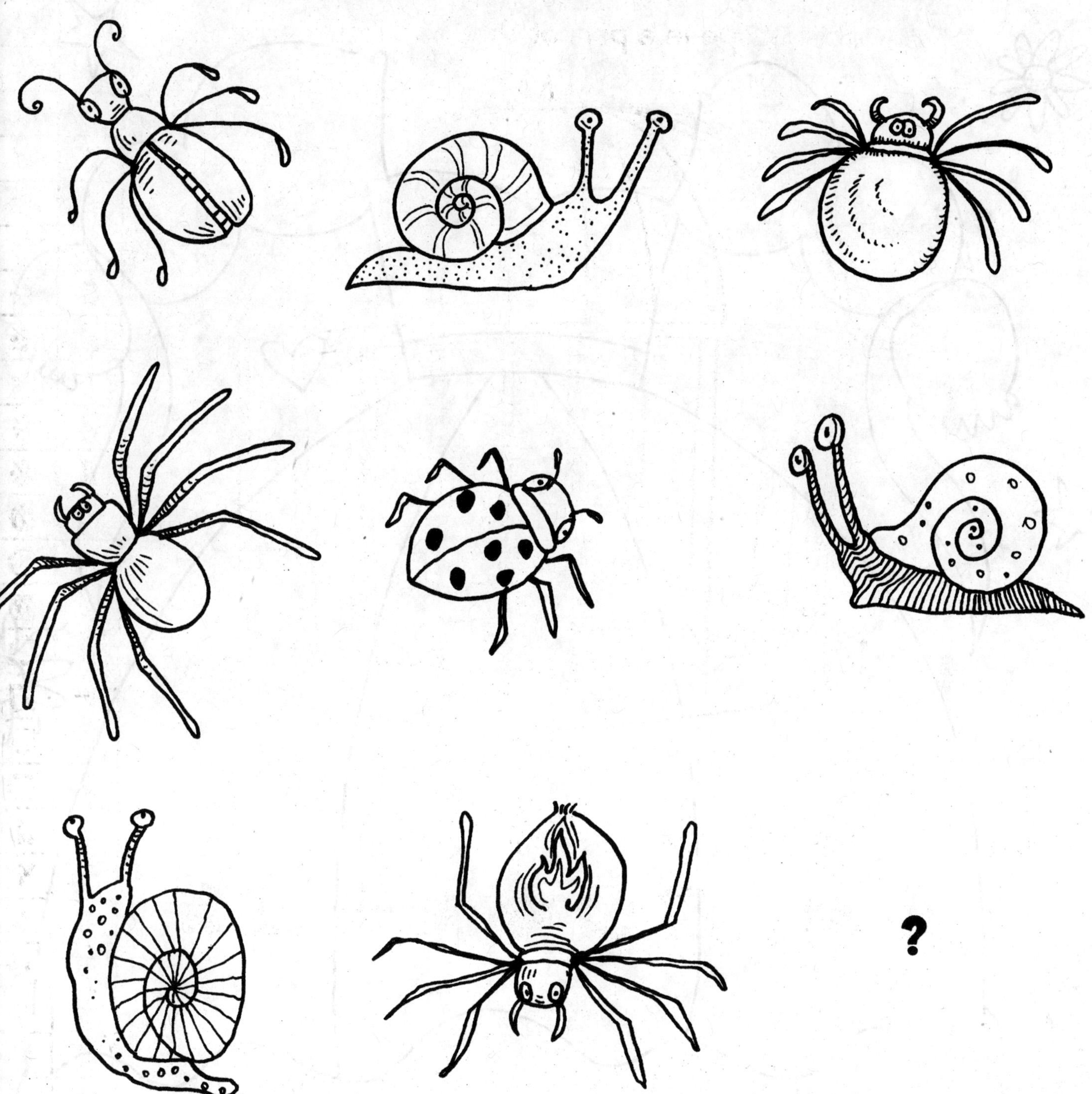

DRESS DESIGNER

Add the details to make this ball gown extra special.

PRETTY POLLY

Reunite Pirate Melville with his parrot, Moby, by counting in threes, starting at the number 3.

START

54	51	48	45	12	9	6	3
57	66	69	42	15	18	21	26
60	63	72	39	36	27	24	32
		75	78	33	30		
		85	81	35			
			84	87			
102	99	96	93	90	94		

FINISH

FORTUNE TELLING

Cross out every other letter, starting with the letter that's blackest, to find the names of two scary characters you don't want to meet.

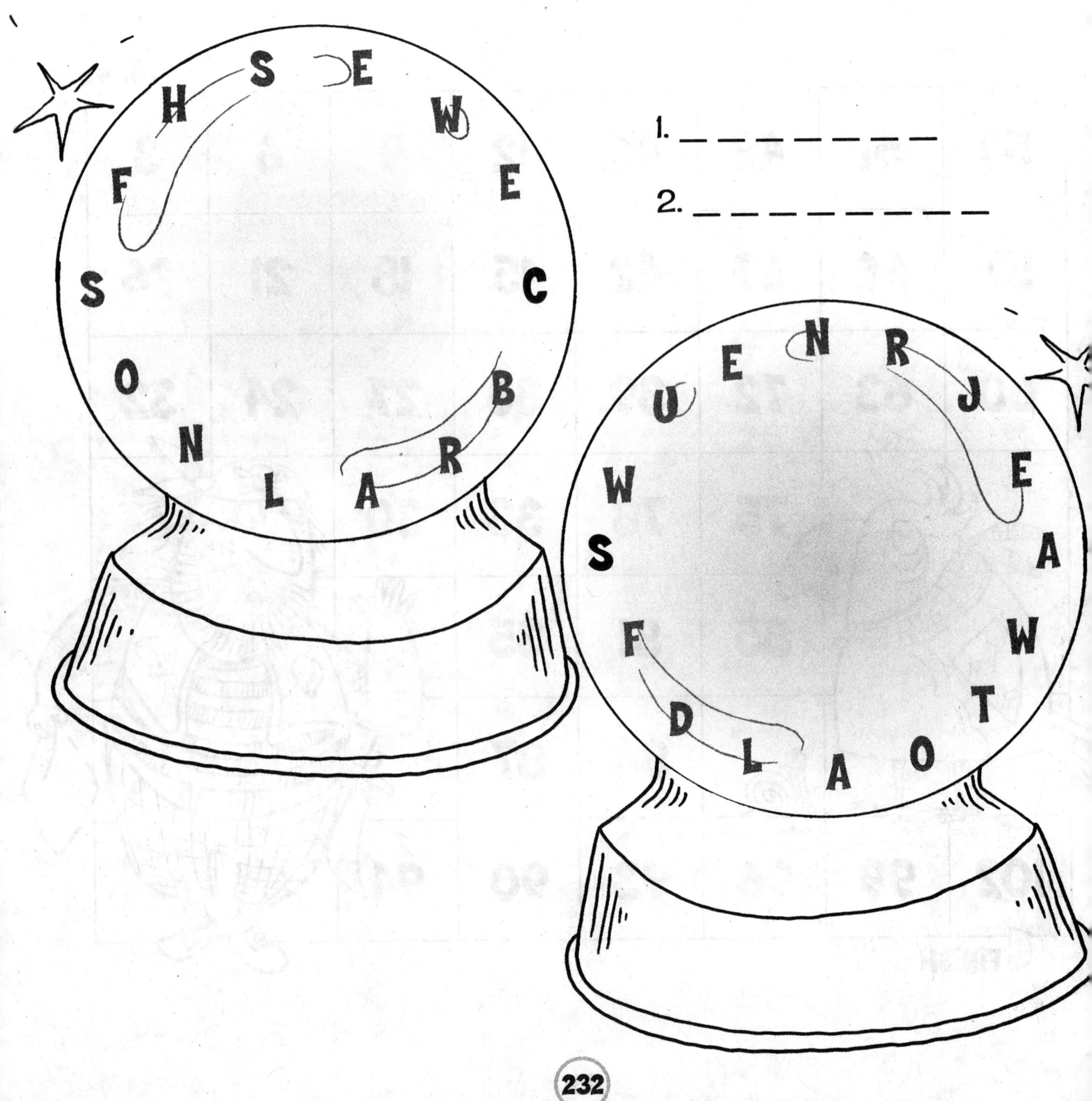

TOO TROO

Which of the small pictures of Troodon matches the main picture?

CAGE CODE

Solve the sums and cross out each answer in the grid. You should have four remaining numbers to unlock the tiger's cage door.

71 x 2 =

1000 ÷ 100 =

900 – 6 =

25 x 100 =

2468 ÷ 2 =

999 ÷ 3 =

416 x 2 =

11 x 11 =

7 x 30 =

60 ÷ 5 =

1	1	8	3	2
0	2	6	2	1
3	3	3	5	2
1	4	2	0	1
9	2	1	0	2

Enter code here

SEADOG SUDOKU

Fill in the puzzle so that every row, column and mini-grid has each of the six pirate pictures.

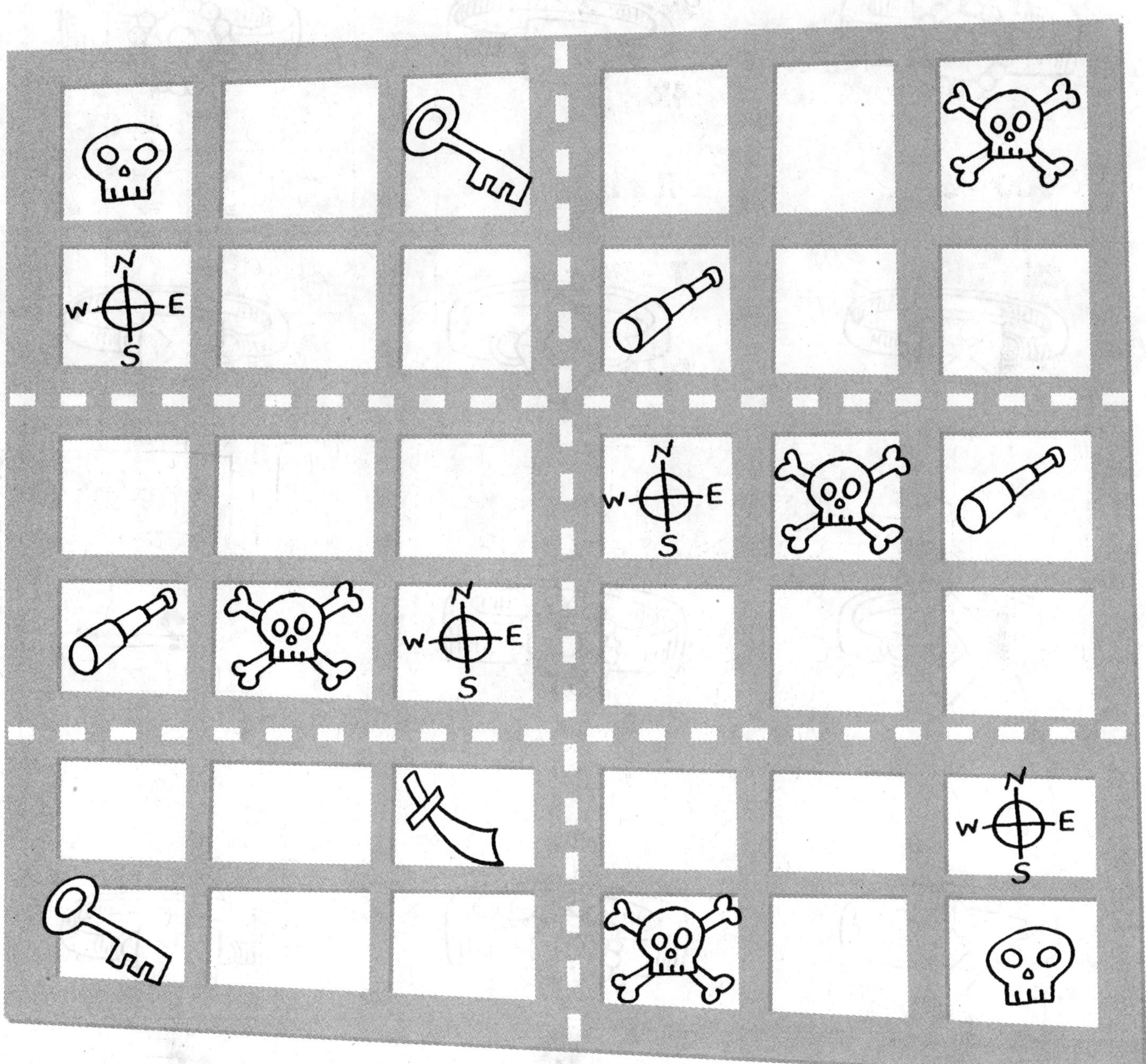

RING RING

What completes the pattern here?

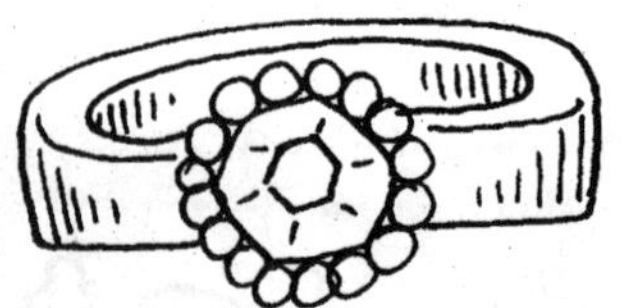

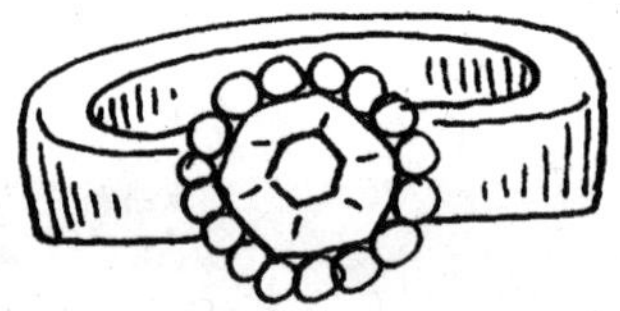

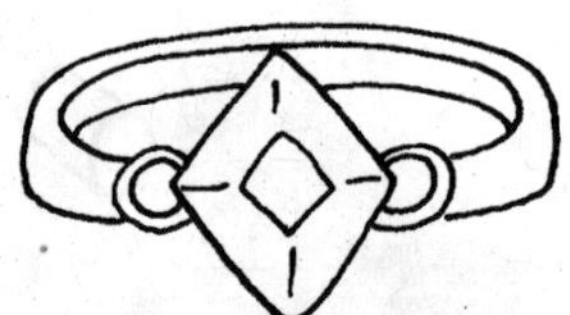

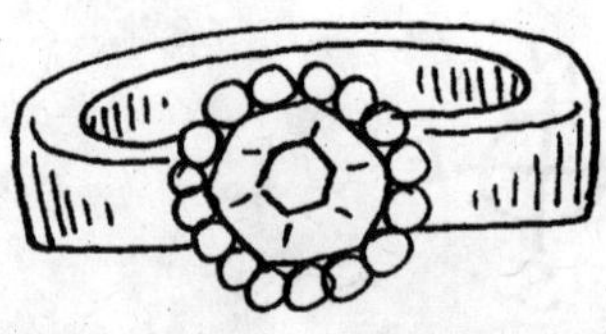

?

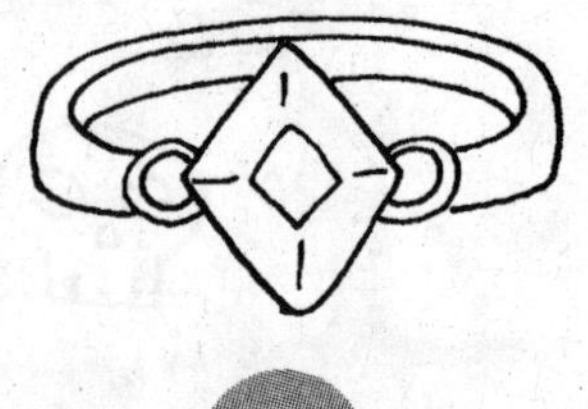

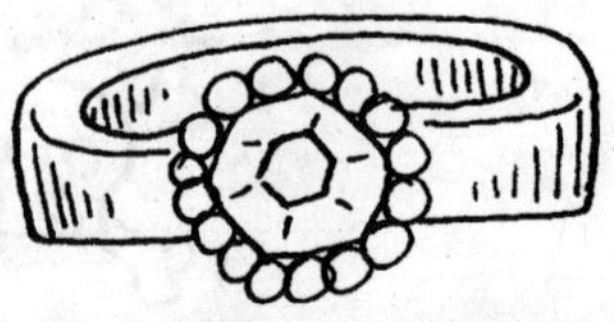

HATCHING OUT

What creatures are coming out of these eggs?

BEASTLY BEING

Which of the groups of words cannot be rearranged to spell GARGOYLE correctly?

GGOLYARE

LAYGOREG

GREGOYAL

GOGLEYOR

GLOGARYE

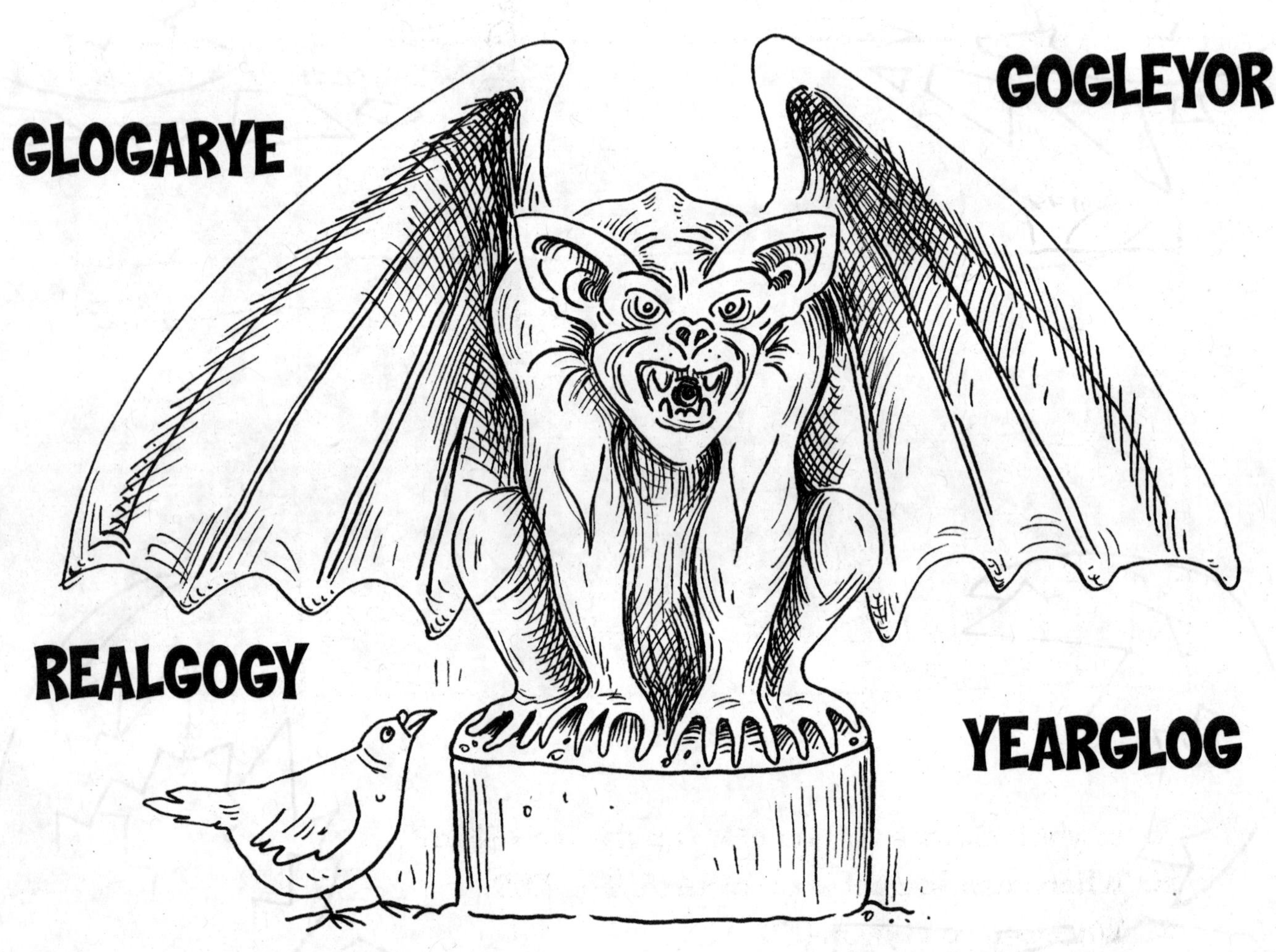

REALGOGY

YEARGLOG

DINOSAUR WORLD

Answer the questions using the map and grid references.

1. In which square do you climb up the Dino Slide?
2. Where can you eat your picnic, E3 or E5?
3. What can you buy in B2?
4. Which dinosaur welcomes you on a walk at B4?

ON SAFARI

What amazing African creatures have you spotted through your binoculars?

BARREL OF FUN

How many times can you find the word AHOY hidden in the grid?

A	A	Y	Y	H	A	O	A	Y	H	O	Y
A	H	A	O	A	A	H	H	O	O	H	A
O	H	A	H	O	H	A	O	A	Y	A	Y
A	H	Y	H	O	H	O	H	O	O	Y	O
A	H	A	O	O	Y	Y	O	Y	H	H	H
H	Y	H	Y	A	O	Y	H	H	A	A	H
Y	A	O	A	H	Y	Y	A	Y	O	O	O
A	H	Y	H	A	H	O	Y	A	O	H	A
Y	O	O	H	A	H	A	H	O	A	Y	H
A	H	A	A	H	O	Y	A	O	O	H	A
H	O	Y	H	O	A	H	O	O	A	O	H
O	H	H	Y	H	O	Y	O	H	O	Y	O
A	O	H	O	Y	A	H	Y	O	H	A	H
A	H	A	H	A	Y	O	H	O	Y	O	O

RIGHT ROYAL WRONGS

Can you spot six things that are wrong in this picture?

TREE TIMES TABLE

Work out the answers to the sums using the number code.
Write the answers as numbers.

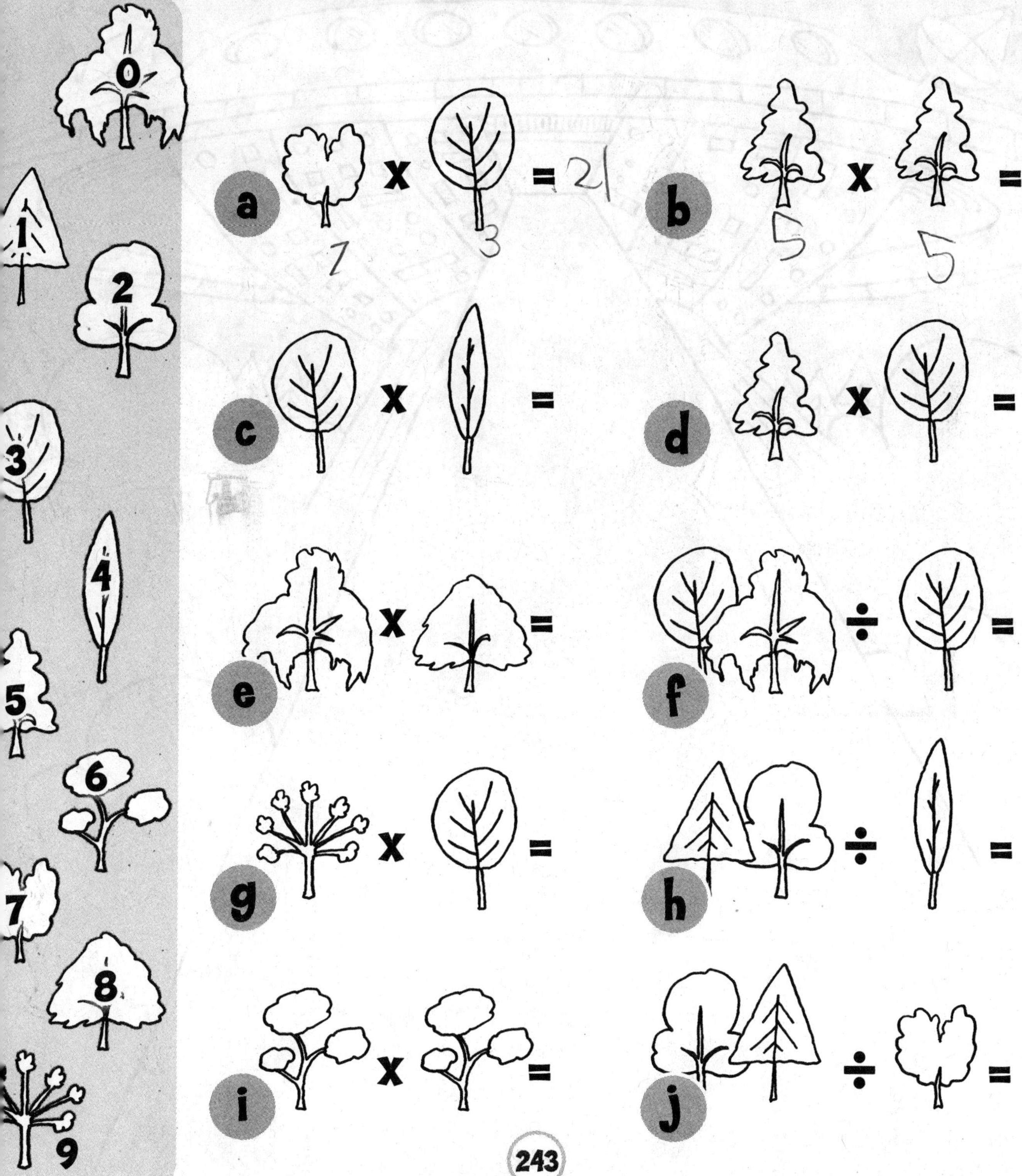

ALIENS HAVE LANDED

Aliens have landed from another planet! Draw them here.

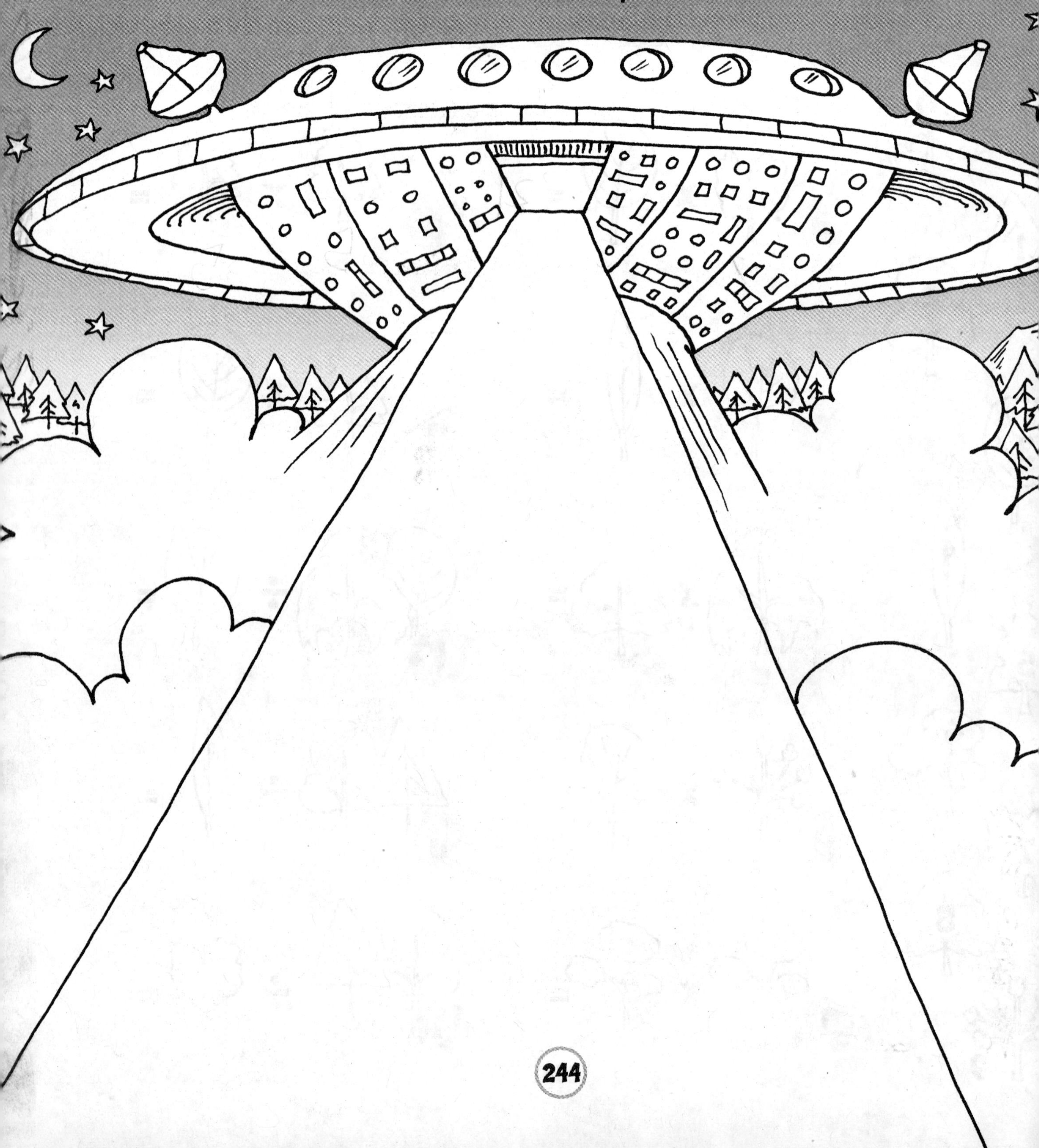

TIME OUT

Write down the letters shown by the minute hand, then the hour hand, for each listed time. They will spell out the names of two dinosaurs.

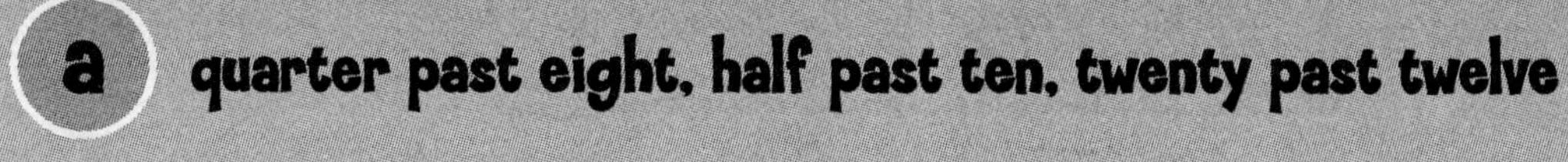

a **quarter past eight, half past ten, twenty past twelve**

_ _ _ _ _ _ _ _ _ _ _ _

b **five to seven, ten past nine, twenty five past one**

_ _ _ _ _ _ _ _ _ _ _ _

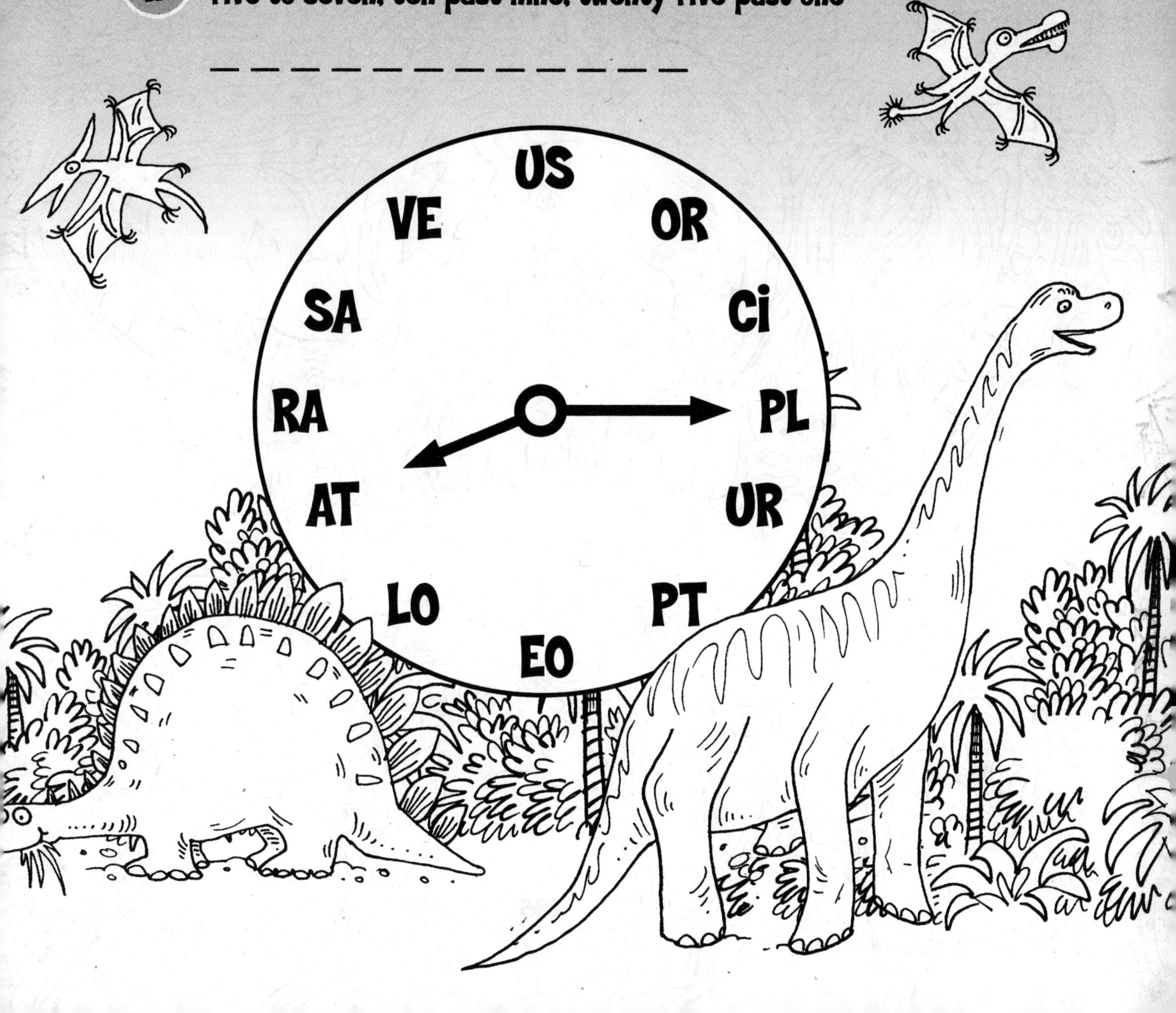

US
VE OR
SA Ci
RA PL
AT UR
LO PT
EO

CREATURE CARVINGS

How many creatures are carved on this tree trunk?

T-SHIRT TREASURES

Add logos, patterns and lots of embellishments to these T-shirts. Which one is your favourite?

WISH ME LUCK

How many lucky horseshoes can you count in the royal stables?

BEETLE MANIA

Which of these stag beetle silhouettes matches the main picture?

MONSTER LAUGHS

Cross out the words using the instructions below. The words left will be the answer to the joke.

Why did the monster eat a torch?

1. Any word with more than 7 letters.
2. Words that begin with T.
3. Words containing the letter O.

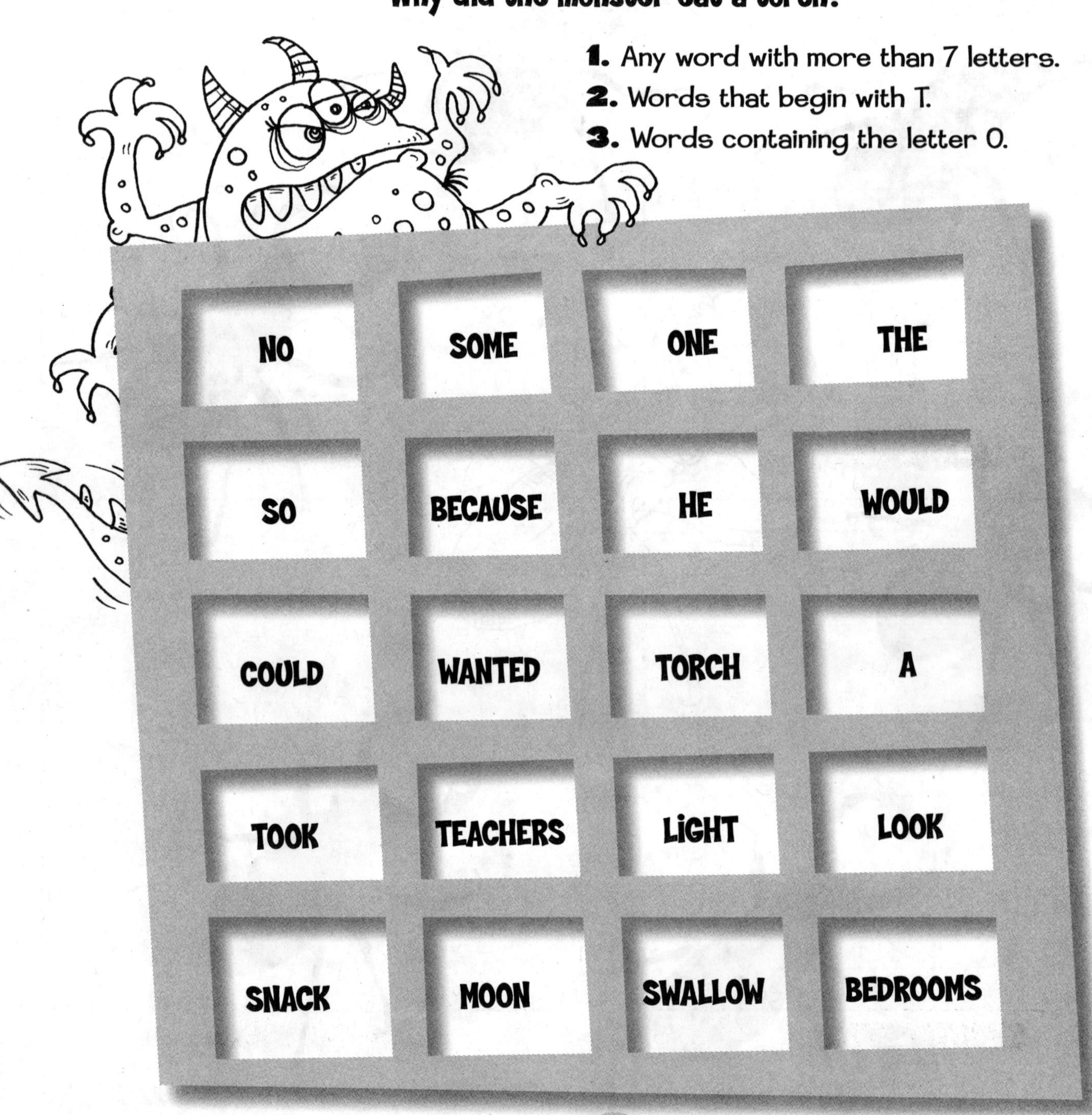

NEW DISCOVERIES

Draw what you think these crazy dinosaurs would look like.

ALLIGATOSAURUS

SPIKODON

SHOOTORAPTOR

STRIPEOSAURUS

NEW FACES

There are three new animals in the bottom picture. Can you spot them all?

PIRATE LOGIC

Read the clues carefully and work out which Captain owns each ship, what colour parrot he has, and what his parrot is called.

1. Captain Barnacle is the captain of the first ship.
2. The parrot called Pesky lives on ship 2.
3. Captain Scablegs has a parrot called Potty.
4. The red parrot is called Perky.
5. Captain Greybeard's parrot isn't the green one.
6. One of the parrots is blue.

	Ship 1	Ship 2	Ship 3
Pirate			
Parrot			
Colour			

DESIGN A DINOSAUR

Doodle your own dinosaur by joining up these bones.

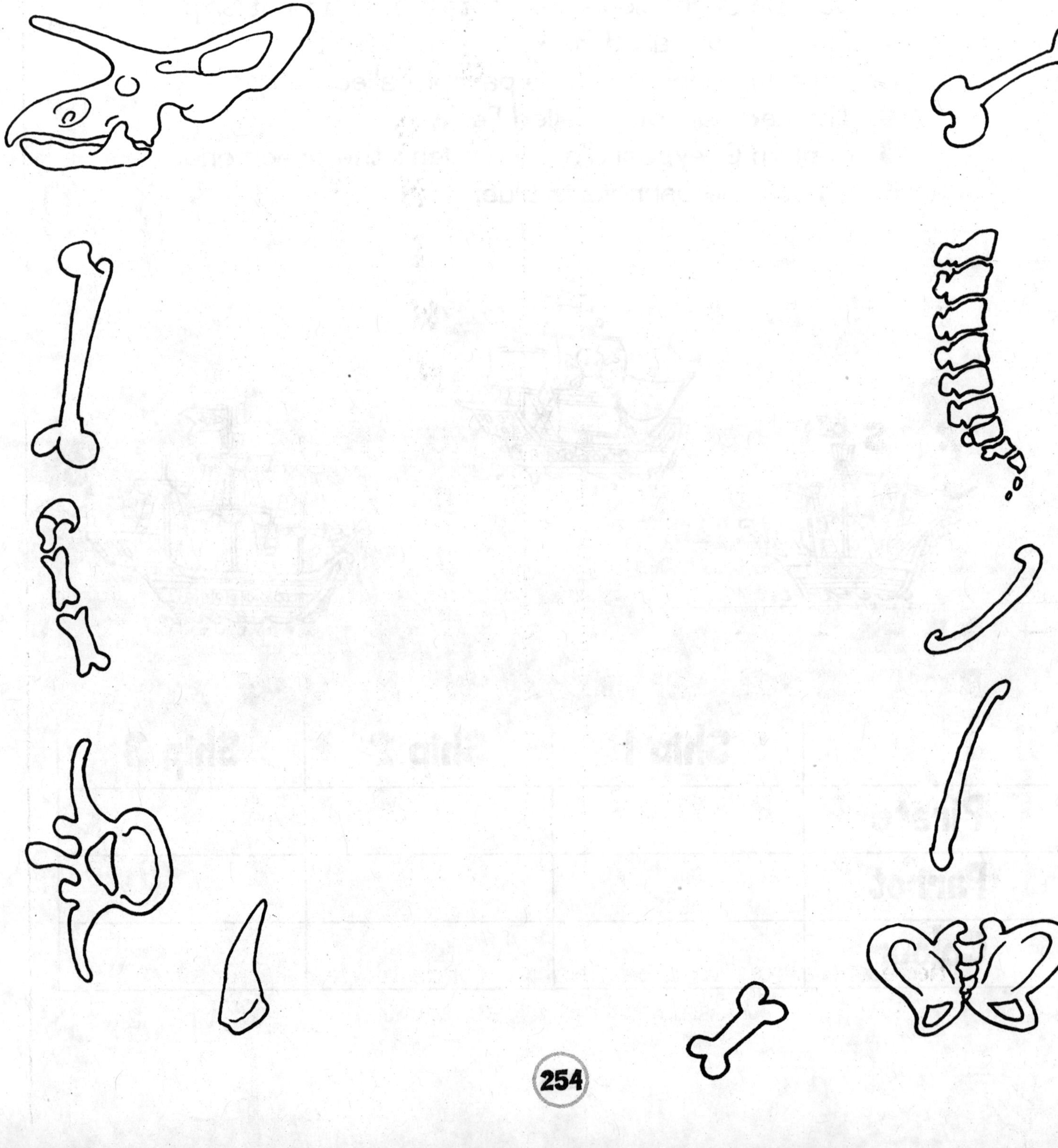

NATURE HUNT

Find the names of ten trees hidden in the wordsearch grid.
There is no list to help you!

W	A	R	U	T	W	I	L	L	O	W
S	B	E	E	C	H	U	E	T	L	G
Y	O	R	S	B	B	A	Q	E	N	R
C	A	X	A	P	F	Q	M	P	H	V
A	V	R	C	N	J	T	I	S	Z	P
M	K	G	A	W	C	L	W	O	F	O
O	A	K	T	B	C	H	M	I	T	P
R	S	Y	L	R	X	K	C	Y	G	L
E	M	R	D	Y	U	F	D	L	K	A
Z	C	H	E	S	T	N	U	T	N	R
G	L	E	K	P	N	G	K	E	X	M
B	A	S	H	R	Z	I	W	H	U	F
J	H	A	F	U	O	P	I	N	E	L
E	U	D	B	C	I	S	C	J	D	Q
A	P	P	L	E	T	P	C	V	K	E

There are also five tree-related words hidden diagonally.
Can you find those, too?

CHAIN REACTION

Which of the jigsaw pieces finishes the puzzle?

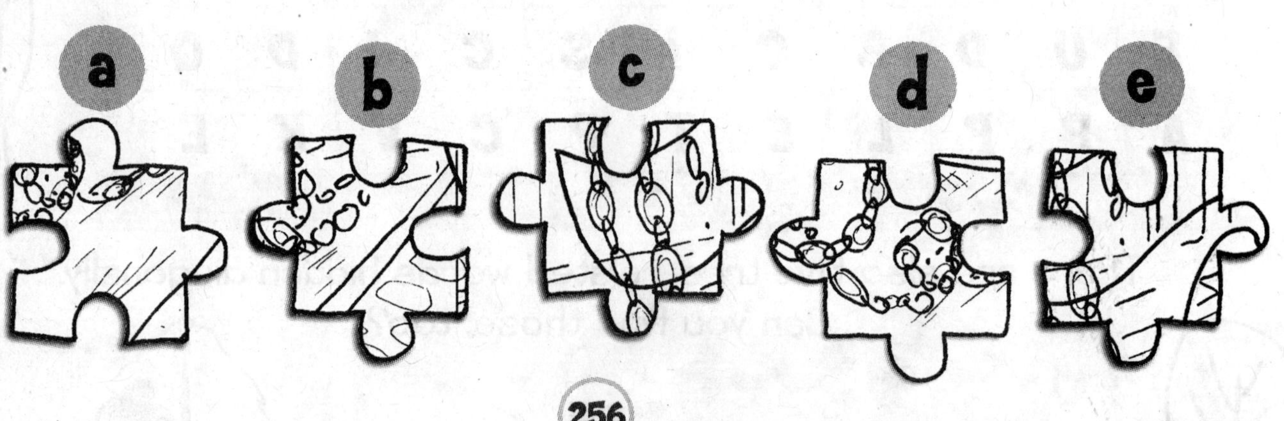

FOSSIL FINDER

If A=1, B=2, C=3 and so on, can you label the boxes of bones correctly?

4.5.9.14.15.14. 25.3.8.21.19

_ _ _ _ _ _ _ _ _ _ _ _

1.14.11.25.12.15. 19.1.21.18.21.19

_ _ _ _ _ _ _ _ _ _ _ _

4.9.16.12.15. 4.15.3.21.19

_ _ _ _ _ _ _ _ _ _ _ _

9.7.21.1.14. 15.4.15.14

_ _ _ _ _ _ _ _ _ _ _

19.16.9.14.15. 19.1.21.18.21.19

_ _ _ _ _ _ _ _ _ _ _ _ _

15.22.9.18. 1.16.20.15.18

_ _ _ _ _ _ _ _ _ _ _

MONKEY PUZZLE

Use the letter pairs on the coconuts to help the monkey spell the names of three of the largest animals in the world.

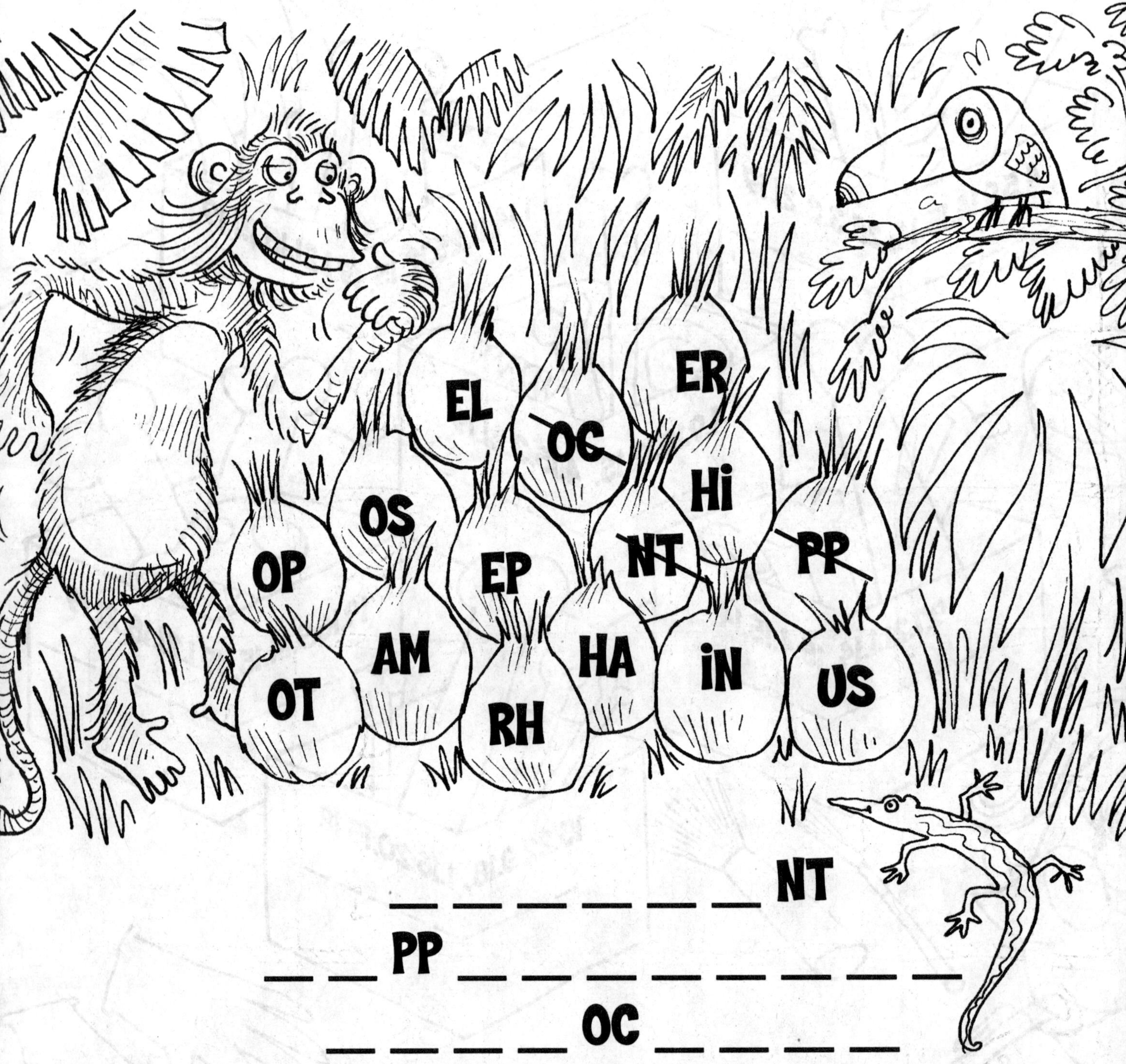

FINDING YOUR WAY

Find the correct path from start to finish, following the pictures in this order:

1 2 3

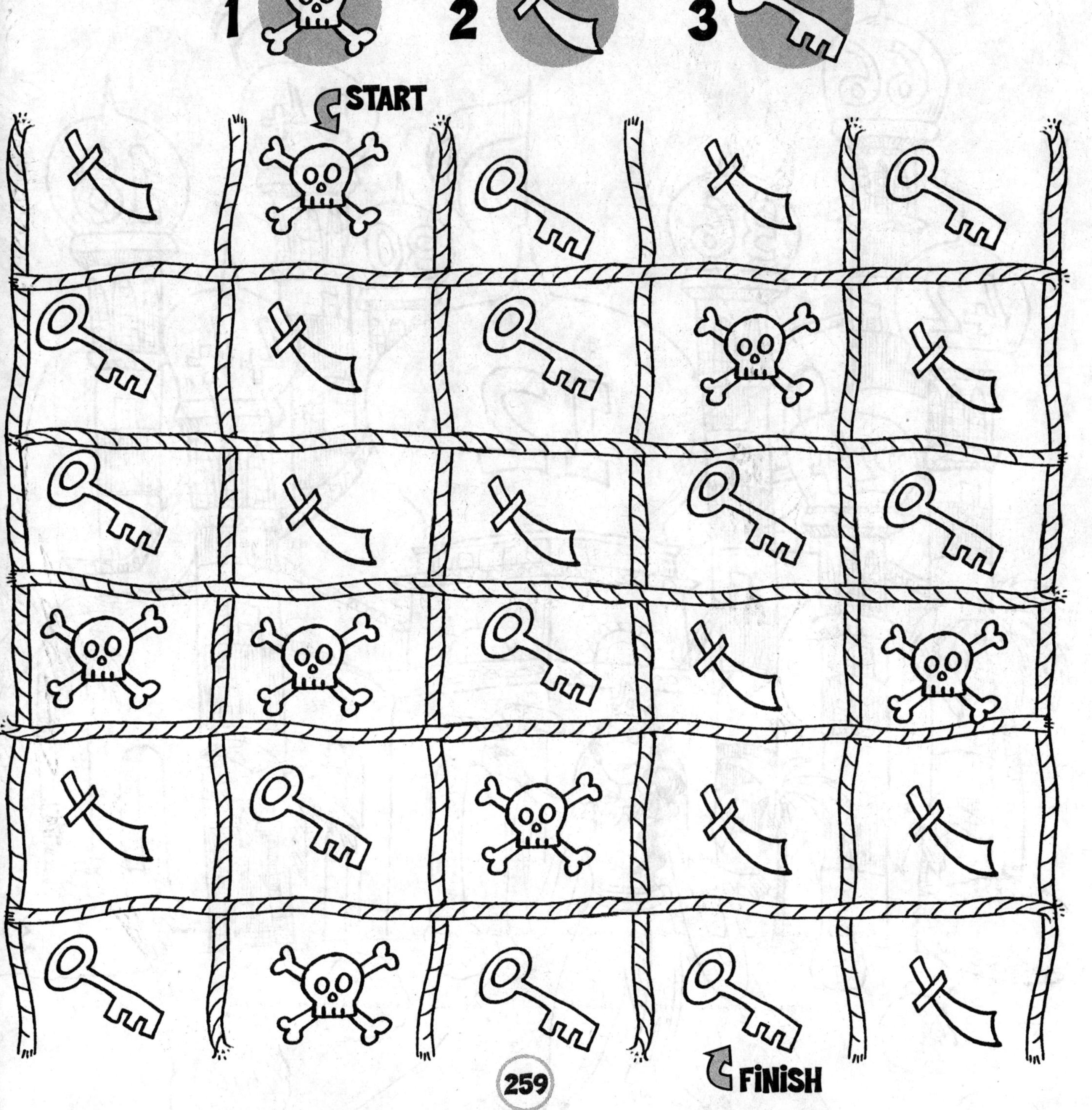

MYSTICAL MATHS

Which of Princess Sanjana's palace towers does NOT have a number from the 6 times table?

UNDER COVER

Draw a background for each creature, and then add some patterns on the bodies to keep them camouflaged.

MEET THE MISFITS!

Study the sequence of pictures correctly and work out which of these creepy females finishes the pattern: a, b or c?

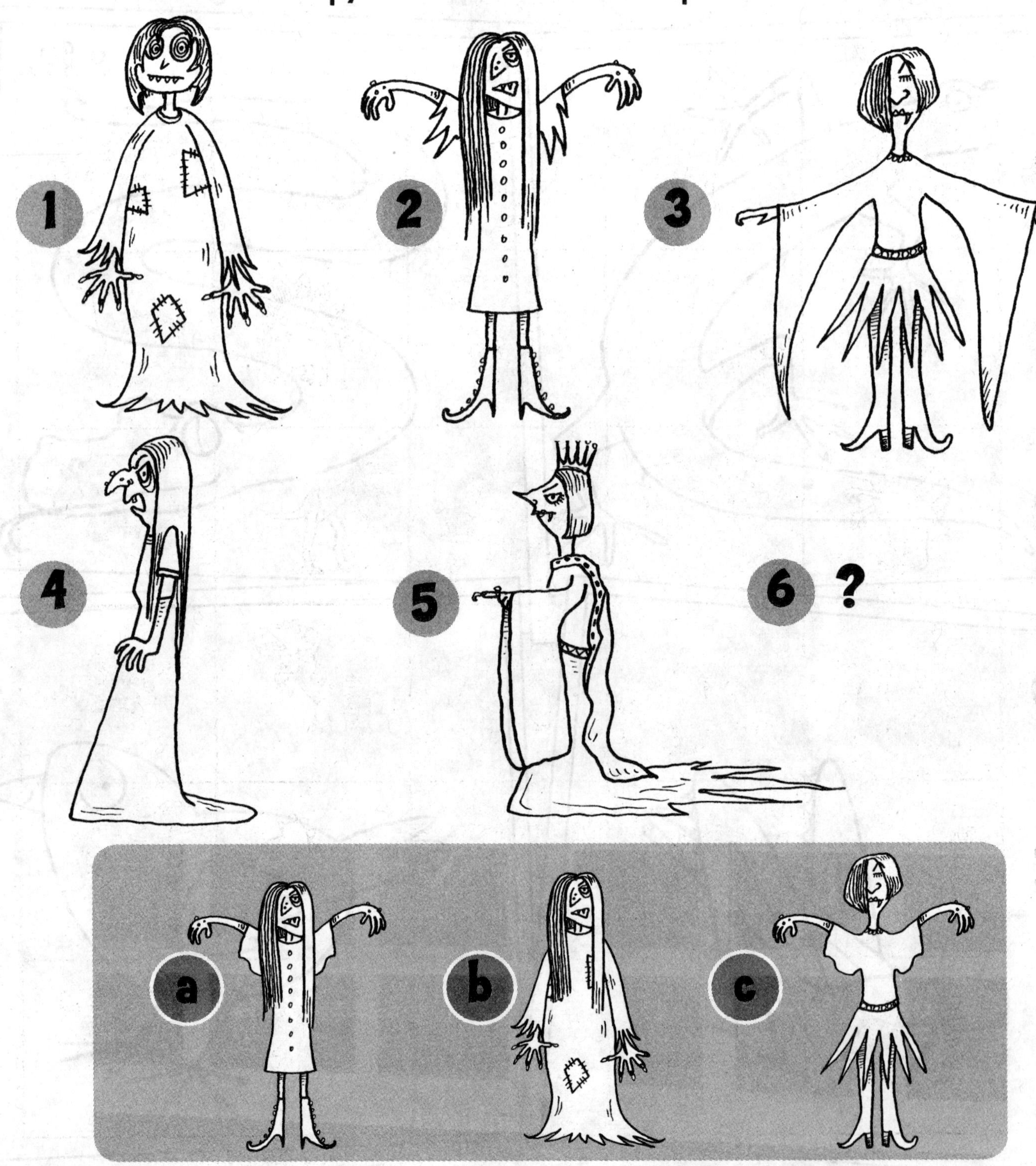

DINO DAZE

Find a path from row A to row F by following the tails of the dinosaurs. If it points down, you move down, or if it points sideways, follow it sideways.

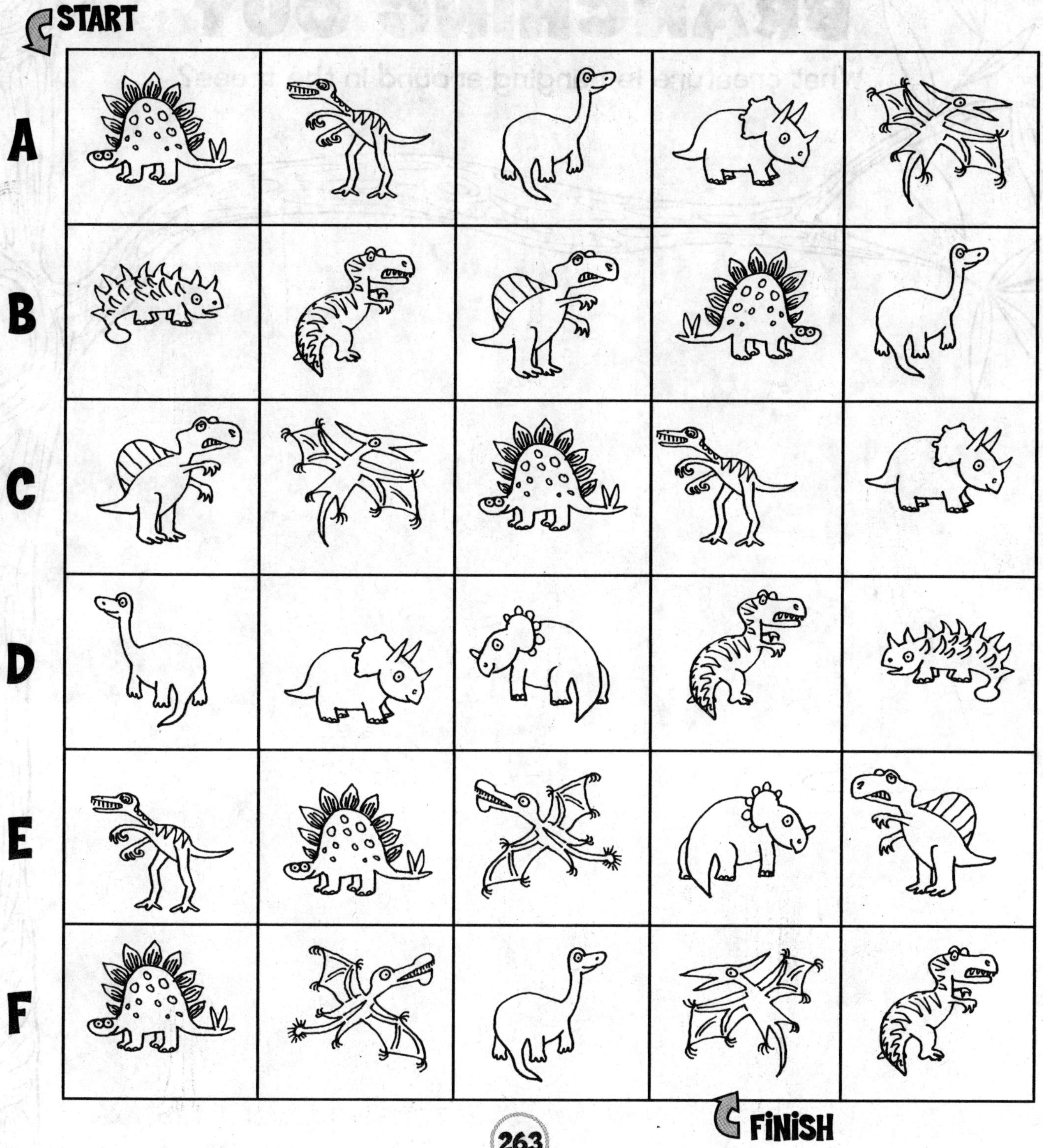

START

A

B

C

D

E

F

FINISH

BRANCHING OUT

What creature is hanging around in the trees?

SAFE HARBOUR

Batten down the hatches! Follow the directions across the stormy seas and draw an X in the harbour where the pirates should land.

1. Sail east for two squares.
2. Head north three squares.
3. Follow your course eastwards for two more squares.
4. Head south and cast your anchor in safe waters.

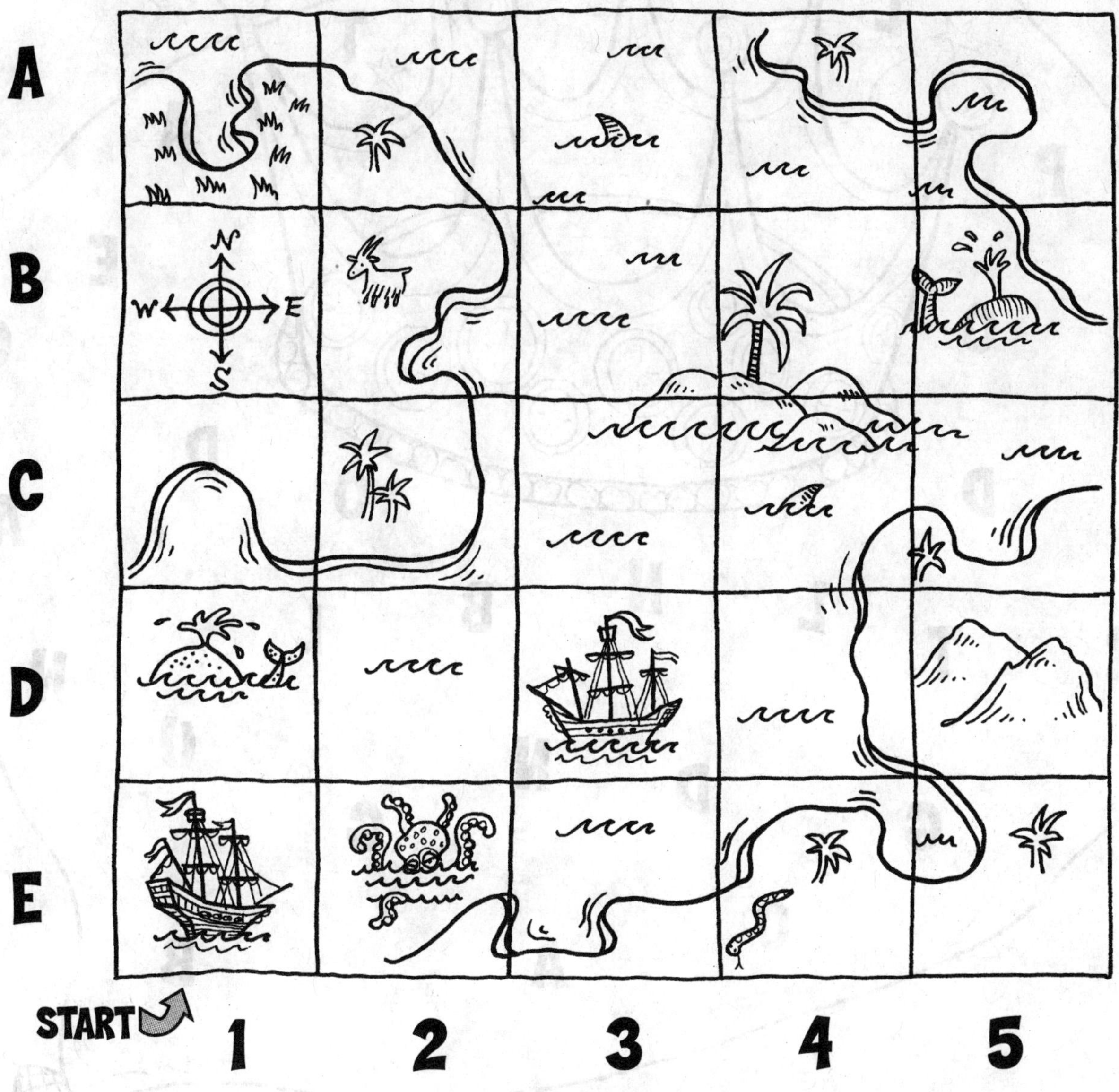

CROWNING GLORY

Cross out any letter that appears more than once
to find where Princess Annalise lives.

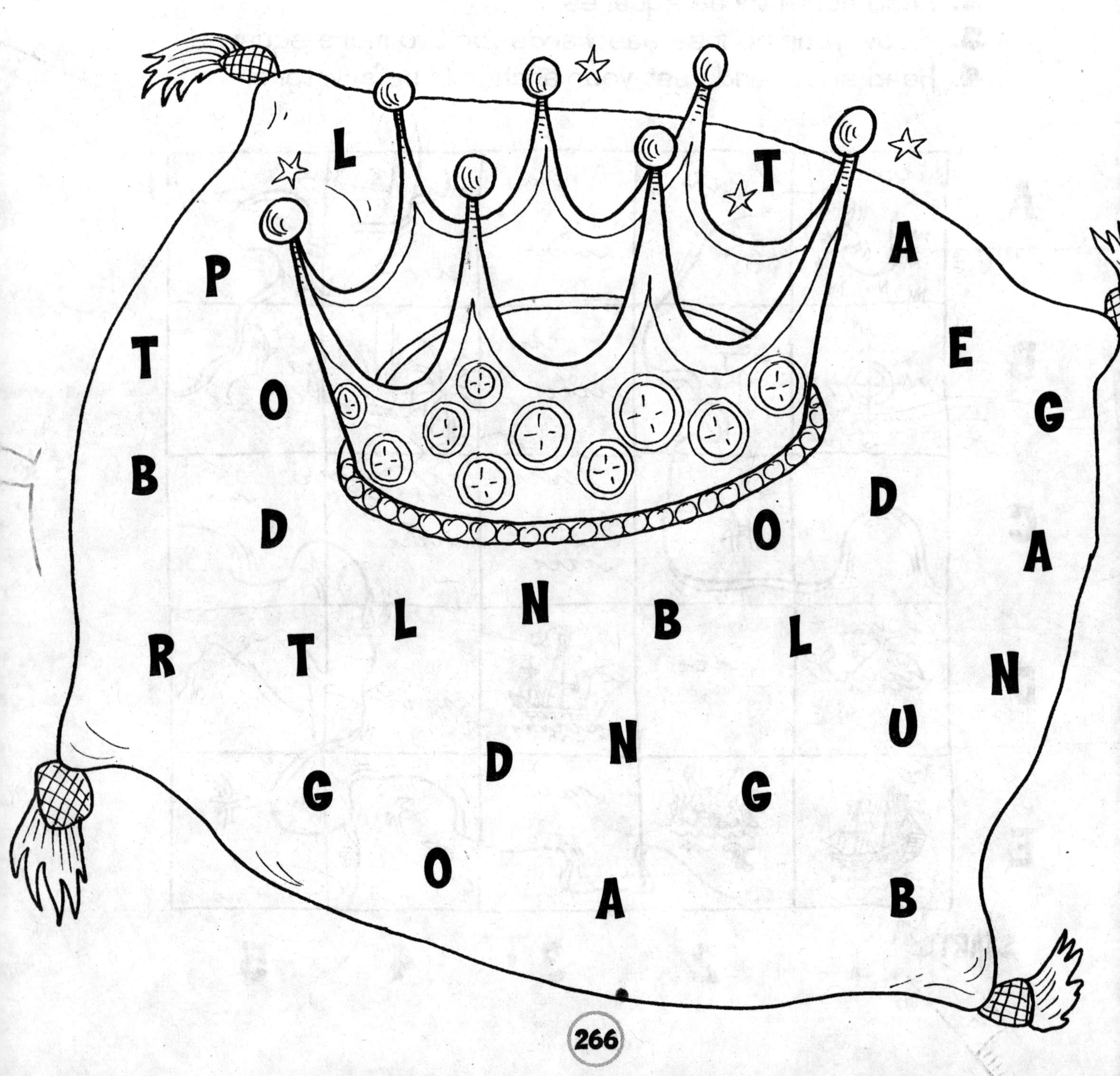

THROUGH THE LOOKING GLASS

Which is the only one of the magnified images that could be part of the main picture?

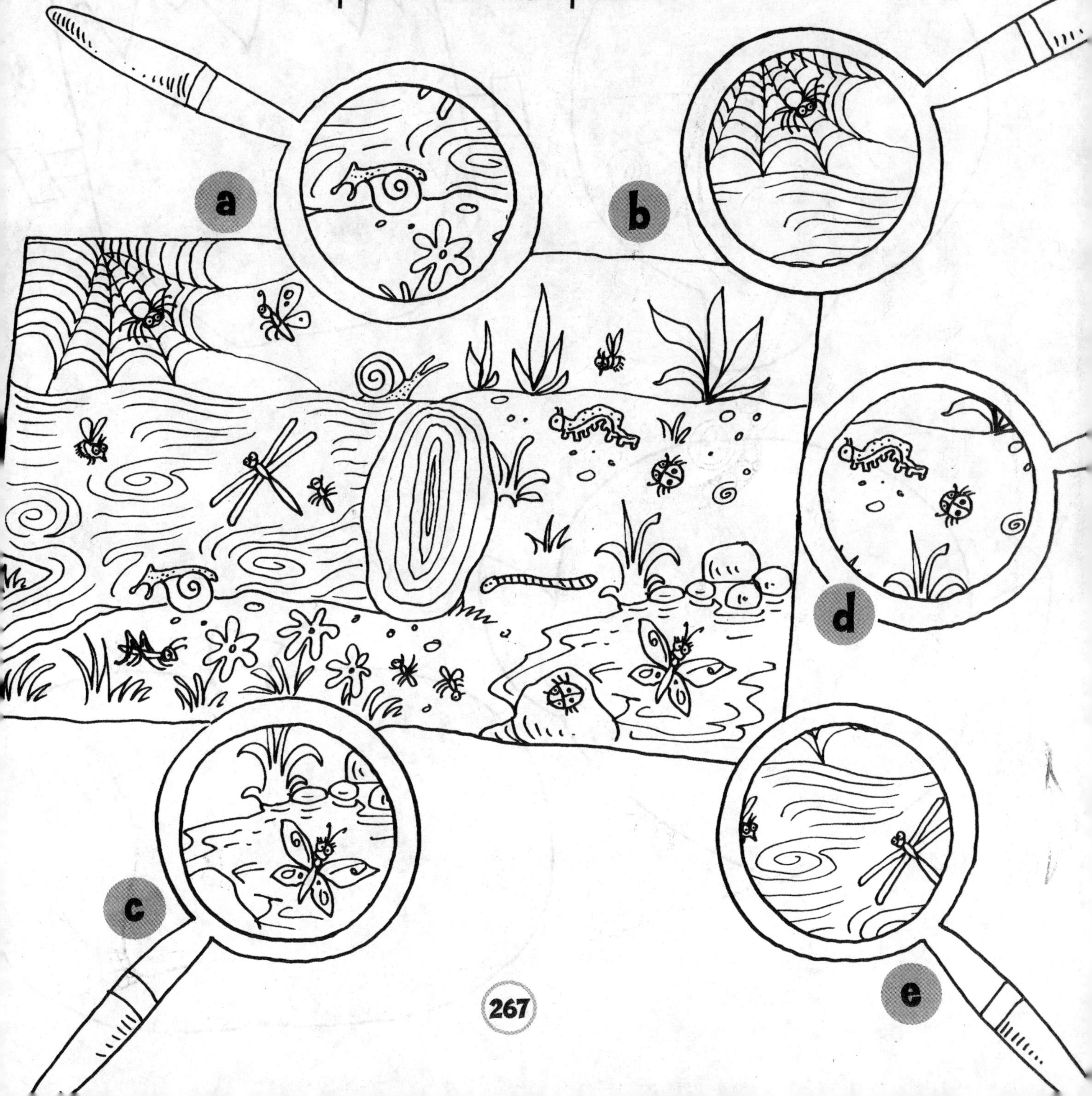

a

b

d

c

e

TRICK OR TREAT?

Draw scary faces on these Hallowe'en masks to freak out the neighbours!

DINO-DOKU

Fill in the puzzle so that every row, column and mini-grid has each of the six dino pictures.

CAT CONUNDRUM
Which of the groups of words cannot be rearranged to correctly spell a big cat?
ARGUJA
THERMAP
GRITE
REPNTAH
HETHACE
OGURAC
DRAPOLE

WANTED!

Design a poster to catch the world's most wanted pirate.

Pirate ________________________________

Distinguishing features ____________________

____

____

Last seen ______________________________

Reward ________________________________

MIRROR MIRROR

Can you read the answer to the joke in Princess Hannah's mirror?

Where did the ice queen go to dance?

The snow ball!

AS THE CROW FLIES

Which of the crows has flown the farthest from the nests? Add up the numbers to find out.

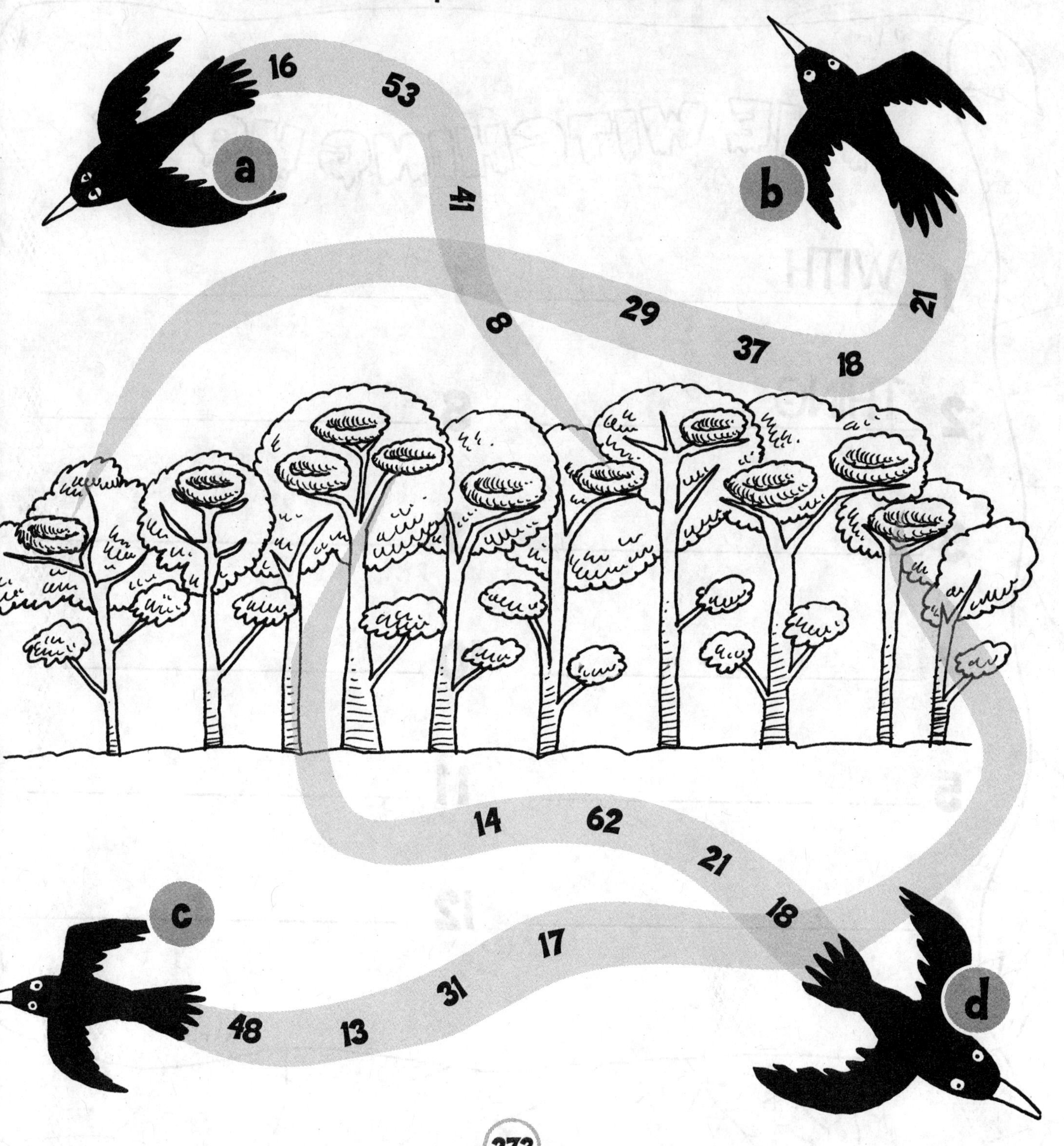

SPOOKY SPELLINGS

How many smaller words can you make from the letters below?

THE WITCHING HOUR

1 WITH

2 THING

3

4

5

6

7

8

9

10

11

12

FLYING HIGH

What would flying reptiles look like if you were in charge?
Add feathers, claws, teeth and patterns.

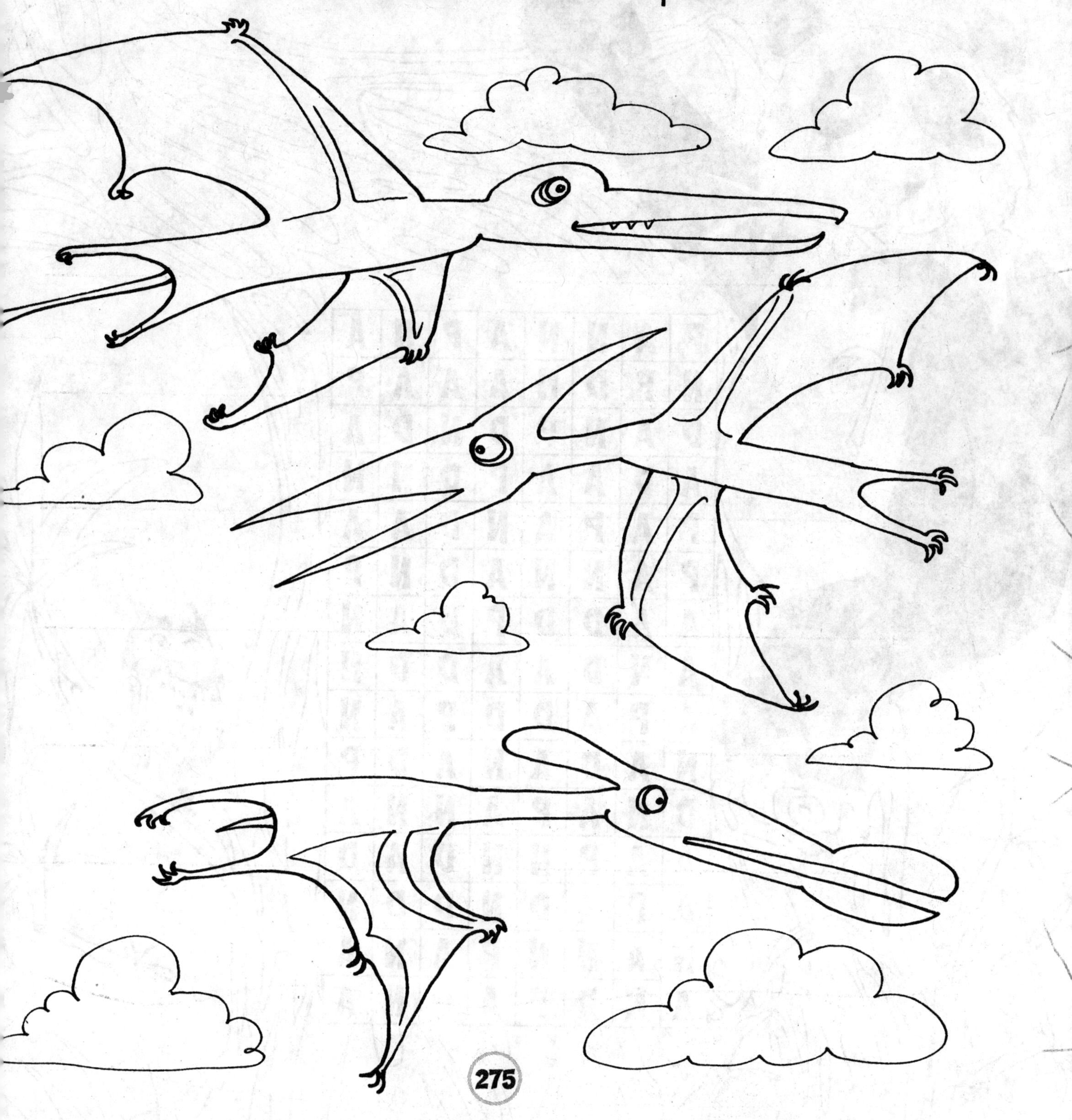

REALLY RARE

Find the word PANDA hidden only once in the grid.

P	A	N	N	A	P	N	A
N	P	D	N	A	A	A	P
D	A	N	P	D	N	D	A
A	D	A	A	P	D	N	N
P	A	P	A	N	D	A	A
P	A	N	N	A	D	N	P
A	A	D	D	P	D	A	N
A	N	D	A	A	D	D	N
A	P	A	D	D	P	A	N
N	A	D	A	N	A	D	P
D	N	A	P	A	N	N	A
A	A	P	N	N	D	A	D
D	P	A	D	N	D	D	N
N	A	N	N	P	A	N	A
A	N	D	P	A	D	N	A

RUFUS REDBEARD

Use the clues to work out which of the flags belongs to Rufus Redbeard.

1. It has a single skull on it.
2. It doesn't show any weapons.
3. The skull is facing forwards.
4. It only shows two bones.

a  b  c

d  e  f

g  h  i

PRINCESS SUDOKU

Fill in the puzzle so that every row, column and mini-grid has each of the six pictures.

UGLY BUG BALL

Which three bugs have made their way into the ugly bug ball in the bottom picture?

WHO GOES THERE?

What are the people running away from? Tilt the page towards you to read the answer.

THUMBS UP

This Iguanodon likes correct spelling! Tick five dinosaur names that are spelt properly.

- ☐ BRACHIASAURUS
- ☐ TRISERATOPS
- ☐ VELOCIRAPTOR
- ☐ ALLASAURUS
- ☐ GIGANTOSAURUS
- ☐ STEGGOSAURUS
- ☐ PTERANODON
- ☐ TYRANNOSAURUS
- ☐ SPINOSAURUS

EAGLE EYES
Follow the tangled lines to see which eagle belongs in each nest.
a
2
1
b
c
4
3
d
282

DEADLY DICE

Do the sums shown on the skull dice to see which roll is the highest. Each time, do the adding part of the sum and then the multiplication.

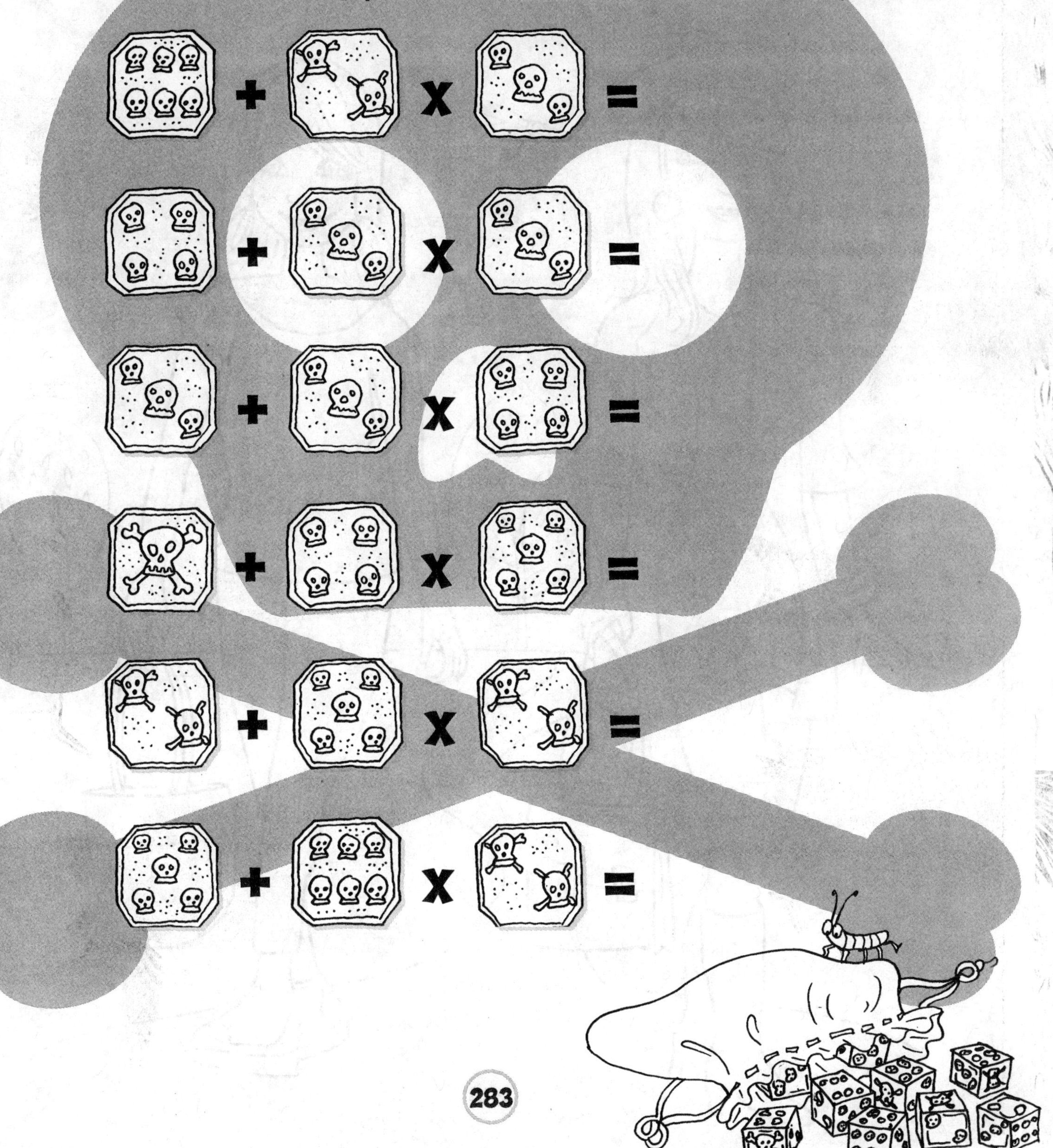

FASHION BY YOU

Use your favourite colours and patterns to finish these clothes, and then add accessories to match.

MAKING TRACKS

Why do bears have fur coats? Work out the answer using the picture code.

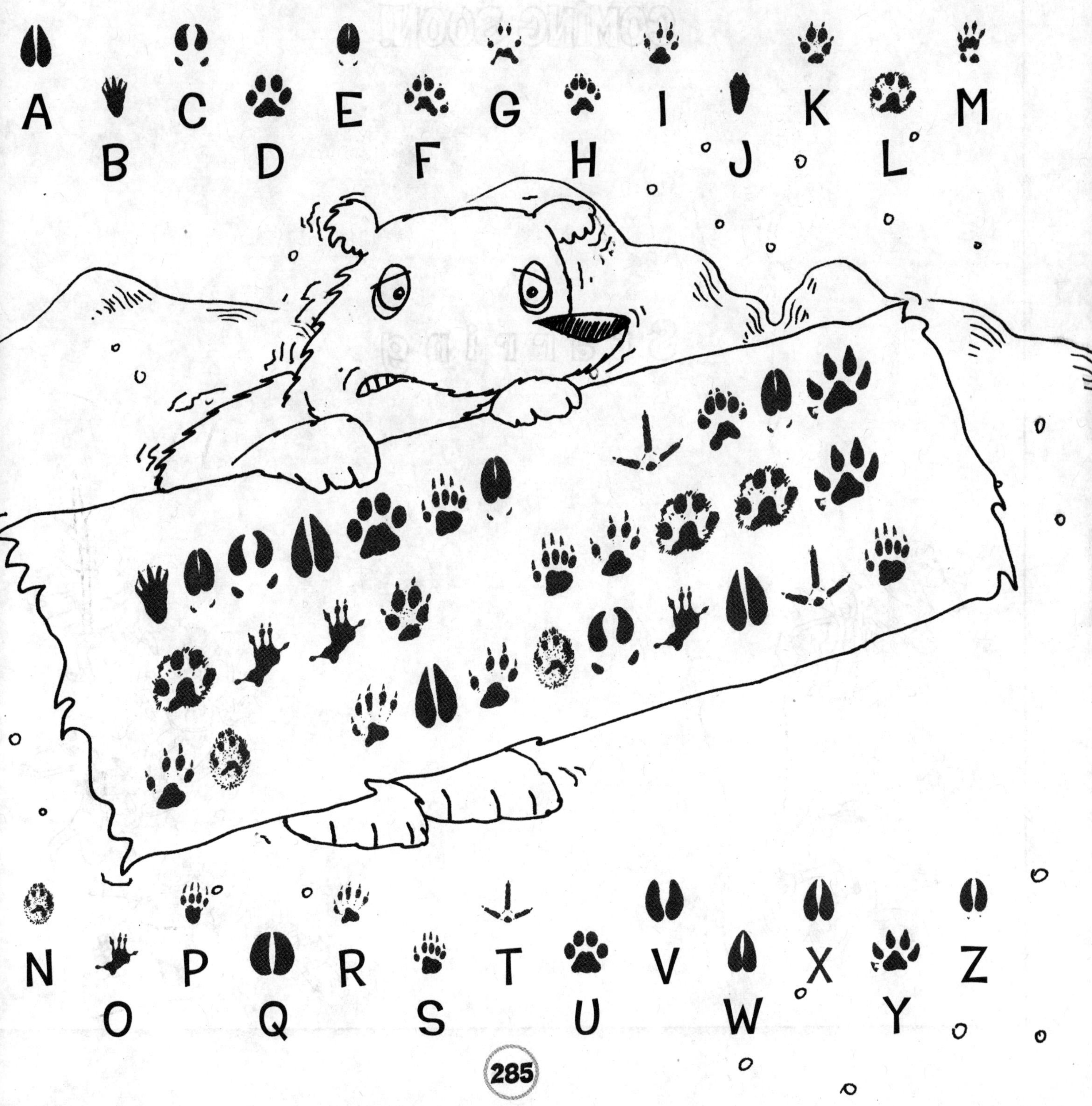

SCARY MOVIE

Finish the poster for a horror movie. What will be the scary star?

COMING SOON!

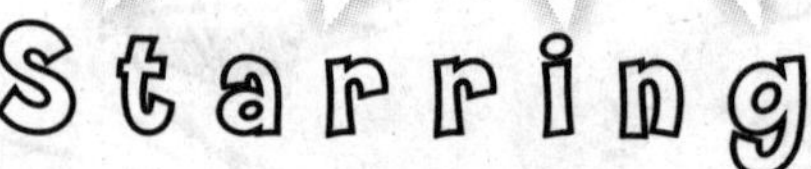

ON THEIR TRAIL

Starting at J, find all of the listed dinosaur words in one long, continuous trail through the grid. They're not in the listed order, though!

TRIASSIC	JAWS	REPTILE	SCAVENGER
CRETACEOUS	EXTINCT	PREDATOR	PREHISTORIC
JURASSIC	FOSSIL	HERBIVORE	
	CLAW	CARNIVORE	

START

J	U	R	A	S	E	T	A	C	E
R	P	C	I	S	R	H	S	U	O
E	E	P	L	E	C	E	T	O	R
D	R	T	I	I	B	R	S	C	I
A	S	W	A	V	E	H	I	T	R
T	O	R	J	O	R	S	S	A	I
A	L	C	E	R	P	I	O	S	S
W	E	N	G	E	R	C	F	L	I
S	V	N	I	V	O	R	E	E	X
C	A	R	A	C	T	C	N	I	T

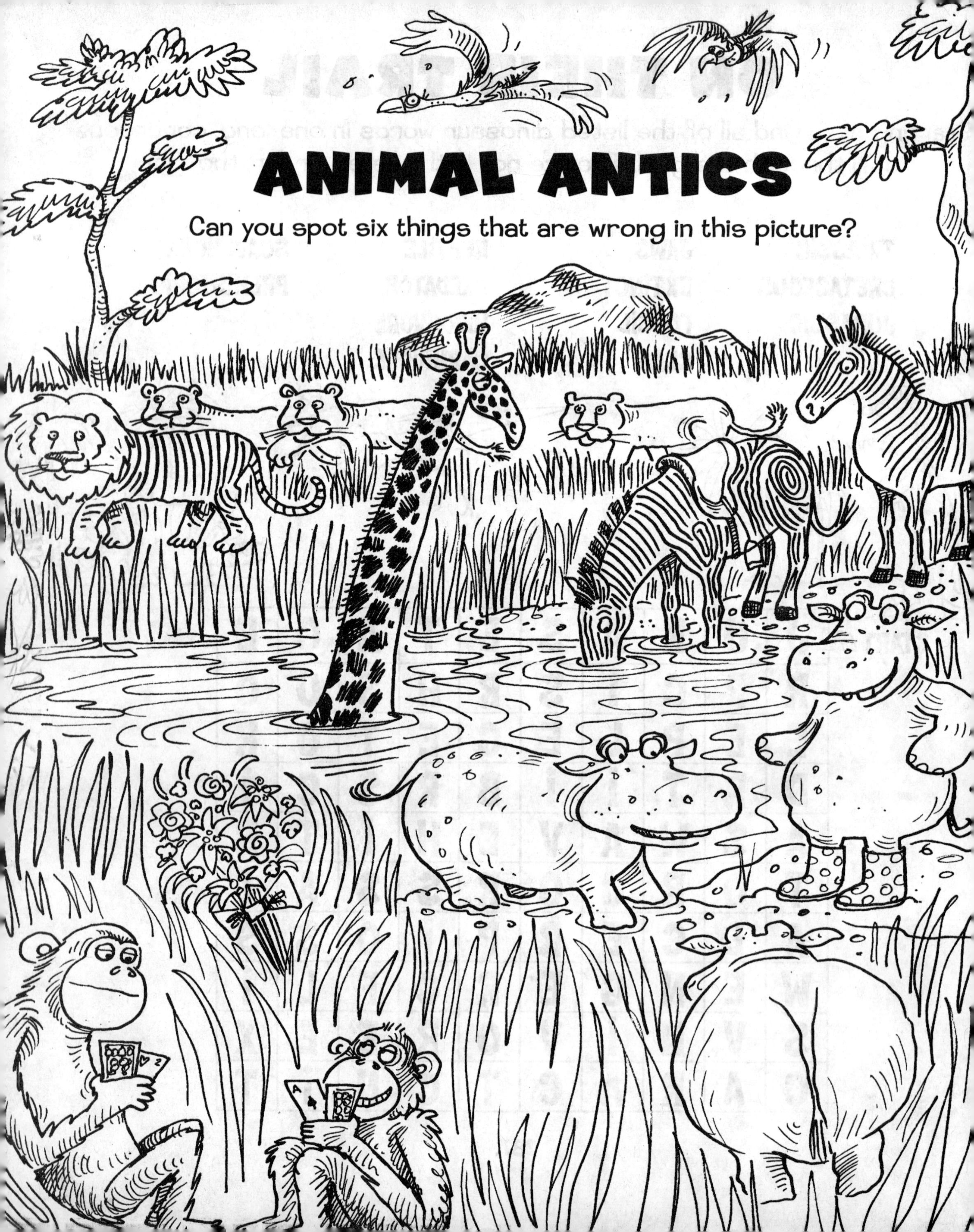

ANIMAL ANTICS
Can you spot six things that are wrong in this picture?

CASTAWAY

Imagine you've been cast away on a desert island. Draw the things you would most like to have with you.

SHOE SUMS

Work out the answers to the sums using the number code.
What do all the answers have in common?

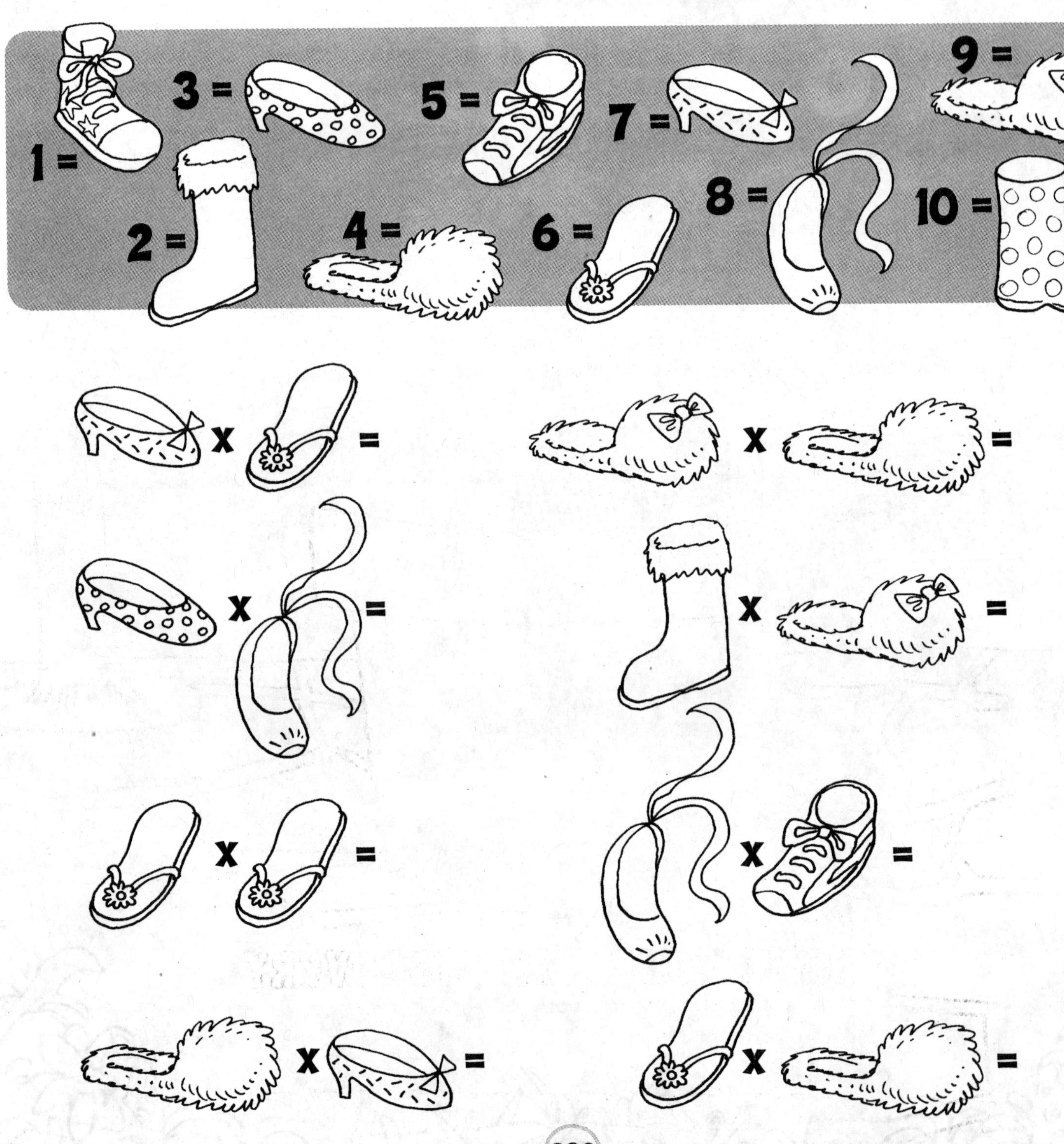

GROW YOUR OWN
If you could design your own new plant, what would it look like?
Would it have flowers, or spikes, or bug-traps?
NAME YOUR NEW DISCOVERY

MIND THE MINOTAUR

Can you find your way through the maze to escape the clutches of the angry minotaur?

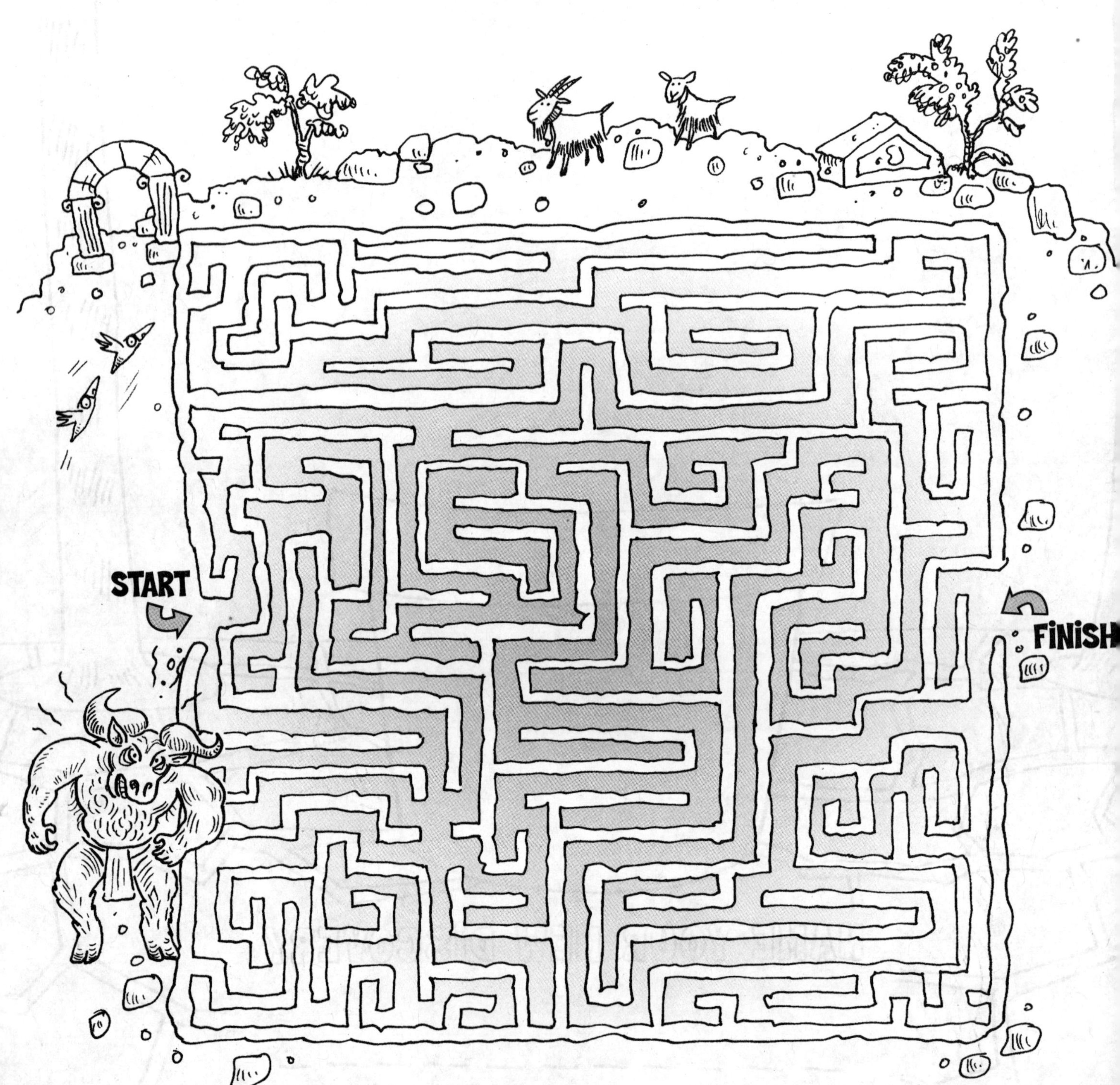

EGGS-ACTLY

Fill this nest with dinosaur eggs and babies hatching out of them.

WHOSE HORSE?

Use the clues to find out which horse of which colour belongs to each rider.

1. Ben's horse is called Niko. It isn't grey.
2. Charlie's horse isn't black or called Gunner.
3. The horse called Dario is chestnut.

	Chestnut	Grey	Black	Niko	Gunner	Dario
Joe						
Charlie						
Ben						

A MESS OF MUSKETS

How many muskets are there in this pile?

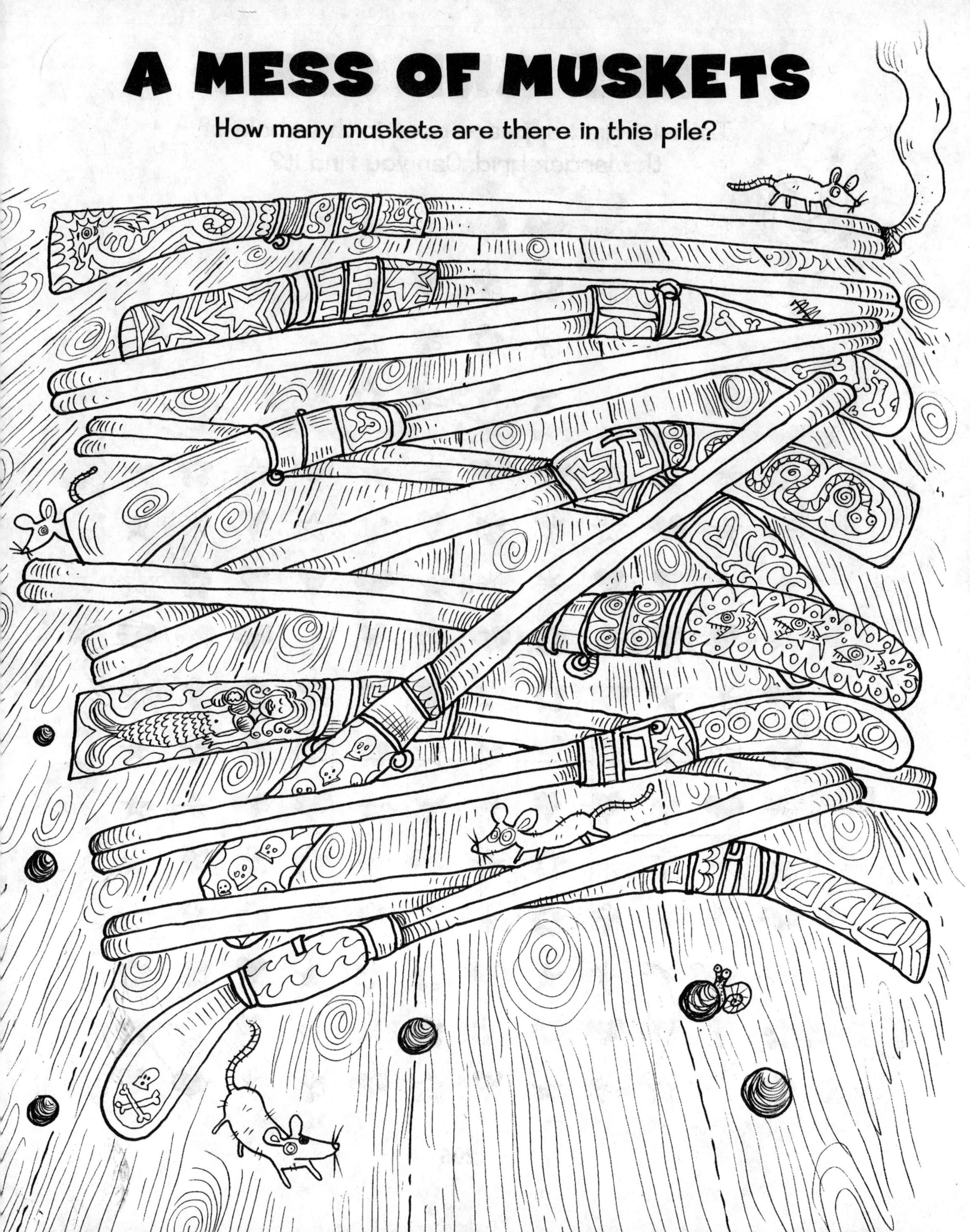

HIDE AND SEEK

The mini-grid appears once in the whole of the larger grid. Can you find it?

✤	✳	★	✳	♥	♥	✳	★	♥	☆	✿	★
✳	★	♥	☆	✤	✤	♥	✤	☆	♥	✳	★
★	☆	♥	♥	✳	✳	★	♥	♥	♥	✿	☆
✳	♥	♥	✳	✿	♥	☆	♥	✳	♥	♥	♥
♥	✳	★	♥	✿	✤	♥	♥	✤	✿	✤	☆
✿	☆	★	☆	♥	✤	☆	✿	✤	✿	✤	★
✳	♥	✤	♥	♥	✳	✤	★	♥	♥	✳	★
★	✳	✤	✳	✿	★	♥	✳	✿	✤	♥	★
♥	✤	✳	✤	✿	✳	☆	✤	✳	✿	✤	☆
☆	☆	♥	✳	★	♥	✿	✤	★	♥	✤	✿
✿	♥	♥	♥	♥	✤	✿	✳	☆	♥	☆	✿
✿	✳	☆	✤	★	♥	☆	♥	✤	✳	♥	♥

HOME SWEET HOME

In each row, cross out any letter that appears twice. The remaining letters spell animal homes - can you match them to the correct creatures?

P P S C T A T W V O O E S W

Y A Y H C i C V T T E A L L

M O O W U E B U K K M

C F F H P O P L U U T R R C

H A L A O T T D i i G V E V H

Y N X X E S L T L B B Y M M

TOXIC TERROR

Which of the small pictures matches the main picture of the Toxic Terror?

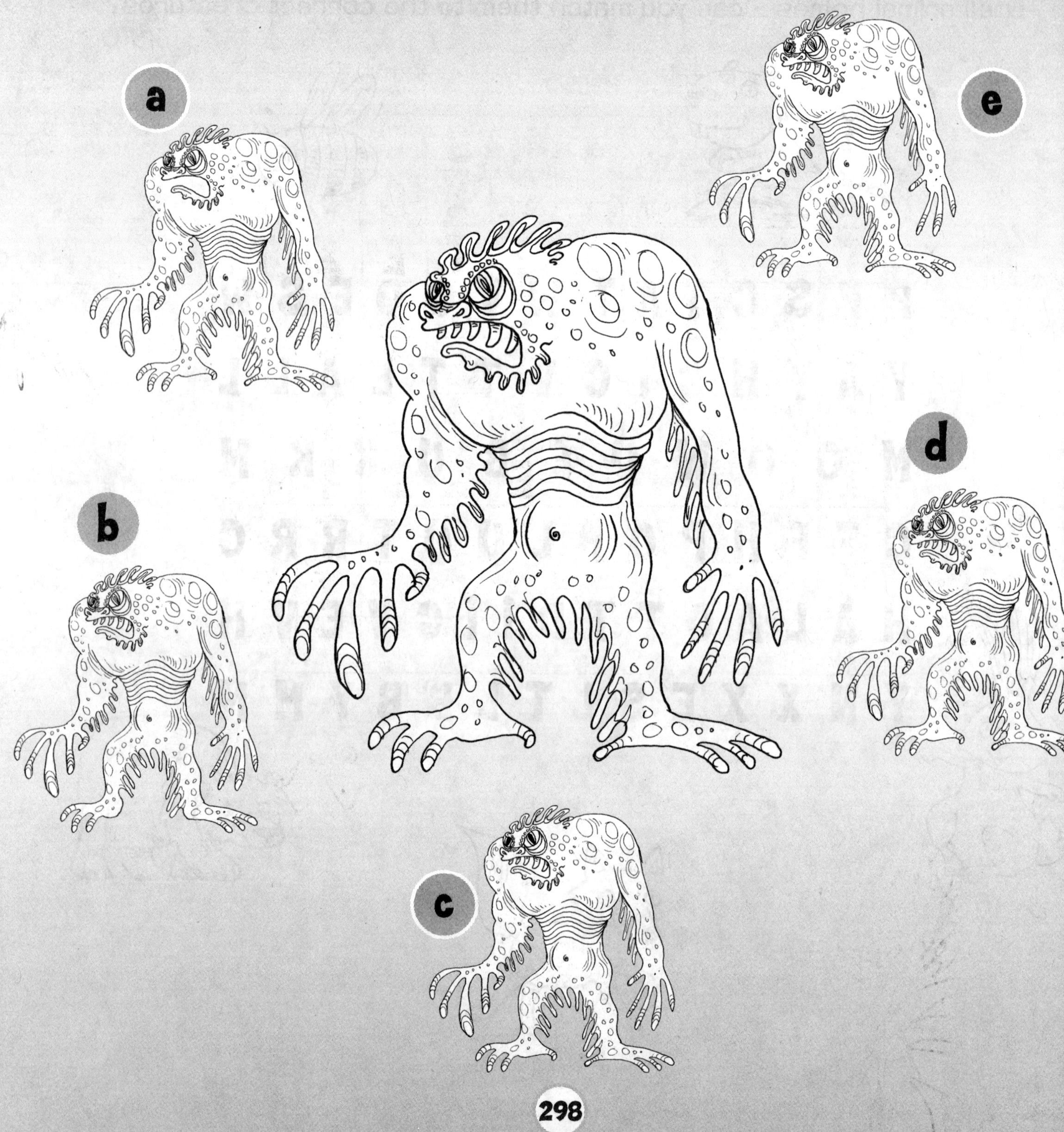

GOING, GOING, GONE

Can you find the word EXTINCT hidden just once in this grid? Look up, down, across and diagonally.

E	X	E	T	I	N	C	T	E	C
X	I	N	C	T	E	X	C	I	T
T	T	X	E	X	I	T	E	X	T
E	X	T	T	X	E	T	X	E	E
T	X	I	N	C	T	E	T	X	X
E	X	T	C	E	T	I	I	I	T
X	E	T	I	X	E	X	C	T	E
C	X	I	N	N	X	N	I	T	X
I	I	T	C	N	C	C	T	X	E
T	T	C	T	T	C	T	E	X	T

MIAOW MIX

Make up a crazy pet that is a mixture of a cat, a dog and a mouse.

CODE CRACKER

Solve the sums and cross out each answer in the grid. You should have four remaining numbers to unlock the code on the treasure chest.

50 x 50 =
1800 ÷ 9 =
1234 + 1234 =
6 x 70 =
3000 – 123 =
12 x 12 =
1998 ÷ 2 =

1000 – 55 =
9876 – 22 =
11 x 11 =
8 x 800 =
5555 + 4321 =
448 ÷ 2 =
100 – 36 =

2	8	7	7	3	9	9	9
4	2	0	2	0	0	6	8
4	2	9	4	5	9	4	7
1	2	1	6	5	0	0	6
6	4	9	8	5	4	0	7

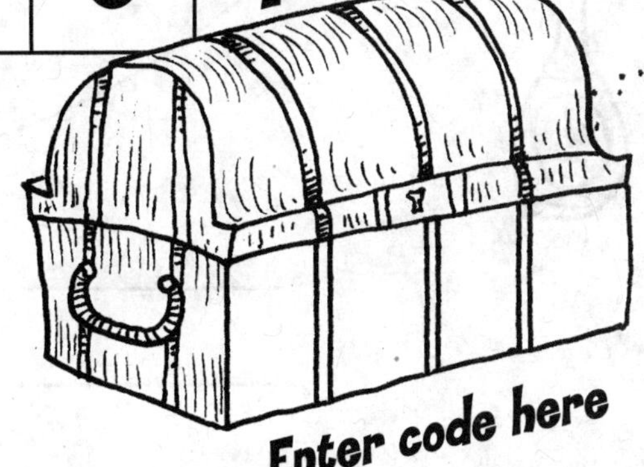

SHOPPING TRIP

Work out how much it will cost to buy all of the goodies in the circle.

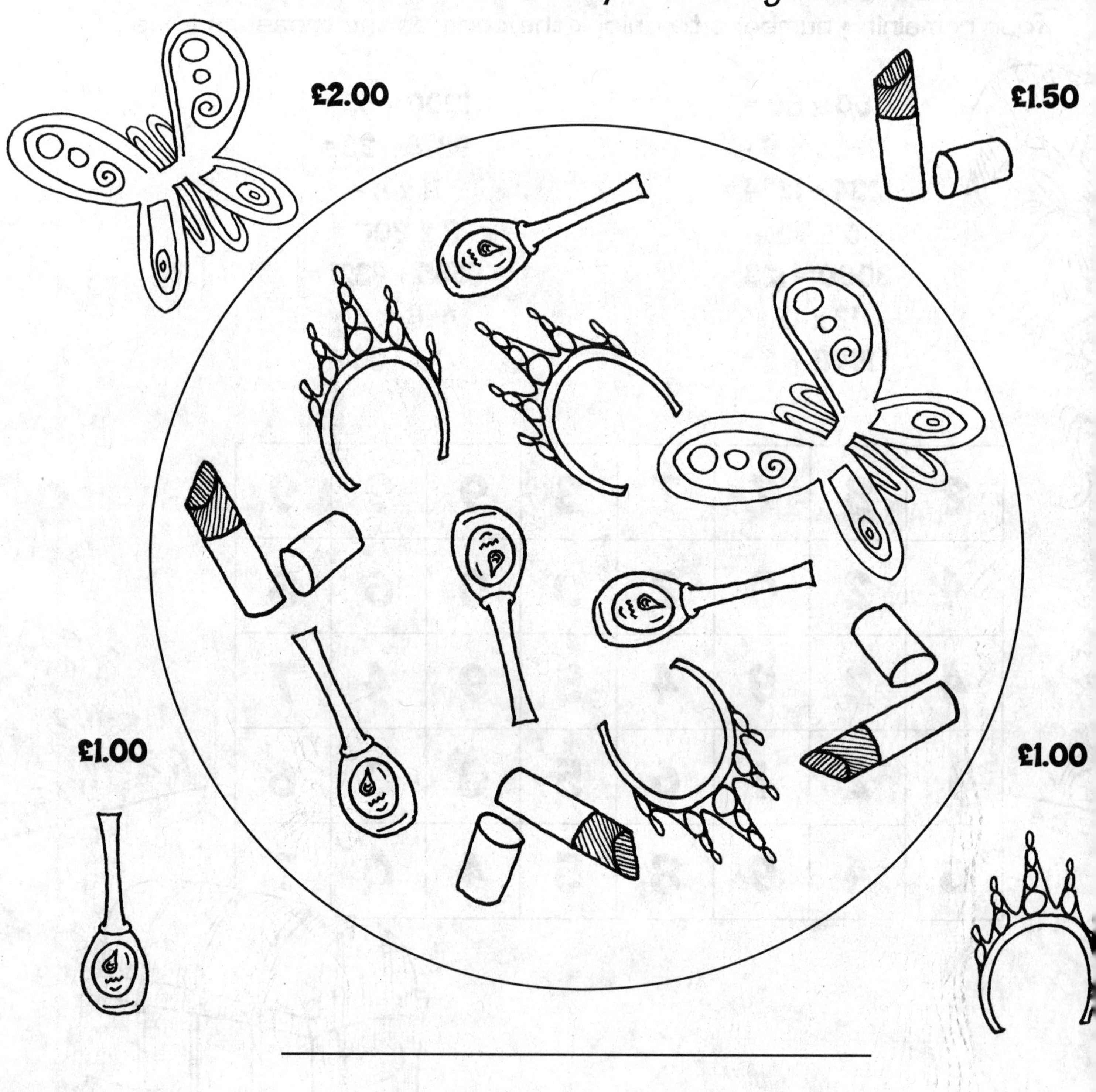

MEMORY TEST

Study this scene and then turn the page to see how many questions you can answer from memory.

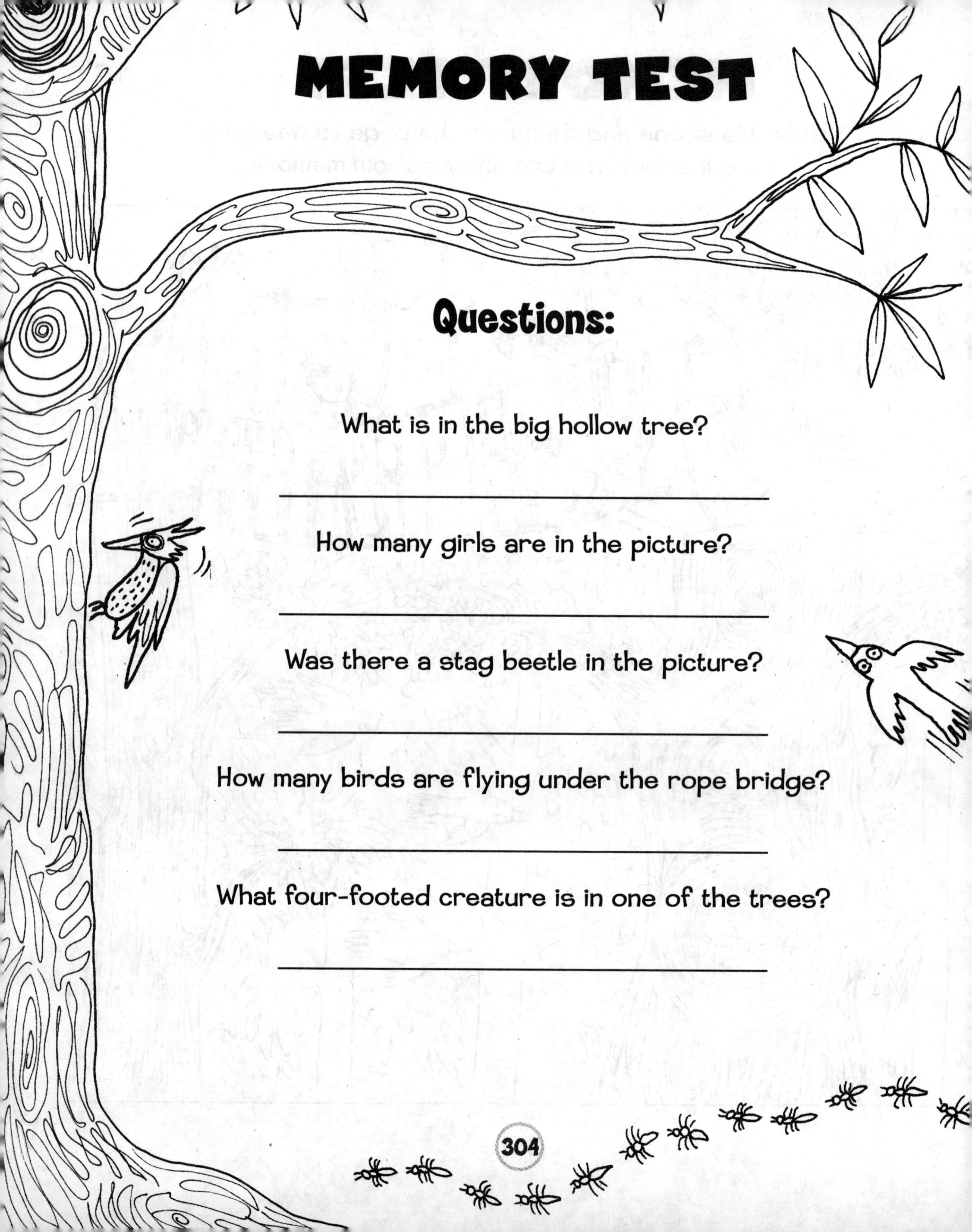

MEMORY TEST

Questions:

What is in the big hollow tree?

____

How many girls are in the picture?

____

Was there a stag beetle in the picture?

____

How many birds are flying under the rope bridge?

____

What four-footed creature is in one of the trees?

____

TWO BY TWO

Circle the letters under the two-legged dinosaurs to spell the name of a dinosaur hunter.

HMMMM, TRICKY

Which of these hummingbirds does not have an identical twin?

WHICH WAY NOW?

Answer the sums correctly to work your way through the compasses from start to finish.

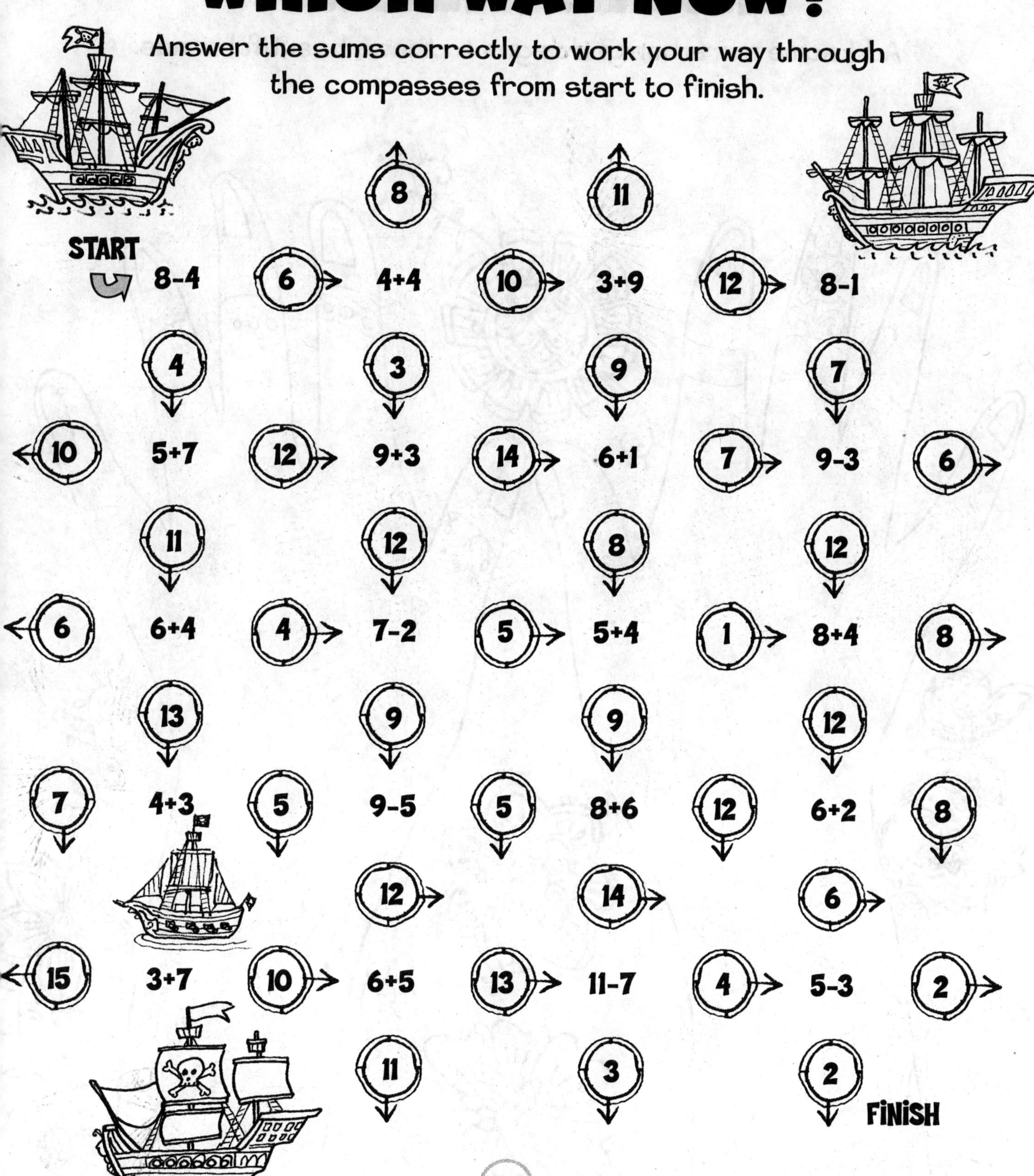

HAPPY HENNA

Add some more henna designs to these beautiful hands.

SPELLING BEE

Which of these words are spelt correctly? And can you correct the other spellings on the spare lines?

wolf ✓ ✗

potatos ✓ ✗

puppys ✓ ✗

fungus ✓ ✗

telescope ✓ ✗

meateorite ✓ ✗

beatiful ✓ ✗

garden ✓ ✗

fierce ✓ ✗

cobbweb ✓ ✗

volcanoe ✓ ✗

CREEPY CASTLE

Add windows, doors and lots of creepy ghosts and ghouls to turn this into the most haunted building in the neighbourhood.

COME FLY WITH ME

Each of these flying reptiles has a matching twin - except one. Can you spot the odd one out?

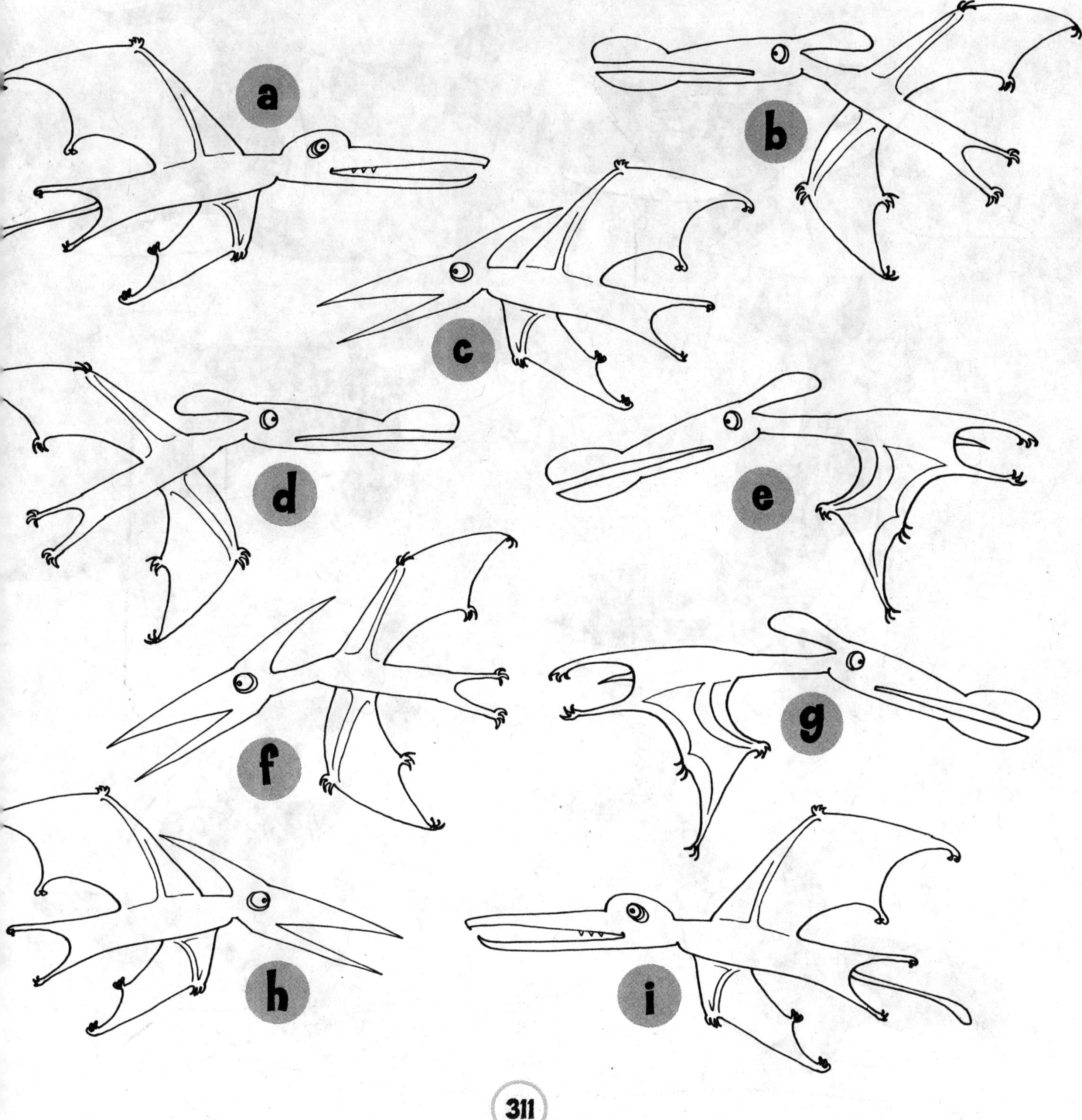

BIG IS BEST

Which killer whale has the sum equalling the biggest number?

FLYING THE FLAG

Design your own pirate flag using the examples around the edge to give you some ideas.

SHADY LADY

Which of the silhouettes matches the picture of the ballerina?

GOTCHA!

This bug is having his lunch... but who is about to gobble him up?

GONE APE

King Kong has gone crazy and ripped up all these sums. Can you match the equations into pairs, like the example?

DINO PARK

Draw a map for your very own dinosaur theme park.

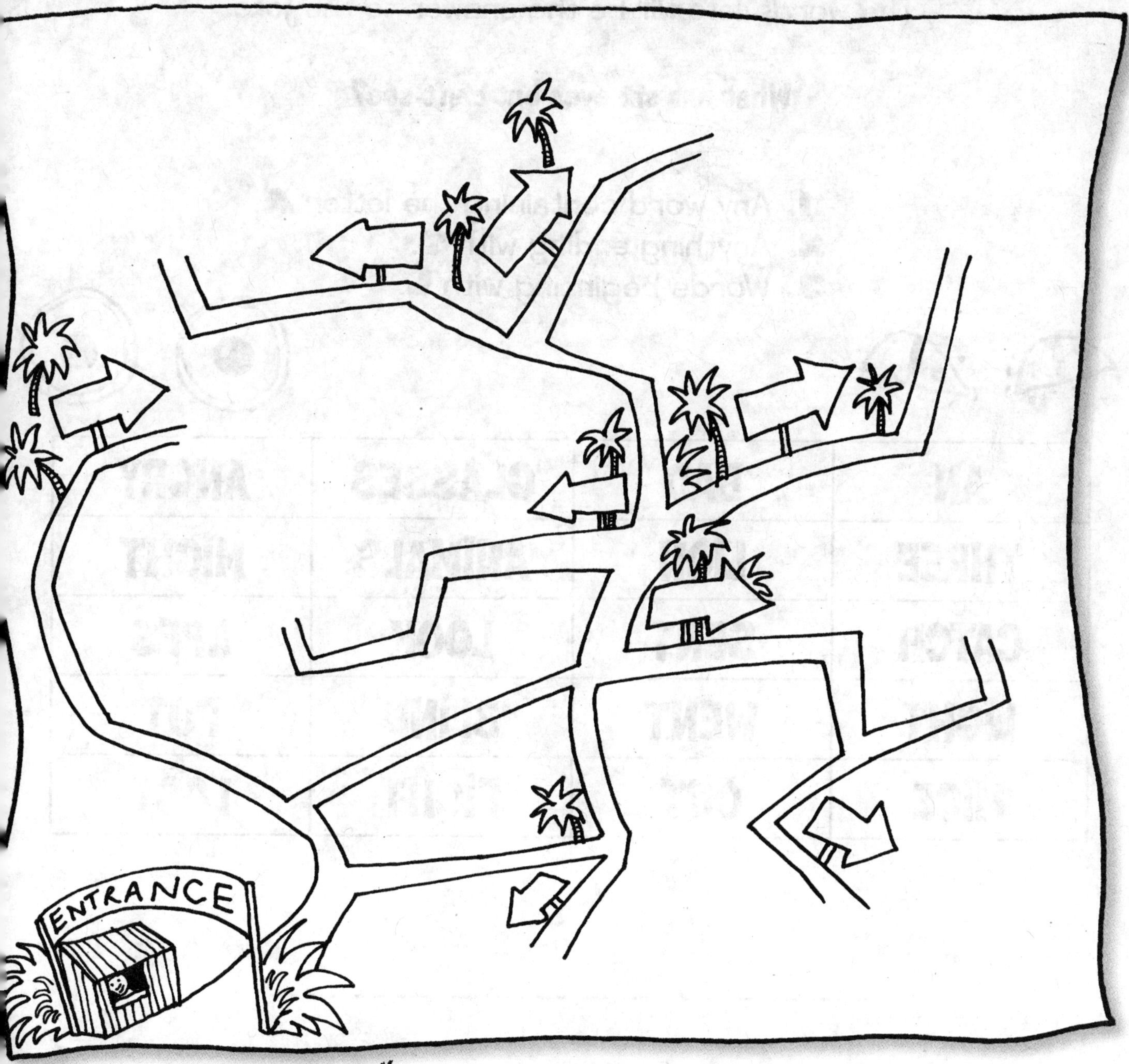

I SEE!

Cross out the words using the instructions below.
The words left will be the answer to the joke.

What has six eyes but can't see?

1. Any word containing the letter **A**.
2. Anything ending with **T**.
3. Words beginning with **L**.

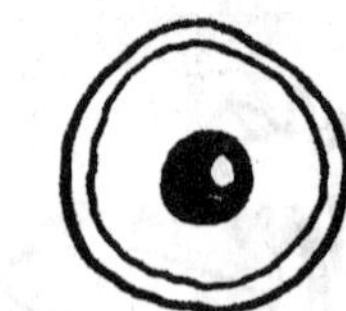

AN	BAD	GLASSES	ANGRY
THREE	LION	ANIMALS	MIGHT
CATCH	SENT	LOOK	APES
LIGHT	WENT	BLIND	PUT
MICE	OUT	FIGHT	LOST

_ _ _ _ _   _ _ _ _ _ _ _ _ _ _

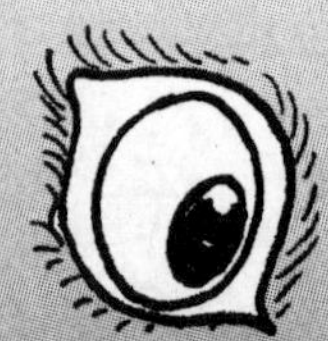
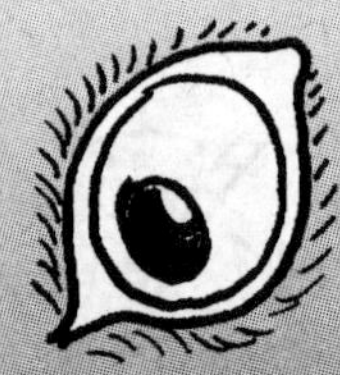

ISLAND HOPPING

Use the three-letter words to fill in the gaps and make the names of six islands.

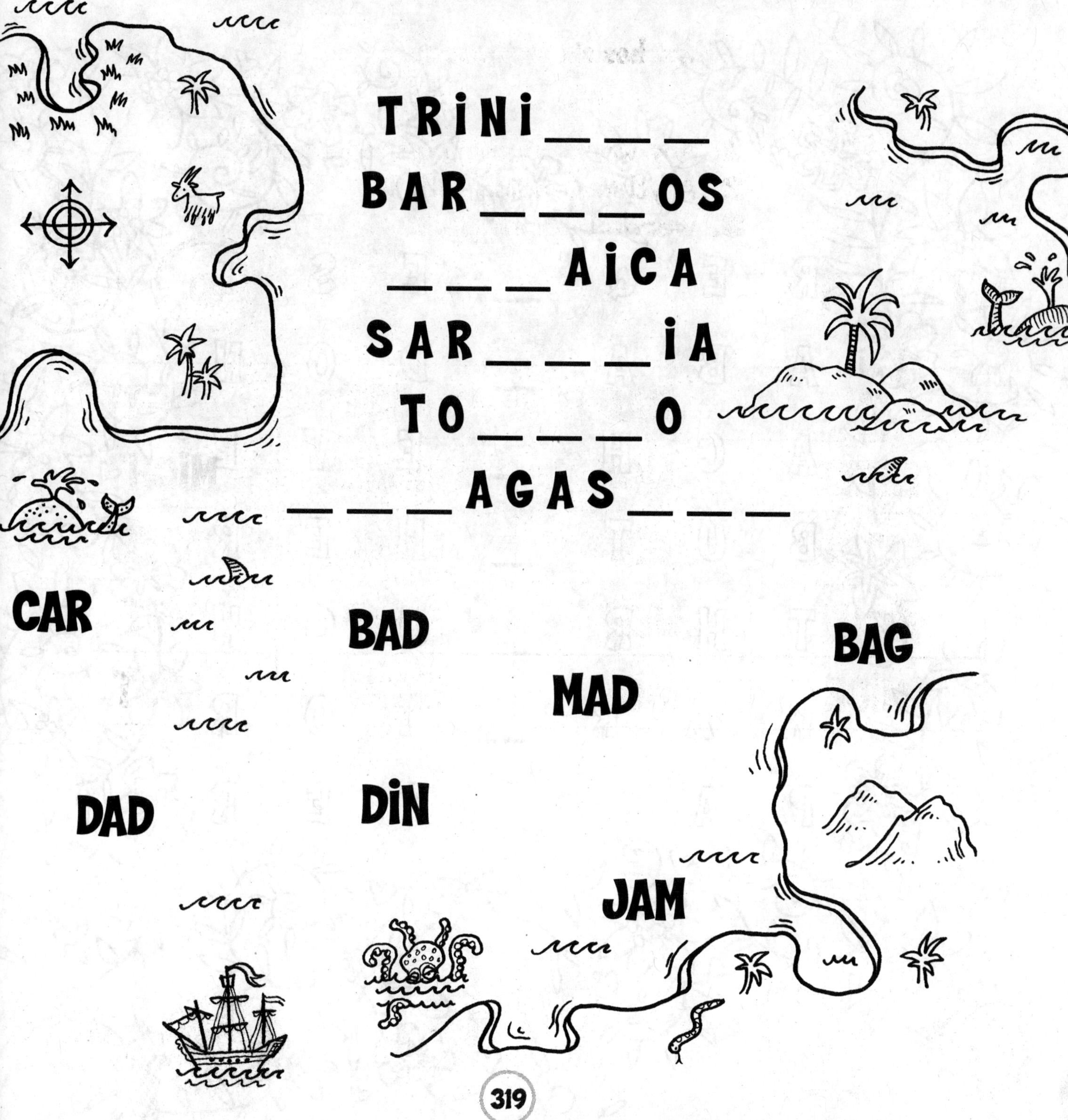

TRINI _ _ _

BAR _ _ _ OS

_ _ _ AICA

SAR _ _ _ IA

TO _ _ _ O

_ _ _ AGAS _ _ _

CAR

BAD

BAG

MAD

DAD

DIN

JAM

IN THE MIDDLE

Fill in the missing letters to complete the 7-letter words and spell the name of Princess Leonie's dream pet.

IN THEIR PRIME

There are 25 prime numbers below 100 - can you colour every cell that contains a prime number?

3	13	23	6	11	68	9	79	22
7	66	63	99	17	18	24		
25	16		5	15	35	45	67	72
88	26	19		27	61	14	33	
19	12	89	90	93	97	74	73	71
55	57	77		4	2		28	
83		75	81	82	37	38	40	41
	52	8	87	91	94	96	53	
56	92	47	29	46	49		43	51
59	63	70	20	99	31	21	10	

LOOK OUT!

Take a careful look at the picture to see if you can spot all of the items from the list.

VERY FUNNY

Colour in all the squares containing the letters F, M and R. The letters you have left will spell out the answer to the joke.

Why do Velociraptors eat raw meat?

F	R	M	F	R	M	F	M	M	F	R	F
F	B	R	E	F	R	M	M	F	R	M	R
M	F	F	M	R	C	F	A	R	F	R	U
R	R	M	F	M	R	S	F	E	M	F	M
M	M	R	R	F	M	R	R	F	R	M	R
T	F	M	H	M	F	E	M	R	Y	R	F
R	M	F	R	F	R	M	F	F	M	F	M
F	D	M	M	O	M	R	N	F	R	T	R
M	R	K	F	R	N	F	F	O	R	M	W
H	M	F	R	O	F	M	W	M	F	M	R
M	F	R	F	M	R	F	R	M	T	O	F
F	C	F	M	O	M	O	F	K	R	F	R

SPOTS AND STRIPES

Add patterns to these animals - but use your imagination. Try zebra stripes on a leopard!

ID PARADE

Study the sequence of pictures correctly and work out which pirate finishes the pattern: a, b or c?

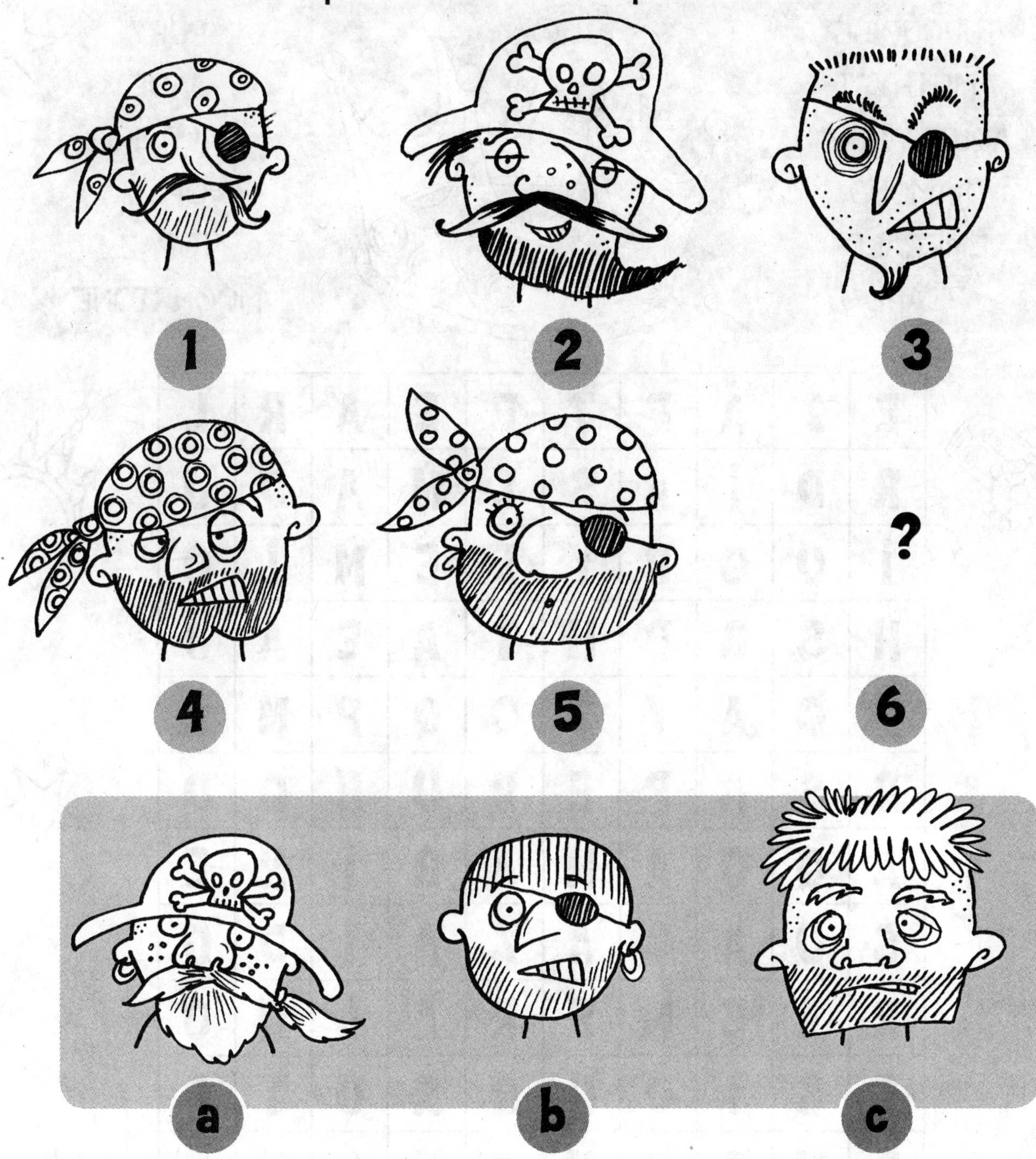

HIDDEN GEMS

Find each of the gems hidden in the wordsearch grid.

TURQUOISE
AMETHYST
AQUAMARINE
DIAMOND
EMERALD
PEARL

RUBY
JADE
SAPPHIRE
OPAL
TOPAZ
MOONSTONE

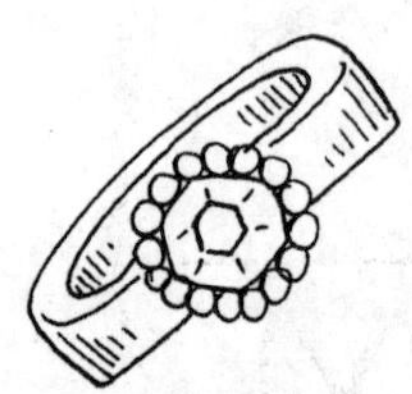

E	Z	A	P	T	P	E	A	R	L
R	D	I	A	S	E	M	A	D	J
I	U	G	R	Y	L	E	M	I	O
H	S	B	P	H	T	A	E	A	J
P	G	A	Y	T	O	Q	P	M	A
P	S	A	P	E	P	U	H	O	D
A	Q	U	A	M	A	R	I	N	E
S	U	A	G	A	Z	A	I	D	U
R	A	E	M	E	R	A	L	D	O
E	S	I	O	U	Q	R	U	T	P
B	M	O	O	N	S	T	O	N	E

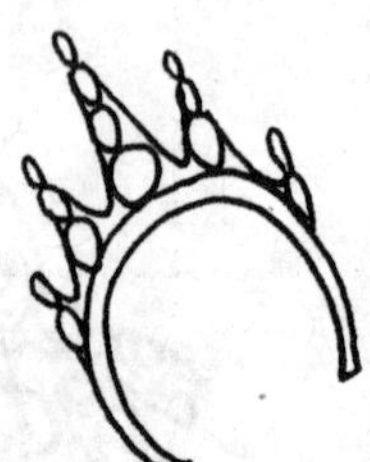

FOOTPRINTS

Find the correct path from start to finish, following the footprints in this order in any direction:

1)  2)  3) 

START

FINISH

WITCH'S BREW

If A=1, B=2, C=3 and so on, can you work out what ingredients are being used to make the witch's potions?

USE YOUR HEAD

How many smaller words can you make from the this dinosaur's name?

PACHYCEPHALOSAURUS

1 HAPPY

2 LOSER

3

4

5

6

7

8

9

10

11

12

PENGUIN PARADE

Find the small squares in the main picture and write the grid reference for each one. The first one has been done for you.

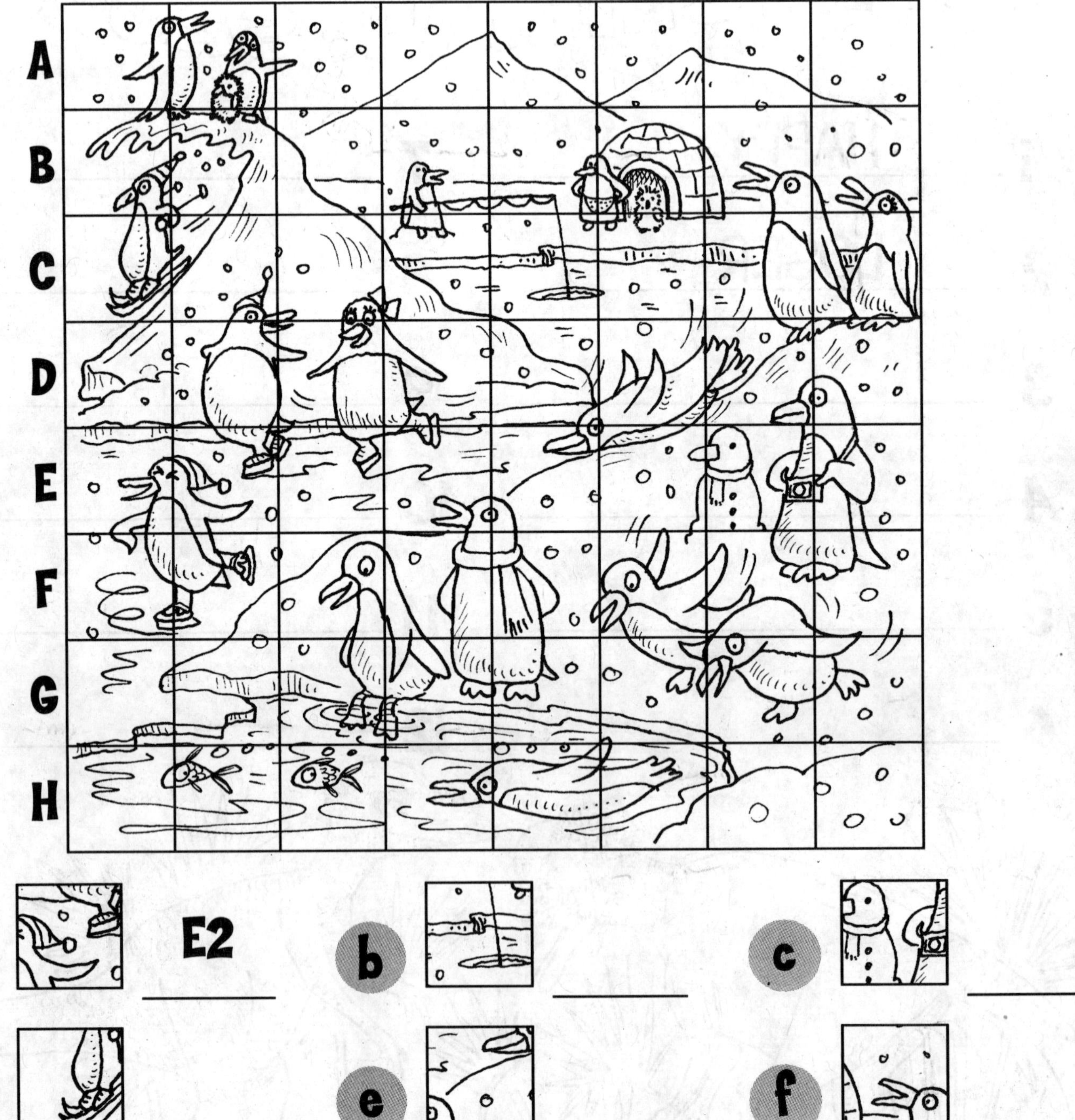

FOLLOW THE TRAIL

Which of the peg-legged pirates has found the treasure?

HAPPY BIRTHDAY

Finish these scrummy cakes with icing and decorations.
Add birthday candles if you like!

COLOUR CRACKER

Colour in all the squares containing D, L or M and use the remaining letters to find the answer to the joke.

What is green and can jump a mile in a minute?

D	A	L	L	M	L	D	M	M	D
L	D	G	M	R	A	D	L	L	L
D	M	L	M	D	M	S	S	L	D
L	D	H	O	M	D	L	M	L	D
M	M	D	L	P	P	D	D	M	L
D	L	L	M	L	D	M	E	R	M
W	D	L	D	i	D	L	T	M	H
L	M	L	L	D	L	D	M	M	L
D	H	M	i	L	L	M	C	C	D
M	D	U	L	L	L	P	D	L	S	M

MAKE A MONSTER

This monster is nowhere near scary enough! What will you add to make it more scream-some?

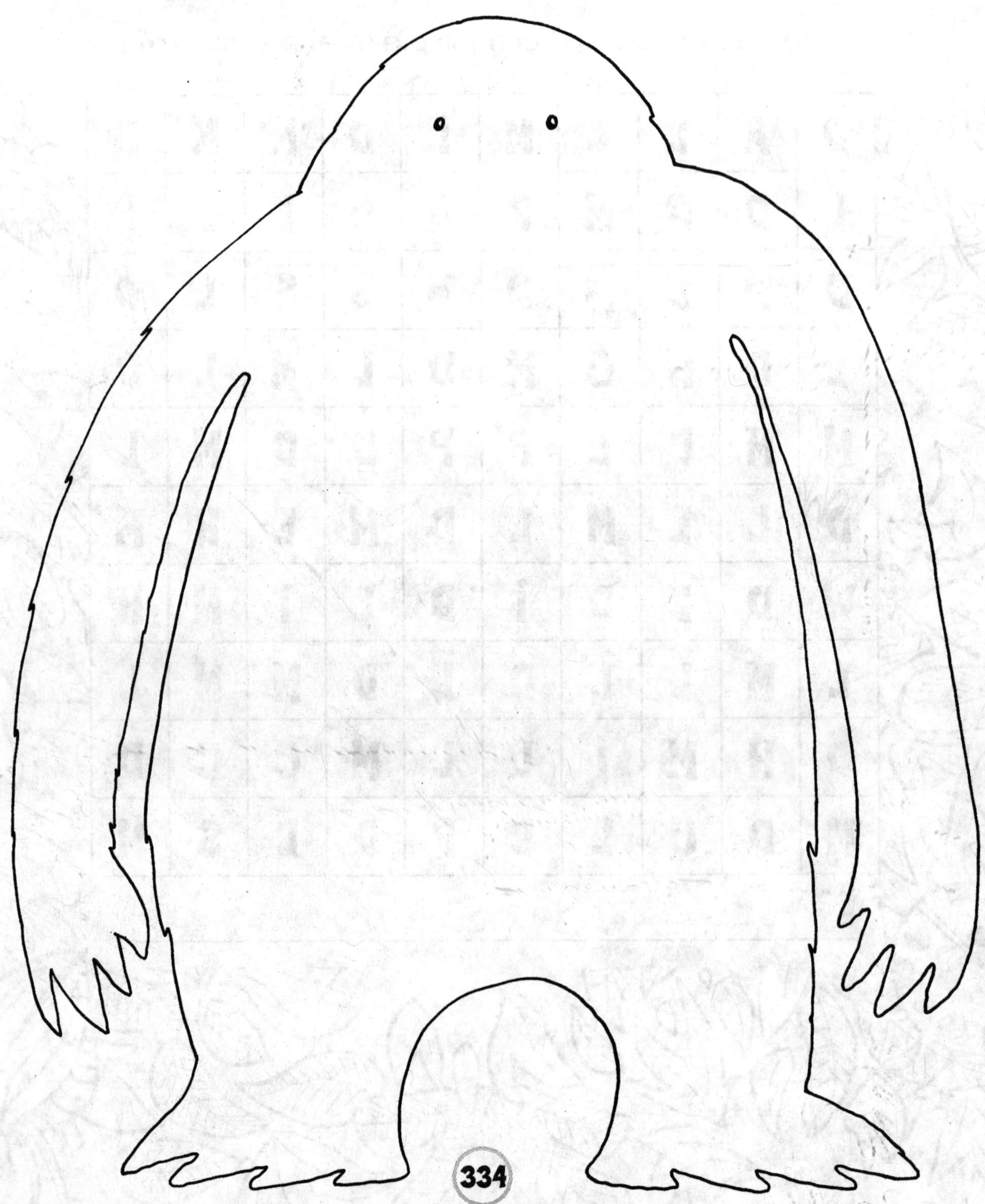

FOSSIL FRIEND

Cross out every other letter, starting with L, to find a flying creature from the age of the dinosaurs.

A B R I C N H T A C E M

O I P N T V E W R S Y U X

The creature is: _ _ _ _ _ _ _ _ _ _ _ _ _ _ _

COOL FOR CATS

Find the names of these beautiful creatures hidden in the grid.

BOBCAT	JAGUAR	OCELOT
CARACAL	LEOPARD	SERVAL
CHEETAH	LiON	TiGER
COUGAR	LYNX	WiLDCAT

L	J	A	G	C	A	R	A	C	A	L	L
N	O	C	E	L	O	T	Y	H	W	E	C
X	H	L	V	A	i	X	T	L	i	O	N
T	C	i	O	G	C	L	i	G	L	P	X
B	H	O	E	L	H	J	S	V	A	A	T
O	E	R	U	S	A	E	E	T	B	R	L
B	E	Y	T	G	E	L	R	X	O	D	E
C	H	E	E	T	A	H	V	L	B	C	O
A	J	L	S	E	L	R	A	U	G	A	J
T	Y	A	E	Y	E	E	L	O	T	Y	B
C	V	A	N	W	i	L	D	C	A	T	O
H	T	X	J	A	G	X	B	O	B	C	B

WALK THE PLANK!

Can you spot six differences between these two pirate scenes?

ONCE UPON A TIME

How many smaller words can you make from the letters below?

FAIRY GODMOTHER

1 FAIR

2 MOTH

3

4

5

6

7

8

9

10

11

12

WHATEVER THE WEATHER

Look out of this window and draw your favourite kind of weather - is it snowy or sunny, windy or wet?

LOSING YOUR HEAD

Work out which of the heads originally belonged to the poor headless horseman!

1. He had a moustache but no beard.
2. He had straight hair.
3. He did not wear a bowtie.

DINOSAUR MASH-UP

What would a Stegosaurus look like if it got mixed up with a Triceratops?

RACCOON PONTOON

Find two raccoons on this page that have numbers that add up to 21.

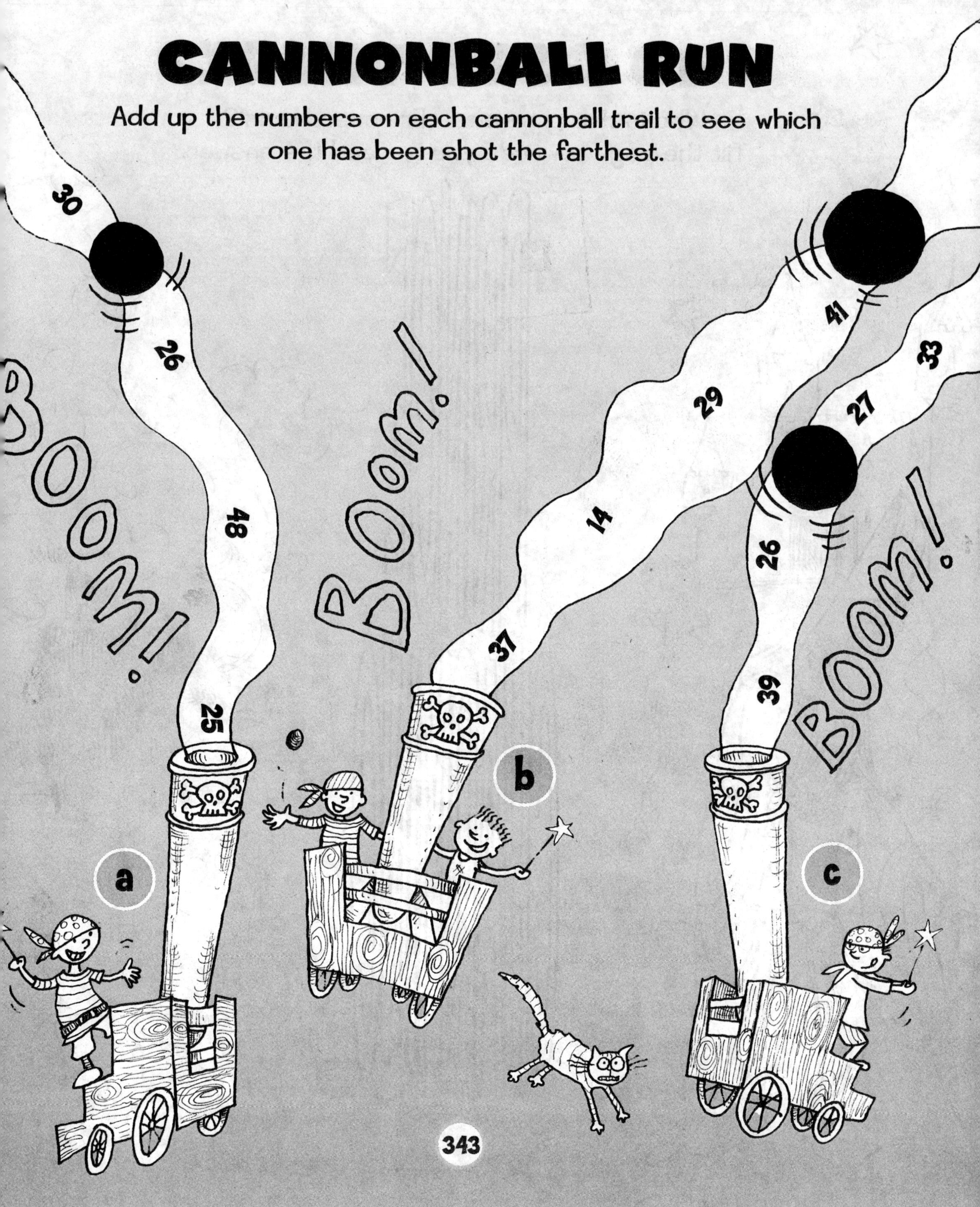
CANNONBALL RUN
Add up the numbers on each cannonball trail to see which one has been shot the farthest.
30
26
48
25
Boom!
a
Boom!
37
14
29
41
b
Boom!
33
27
26
39
c

WHO GOES THERE?

Who is riding towards Princess Naomi?
Tilt the page towards you to read the answer.

PRINCE CHARMING

A RARE FIND

Some orchids are extremely rare. Can you find the word ORCHID hidden just once in the grid?

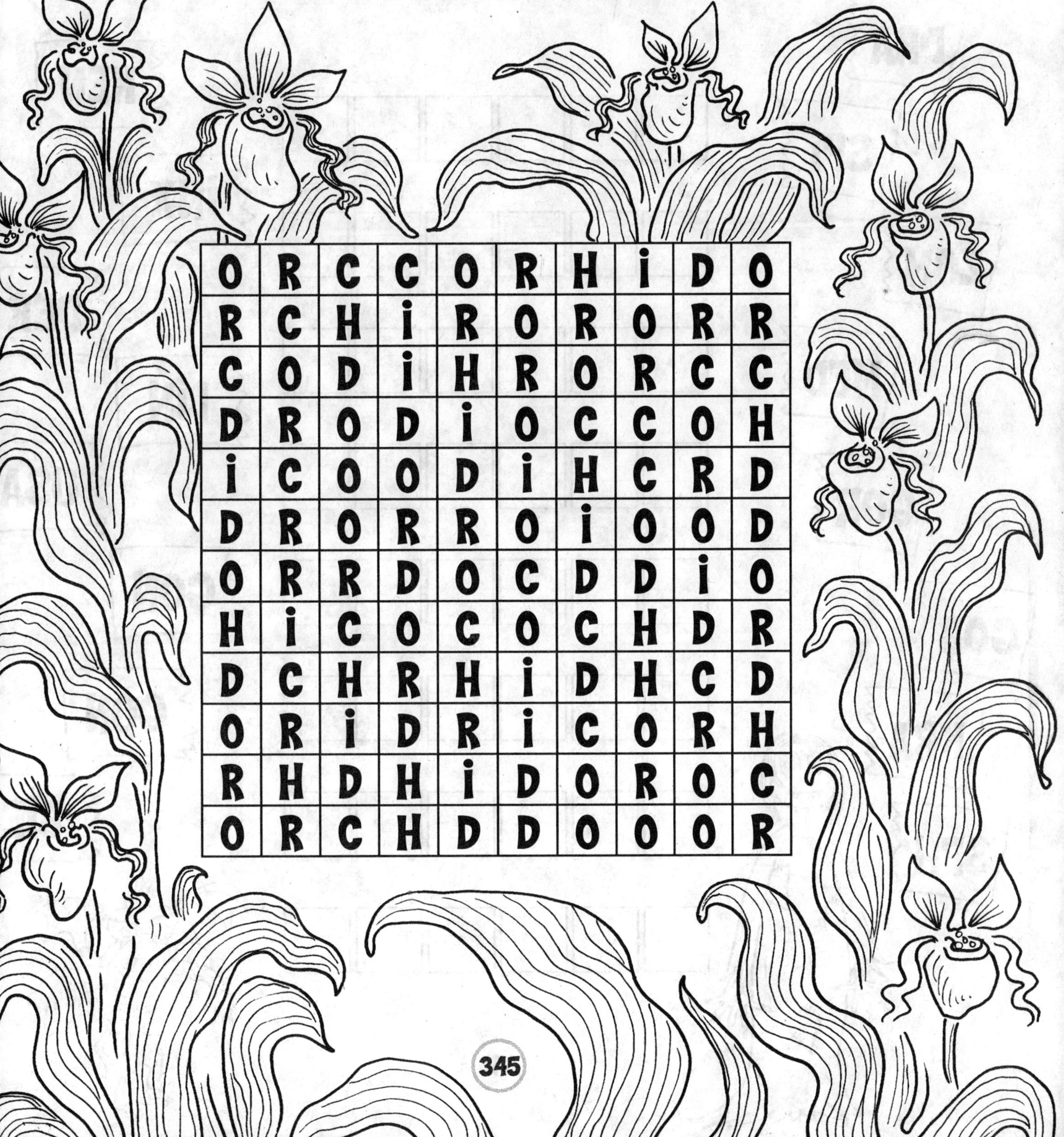

O	R	C	C	O	R	H	I	D	O
R	C	H	I	R	O	R	O	R	R
C	O	D	I	H	R	O	R	C	C
D	R	O	D	I	O	C	C	O	H
I	C	O	O	D	I	H	C	R	D
D	R	O	R	R	O	I	O	O	D
O	R	R	D	O	C	D	D	I	O
H	I	C	O	C	O	C	H	D	R
D	C	H	R	H	I	D	H	C	D
O	R	I	D	R	I	C	O	R	H
R	H	D	H	I	D	O	R	O	C
O	R	C	H	D	D	O	O	O	R

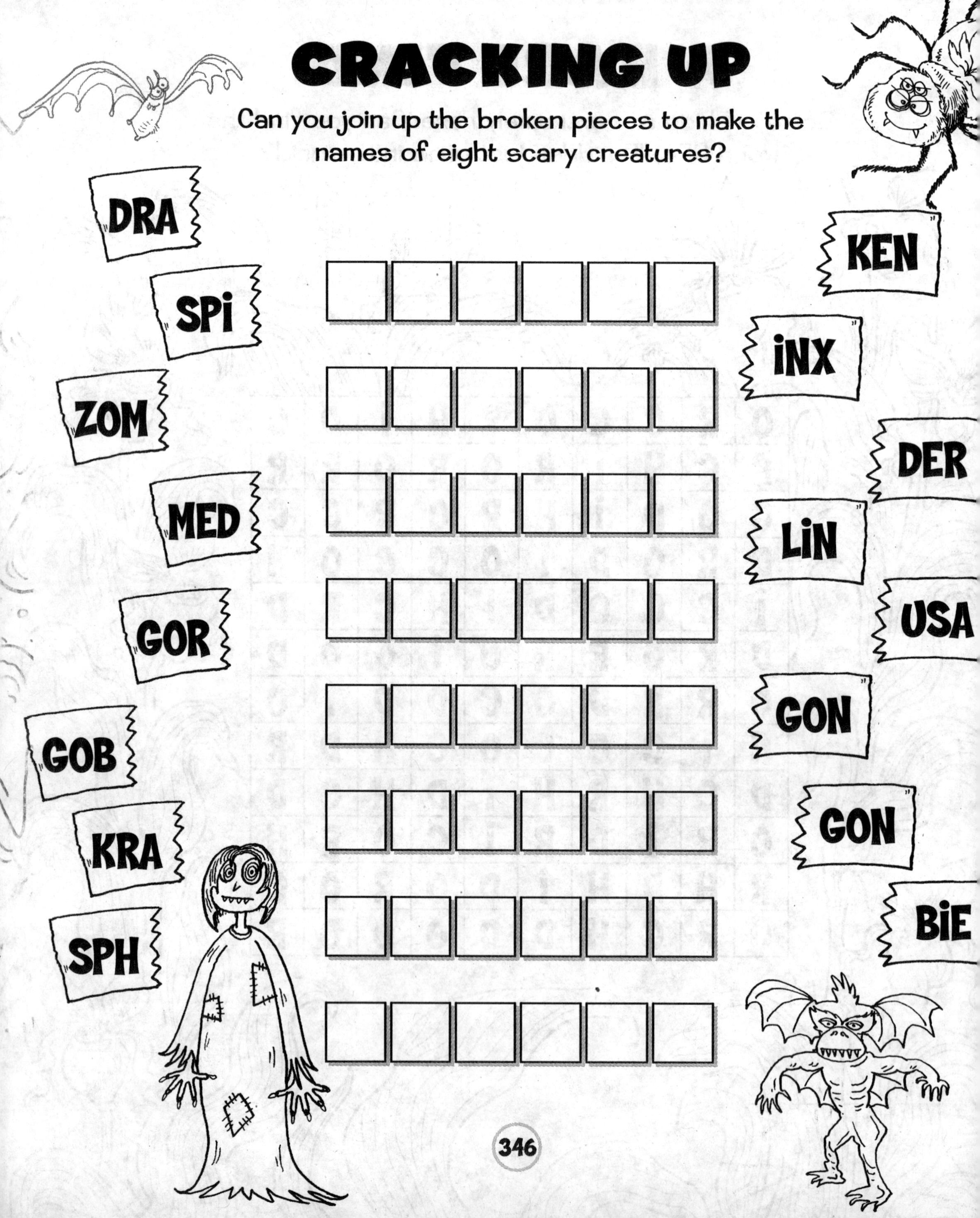

CRACKING UP

Can you join up the broken pieces to make the names of eight scary creatures?

ON DISPLAY

Help the museum curator unscramble the letters to put a proper sign by her dinosaur display.

IN THE JUNGLE

Zoologists find new creatures in the deepest jungle. What is hiding here?

TAKE A LOOK

Take a careful look at the picture to see if you can spot all of the items from the list below.

Find these items!

GRIDLOCKED

Colour in all the squares containing O, M or B and use the remaining letters to spell out a classic fairy tale.

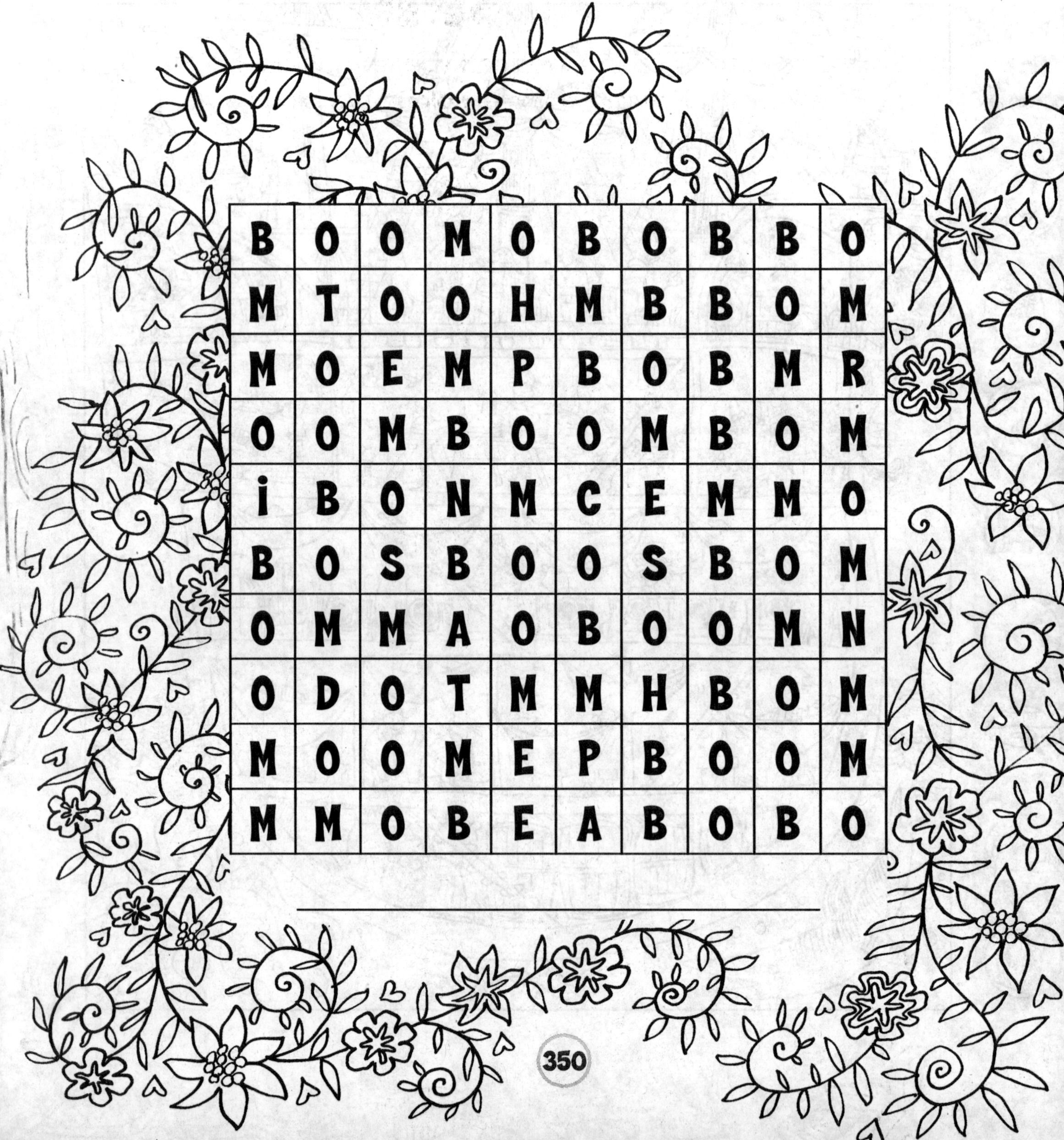

B	O	O	M	O	B	O	B	B	O
M	T	O	O	H	M	B	B	O	M
M	O	E	M	P	B	O	B	M	R
O	O	M	B	O	O	M	B	O	M
I	B	O	N	M	C	E	M	M	O
B	O	S	B	O	O	S	B	O	M
O	M	M	A	O	B	O	O	M	N
O	D	O	T	M	M	H	B	O	M
M	O	O	M	E	P	B	O	O	M
M	M	O	B	E	A	B	O	B	O

I SPIED A SPIDER

How many camouflaged spiders can you spy in this leafy pile? Once you've counted them, colour the picture.

MUMMY MATHS

This mummy isn't very clever. Can you help it find the correct scarab beetle to open the Book of the Dead?

MIND THE GAPS

Use the three-letter words from the list to fill the gaps and complete the dinosaur names.

ALL CAN HER PAT RAP

BAR DIP NOT PIN TIN

GIGA _ _ _ OSAURUS

_ _ _ YONYX

VELOCI _ _ _ TOR

ACRO _ _ _ THOSAURUS

_ _ _ OSAURUS

S _ _ _ OSAURUS

_ _ _ RERASAURUS

ARGEN _ _ _ OSAURUS

_ _ _ PLODOCUS

A _ _ _ TOSAURUS

PETS WIN PRIZES

Draw your favourite pets winning Best in Class!

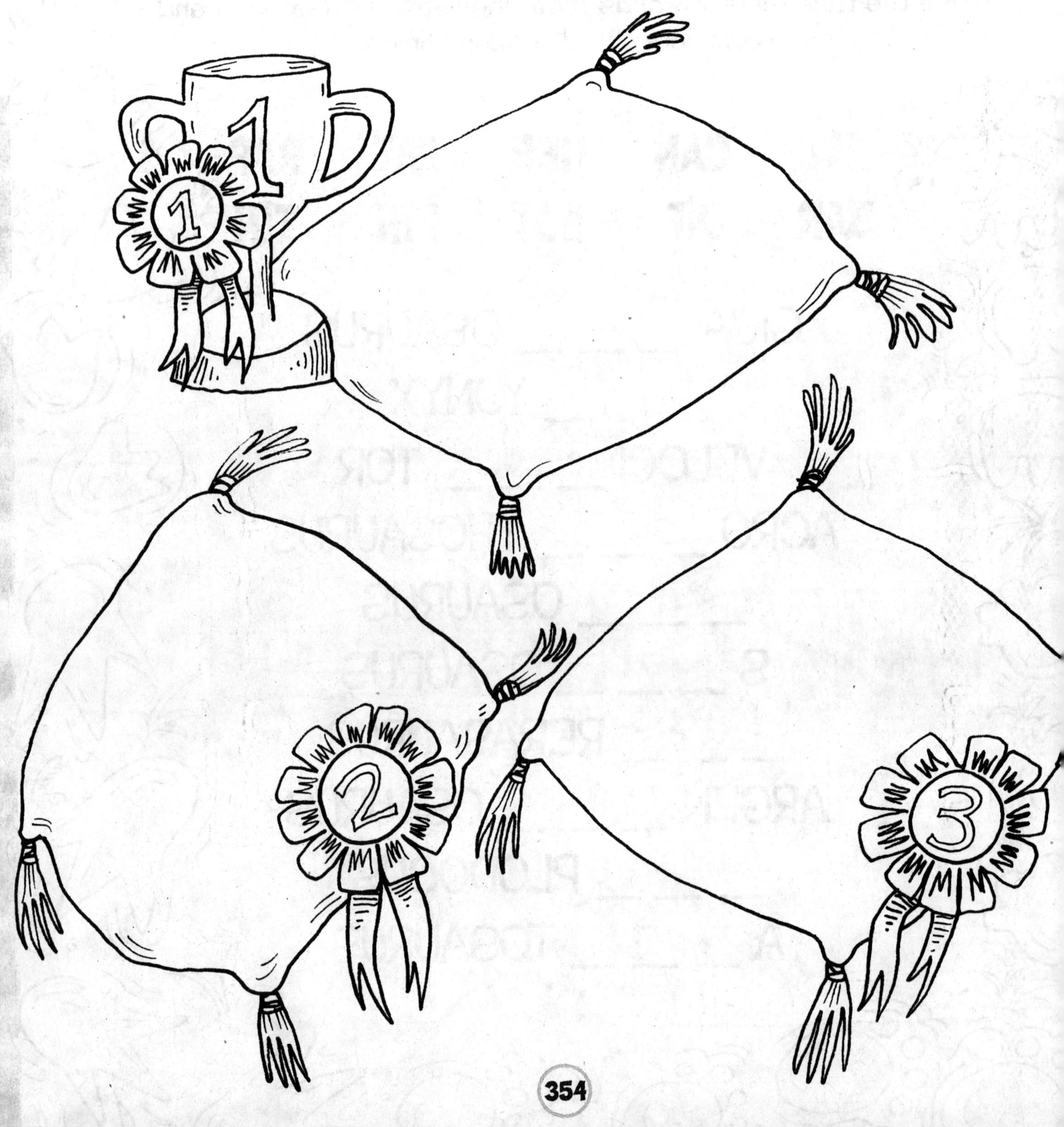

ALL AT SEA

Help the pirate row to the safety of the island by finding a way through the maze.

WHERE OH WHERE?

Crack the code to find out where Princess Dulcibella is dreaming she might go.

FANGS A LOT

Which of the numbers on Dracula's cape are NOT in the nine times table?

18

54 63 72

81 27 89

52

66 36 45

31 47 99

MAP IT OUT

Draw your own map to remind you where to find your buried treasure.

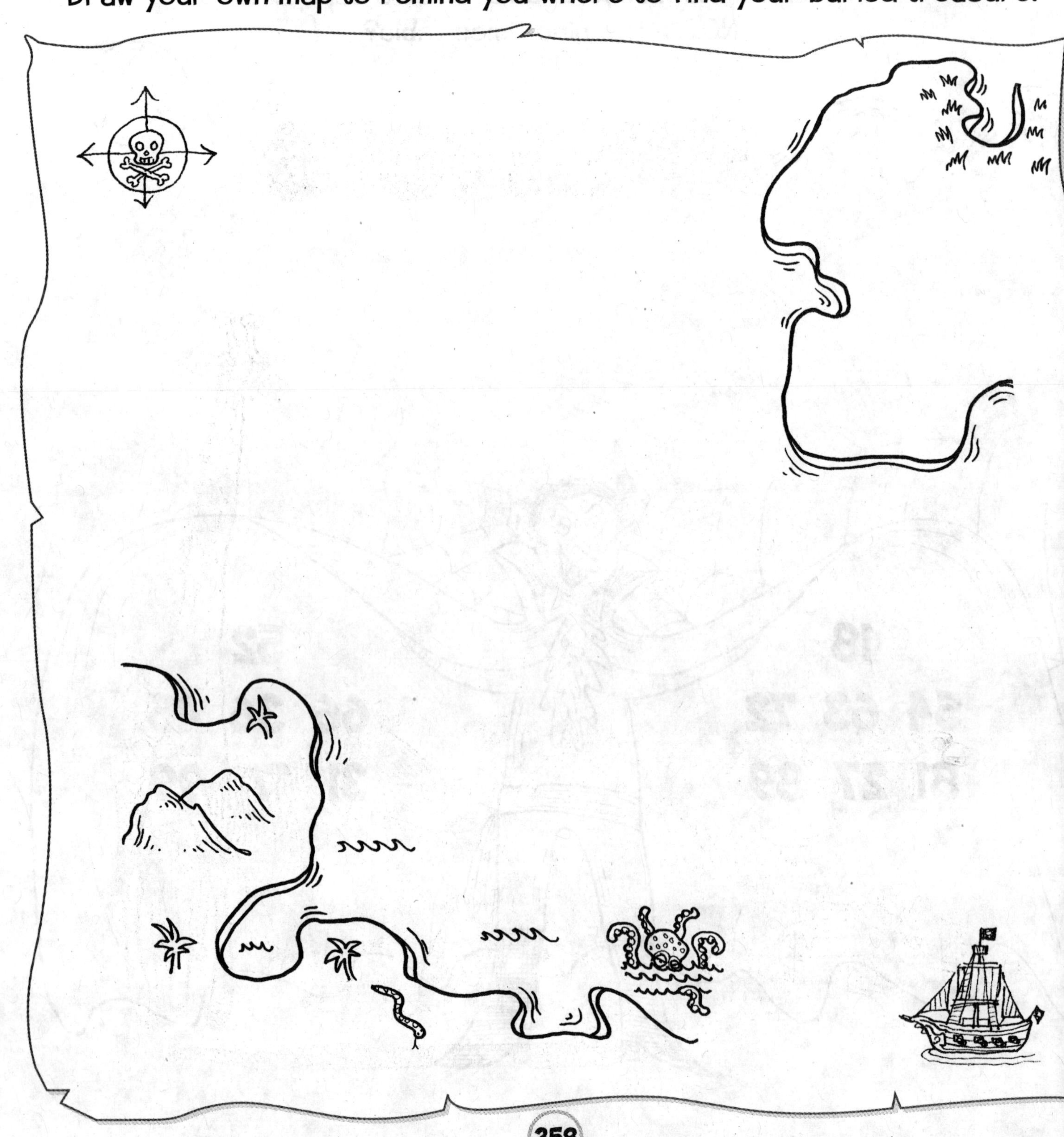

Answers

3 MONSTER MAD

c

4 iN THE SWiM

d

5 AT THE MATCH

6 BUGOKU

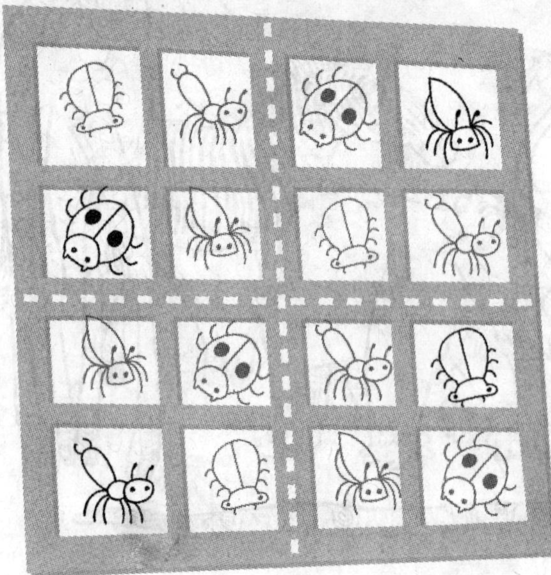

7 MOON WALK

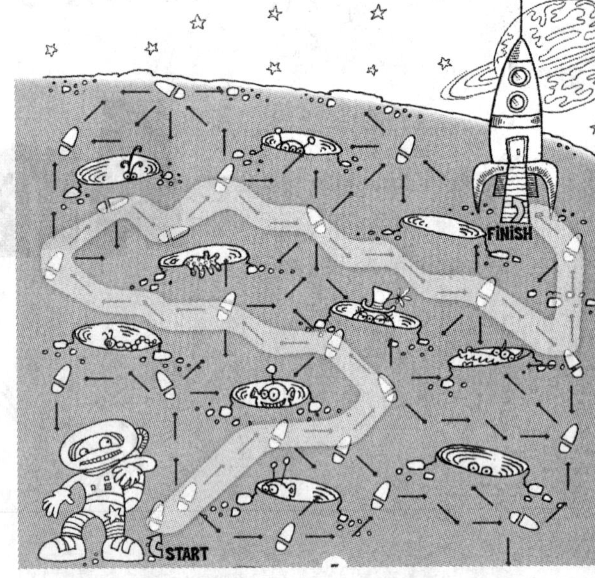

8 THiRSTY WORK

f

9 A DAY AT THE ZOO

10 SPY SCHOOL

Knock! Knock!
Who's there?
Sadie...
Sadie who?
Sadie secret code or you can't come in!

11 A WALK IN THE PARK

1. Eating their picnics **2.** D3
3. Reindeer **4.** E2

12 CAPITAL LETTERS

BELGIUM = Brussels
FINLAND = Helsinki
CHINA = Beijing
JAMAICA = Kingston
UNITED KINGDOM = London

13 UNDER COVER

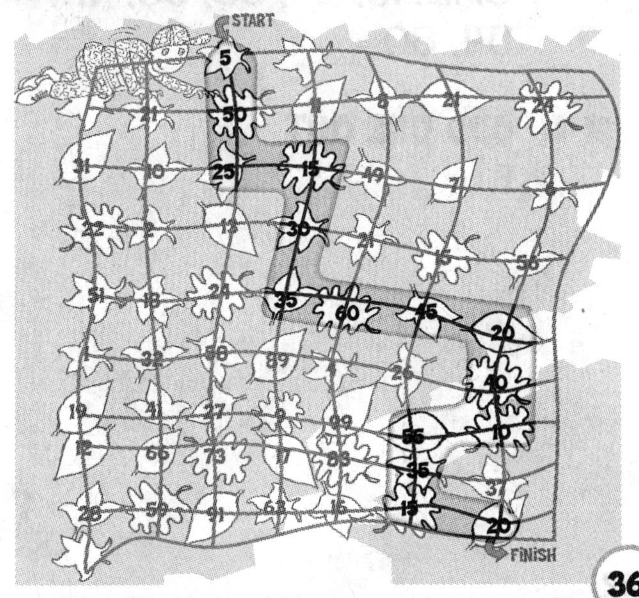

14 NUMBER CRUNCH

= 1 = 2
= 3 = 7

15 HAUNTED HOUSE

16 FREEZE POPS

84

17 ANIMAL BREAKOUT

Code = 6324

18 PIRATE PARADE

b and e

19 ALPHADOKU

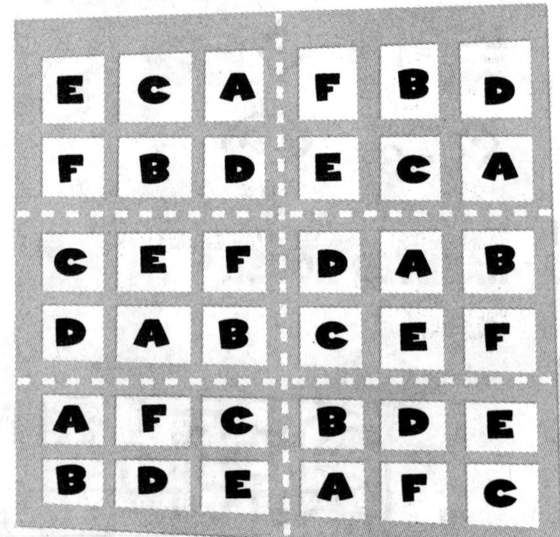

E	C	A	F	B	D
F	B	D	E	C	A
C	E	F	D	A	B
D	A	B	C	E	F
A	F	C	B	D	E
B	D	E	A	F	C

20 SPOT THE DIFFERENCE

21 MENU MIX UP

BANANA BURGER
CARROT ORANGE
PEANUT SALMON
TOMATO TRIFLE
TURKEY POTATO

22 WORLD RECORDS

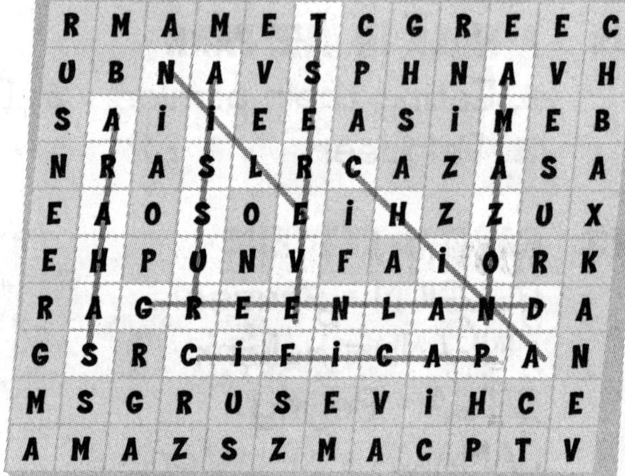

R	M	A	M	E	T	C	G	R	E	E	C
U	B	N	A	V	S	P	H	N	A	V	H
S	A	I	I	E	E	A	S	I	M	E	B
N	R	A	S	L	R	C	A	Z	A	S	A
E	A	O	S	O	E	I	H	Z	Z	U	X
E	H	P	U	N	V	F	A	I	O	R	K
R	A	G	R	E	E	N	L	A	N	D	A
G	S	R	C	I	F	I	C	A	P	A	N
M	S	G	R	U	S	E	V	I	H	C	E
A	M	A	Z	S	Z	M	A	C	P	T	V

23 PLANET SIX

6, 12, 18, 24, 30, 36, 42, 48, 54, 60

24 ODD ONE OUT

f

25 GRIDLOCKED

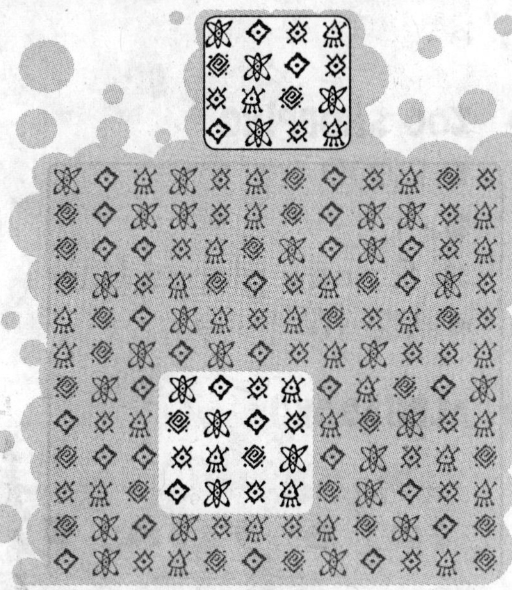

26 FOOTBALL FRACTIONS

a = 2 b = 5
c = 3 d = 4
e = 6

27 CLASS ACT

1. The Solar System
2. Man
3. 5
4. 10:30
5. Flowers
6. 2
7. Fish
8. 3
9. Spots
10. Fish-shaped

29 FAIRY TALES

Here are some you might have thought of:
one, pat, tea, cat, put, none, pout, pint, cone, open, tape, meat, pounce, peanut, coupon

30 SUDOKU

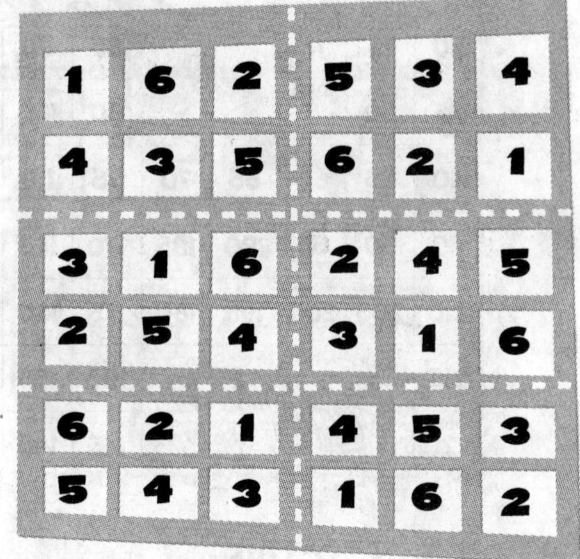

31 OUT OF ORDER

2, 6, 1, 3, 4, 5

32 TREASURE HUNT

C1 - by the cacti

33 DOUBLE TROUBLE
Pelican; swallow
Vulture; peacock
Ostrich; chicken
Penguin; sparrow

34 TIGER TABLES

35 DINO-DETECTIVE
IGUANODON

36 PLANE SAILING
c

37 ON THE MOVE
Bicycle; tractor; yacht; train; aeroplane; speedboat; motorbike; helicopter

38 FEEDING FRENZY
e

39 ZOO SHOPPING
1. £7.00
2. 4
3. 2 snow globes (£8)
4. £2.45

40 ALPHADOKU

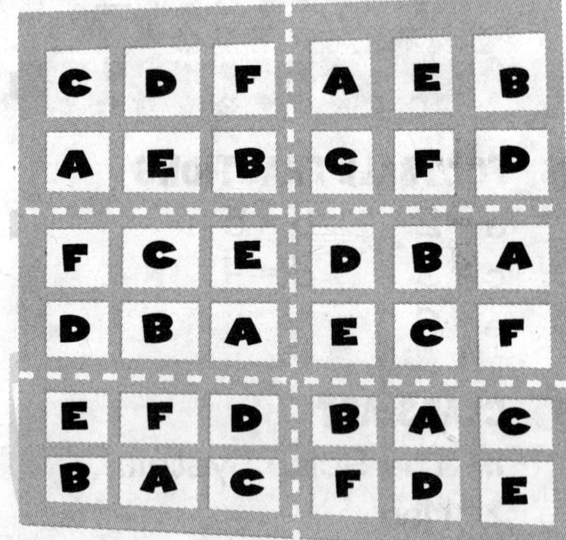

41 WHAT NEXT?
c

42 FOOD FOR THOUGHT

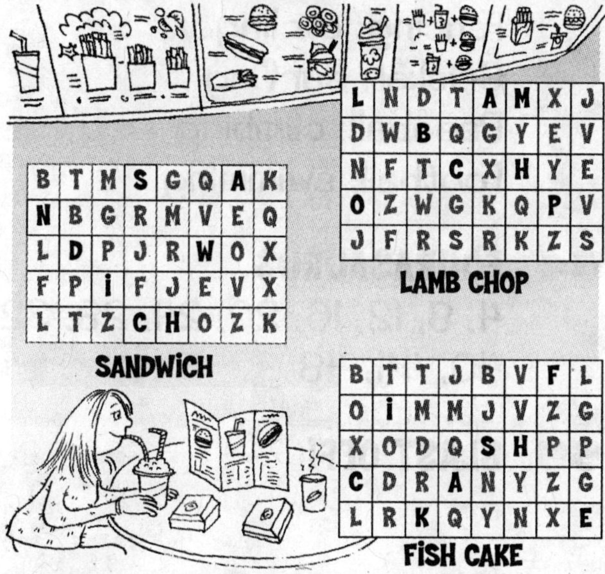

43 HOLiDAY HUNT

44 GRiDLOCKED

45 SPY SCHOOL

South America

46 FEEDiNG TiME

Code = 1635

47 CAMPSiTE CHALLENGE

48 SPACED OUT

Uranus; Jupiter; Mercury; Neptune; Asteroid; Meteor

49 BUGOKU

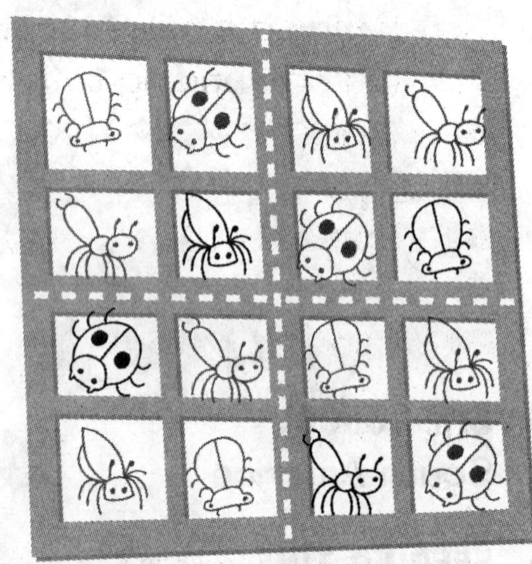

50 SPY SCHOOL

WHAT WORKS UNDERCOVER, SPEAKS MANY LANGUAGES, AND HAS EIGHT LEGS?
A SPY-DER!

51 PIECES OF EIGHT

a

52 SNACK SUMS

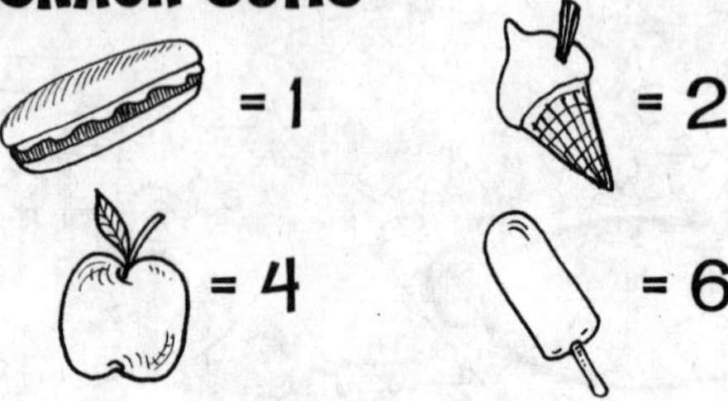

53 DOUBLE TROUBLE

Fencing; cycling
Cricket; surfing
Baseball; climbing
Football; swimming

54 FOURASAURUS

4, 8, 12, 16, 20, 24, 28, 32, 36, 40, 44, 48

55 BLAST OFF!

e

56 RIGGING RIDDLE

MAST-MALT-MALL-MAIL-SAIL

57 NUMBER MAZE

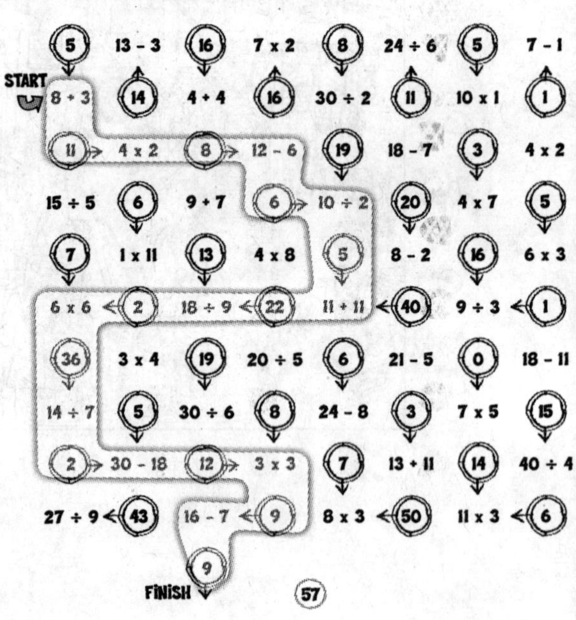

58 **ELEPHANT RIDE**

e

59 **ANIMAL MIX UP**

MONKEY
JAGUAR
MARMOT
GERBIL
GIBBON
COYOTE
BADGER
TURTLE
PYTHON
WALRUS

60 **ALPHADOKU**

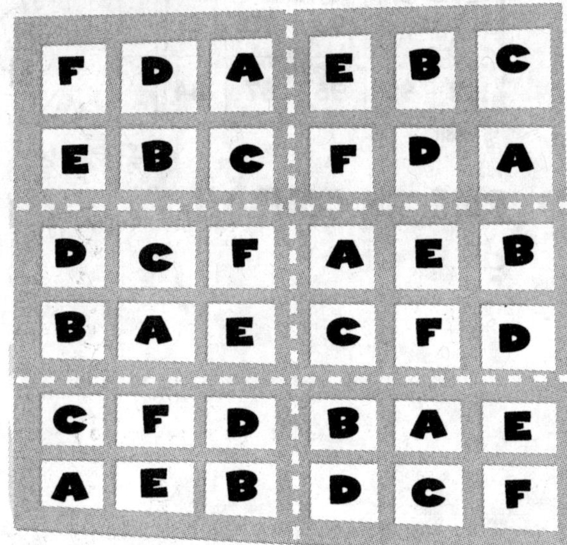

61 **STATION SLEUTH**

1. 3
2. 3:13
3. Paris
4. 3
5. Reading a newspaper (or pretending to!)
6. Right
7. Lips
8. Books
9. Guitar
10. 1 and 2

63 **FAIRY DUST**

c and e

64 **ENDANGERED SPECIES**

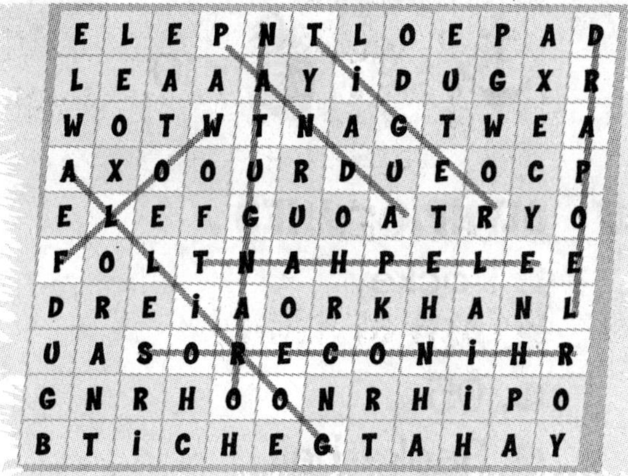

65 A BUG'S LIFE

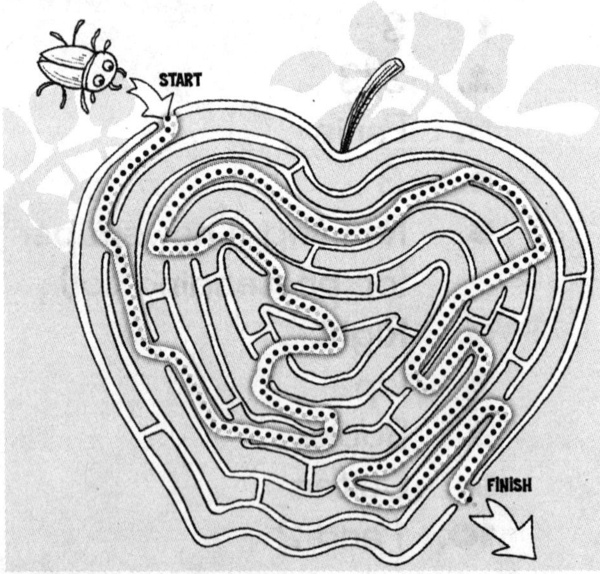

66 NUMBER CRUNCH

= 3 = 6

= 8 = 10

67 OLYMPIC GAMES

1. Hockey
2. A5
3. D5
4. Basketball

68 JET SETTERS

Here are some you might have thought of:
dad, wet, two, owl, nut, tear, deal, down, hurt, wear, lead, heard, learn, under, throw

69 MAGICAL MARVIN

70 RIDE 'EM COWBOY!

d

71 FOODOKU

72 FLOWER FAIRIES

73 SPY SCHOOL

GO TO THE LIBRARY

74 SEA LIFE SQUARES

Lobster; dolphin

75 CRAZY CRABS

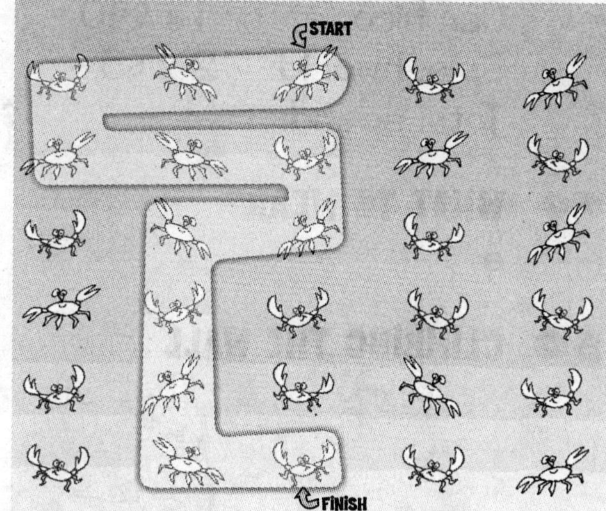

76 MAP MIX UP

MEXICO FRANCE
CANADA TURKEY
SWEDEN POLAND
ISRAEL RUSSIA
GREECE KUWAIT

77 MONSTER TRUCK

d

78 TAKING A TRIP

Flight tickets:	3 x $100 =	$300
Suitcases:	4 x $10 =	$40
Train tickets:	3 x $60 =	$180
Car hire:	1 x $40 =	$40
Splashworld:	2 x $5 =	$10
Total spend:		$570

79 WHAT TO WEAR?

e

80 CLIMBING THE WALL

81 TIDY UP TIME

52 leaves; 9 bugs

82 SPOT THE DIFFERENCE

83 SUDOKU

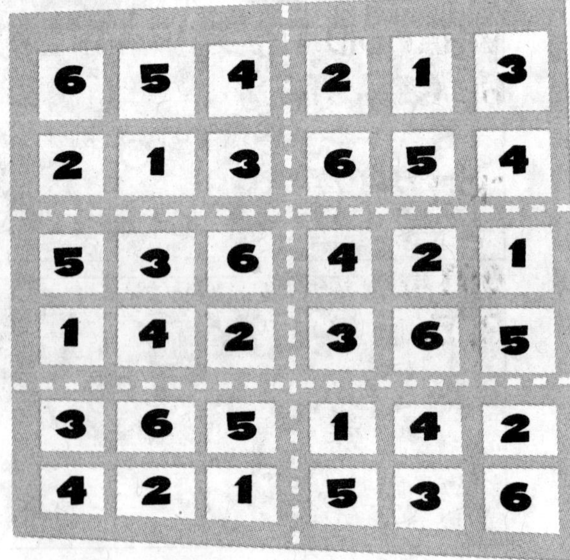

6	5	4	2	1	3
2	1	3	6	5	4
5	3	6	4	2	1
1	4	2	3	6	5
3	6	5	1	4	2
4	2	1	5	3	6

84 CHEEKY MONKEYS

d

85 IN THE LAB

a

86 TROPICAL PARADISE

87 SPY SCHOOL

WHAT DID THE SPY SAY WHEN HE GOT STUCK IN SEAWEED?

"KELP! KELP!"

88 OUT OF ORDER

3, 5, 6, 2, 1, 4

89 GRIDLOCKED

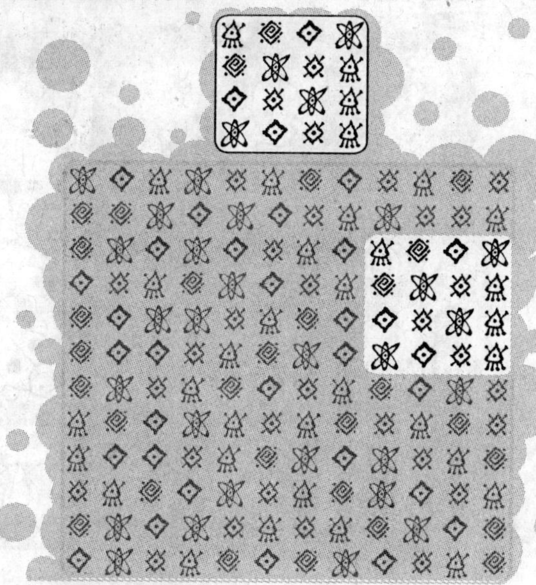

90 JEWEL THIEF

3964

91 FLYING FUN

1. 9
2. Flying
3. 2
4. 3
5. Stripes
6. Hot dogs and ice cream
7. 8
8. Saturday
9. 6
10. 2

93 DELICIOUS DESSERTS

b and f

94 BUGOKU

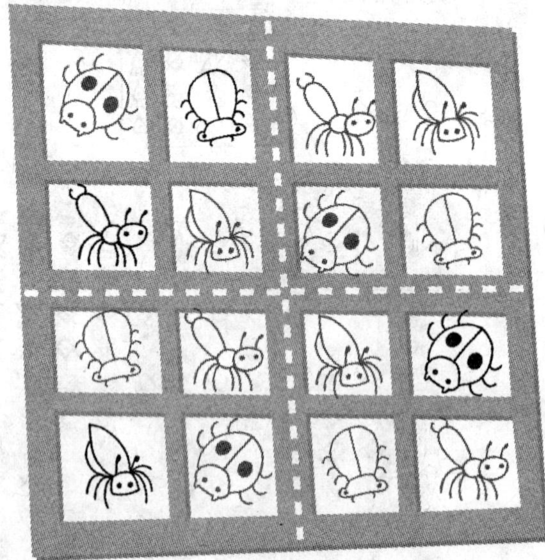

95 TREASURE HUNT

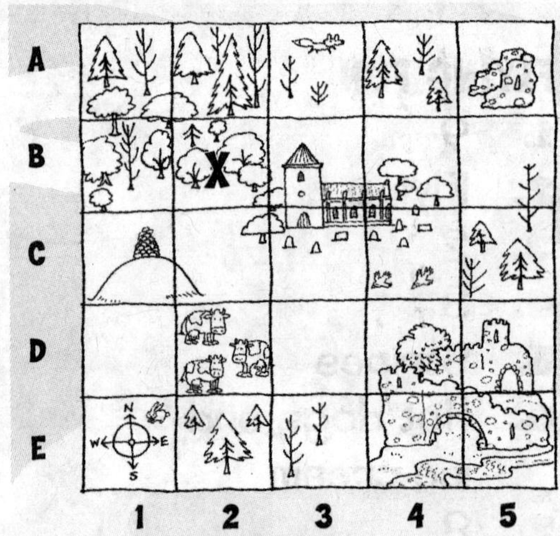

96 CREEPY CRAWLIES

BUMBLEBEE
LADYBIRD
CENTIPEDE
BUTTERFLY

97 FIRE DRILL

98 LIBRARY CODES

Geography books

99 PLAY TIME

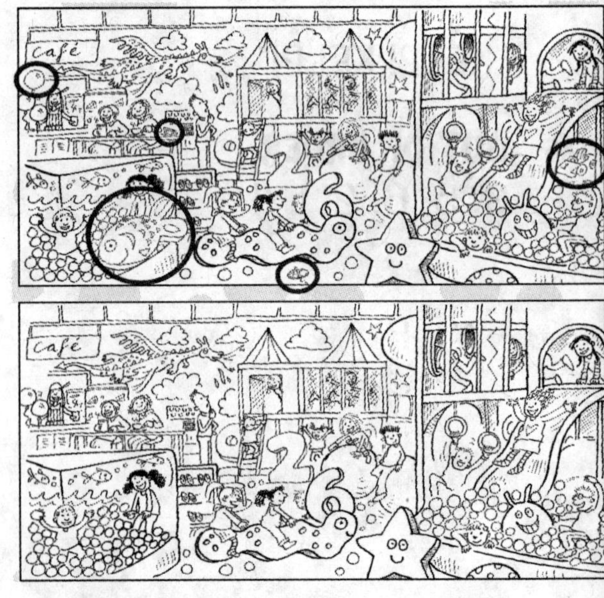

100 ALPHADOKU

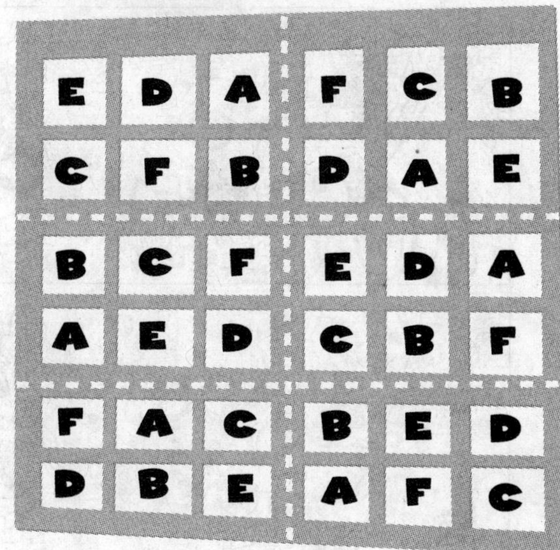

101 TOTALLY TROPICAL

40

102 PARTY BAGS

1. Toy lizard (1.00), stars x 2 (20p), elephant (50p)
   Total: £1.70
2. Hat (2.50), lolly (75p), pencil (75p)
   Total: £4.00
3. Hat (2.50), star (10p), elephant (50p), pencil (75p), lizard (1.00), lolly (75p)
   Total: £5.60

103 FANTASTIC GYMNASTICS

104 SUMMER OLYMPICS

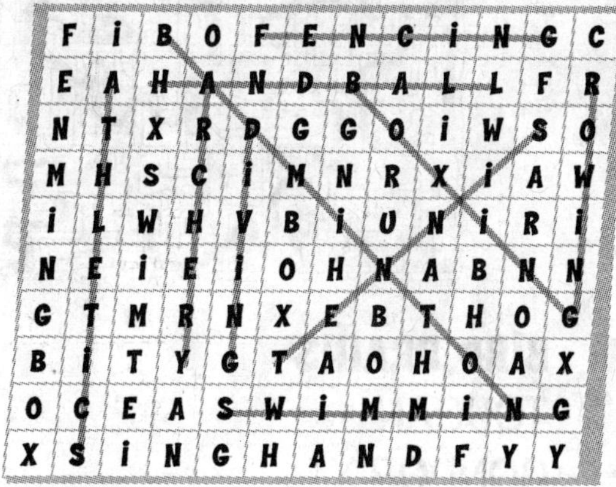

105 WHAT NEXT?

b

106 CASTLE CAPERS

1. Church
2. D4
3. E3
4. Horses

107 COOL CALCULATIONS

3 lollies @ 50p = £1.50
2 lollies @ 90p = £1.80
3 lollies @ 75p = £2.25
2 lollies @ 65p = £1.30
Total = £6.85

108 CHILL-OUT TIME

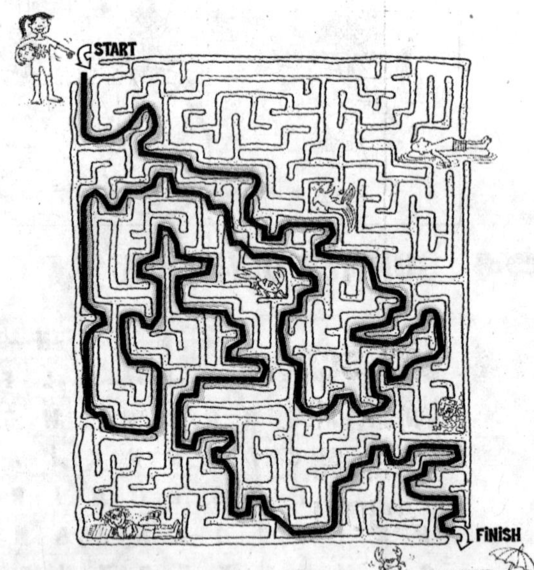

109 BIRD BRAINS

TOUCAN
CONDOR
MAGPIE
PIGEON
FALCON
PARROT
THRUSH
TURKEY
PUFFIN
CUCKOO

110 SPOT THE DIFFERENCE

111 FOODOKU

112 RAINY-DAY PUZZLE

Here are some you might have thought of: **din, ran, son, acid, sign, gong, grin, again, drain, grain, grant, snort, short, string, training**

113 FAIRY TALE

d

114 NUMBER CRUNCH

115 DINO CLUB

a

116 POPSICLE PUZZLER

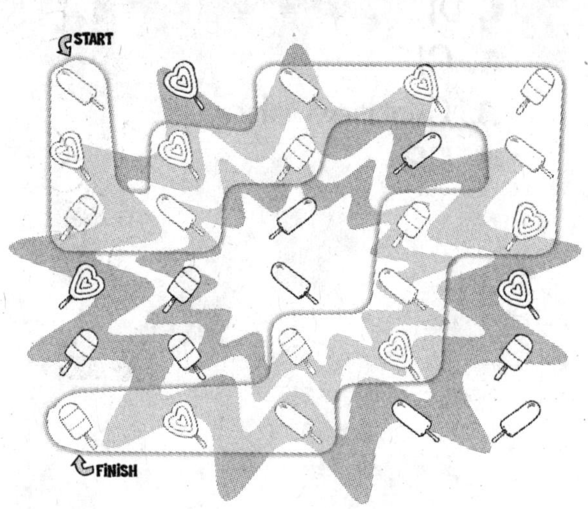

117 OCTOPLUS

8562

118 TREASURE HUNT

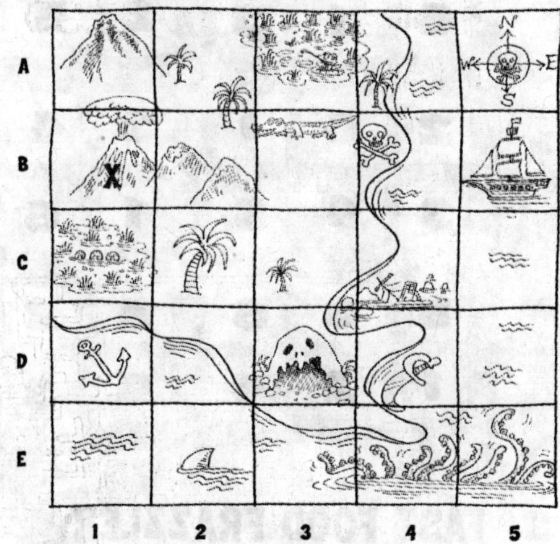

119 SPY SCHOOL

WHAT DO YOU CALL A SPY WHO HIDES AT THE BEACH? SANDY!

120 IN A TWIRL

8, 16, 24, 32, 40, 48, 56, 64, 72, 80, 88, 96

121 BEAUTIFUL BUTTERFLIES

e

122 SUDOKU

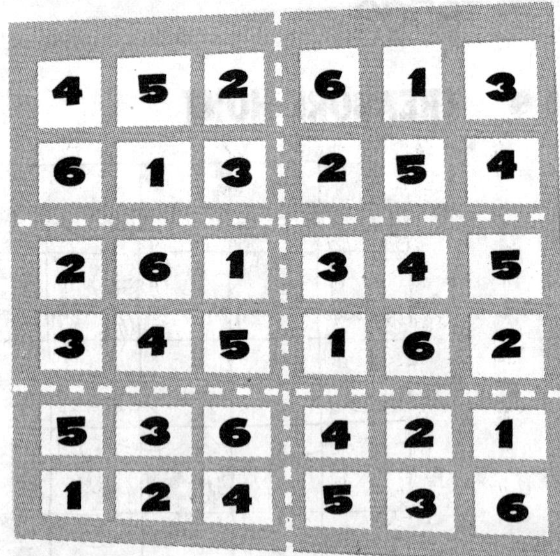

4	5	2	6	1	3
6	1	3	2	5	4
2	6	1	3	4	5
3	4	5	1	6	2
5	3	6	4	2	1
1	2	4	5	3	6

123 FAST FOOD FRAZZLER

1. 3
2. Man
3. Ladies
4. Burger and hotdog
5. 2
6. Woman
7. 2
8. Plant
9. Train
10. 2

125 GRIDLOCKED

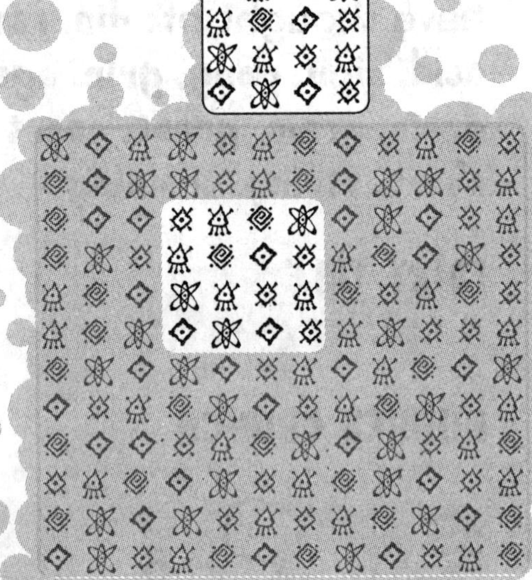

126 FIRE STARTERS

a and e

127 OUT OF ORDER

4, 3, 6, 2, 5, 1

128 SHOPPING TRIP

1. D1
2. C1
3. Clothes shop
4. E3

129 SNAIL TRAIL

130 ROLL THE DICE

462 + 135 = 597
124 + 632 = 756
541 + 123 = 664
653 + 154 = 807
246 + 645 + 891

131 JUNGLE FEVER

BY THE TARANTULAS

132 CIRCUS SEVENS

	1	17	12	28	35	42
		11	16	21	25	49
			START 7	14	33	56
37		41	44	52	50	63
	FINISH 105	98	91	84	77	70
			96	90	79	75
			100	95	83	88

133 WITCH NEXT?

b

134 SPOT THE DIFFERENCE

135 NUMBER CRUNCH

136 CAMPING TRIP

HIKE-BIKE-BAKE-CAKE-CAME-CAMP

137 GHASTLY GHOSTS

31 ghosts; 11 bats

138 PARTY PUZZLE

139 PAINTER'S PALETTE

Orange, violet, scarlet

140 ALL CHANGE

C

141 FLYING FARTHEST

The top plane has flown farthest (68 compared to 55 and 59)

142 FOODOKU

143 TRACK SIDE

144 HIDDEN GNOMES

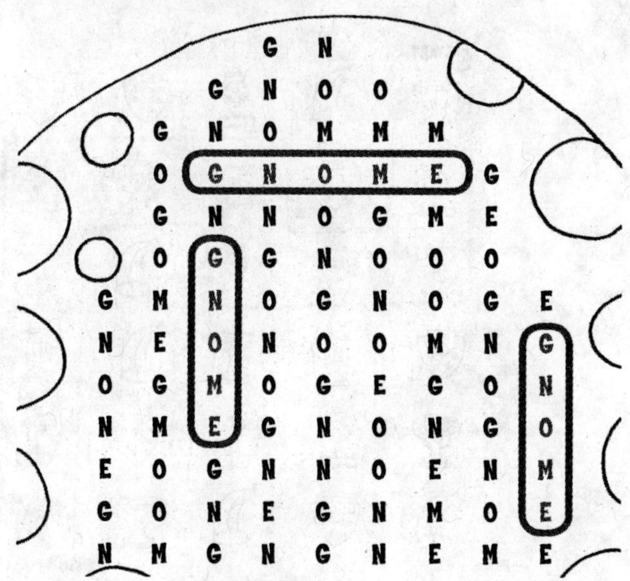

145 TEEPEE TEASER

f

146 FARMER BEN'S HEN

147 EATEN EIGHTS

11 apples

148 JUNGLE TREASURE

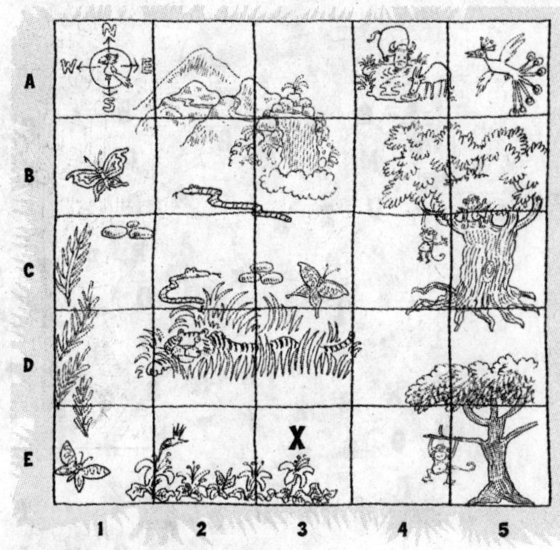

149 BUGOKU

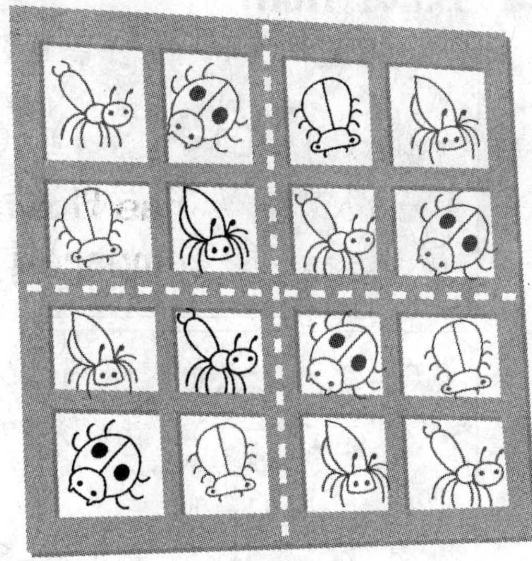

150 BEAT THE TEACHER

The answer is 143

151 GARDEN PARTY
a

152 PET CiTY

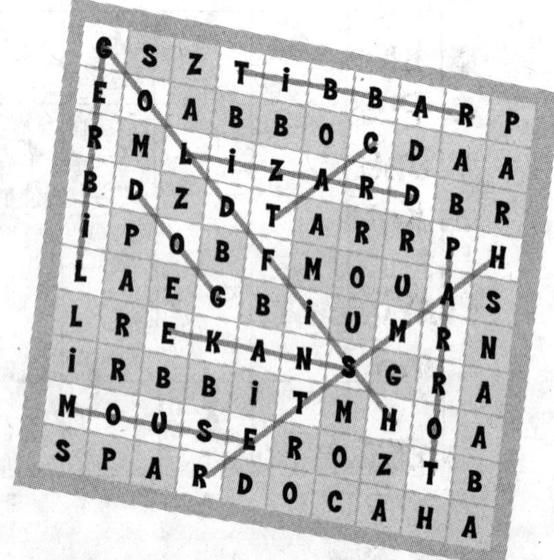

153 FANCY THAT!

154 TROPHY CABiNET

155 JURASSiC PARK
Here are some you might have thought of:
pod, cup, lip, cod, old, lid, oil, clip, idol, dodo, cold, loud, cool, soup, solid

156 SPY SCHOOL
WHY DID THE SILLY SPY GO TO NIGHT SCHOOL?
HE WANTED TO LEARN TO READ IN THE DARK.

157 AT THE BALLET
c and f

158 SKi RUN

11, 22, 33, 44, 55, 66, 77, 88, 99, 110

159 SPOT THE DiFFERENCE

160 DOWN ON THE FARM

1. Scarecrow
2. D4
3. 1
4. E2, E3 and C4

161 LE PUZZLE

1. Puzzle
2. Bottle
3. Giggle
4. Riddle
5. Little
6. Puddle
7. Battle
8. Kettle

162 PLAYiNG SNAP

a and e

163 SWEET TREAT

1. 3
2. Cat
3. Girl
4. 4
5. Pumpkins
6. Roof
7. No
8. A deer
9. No
10. 6

165 SPY SCHOOL

FIND THE SECRET WEAPON

166 **KAYAK COURSE**
The kayaker in the middle scores the most (46 compared to 42 and 40)

167 **AT THE AQUARIUM**
1. AU$ 6.50
2. 2 lionfish
3. 10
4. AU$ 2.50

168 **FOUR-TUNE TELLER**
4, 8, 12, 16, 20, 24, 40

169 **FAIRY TALE**
b

170 **LET IT SNOW!**

171 **PRETTY POLLY**
Here are some you might have thought of:
fog, pit,
got, pie,
chef, gift,
pest, fist,
feet, poet,
site, goes,
chest, spite,
cheese

172 **BRAIN TEST**
EASY-EAST-CAST-CART-CARD-HARD

173 **NUMBER CRUNCH**
= 3 = 4
= 6 = 7

174 FAIRY TREASURE

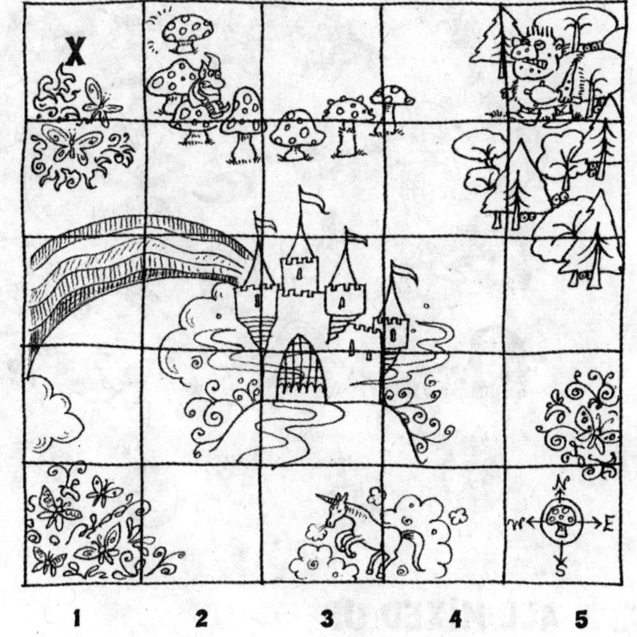

175 ALPHADOKU

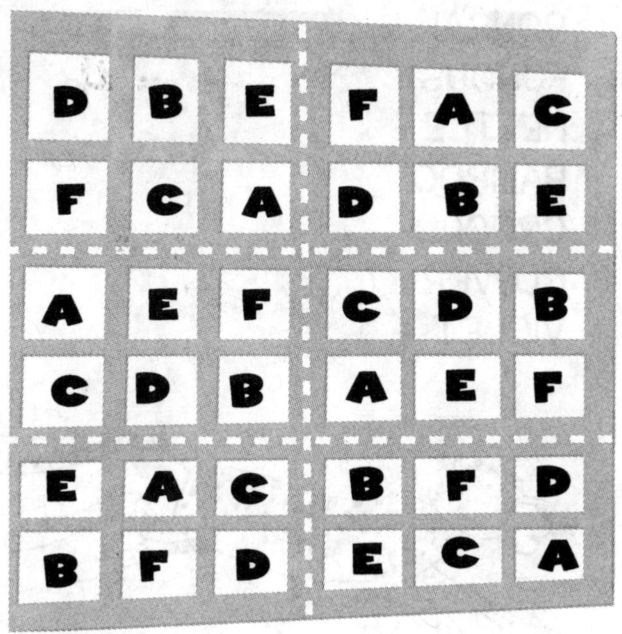

D	B	E	F	A	C
F	C	A	D	B	E
A	E	F	C	D	B
C	D	B	A	E	F
E	A	C	B	F	D
B	F	D	E	C	A

176 SIX CHICKS IN A FIX

177 ANIMALS OF THE WORLD

PLATYPUS (Australia)
BOBCAT (North America)
MEERKAT (Africa)
ORANGUTAN (Asia)
PINE MARTEN (Europe)
ANTEATER (South America)

178 HIDE AND SEEK

7 recorders

179 GOiNG APE

181 PiRATE PAiRS

180 MiSSiNG MONSTER

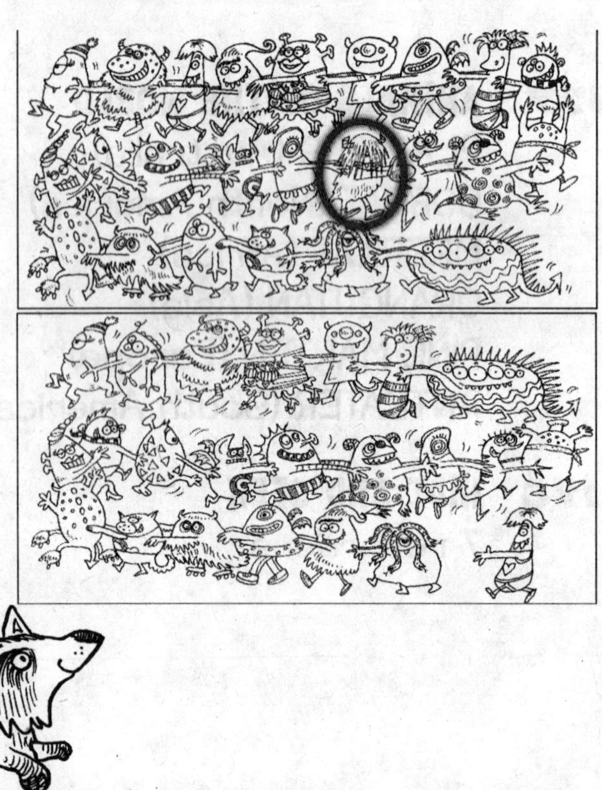

183 ALL MiXED UP

CACTUS
WILLOW
ORCHID
BONSAI
FUNGUS
NETTLE
BAMBOO
CROCUS
CLOVER
VIOLET

185 JURASSIC JOKE

Tyrannosaurus wrecks!

186 EGGS-ACTLY

Toucan

187 WEIRD SEARCH

Z	L	V	A	M	P	I	R	E	G
W	L	W	I	Z	L	G	F	G	Z
O	I	O	A	G	L	L	H	N	O
E	E	Z	G	H	O	O	D	A	M
W	W	Z	A	W	R	W	G	I	B
O	G	W	E	R	T	I	W	T	I
L	G	R	I	E	D	Z	E	R	E
L	E	R	Y	T	E	V	R	A	R
W	E	E	F	W	C	A	E	M	A
W	G	H	T	S	O	H	G	E	W

188 POLLEN COUNT

a 29
b 13
c 12
d 97

190 OUT OF THIS WORLD!

b

192 SEEING STRIPES

d

193 THE NAME GAME

Gonzalo

194 BUTTERFLY BONANZA

h

197 TRICERATOPS TRAIL

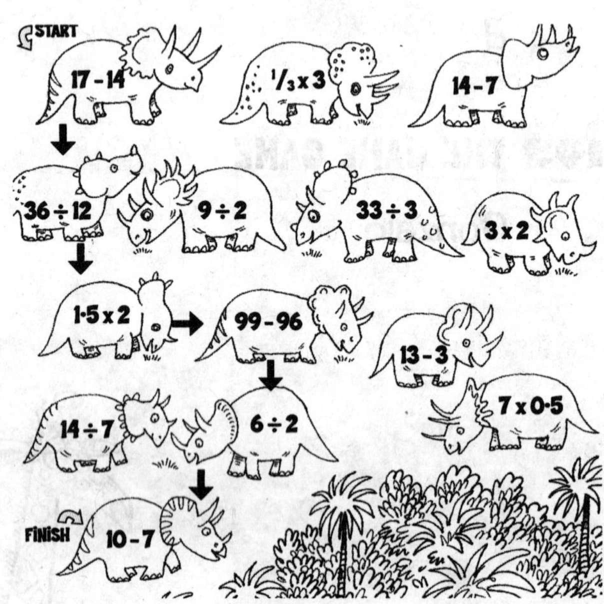

199 IN A MUDDLE

Bermuda

201 BIG IS BEAUTIFUL

7 x 3 x 2 = 42

203 MUNCH TIME

e

204 THE RIGHT FIT

The circled letters spell hedgehog.

H	O	R	N	B	I	L	L
E	L	E	P	H	A	N	T
A	A	R	D	V	A	R	K
F	L	A	M	I	N	G	O
P	A	R	A	K	E	E	T
C	H	I	P	M	U	N	K
M	O	N	G	O	O	S	E
B	U	L	L	F	R	O	G

206 FAIRY FOOD

a

207 HONEY TRAP

2 bees are going back to the hive.

208 ON REFLECTION

What do vampire movie stars receive in the post?
Fang mail!

210 FEEDING TIME

Deer, lion, puma, seal, wolf, boar

211 MAGGOTY MATHS

40 + 63 = 103
72 - 53 = 19
81 ÷ 9 = 9
5 x 6 = 30
27 + 27 = 54
86 - 39 = 47
7 x 3 = 21
48 ÷ 6 = 8

212 IVORY TOWER

b

213 A BIRD'S EYE VIEW

e

215 MEGALOSAURUS MATHS

a = h
b = e
c = g
d = f

216 MONSTER MATCH

b and f

217 LAND AHOY!

218 DANDELION CLOCK

Lunchtime

219 A-MAZING

221 DINOSAURS AND DRAGONS

222 PAIR UP THE PETS

Annika has a brown dog.
Luke has a black cat.
Freddie has a white hamster.

224 SHOE SHUFFLE

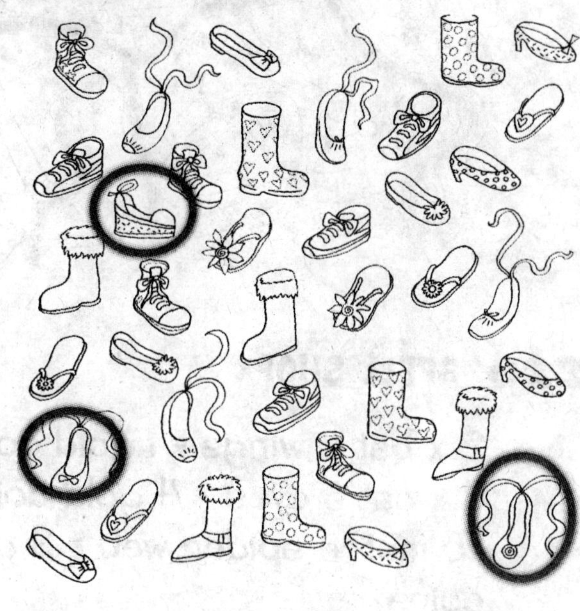

225 GOING UNDERGROUND

Mole, groundhog, badger

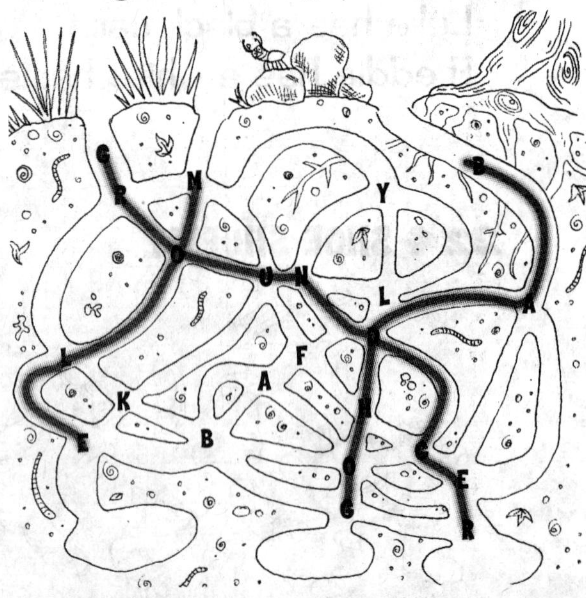

226 SPELL SHOP

2 x bat's wings = 1 gold coin
4 x cat's eyes = 4 gold coins
1.5 metre spider web = 3 gold coins
1 jar of nightfall = 7 gold coins

Total = 15 gold coins

228 THINK ABOUT IT

A polygon!

229 MINI BEASTS

A beetle (each row and column has one of each creature)

231 PRETTY POLLY

232 FORTUNE TELLING

Banshee, werewolf

233 TOO TROO

9

234 CAGE CODE

6924

235 SEADOG SUDOKU

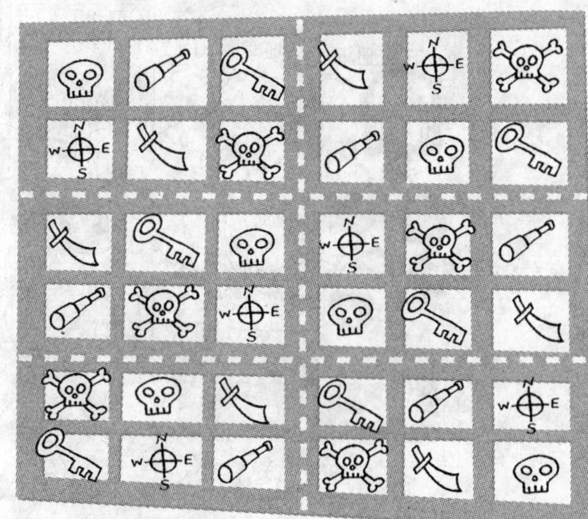

236 RING RING

Ring a (each column has one of each design, each row has the same design at both ends)

238 BEASTLY BEING

GOGLEYOR

239 DINOSAUR WORLD

1. D1
2. E3
3. Ice cream
4. T. rex

241 BARREL OF FUN

A	A	Y	Y	H	A	O	A	Y	H	O	Y
A	H	A	O	A	A	H	H	O	O	H	A
O	H	A	H	O	H	A	O	A	Y	A	Y
A	H	Y	H	O	H	O	H	O	O	Y	O
A	H	A	O	O	Y	Y	O	Y	H	H	H
H	Y	H	Y	A	O	Y	H	H	A	A	H
Y	A	O	A	H	Y	Y	A	Y	O	O	O
A	H	Y	H	A	H	O	Y	A	O	H	A
Y	O	O	H	A	H	A	H	O	A	Y	H
A	H	A	A	H	O	Y	A	O	O	H	A
H	O	Y	H	O	A	H	O	O	A	O	H
O	H	H	Y	H	O	Y	O	H	O	Y	O
A	O	H	O	Y	A	H	Y	O	H	A	H
A	H	A	H	A	Y	O	H	O	Y	O	O

242 RIGHT ROYAL WRONGS

1. The bird is flying upside down
2. One guest has a sleeping cat on her hat
3. The bride's bouquet is made of fish
4. The groom's crown is on upside down
5. Another guest is wearing snorkelling gear
6. There is a monkey swinging from the bunting!

243 TREE TIMES TABLE

a $7 \times 3 = 21$
b $5 \times 5 = 25$
c $3 \times 4 = 12$
d $5 \times 3 = 15$
e $0 \times 8 = 0$
f $30 \div 3 = 10$
g $9 \times 3 = 27$
h $12 \div 4 = 3$
i $6 \times 6 = 36$
j $2 \div 7 = 3$

245 TIME OUT

a Plateosaurus
b Velociraptor

246 CREATURE CARVINGS

26 (not including the owl sitting on a branch!)

248 WISH ME LUCK

249 BEETLE MANIA

d

250 MONSTER LAUGHS

Because he wanted a light snack!

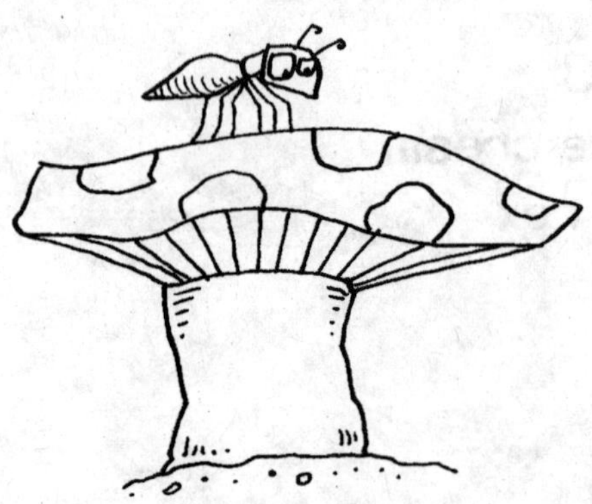

252 NEW FACES

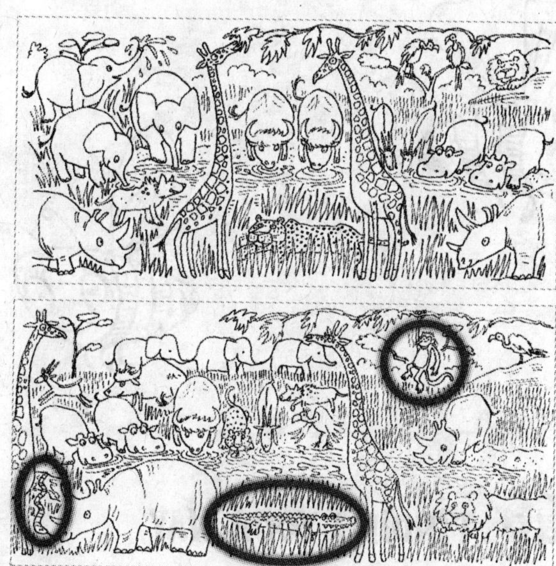

253 PIRATE LOGIC

Ship 1 is owned by Captain Barnacle who has a red parrot called Perky.
Ship 2 is owned by Captain Greybeard who has a blue parrot called Pesky.
Ship 3 is owned by Captain Scablegs who has a green parrot called Potty.

255 NATURE HUNT

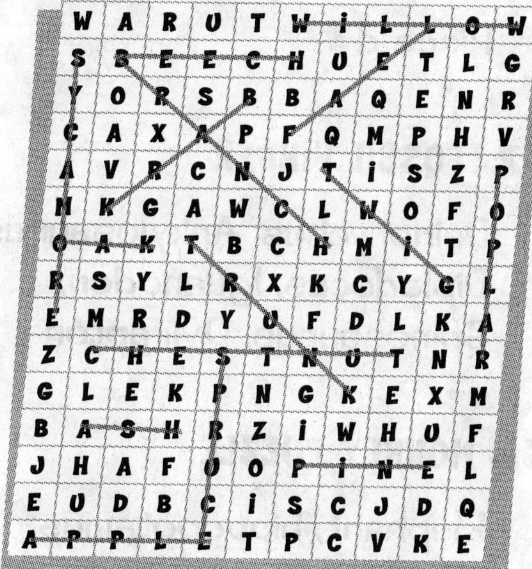

256 CHAIN REACTION

Piece d

257 FOSSIL FINDER

Deinonychus, Ankylosaurus, Diplodocus, Iguanodon, Spinosaurus, Oviraptor

258 MONKEY PUZZLE

Elephant, hippopotamus, rhinoceros

259 FINDING YOUR WAY

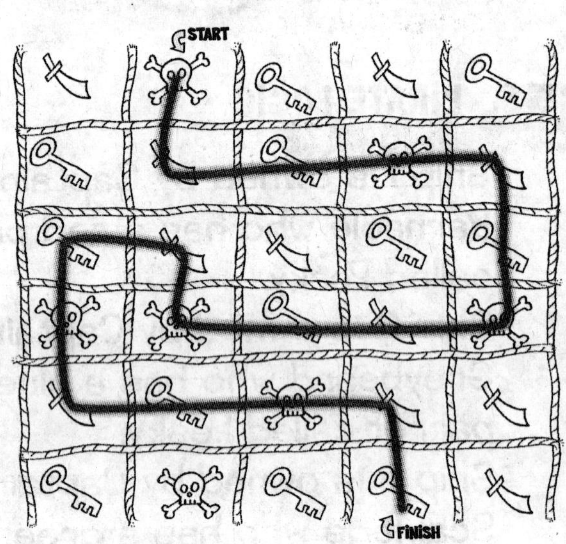

260 MYSTICAL MATHS

44

262 MEET THE MISFITS

Female a (follow the patterns: the ladies have alternate long sleeves and short sleeves, alternate short hair and long hair, and alternate ragged hem or straight hem)

263 DINO DAZE

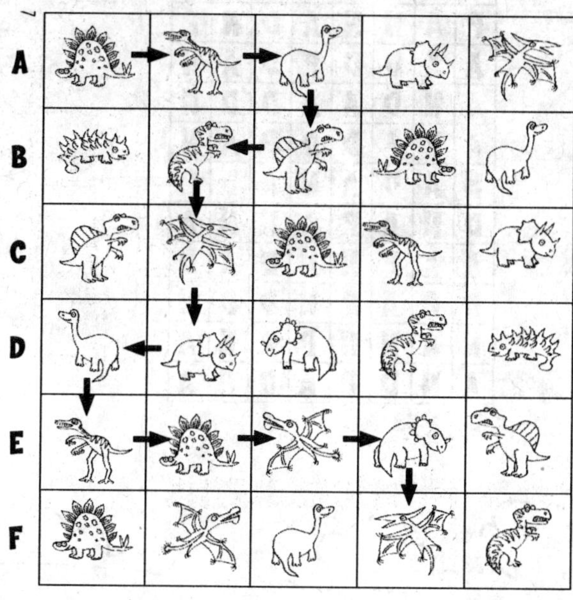

265 SAFE HARBOUR

The pirates should land in C5.

266 CROWNING GLORY

Peru

267 THROUGH THE LOOKING GLASS

e

269 DINO-DOKU

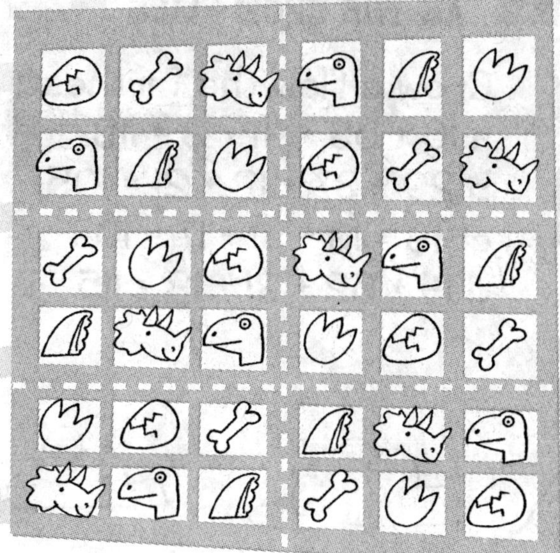

270 CAT CONUNDRUM

THERMAP doesn't unscramble to spell a big cat. The others can be rearranged to spell jaguar, tiger, cheetah, leopard, ocelot and cougar.

272 MIRROR MIRROR

The snow ball!

273 AS THE CROW FLIES

Crow a flew the farthest:

a 16 + 53 + 41 + 8 = 118
b 29 + 37 + 18 + 21 = 105
c 48 + 13 + 31 + 17 = 109
d 14 + 62 + 21 + 18 = 115

274 SPOOKY SPELLINGS

Here are some you might have thought of:

NUT, WET, GNU,
HIGH, WRITE, TWIG,
UNIT, HURT, TWIN,
WING, GRUNT, TRUTH,
NIGHT, THOUGH, THROUGH

276 REALLY RARE

P	A	N	N	A	P	N	A
N	P	D	N	A	A	A	P
D	A	N	P	D	N	D	A
A	D	A	A	P	D	N	N
P	A	P	A	N	D	A	A
P	A	N	N	A	D	N	P
A	A	D	D	P	D	A	N
A	N	D	A	A	D	D	N
A	P	A	D	D	P	A	N
N	A	D	A	N	A	D	P
D	N	A	P	A	N	N	A
A	A	P	N	N	D	A	D
D	P	A	D	N	D	D	N
N	A	N	N	P	A	N	A
A	N	D	P	A	D	N	A

277 RUFUS REDBEARD

g

278 PRINCESS SUDOKU

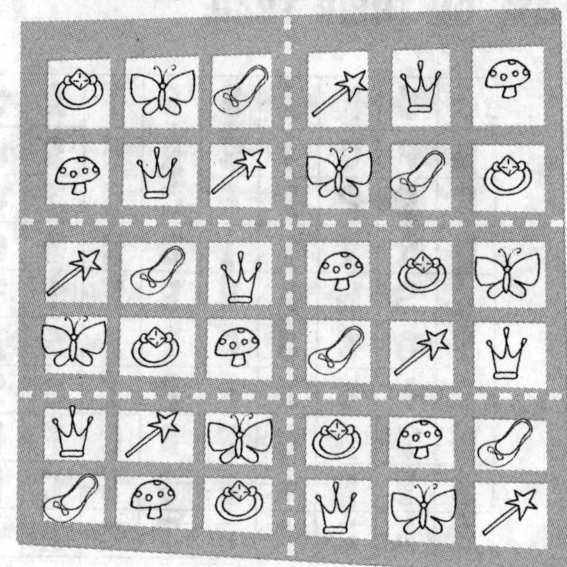

279 UGLY BUG BALL

280 WHO GOES THERE?

Godzilla

281 THUMBS UP

These five are spelt correctly:
Velociraptor, Gigantosaurus, Pteranodon, Tyrannosaurus, Spinosaurus

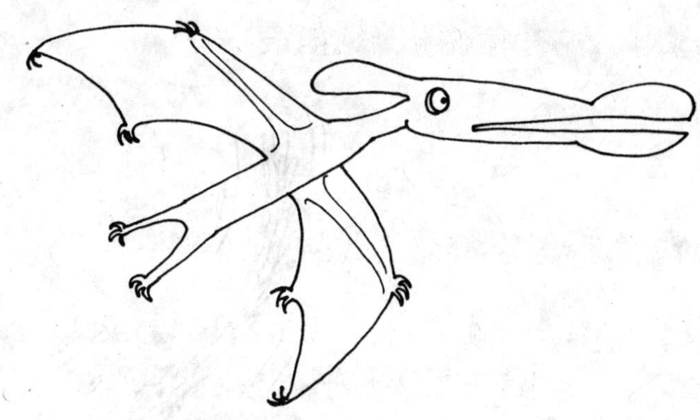

282 EAGLE EYES

a belongs to 4
b belongs to 2
c belongs to 1
d belongs to 3

283 DEADLY DICE

1 + 4 x 5 is the highest:
6 + 2 x 3 = 24
4 + 3 x 3 = 21
3 + 3 x 4 = 24
1 + 4 x 5 = 25
2 + 5 x 2 = 14
5 + 6 x 2 = 22

285 MAKING TRACKS

Because they look silly in raincoats!

287 ON THEIR TRAIL

J	U	R	A	S	E	T	A	C	E
R	P	C	I	S	R	H	S	U	O
E	E	P	L	E	C	E	T	O	R
D	R	T	I	I	B	R	S	C	I
A	S	W	A	V	E	H	I	T	R
T	O	R	J	O	R	S	S	A	I
A	L	C	E	R	P	I	O	S	S
W	E	N	G	E	R	C	F	L	I
S	V	N	I	V	O	R	E	E	X
C	A	R	A	C	T	C	N	I	T

288 ANIMAL ANTICS

1. The lion has tiger stripes.
2. The giraffe is up to his neck in water.
3. The zebra has a saddle on.
4. A hippo is wearing wellies.
5. There is a bouquet of flowers in the reeds.
6. The chimps are playing cards.

290 SHOE SUMS

All the answers are even numbers.

7 x 6 = 42
9 x 4 = 36
3 x 8 = 24
2 x 9 = 18
6 x 6 = 36
8 x 5 = 40
4 x 7 = 28
6 x 4 = 24

292 MIND THE MINOTAUR

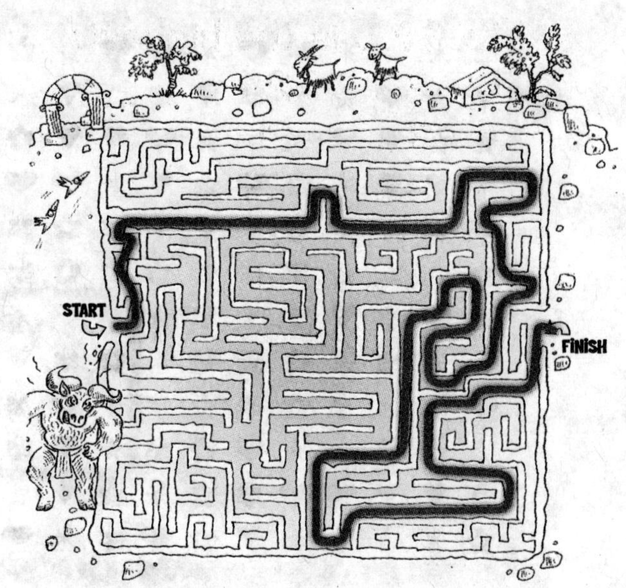

294 WHOSE HORSE?

Joe has a grey horse called Gunner.
Charlie has a chestnut horse called Dario.
Ben has a black horse called Niko.

295 A MESS OF MUSKETS

12

296 HIDE AND SEEK

297 HOME SWEET HOME

Cave = bear
Hive = bee
Web = spider
Hole = fox
Lodge = beaver
Nest = bird

298 TOXIC TERROR

d

299 GOING, GOING, GONE

E	X	E	T	i	N	C	T	E	C
X	i	N	C	T	E	X	C	i	T
T	T	X	E	X	i	T	E	X	T
E	X	T	T	X	E	T	X	E	E
T	X	i	N	C	T	E	T	X	X
E	X	T	C	E	T	i	i	i	T
X	E	T	i	X	E	X	C	T	E
C	X	i	N	N	X	N	i	T	X
i	i	T	C	N	C	C	T	X	E
T	T	C	T	T	C	T	E	X	T

301 CODE CRACKER

50 x 50 = 2500
1800 ÷ 9 = 200
1234 + 1234 = 2468
6 x 70 = 420
3000 - 123 = 2877
12 x 12 = 144
1998 ÷ 2 = 999
1000 - 55 = 945
9876 - 22 = 9854
11 x 11 = 121
8 x 800 = 6400
5555 + 4321 = 9876
448 ÷ 2 = 224
100 - 36 = 64
Code is 3597

302 SHOPPING TRIP

£2 + £4.50 + £4 + £3 = £13.50

304 MEMORY TEST

An owl
2
Yes (on the right-hand tree trunk)
3
Squirrel

305 TWO BY TWO

Paleontologist

306 HMMMM, TRICKY

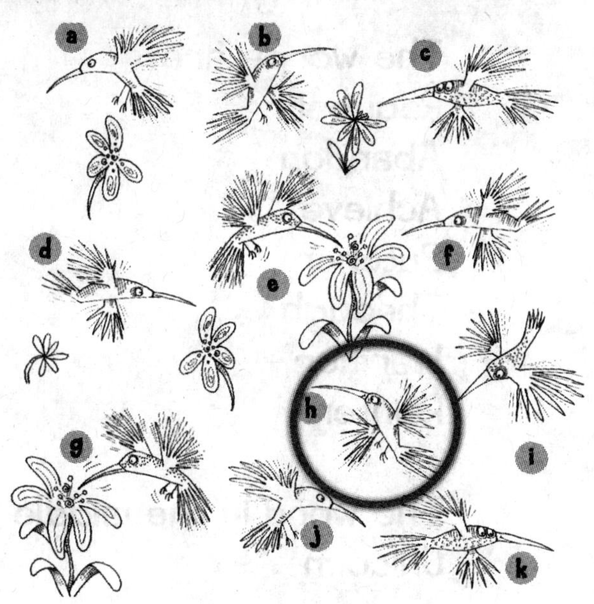

307 WHICH WAY NOW?

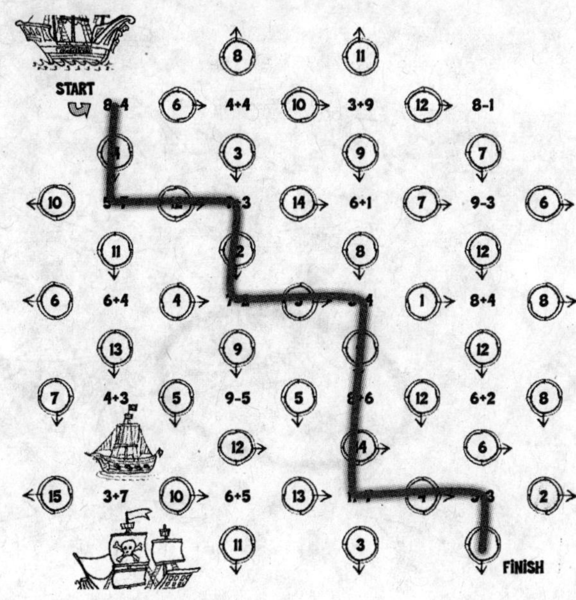

309 SPELLING BEE

These words are spelt correctly:
wolf, telescope, fungus, garden, fierce
The incorrect ones should be spelt like this:
potatoes, puppies, meteorite, beautiful, cobweb, volcano

311 COME FLY WITH ME

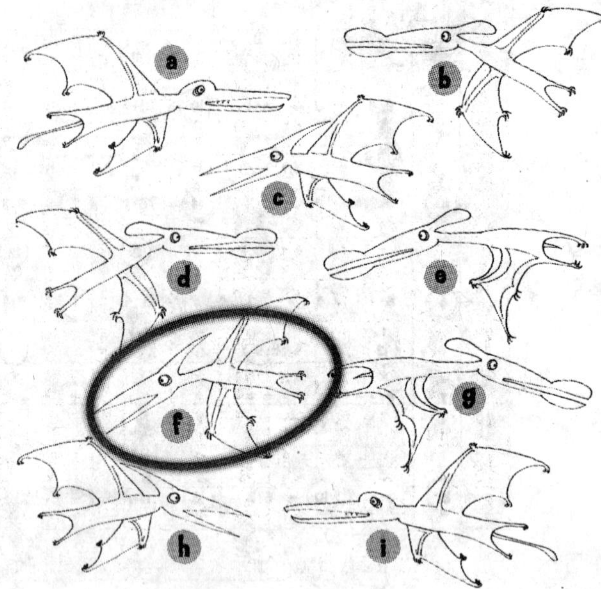

312 BIG IS BEST

Sum b because
a = 135
b = 150
c = 142
d = 137
e = 144
f = 140

314 SHADY LADY

e

316 GONE APE

3 x 4 = 2 x 6
12½ + 12½ = 5 x 5
35 " 5 = ½ x 14
25 x 2 = 0.5 x 100
6 x 6 = 50 - 14

318 I SEE!

Three blind mice!

319 ISLAND HOPPING

Trinidad, Barbados, Jamaica, Sardinia, Tobago, Madagascar

320 IN THE MIDDLE

The words are:
Request
Abandon
Achieve
Butcher
Through
Warrior
Painter

The word in the middle is Unicorn

321 iN THEiR PRiME

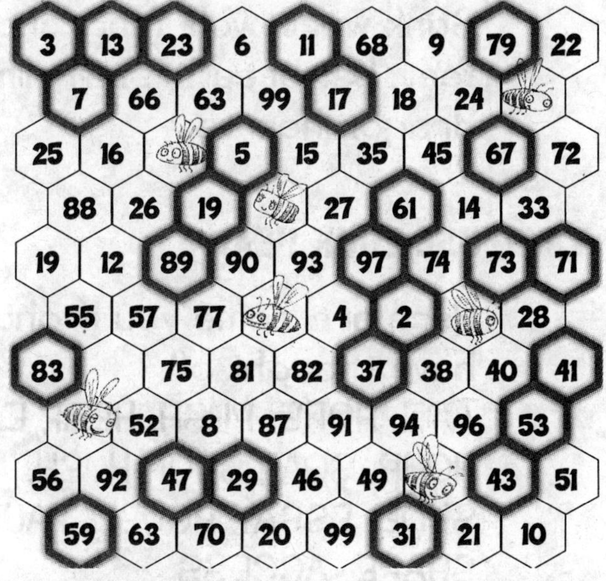

323 VERY FUNNY

F	R	M	F	R	M	F	M	M	F	R	F
F	B	R	E	F	R	M	M	F	R	M	R
M	F	F	M	R	C	F	A	R	F	R	U
R	R	M	F	M	R	S	F	E	M	F	M
M	M	R	R	F	M	R	R	F	R	M	R
T	F	M	H	M	F	E	M	R	Y	R	F
R	M	F	R	F	R	M	F	F	M	F	M
F	D	M	M	O	M	R	N	F	R	T	R
M	R	K	F	R	N	F	F	O	R	M	W
H	M	F	R	O	F	M	W	M	F	M	R
M	F	R	F	M	R	F	R	M	T	O	F
F	C	F	M	O	M	O	F	K	R	F	R

Because they don't know how to cook

322 LOOK OUT!

325 iD PARADE

Pirate c (The pattern is patch, no patch, patch, no patch... and head gear, head gear, no head gear... so the next pirate must have no patch and nothing on his head).

326 HIDDEN GEMS

E	Z	A	P	T	P	E	A	R	L
R	D	I	A	S	E	M	A	D	J
I	U	G	R	Y	L	E	M	I	O
H	S	B	P	H	T	A	E	A	J
P	G	A	Y	T	O	Q	P	M	A
P	S	A	P	E	P	U	H	O	D
A	Q	U	A	M	A	R	I	N	E
S	U	A	G	A	Z	A	I	D	U
R	A	E	M	E	R	A	L	D	O
E	S	I	O	U	Q	R	U	T	P
B	M	O	O	N	S	T	O	N	E

327 FOOTPRINTS

328 WITCH'S BREW

Stink wort, wolf fang, crow's feet, bat breath, snail slime, dragon hearts

329 USE YOUR HEAD

Here are some you might have thought of:
APE, HOPE, PUSH, HEAP, EASY, HOUR, SOAP, SHOP, HUSH, SHOE, ESSAY, HOUSE, PAUSE, SHAPE, ACCESS

330 PENGUIN PARADE

a = E2 b = C5 c = E7
d = C1 e = E5 f = B7

331 FOLLOW THE TRAIL

b

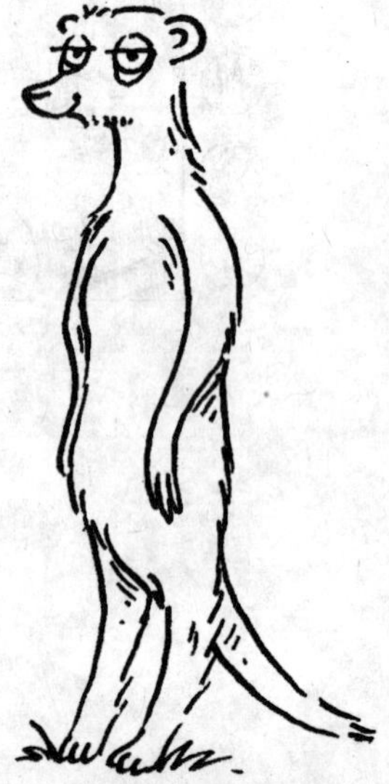

333 COLOUR CRACKER

D	A	L	L	M	L	D	M	M	D
L	D	G	M	R	A	D	L	L	L
D	M	L	M	D	M	S	S	L	D
L	D	H	O	M	D	L	M	L	D
M	M	D	L	P	P	D	D	M	L
D	L	L	M	L	D	M	E	R	M
W	D	L	D	i	D	L	T	M	H
L	M	L	L	D	L	D	M	M	L
D	H	M	i	L	L	M	C	C	D
M	D	U	L	L	P	D	L	S	M

A grasshopper with hiccups

335 FOSSiL FRiEND

Archaeopteryx

336 COOL FOR CATS

L	J	A	G	C	A	R	A	C	A	L	L
N	O	C	E	L	O	T	Y	H	W	E	C
X	H	L	V	A	i	X	T	L	i	O	N
T	C	i	O	G	C	L	i	G	L	P	X
B	H	O	E	L	H	J	S	V	A	A	T
O	E	R	U	S	A	E	E	T	B	R	L
B	E	Y	T	G	E	L	R	X	O	D	E
C	H	E	E	T	A	H	V	L	B	C	O
A	J	L	S	E	L	R	A	U	G	A	J
T	Y	A	E	Y	E	E	L	O	T	Y	B
C	V	A	N	W	i	L	D	C	A	T	O
H	T	X	J	A	G	X	B	O	B	C	B

337 WALK THE PLANK!

338 ONCE UPON A TiME

Here are some you might have thought of:
POT, OUT, ACE, PIN, POEM, INTO, NOON, OPEN, MENU, TEMPO, INPUT, ONION, POUNCE, OPTION, MOTION

340 LOSiNG YOUR HEAD

d

342 RACCOON PONTOON

343 CANNONBALL RUN

Cannonball a was shot the farthest.

a 30 + 26 + 48 + 25 = 129

b 37 + 14 + 29 + 41 = 121

c 39 + 26 + 27 + 33 = 125

344 WHO GOES THERE?

Prince Charming

345 A RARE FiND

O	R	C	C	O	R	H	i	D	O
R	C	H	i	R	O	R	O	R	R
C	O	D	i	H	R	O	R	C	C
D	R	O	D	i	O	C	C	O	H
i	C	O	O	D	i	H	C	R	D
D	R	O	R	R	O	i	O	O	D
O	R	R	D	O	C	D	D	i	O
H	i	C	O	C	O	C	H	D	R
D	C	H	R	H	i	D	H	C	D
O	R	i	D	R	i	C	O	R	H
R	H	D	H	i	D	O	R	O	C
O	R	C	H	D	D	O	O	O	R

346 CRACKiNG UP

Dragon, spider, zombie, medusa, gorgon, goblin, kraken, sphinx

347 ON DiSPLAY

Troodon

349 TAKE A LOOK

350 GRiDLOCKED

B	O	O	M	O	B	O	B	B	O
M	T	O	O	H	M	B	B	O	M
M	O	E	M	P	B	O	B	M	R
O	O	M	B	O	O	M	B	O	M
i	B	O	N	M	C	E	M	M	O
B	O	S	B	O	O	S	B	O	M
O	M	M	A	O	B	O	O	M	N
O	D	O	T	M	M	H	B	O	M
M	O	O	M	E	P	B	O	O	M
M	M	O	B	E	A	B	O	B	O

The Princess and the Pea

351 i SPiED A SPiDER

352 MUMMY MATHS

43 + 34 = 77

353 MIND THE GAPS

GigaNOTosaurus, BARyonyx, VelociRAPtor, ALLosaurus, sPINosaurus, ArgenTINosaurus, DIPlodocus, aPATosaurus

355 ALL AT SEA

356 WHERE OH WHERE?

Over the rainbow

357 FANGS A LOT